THE
BEASTLY
BEATITUDES
OF
BALTHAZAR B

Books by J. P. Donleavy

The Ginger Man
A Singular Man
The Saddest Summer of Samuel S
The Beastly Beatitudes of Balthazar B
The Onion Eaters
A Fairy Tale of New York
The Destinies of Darcy Dancer, Gentleman
Schultz
Leila
Meet My Maker the Mad Molecule
The Unexpurgated Code: A Complete Manual
    of Survival & Manners
De Alfonce Tennis
J. P. Donleavy's Ireland

THE
BEASTLY
BEATITUDES
OF
BALTHAZAR B

J. P. DONLEAVY

THE ATLANTIC MONTHLY PRESS
NEW YORK
·

Copyright © 1968 by J. P. Donleavy

Chapters 1 through 8 were previously published in *The Saturday Evening Post*. Excerpts originally appeared in *Playboy* magazine.

Published simultaneously in Canada

Printed in the United States of America

First Atlantic Monthly Press edition, July 1988

Library of Congress Cataloging-in-Publication Data
Donleavy, J. P. (James Patrick), 1926–
    The beastly beatitudes of Balthazar B.
    I. Title.
PS3507.0686B4   1988   813′.54   88-3415
ISBN 0-87113-225-7

The Atlantic Monthly Press
19 Union Square West
New York, NY 10003

FIRST PRINTING

THE
BEASTLY
BEATITUDES
OF
BALTHAZAR B

1

He was born in Paris in a big white house on a little square off Avenue Foch. Of a mother blond and beautiful and a father quiet and rich.

His nannie wheeled him daily in a high blue pram on pebbled paths under the tall trees. And as May branches were pressing out their green tips of new leaves he was taken on this warm sunny day across the river, through portals, a court-yard and under musty military flags. And there in a god-mother's arms with salt pressed on his lips and a cold dash of water on the skull, he was christened Balthazar.

Made of sudden love this gurgling baby shook tiny tender limbs in ecstasy. Wheeled to the Bois across summer, fists encased in woolly whiteness, skies passed more blue than cloudy beyond the folds of gauze. Under leaves and green, nannie sat near knitting on her folding chair. She waved away the mosquitos and bees and welcomed butterflies. And each day at four, in the thickest hot stillness, we headed home for tea.

Up the cooling steps to winter, her blue cap sat on a bun of brown hair. In a crib in the sun room off the vestibule I crawled. And reached through wooden bars to tug at plants sitting on their white gleaming pedestals. And touched where a chinaman fished forever in the river, to make him move. And he stayed the same. Like the cuddling kissing rocking arms I knew. Until the sweet nut flavour and milk white beauty of my mother's breasts were taken away. And I made my first frown.

2

Winter went away down warming steps to spring. The vestibule plants crushed together against the window. On a June dawn the big black car with the footrests sticking from the fuzzy floor drove west north west from Paris. Through steamy mists rising on the land.

Late afternoon, a western heaven rippled red. Past all the villages between the wide spreading fields shimmering in the sun, lonely steep roofed red tiled cottages and flowering apple trees. And beyond a grey wall and gateway, at the end of a white dirt drive over two little bridges stood a grey and solemn house in the trees. The dusty motor stopped and out stepped nannie and a sailor suited Balthazar. Pierre the chauffeur handed boxes and bags to Heloise and Celeste hurrying from the house. And the little brown and black dog, Spot, jumped and licked and barked.

Under the slate roof and yellowing eaves were rooms and rooms shuttered through winter, leaving a dark summer air stale and cold. A mile away over pastures rose dunes and on the white sandy shore washed the chill waves of the English Channel. And here Balthazar B learned to swim, learned to pray, speak English and to use his potty.

Mornings nannie came up from the dungeon kitchen with an egg basket of baguettes sliced with layers of soft ham in white creamy butter. The primrose pram with its upturned footrest and lacy awning proceeded out the white pebbly drive and down a straight black tarry road to the beach. As Spot raced up and down unseen between furrows under the potato leaves.

Balthazar's fair skinned body was rubbed with oil and he played the day under the big orange parasol. Cloudy skies he ran up and down the dunes with Spot and dug at the roots of the strange sharp clumps of grass. Until the cool of evening, when returned with a bag of shells and one big one to which nannie said you could listen and hear the sea, they sat by his window with Spot a cozy little ball between their ankles and up over the tops of elms and pines they watched for shooting stars.

All the countryside dark and still across vineyards and turnip fields. A dog barks and a candle glows at a farmhouse. The sleeping sound of waves takes the sand away under the feet and washes ankles white and blue with cold. Nannie leans close with big brown eyes and round smiling cheeks. To seal the day, she said. With a kiss. And not to worry little boy about dreams, no big sea away on the shore will come pounding and foaming down the road. Tomorrow mommie and daddy will come. And like a good little boy we must move our bowels and take our drop of iodine in a glass of water and one day just like nannie you'll be able to break an apple in half with your thumbs.

This night a storm swept in from sea and raged through the poplar leaves out the window. To lie snug and warm and safe where out there under the wild sky the world is so cold and wet. When big harm is a big shadow waiting for little boys who have no roof nor mommie nor nannie and daddy to save them. Gentle sheets tucked up round and safe now to go to sleep.

Mommie and daddy came. And two days later a long grey car with a black canvas canopy and gleaming brass radiator. And out stepped a man in helmet and goggles and shiny brown leather gaiters. Bald with a beard and monster teeth he slept in the bedroom at the top of the stairs. Nannie said he was a famous balloonist and hunter and had just come back from darkest Africa from many narrow escapes from wounded lions, slithering pythons who wrapped round you and crocodiles. Who could snap off your head. And that Balthazar was a bad little boy to crawl up the stairs and throw lumps of cheese over the banister at this Uncle Edouard as he lay asleep in bed.

3

A woman came called Fifi. With a flapping wide pink hat and narrow little waist and fluffy lacy frills round her throat. Her skin was smooth and pale. And by early morning Balthazar stole to Uncle Edouard's door and quietly pushed it open. Retreating behind the banister once more to heave lumps of cheese and fling kitchen knives clattering across the floor. Fifi sat up in bed and her shoulders showed. Uncle Edouard foamed at the mouth and his eyes blazed and he shouted I will kill you you little brat.

Harvest days passed, the grapes and orchards ripened. And on a September full moon night there were voices on the porch below. Suddenly shouting and a face slapped in the still summer air. Balthazar woke from sleep and climbed from his bed in the white pale light. All fear. That somewhere else was far away and home. And the little boy in big pyjamas went down the stairs, past the cracks of light and murmurings under the salon door. Lifting the heavy latch to go down the porch steps and run and run on the wet grass along the drive to the black road. Where his feet felt the warmth and stuck in the softened tar. Then hands jumping out of the vast night grabbed him from behind. The strong arms of Pierre. Who carried the struggling little prisoner back to bed.

Next day through a silent morning house, nannie collected clothes and toys. And out on the white pebbly drive Pierre fastened the long thick straps across the black oily cover of the luggage rack. At noon the big dark car passed along the valley of the Seine towards Paris. Counting barges on the snaking river and the tires humming on the road. Pierre's flat backed grey head between his reddened ears hunched over the steering. Tears dropped from nannie's eyes. And Balthazar in white knee stockings and silver buckled shoes clutched his blue stuffed elephant Tillie tightly to his breast. And little dog Spot whined and moaned between his legs.

High in the attic room in the big house in the little Paris square, nannie whispered God love you little boy. His wrists no longer tied to the bed to stop him sucking thumbs. Nor the elastic hat put on his head to keep back his ears. And in

4

strange freedom Balthazar B snuck to watch from the gallery high on the wall down into the dining room. Where candles flickered and incense floated across gleaming plates and crystal glass. His mother in a white flowing gown, leaned elbows on the mantel, a loose long strand of her golden hair fallen on her tan shoulder and her head held in her hand.

Morning wiping sleepy dust from eyes, Balthazar asked nannie why does everyone cry. Because your father has gone away. Where. To where people go. Where do they go. They pass away. Where. To be with God. Why. Because they are dead. What is dead. Dead is when your heart grows cold. Will my heart ever grow cold. Yes God love you little boy.

At this last morning bath, no laugh nor blush as his pecker stood a point in nannie's face. Hair brushed, a white blouse under a black satin suit. And borrowed long black stockings with the little bumps of suspender garters stretched against his thighs.

"I don't want to wear these nannie."

"Don't make such a fuss."

"I don't, I don't, I don't."

"Don't say don't."

"I will I will I will."

"All right all right all right."

"Let me do what I want."

"No."

"I will."

"Yes, I suppose you will."

"What do you mean nannie."

"O God, shut up you brat."

"I am not a brat."

"I know you're not, I know you're not."

Nannie clutched and squeezed and kissed Balthazar. Leaning her face on his little neck and her cold nose nuzzling up against his silky hair and her lips biting the lobe of his ear.

"Nannie, you cry again."

"Yes I do."

"Because you have been beastly horrid to me."

5

"No."

"You have you know. You should never talk to me like that. Because I don't like it."

The downstairs rooms of the house open, the windows closed and shuttered and table lamps lit. Hands reaching out from the shadowy figures and shaking other hands. Uncle Edouard, explorer and balloonist, a tall dark spectre in the hall speaking to passing mourners on their way to the cars. Towards every tiny rosette in a dark lapel he gave a little inclination of the head, a twist of shoulder and smile.

"It is very up to date. Up to date. Very modern. It is as he would like, I am sure. We do not leave a little wine behind in the glass. Ah so, here is this little boy who throws hunks of cheese at his uncle. Is it not so."

"Do not call me little boy."

"Ah so what are we."

"You should not talk with such a loud voice when my father is dead."

"Ah a son like the father. I am sorry, forgive me."

"No."

Uncle Edouard clicked his heels and bowed. Nannie clutching Balthazar's hand and nodding her way on tall black stockinged legs across the white tiles of the vestibule. Legs that lived and were all alive and were my nannie's. Wheeling me from this house under the red berry trees. By the low crochet wire fences, along the criss crossed paths and green dipping swards down Avenue Foch. The iron lamp posts with their frieze of evergreen leaves. All the high black iron fences thick with ivy before the great stone houses. White haired ladies bent watering window plants in their silent scented world. With secretive gardens and rusting shutters. The little iron doors by the pavements that opened into dark cold cellars. Where ghosts and rats and monsters breathed out a chill to passing little boys.

His father's coffin lay covered with a purple cloth behind the glass of this gleaming black vehicle. The trees in their fullest late summer holding a thick shadowy chestnut green-

6

ery over the long line of cars. The red faced man hat in hand, whispering through yellow little teeth, his lips shiny and dry, eyes moist and grey taking mommie's elbow, as she holds my hand. Nannie following and we sit side by side. The dark men place the last of the white lilies, red and pink and purple wreaths and flowers where the casket lies.

The sun glinting on automobiles slowly creeping out and down the narrow road. Turning left and left again and out past a gendarme standing in blue coat, white gloves and shiny belt in Avenue Foch, holding back traffic with his raised white baton. His stiff salute. On the sandy path the little drinking fountain. Nannie would press the button to make it wee wee. The mountainous stone cold shadow of the Arc de Triomphe. Around the Etoile, amid the stream of bicycles under little trees sprouting over the hard ground. Past the great oak doors and thick walls of Paris. Down the Avenue Kléber and the vista of the Eiffel Tower beyond the thatch of chestnut trees. Blue and red awninged cafes on the Trocadero. Up past the high stone wall and above it the tops of tombs and the tall arbour fence of ivy leaves. A uniformed man at the big open iron gate. Pale, blond pillars. A grey marble waiting room. The cars pull up around a short curving cobble stoned road. And between the slabs of marble, links of chains, the sun in a white heaven blinks and gleams. The dark figures alight. And collect. The voice of Uncle Edouard.

"Ah the eternal regrets."

The coffin carried along the path on shoulders, down between the narrow shady row of clipped chestnut trees. Approaching the grey rain stained walls and roof of this mausoleum rearing from the hard sandy ground. Its small stained glass window open. Through an iron rusting fence and gate the coffin lowered down the steep winding stairs. Beads of sweat on straining faces and urgent whispers. The red necks bulging from white stiff collars. Uncle Edouard touching his forehead with a red handkerchief taking sudden command.

"Careful, if you please, monsieur holds the Grand Croix de la Légion d'Honneur, Croix de Guerre and Médaille Militaire, and Chevalier de la Tour et l'Epée and Décoré de l'Ordre de St. Stanislas de Russie."

"What is Uncle Edouard saying, nannie."

"He is telling the gentlemen not to have an accident."

"Why does he wave his hand around his head like that."

"He has just lost his hat and the pall bearer has stepped on it. He is awfully upset."

Hot and hushed in the random rainbow rays of light on the grey and white checkered floor, the black little group assembling tightly one by one. A kneeling stool in front of an altar covered in dusty brown faded photographs. Of shawled women and homburg hatted men. One smilingly smoking a cigar of whom it was said he was a black sheep who had wandered astray in camel hair to watering places everywhere.

"I am hot nannie."

"Shush."

"Why does mommie sway."

"Shush."

"Uncle Edouard is pulling out his."

"My God."

"Tie."

"O shush."

The priest murmuring prayers as heads bow in the stale musty air. The coffin pushed gently sideways on the shelf in the wall. Sprinkled with holy juices. Balthazar's mother's hair so blond against the black, a white hanky held up under her veil. And as the milky marble slab shut the coffin away. Heads were turning one by one to look at Uncle Edouard as he stood his chin lifted and eyes elevated. His black tie decorated with a balloon and gondola beneath which was written, Bon Voyage.

3

At noon the air still, a white light and dust across Paris. Little groups collecting in boulangeries down dark streets. Big cats asleep in shoemakers' windows. Three long black automobiles turning into an entrance in Avenue George V. A pale delicate tree in the midday darkness, long smooth branches reaching up past windows to a playful sky blue.

The air cool inside the high wide thick doors. Balthazar's mother in her black laces, veils and chiffons ascends alone in the tiny lift. There she is as we come puffing up five flights of wide pink marble stairs, curved and gleaming. Uncle Edouard frowning and pursing his lips at the mechanical marvel. Where are we going nannie, now. Who is that man with mommie. These are lawyers. What are lawyers. They are men who look things up in big books.

"Why."

"To be safe."

"Why."

"Because you must always try to be safe."

"Am I safe nannie."

"Yes."

"Are you safe nannie."

"No."

"Why."

"We must be quiet now."

"I don't like lawyers, nannie."

"No one likes lawyers, little boy."

The big brown eyed soft faced man bowed at the door and led these five people and little Balthazar across the red blue and gold carpet of this high domed marble pillared foyer. Down a long oak panelled hall past portraits of ministers, presidents and kings. He held out an arm at a doorway into a

9

wide pale pink low ceilinged room and nodded as each passed
by his secret face and soft silken cuffs held by wafers of golden
links. Three all black straw hatted women entering, each with
thick greying thatches of dark hair bobbed across foreheads,
each fluttering fans against their veiled faces, and taking seats
in the last row of chairs as Uncle Edouard put his cupped
hand to his mouth and emitted a long vibrating belch.

A great glass topped table stacked with ribboned documents and a black strong box with Balthazar's father's name
written in silver. Balthazar's mother in the centre front row of
chairs, crossing her long black stockinged legs, and her hand
tugging the edge of her skirt down on her knee. She turned to
Balthazar, patting the seat next to hers. He shook his head
and held nannie's hand. The door closed and the key turned
in the lock. The lawyer put on his glasses and nodded and
waited and a man came to nannie's ear. He whispered and she
dropped Balthazar's hand, stood and moved towards the door.
Balthazar with blazing eyes and clenched fists.

"Stay nannie, stay with me."

"She cannot little boy."

"She must she must."

Out the window a sudden cooling breeze blowing over the
tree tops. Great grey thundery clouds collecting. Uncle
Edouard raising a right arm and flickering his hand.

"But of course nannie should stay."

The Maître looking over the faces until he nodded towards
Balthazar and then to nannie and then to Uncle Edouard who
leaned forward over her shoulder.

"Balthazar, the little boy, perhaps he would give the signal
to begin, it is technical of course."

"Begin."

"Ah like the father, he has authority as well as anger."

A cool breeze pushed out the heavy green drapes at the
windows. The clouds growing greyer and sky darker as Maître's voice was raised above the honking traffic in the street
below. Who are those three ladies nannie. They are your
aunts from the country. What are they holding. They are

holding jars of honey. Why. Shush you must listen to Maître. What do hotchpot and trustee mean nannie. They mean important things. Why do you squeeze up your forehead nannie, it doesn't make you look nice. I know but shush now.

"I want to wee wee. You must come and hold it for me."

Maître lowering his manuscript. Balthazar standing and pulling nannie by the hand. A young man turning the key and opening the door and leading them along the hall.

"Come in nannie."

"Go yourself."

"No."

"O God."

"You must not say o God. You must hold it for me. I do not want to be unkind to you nannie, but I will shout if you don't. Now that I am awfully rich you must do what I tell you."

Balthazar returning with nannie across these soft carpets. Maître reads on. A heavy rain falling on Paris. Winds sweeping over the chestnut trees and lightning streaking bright blue across the rooftops. Maître flinching at the splintering shatter of thunder. The young man in the grey suit and flattened gleaming black hair closed the windows. Uncle Edouard taking deep breaths and sighing, ah ozone, ozone. The last page turned over. Maître looked over the top of his glasses and laid the white and red beribboned document on his desk. The little assembly sat in stillness. Maître cleared his throat and pulled slowly at the end of his nose.

"Are there any questions, please."

Uncle Edouard putting back his arms and yawning loudly.

"Ah yes, why are men more fond of dogs than other men."

"Monsieur I think that is perhaps on this occasion out of my arrondissement to answer."

"I am happy to withdraw the question. Lawyers, ah yes, they have courage. But only when it is time to send the bill. It is time by my watch for my steam bath. Besides I always like to be only five minutes away from my camembert in case it is the end of the world and only a little Beaujolais is left. Gevrey Chambertin."

The little gathering rose. The young man unlocking the door. Uncle Edouard taking a stance, heel clicking the ladies departure. The jars of honey placed in nannie's hands. The three aunts each in turn patting Balthazar on the head. Their fat black new shoes sticking out from their long black skirts. One held a cane, and had big brown teeth when she smiled.

4

And this evening a fresh green darkness over Paris. Nannie hurried through the figures collected in the doorway. Tightly squeezing Balthazar's hand as they stepped down the grey steps under the ivy entwined glass canopy. Her big eyes full of tears pushing him up on the high black leather seat of Uncle Edouard's car. She stood wiping her hands across her mended greeny tweed travelling skirt. Her eyes crinkling as she tried to smile.

"We'll be going to Dover. You'll see the big white cliffs from the boat."

"Will there be a little boy I can play with in England."

"Yes."

A loud explosion. The motor jumped forward and nannie jumped back. Uncle Edouard ripping off his helmet to stand in front of the machine wagging his finger.

"You, you machine, you are the first self starting machine in Paris and so help me God you will start or I will kick off your fenders."

Uncle Edouard climbing in again. A yessy grin at Balthazar. And again pressing the little black button. A splutter and the machine rumbled and fumed into life. Light gleaming on his mother's golden hair, her black veils clutched around her shoulders. All wan smiles and waves. They push you away, and say goodbye. Then you are lonely and afraid with all the emptiness deeper and deeper everywhere.

The motor passed honking and lights flashing out across Avenue Foch. Uncle Edouard shaking his fist at a terrified automobilist he narrowly missed. They whizzed by the little triangular peak of land at Avenue Bugeaud with a squeal of tires and bumped over the rainbows of cobble stones agleam in the yellow flood of headlights. Uncle Edouard squeezing the black rubber bulb of his squawking horn. At the Place Victor Hugo under the lamplight a dark figure stepping from the curb turned suddenly to raise an umbrella and shout at the approaching motor.

"Infidel, infidel, I am holder of the Carte for War Injury, third class."

"Out of my way Monsieur, I am holder of the Carte d'Auteur Légion Pornographique, avec une palme et deux balles, first class."

Balthazar turning to look as the car sailed past, and an old gentleman swooned back from the road to fall into the lap of a cafe customer and both with table and citron pressé went crashing to the ground. When I bombarded Uncle Edouard with the cheese, he said I was a little brat.

"Why are you not a big brat to do that to that gentleman."

"Ah but I am."

A man in beret and blue overall with a banana long red nose and tiny dark eyes opened back two huge gates. The motor entered a grey stone paved courtyard and rolled to a stop under a vast glass roofed garage lined with motorcars, two wicker gondolas, and tall potted palms.

"Anatole this is my little nephew Balthazar, he is our guest. Come Balthazar, you have not been here before. You will like it."

"I may not."

"Ah you are a persistently disbelieving little chap aren't you. You must be my friend and I will be your friend."

A looming hairy shadow in the half light behind a gently arching palm. Balthazar stops and moves back a frightened step.

"What is that."

"That is the most dangerous bear in the world. The Grizzly."

"Is he real."

"Ah he is stuffed but he is real. He charged out at us in the Yukon. We had no warning. He is eleven feet high and alive he weighed five hundred kilos. He is too big for the house."

14

Uncle Edouard taking off his helmet and brushing his hand lightly down his gay checked suit. From his lapel floated a tiny red balloon, the Légion d'Honneur aloft, which bounced about as he led the way up a metal staircase to a glass door. Anatole opening it and carrying Balthazar's bag.

"What did you do when the bear came after you."

"Of course I dropped to my knee to take aim. Everyone else they ran. I had just time to fire. I knew there would be no hope if I did not at once hit a fatal spot. I aimed for the eye. Bang. He was but ten yards away and coming like a train. I fired again but he was upon me. I jumped to the side. His paw caught me on the shoulder, tearing right through. It was but a shallow scratch only. Of course it made me a trifle nervous. I had only the left arm to fire the rifle into the side of his head. He could not see out of one eye but at such close quarters his claw came down like so and my jacket it was torn in half. The situation was very dangerous. You follow me. It was terrible. I shot again below the ear. At last he went down. It was like an earthquake. The brambles, the roots, clumps of grass all went flying in the sky. I had won. In sadness I came close and aimed between the eyes. Bang. It was all over. He was a brave bear. Afterwards I had a marvellous appetite. A true Frenchman does not reserve all valour for the battle field but for the dinner table."

Down a long dark hall, the walls dressed with spears, crossbows and arrows. Two dogs, their claws tearing at the parquet rushing to jump up on Uncle Edouard, snapping and growling at each other's grey hairy heads.

"Ah hello. Hello. These two. They are Esme and Putsie. They both love me. But they hate one another. If one could cook for the other perhaps it would not be so."

Shiny green walls round a steep winding staircase into a kitchen under an arching brown smoky ceiling. Blackened great iron ranges, copper pots, ladles from the little to the big. Bacon and hams curing on hooks. Gleaming knives spread on a thick chopping table. Sliced red golden carrots and long strips of meat. Uncle Edouard taking up a large knife and flashing the blade back and forth on a thin tapering sharpening steel.

"Now Balthazar watch me."

Uncle Edouard with one hand throwing up a fat blue pink onion. He holds out the knife. A swift pull, and with the left hand he catches half an onion and smiles upon the other half as it skids away across the floor.

"Ah too bad but I have never caught both halves. But Louis the great chef of Metz. He could do it behind his back with a clove of garlic. While he sang the Marseillaise. He had what you call the dexterity."

Steaming on the range two big black iron pots to which Uncle Edouard tip toes smilingly, drawing his neck like a turtle into his long leather motoring coat. Lifting the lid of one and sniffing. Then the other where a pig's ear peeked from the edge of the vaporous vessel.

"Odette, my God. An aroma fit for, how can I say. A clochard's dream. Such consommé."

"But Monsieur le Baron, I have merely scraped together a few ingredients, as always."

Uncle Edouard with a great bow and sweep, bending to kiss Odette's hand as she raised the other shrinking to her breast and cackled shyly from a toothless mouth. And Balthazar led along a gloomy corridor by this large jaunty uncle.

"Why does not everyone call you Baron."

"To be Monsieur is to be everything already. I am too, your godfather. I am your father's first cousin. It is proper that families remain thick like a good soup so nourishing on a cold day. And here, this is the first private lift in Paris. Out of order, of course. It is man's destiny to go upwards. Even at the most intimate of times."

That night from covers tucked tightly at Balthazar's throat, the world was dark and deep. Under the whitish waves of the English Channel did there swim these turtles cooking. Were they awfully afraid to boil and simmer out of a cold sea and go up Uncle Edouard's twitching nose. Please God make me and

16

nannie go upwards and bring her safe back to me. Even when she is a little sweaty and I do not like the smell.

At dawns to wake in Uncle Edouard's big musty house, and see the shadowy cupboard carved with sheaves of wheat and grapes and leaves of vines. To push the pearl in the black ebony button by the bed. And wonder. To ask why of Uncle Edouard, could not my father do tricks like you. Ah but he did, but they were with the contract, and presto you are a very rich little boy.

A gentle knock. As each morning came a big black and gold leaved Welsh tray carrying a hot white pitcher of milk and white pot of coffee. A small basket of cut bread of crackling crust on the starched linen. Earthenware tub of butter. White white saucers of peach and strawberry preserve. And Balthazar sat thin little elbows tucked beside him. Saying a shy merci beaucoup to the dark thin person who each morning smiled and said bonjour little gentleman.

Down a half landing his bare feet on the silk brightness of Persian carpet and through a glass door was a large tiled room filled with contortions of gleaming pipes. Center stood a canopied iron pissoir as on the boulevards and next to it a frosted glass cage where Uncle Edouard showered. And by one wall a great green glass tub on golden lion paws. The thin dark servant had come to turn the huge gold taps and fill the tub.

"Madame."

"I am mademoiselle."

"Pardon. Mademoiselle what are all the tubes and rubber bottles and clips."

"Ah the Baron is fond of the Enema Anglais."

"What is that."

"Like cognac it is not for little gentlemen."

"Why."

"Never mind but at ten this morning you go and wait for your uncle in the library."

The walls oak panelled and lined with tall books. A globe of the world with a sea all blue and land all colors stood higher than Balthazar's head. Lifting a big book from the desk and opening it across his lap in the high backed leather chair. Photographs of chaps in fur hoods and mittens and fat boots standing on the snow near steaming waters. The kissing sound that Uncle Edouard makes with his teeth as he comes through the door. Bending his head around the chair and smiling at Balthazar.

"Good. You read of the Icelandic exploration. He is Alpert, he is Dubois. My beloved confreres. They are lost forever beyond the arctic circle. Death is painless in such frozen wastes. But come. Today you will see something."

The sun shining whitely on Paris this mid September. The air shimmering and still. In the big motor Uncle Edouard cruised down the boulevard bumping on the cobbles. Across the Seine with plowing barges in its grey green water. And past the wine market to the Aquarium of the Jardin des Plantes. Walking along the gravel paths between the rows of closely clipped chestnut trees. Other little children squatting over their games around plots of blossoms flaming from the ground.

"Uncle Edouard."

"Yes little boy."

"What is the Enema Anglais."

"Ah ha. To whom have you been talking."

"No one."

"You have loyalty. Good."

"Do you Uncle have the Enema Anglais, is that good."

"In England it is for the thrill. But for me it is science."

"What is it."

"A delicate matter."

"Why."

"I am the first to make the first official illegal flight across the sixteenth arrondissement north to south. And for that achievement I use the ballast au naturelle. For three days before I dine in the best restaurants of Paris. And when necessary to achieve further ascent there is the jettison of the bowel. But the trouble was grave. Came the scream of ordure from below. The newspaper carried the headline, The Affaire Balloon Merde. Now before I go aloft I have the Enema Anglais. And then there is no question of the ballast of the bowel."

A moist and steamy air under the high arching greenhouse glass. Pots and palms and vines, orchids and water lilies. They walked hand in hand through a dark long passage. A brown door and into a sky lighted room. A gentleman with a great beak of nose and thin greying hair. His deep voice booming as he shook hands with Uncle Edouard and bowed to the big blue widening eyes on the pale face of Balthazar. Whose small bared knees touched, thin stems joined between his white stockings and short flannel trousers. The air scented with the sharp sweet smell of lifeless life pinned, tacked and pickled.

"Perhaps it is a biology lesson I bring my nephew to. The eels, Professor, how do they go."

"They continue to go down each other's gullet."

"Perhaps you would tell Balthazar the history."

"It is short. They eat each other alive to live and soon there will be but one left."

"And ah Professor, shall we not come and seize him. We will eat him."

"When he is smoked. Dear Edouard."

"Your point well taken, Professor. And the palate chilled with Chablis."

The days ticked by and chimed on the great grandfather clock in the library. With trips around Paris. To the zoo. Where citizens collected in front of the monkey cages cheering the passions of the apes. And when Uncle Edouard said.

"They are but amateurs at love."

"And you Monsieur, you are a professional frissonist. Perhaps you give lessons."

The little crowd laughed. And later under the bright blue awninged cafe by the Bois, Uncle Edouard quaffed the Vichy water as Balthazar scooped up the raspberry ice cream. Back at Uncle Edouard's house, Balthazar passing the strange room of

Fifi who did not emerge, and he heard Uncle Edouard. Long live suppositories, my Fifi, you must shove the cure up the arse for the best results, so as not to ruin the stomach with the pills. The door opened and Uncle Edouard shook his head back and forth, my Fifi is poorly. And Balthazar stepped behind a jardiniere as Uncle Edouard went down the hall.

Nannie sent a postcard from Folkestone with a green stamp and picture of a soldier in red coat with a big black tall hat and you could not see his eyes as he stood with a gun. And remembering a story of olden days when men came to take prisoners out to a big knife which dropped on their necks. And nannie said the heads say words as they roll.

Now this Sunday morning scented with coffee and baking bread. Servants dressed for mass. All silent through the sunless house. Awnings down over windows. Concierges taking momentary eyes away from tenants to feed their canaries. Bells pealing across Paris. Boulangeries laying out their sweet cakes. While old ladies lean between their plants to stare into the street.

The library of Uncle Edouard's house where the Baron, festooned with pitons and coils of rope, clung photographed to the sides of mountains and waving from gondolas prepared for the ascent. The grandfather clock with its little ship rocking the seconds away on a tempestuous sea, struck ten o'clock. And Balthazar sat upright at a sudden sound of loud barking, growling and screaming. He stepped out past the open thick oak door and tip toed up the spiral stairs. Other hurrying feet through the halls and coming up from the kitchen. At the floor above and down the hall from the ablution room, the open door of Uncle Edouard's bedchamber flanked by the two terror stricken servant girls. Sound of glass breaking. Anatole pushing by followed by Odette, and Balthazar peeking between the two.

In the panelled bedroom a canopied four poster festooned with blue satin and crimson tassels. Fifi, Uncle Edouard's unseen strange mistress of the rubbery white skin and kinky hair, clutching bedclothes high to her naked shoulders. The dogs Esme and Putsie flying round like a wheel and tearing at each other's throats. The bright red eiderdown rent. The room afloat with feathers and the growling and slashing and clacking of teeth. The two dogs from the back of a sofa chair leaping to the mantelpiece and felling the photographs. Brushes, perfume bottles tumbling as the doggies sailed across the boudoir table, to briefly sally half way up the only thin panel of green brocaded wall.

The little group aghast. Fingernails in mouths, where a tremulous joy tugged in the corner of lips at the sight of this canine chaos. Anatole in pursuit and tripping over a stool to bounce on his long nosed face. As Fifi raised the cry.

"Edouard, Edouard."

Heavy padding feet coming down the hall. Hunter balloonist explorer Uncle Edouard appeared dripping water from hairy shoulders, a towel held wrapped around his middle. The gathering making way for the master of the house.

"My God Fifi it is like a blizzard."

"Stop them."

"What happened."

Uncle Edouard pursuing the doggie antagonists as they travelled up and down the chaise longue, skidding across the inlay. Now locked in each other's jaws and rolling under the bed.

"Ah ha. It is the Yukon once more."

"Stop them."

"Of course I am. How did it start."

"Esme was sleeping under the eiderdown and Putsie went to crawl in there as well. There was the confrontation in the dark."

"Yikes."

Anatole with a fire tongs forcing them out from under the bed and with a flash of hands Uncle Edouard on his knees seized both doggies by the scruff of the neck and stood triumphantly holding them high and apart from each other in either hand. The two snarling animals shaking and snapping in the air.

A great awful silence. Fifi, eyes wide, slowly raising her hands to cover her face. A little victory smile on the face of Anatole. Slow intakes of breath as the two servant girls covered mouths with their spread out fingers. And Odette the cook announcing.

"But Monsieur le Baron is naked."

There are
More of
Merry matters
Later.

5

And Monday this fading September his mother returned from Bad Gastein in the Austrian Alps. Pierre came to collect Balthazar in a long silver motor. The thermometer on the ivy clad wall of Uncle Edouard's courtyard read seventeen degrees centigrade. And Pierre put a knuckle under the chin of the passing thin dark servant girl with her basket full of vegetables.

"Ah my sweet you would be a nice little pigeon out of your coop."

The swallows dipped and swooped over the dark greenness of the chestnut trees. And the car went detouring a long route down Avenue d'Iéna past the Palais de Chaillot. Where nannie had taken Balthazar to see the fountains Uncle Edouard called the grand pissoir and Balthazar said who makes all that wee wee.

This afternoon to take tea and petits fours on the window seat of the salon in the big house off Avenue Foch. A soft sunlight passing down the grey rooftops and spreading warmth amid the coloured cozy cushions. Little dog Spot jumped and licked Balthazar's face and knees. His mother kissed him on the cheeks and brushed back his hair with her hand. Her skin browned and smooth. And Balthazar frowned and turned away from the swellings of her breasts. A cigarette at the end of a long holder she tapped with a gleaming sharp nail. To raise her chin and look down her cheeks from her fluttering white lidded eyes.

"You will like little English boys. They all go away from their country castles to school. They go in big black cars. Their nannies go too with boxes of goodies. Chocolate and jams, biscuits and turkish delights."

"I want to stay with Uncle Edouard."

"Absurd. He is a great fool."

"He is not."

"He was but one day in America off the boat before he was sold a bridge to Brooklyn. He wanted to jump by parachute into the river, privately. It was too bad he was arrested."

"He is an explorer."

"What. For little tidbits of fluff he picks up on the boulevards to call mistresses. At school you will be taught golf. And that will be nice. You will write often to your mommie, won't you."

"No."

"Why."

"Because I don't like you."

On the lonely grey Tuesday. Rain pouring on Paris. Dreams at night of eels with other eels' tails sticking out of their mouths in a whole great ocean of long grey devouring things waving up like seaweed to bite at one swimming and swimming. And in the morning dressed. Gusts of wind bending the branches and turning up the silver sides of leaves. Uncle Edouard at the bottom of the iron staircase in the courtyard. Patting Balthazar on the head.

"Ah little boy you must not mind, one day it will all only seem as a dream. Remember you go to learn about fair play in England. There they make life like a game and they say play the game. I am glad you have liked it here and you will come back of course."

The big long black motor stopped in the courtyard. Pierre, his father's chauffeur, stepping out. Inside sat nannie. And suddenly Balthazar turned and ran. Up the stairs and down the hall. And nannie, Pierre and Uncle Edouard went searching up through the house. Pierre found him a half hour later crouching hidden in a laundry basket. Struggling and tugging, he was pulled along, his small black shoes digging and dragging on the carpets. His hand catching wherever he could hold and with the other he squeezed his elephant Tillie tightly to his cheek.

Down the iron stairs again to the courtyard, kicking Pierre's

24

shins. The big arms holding him firmly, like the night he was grabbed up from the dark country road. Uncle Edouard's voice and strange sad wave as the others of the house watched from a window.

"O do not hurt the little boy, do not hurt him please."

The kicks rained upon Pierre's leather gaitered shins. And he swept Balthazar up and laid him into the arms of nannie. Her tear streaked face as she sat nodding out the car door. A civil goodbye to Uncle Edouard who stood solemnly holding up a motionless hand. The motor pulled out the gates and turning right, crossed over Avenue Kléber to speed towards the Arc de Triomphe. When suddenly nannie put her hand to her lips and called through the little fanlight to Pierre to please go back down to the white house off Avenue Foch again.

Nannie's dark blue cape flew out from her as she ran through the gate and went tripping up the steps. Beyond the glass within the shadows of the house, Balthazar saw her handed a white envelope. Figures following as she stopped a moment under the ivy entwined glass canopy that shielded the grey steps from the pouring rain. Nannie rushed to the open car door and waved back to the figures emerging on the porch. With a great sigh she tucked the envelope in her bag. Pierre leans forward to release the brake and says to Dunkirk.

With a honk of the squawking horn, the big black car, streaming rain, rolled away from the shuttered house in the little square. Under the canopy cook waved and maid waved and Balthazar in the car's back window stuck out his tongue. Slowly the women on the porch dropped their hands to suddenly raise them again. As Spot the little brown eyed dog came dashing between their skirts and down the steps after the car. Which went faster and faster. And Balthazar screamed stop stop.

Through puddles across grass verges along the Bois to Porte Maillot. The wet little brown and black creature watching up at the back car window as its small legs churned away on the grey cobbles. All along the Boulevard heading north. Pedestri-

25

ans stopping to turn and look from under their umbrellas. And Balthazar said o nannie nannie please wait for him, please.

At a grey deserted cross road, the tired little dog came to a stop. He stood there looking left and right and growing smaller and smaller. To leave a bleak empty space behind on the road. Through the flickering of Balthazar's tears all the way to Chantilly and across the river Oise.

And this next morning out on the Channel a smell of fumes of oil and breath and vomit. As Balthazar led nannie out along the ship's rail and they stood against the bulkhead lashed by sheets of wind and mists of spray from a grey wild sea. A gentleman stood a little away and smiled at nannie.

"Why does that gentleman look at you like that and smile nannie."

"It is what gentlemen do."

"He is looking at your skirt where you have your big mend."

"Yes."

"Why."

"Because he thinks that perhaps I would make a good wife who can cook and sew."

The deck heaving in the long curving foaming swells speeding on the sea. Nannie held a hand to her mouth as she vomited. Balthazar gave her his hanky and put an arm close around her. Pierre in his dark suiting and gleaming leather gaiters was drinking brandy two decks below in the first class bar.

In the grey dark tumbling heavens ahead were explosions of light flashing up from the horizon. The sound of crashing chairs and pots and broken glass as the little ship pitched and crashed into the rising walls of water. Nannie gave out with anguished gasps through the brown and green liquids spewing from her mouth.

A steward came and helped take nannie back to the cabin where she lay eyes closed on the bunk. At a little lamp Balthazar read the newspaper, his stockinged legs crossed

26

jigging his black gleaming silver buckled shoe. He rang for a lemon flavoured mineral water and a thin piece of ham between slices of white bread. Brought by the gentle white jacketed steward. Who smiled kindly and bowed and said he would be delighted to be of further help if anything was needed for madam. And Balthazar smiled and said he called you madam nannie.

Balthazar clutching the broad wood railing on deck. Ahead the white cliffs and sea gulls soaring in the grey sky. Dark castle walls on the hill. Two little lighthouses atop the ends of the great concrete breakwaters. Fishermen in yellow and black oil skins waved and pointed at the tossing packet boat and crouched as a wall of sea crashed. Ships' bells cutting speed. And in the strange silence the little vessel heaved between the lights and across into the sheltered waters.

The safe harbour full of fishing boats and bereft coasters. Under hovering bleak cranes, lines were cast to shore. Dark sheds and railway sidings. The grey slate roofs of the red bricked buildings on the hillside. All chill wet and grim and England.

Pierre signing yellow sheets of paper for a grey uniformed man. Black dressed and capped customs with gold circles around their sleeves. The strange tall hats on the ruddy faced smiling policemen. Nannie no longer green but white and wan as Balthazar helped her unsteadily down the bumpy gangway.

Another grey uniformed man bowed them welcome into the big black car. To bump across the dockyard and between two tall great green wooden gates. Through the town with bricked in flower gardens in front of the houses all called Sunnyside. And suddenly out to the gently rolling green hills and hedgerowed fields. Why is England so small nannie and all the trees in the fields with the cows.

Nannie read out directions to Pierre from a book. Stopping to see signposts through little villages neat silent and green. Up over hills and under canopies of trees. To take tea at an inn. Hot scones and strawberry jam. Pierre across the hall

27

nodding about to cloth capped men in tweed jackets with little knots of scarfs tied at their throats. They stood in the smoke close under twisted ancient beams and swirled tall jars of drink.

"Nannie they look like they drink wee wee."

"That's a very naughty thing to say."

At this great entrance with lions and shields high up, a drive went winding between thick green shrubberies. On and on turning and twisting until they came into a clearing. A great grey massive building. A group of boys their white knees and short trousers. Led hangdog along the road. And who turned and looked at him as the big car passed. To stop beside a tall brown door at the top of three granite steps.

"I don't want to stay here, nannie. I don't like it."

"You will like it. Look see, other little boys there. Nice little English boys."

Inside the lost gloomy greyness a group of heads crowded at the window looking out. Grins on the front row faces. Pierre's feet crunching on the gravel, unloading trunk and tuck box. Nannie pressing the big brass button. A grey haired woman opening the door. Balthazar shrinking in the car. Nannie returning down the wide grey steps, her face and eyes white and tearful.

"Come Balthazar."

"No."

"You must. You must for me."

Balthazar came from the car. His black little overcoat wrapped tightly round him. Blue Tillie clutched to his breast. A bell tolling time in a spire above the roof. Pierre carrying his trunk and box into the shadowy hallway. And Balthazar following nannie to the click of heels down the long panelled hall as a tall thin man approached. Smiled. Offered down a hand to Balthazar. And nannie suddenly turned and bent to touch her lips on the silken blond hair. And then she and Pierre were gone. The sound of the car starting and fading away in this lonely ungentle world.

"Come Balthazar, meet some of your dormitory mates. That's a good chap, this way."

In an oaken door. A large room of high windows, tables, chairs and benches. The wood gouged with initials and names. The walls kicked and scarred. A banana peel on the window sill and a plate of carrots on the floor. And a little group, the grinners at the window. Who approached unsmiling and sidled round like grazing cattle. One hand was put forward in greeting.

"There you are, this is Balthazar. He is from France, boys. Welcome him. No nonsense now. Beefy is another Balthazar but we call him Beefy, don't we Beefy. And you Duffer when you stop picking your nose you show Balthazar here the way about. What is the ablative of fossa."

"Fossa sir."

"Good chap."

The door closed. The little group grinning again. Duffer feeling the fabric of Balthazar's overcoat. A small dark boy of glittering eyes stepped close to touch Tillie's pink trunk and Balthazar twitched his shoulder away.

"New boy."

Balthazar looking round at the hard faces and stepping back and squeezing close Tillie.

"New boy give us this elephant. We don't have toys here. New boy. You must give us this elephant."

"No."

"New boy give us this elephant."

"No."

The little circle tightened about Balthazar. Of narrow eyed boys. Pudgy hands reaching and pulling at Tillie tightly clutched in the crook of his arm.

"Give us this elephant new boy if you know what's good for you."

Balthazar clenching his jaw. A thump thump thump in his breast. Laurel leaves touching the squares of window pane beyond the teeth showing faces. A grimy hand tugging at Tillie's trunk. Other fingers prising open the crook of his elbow. The figures closed in. Breathing up against his eyes. Balthazar shaking himself back and forth from the grasping hands and turning towards the door for escape where another grinning monster stood with big lips open.

"You can't get out of here new boy."

Balthazar raised a little fist and struck out in front of him. The faces closed in again. A hand pushed hard at his chest. He went backwards over a boy crouching behind his knees. Tillie pulled from his hands as he fell. His head banged the floor and stars danced across a sudden blackness. His eyes opened and above him Tillie's grey stuffing dropped down as it was stretched and torn to pieces between the laughing hands.

Balthazar rose shouting and flailing his arms. The door handle turning. A sudden scuffling commotion. Then silence. A row of little boys seated gently at their desks, perusing Latin and Greek grammars, faces contorted in thought. All the studious eyebrows raised towards the opening door.

"What's this nonsense going on in here. What's the dreadful meaning of this."

Balthazar was led away. Down the long dark corridor. His chest trembling with his breath. Through a swing door into a large room with panelled walls and ceiling. A great crystal chandelier on a chain. A woman in a white apron brought a cup of brown tea. And slice of buttered toast. He sat alone among the dining tables. Out the window a terrace. Faint shouts and smack of a stick against a ball. A hill sweeping steeply down to the tops of trees. The sky was grey and purple and flashed with light and there came a distant rumble of a thundery world.

Balthazar taken from the dining room by the white aproned woman. Down the hall and up two flights of stairs. To sit in a big leather chair in the housemaster's study. The thin tall man in a dark checked coat and grey flannel trousers. A bright yellow tweed tie. And his polished boots cracked and scarred. The desk lamp spreading out its dim light as long thin fingers turned over papers. The wind brushing a fir branch against the window glassy and black.

"I am your housemaster. Who pushed you down."

"I do not know."

"The elements of leadership sometimes are found in a little scuffling. We mold little leaders here. Did you get a cup of tea."

"Yes."

"Did you enjoy your little tea."

"It was quite reasonable."

"You speak English well. Who taught you."

"My nannie."

"Good show. You look a dear little chap."

"Do not speak to me like that."

"I beg your pardon."

"I do not want to be called a dear little chap. I am a small human being."

"I see. Well perhaps it's time we took you to your dormitory. Our small human being will be playing golf tomorrow. Do you read your bible."

"No."

"Well we are keen on scripture here. And you must address me as sir. We are not unkind but we stand for no nonsense. Play the game. Play it well. Play it fairly. And avoid smutty talk and companions."

"I do not understand the word smutty."

"Pity. Smutty. You will recognise it when it comes. And know we shan't stand for it."

"What is smutty."

"You mean what is smutty, sir."

"What is smutty, sir."

"That's better. Smutty. Hmmmm. A smear upon the spirit. Concerning things between the legs. There shall be no groping there, you can be sure of that. We shall have no Frenchiness either. When smuttiness comes smite it."

"What is smite."

"Smite, smote, smitten. To strike powerfully. And here we

smite smut. Let there be no question about that. Our little golfers knock it for a loop. You are a clever little chap, I can see that. But we don't want cleverness to become slipperiness."

"I do not understand you."

"Quite simple, we run a school here to mold leaders. Boys here are of the very best families. Little princes and lords with few exceptions."

"I am not a prince or lord."

"We make allowances for that. Commoners are given every opportunity."

"I want my elephant back."

"You mean sir."

"Sir."

"We don't have toys here you know. Boys grow up here. And we will stamp out this groping between other boys' legs. We'll have done with that. Gung ho. That's the cry. You French tend to run under heavy mortaring. You lack gung ho."

"How dare you say that."

"What. Come come. You must learn to take criticism on the chin. Quite understandably you want to put up a little show for your countrymen. Mustn't blind yourself however. Must not do that. From this school you will bring gung ho back to France. Carry that thought with you during your years here. Up you get now. Matron's waiting in the hall. Your number is fifty seven. Always answer with your name and number. You'll get used to it here."

The matron, towels over her arm, led Balthazar along the hall, down a stair and into a high ceilinged long room. A wide shiny aisle of floorboards dividing two rows of beds standing against the grey walls. Matron stopped near one of the tall windows framing the edge of tree tops against a clearing sky. A pinkish mist of white swirling clouds over the countryside. Boys reading, polishing shoes, and tidying lockers. They focused eyes up at the ceiling or down into their laps.

"Here we are now. You'll soon muck in."

32

The matron in her grey tweed skirt and sweater, vast bosoms bumping Balthazar on the shoulder, patted him gently on the head. She smiled around her, nodding east and west. And disappeared out the door where a strange red light glowed from the great window of the staircase.

Balthazar reached to touch his crocodile grooming case on the blue blanket. A toothbrush and toothpaste laid upon a towel, and neatly folded across his pillow, his golden silk pyjamas. Standing now tears all dried, a taste of salt at the corner of the lips, legs atremble and cold. His lungs shuddering faintly as he caught in mouthfuls of air.

Not to look up ere some crushing horror descend at the back of one's ears. Nor move too soon ere a large monster snort new fire. But now to turn gently and up from brave but shy eyes to see. On the next bed sitting a plump little boy. His carrot haired head bent over as he sewed carefully with needle and thread. He looked up and smiled. His eyes were brown and his cheeks big and red. And in his hands, all nearly joined back together again, was Tillie.

Hello
Now
To any
Wondrous
Little men.

6

Each fortnight Beefy's granny sent Swiss chocolate. And little blocks were pushed across to Balthazar in the dark. Lights out and Crunch the housemaster patrolled the dim corridors. At full moon he walked a rapid tight circle at the distant end of the hall, nervously entwining his hands and mumbling.

"We will stamp out smuttiness. We shall have straight little backs and sound bottoms. No smut here."

October trees dropping their brown leaves on the wet grass. Chill damp dawn mornings the little boys rose shivering and clutching towels to hunch to the tub room. The still dark countryside out the window. Wintering thrushes asleep.

The screams and agonised faces as the white bodies cast themselves into the big baths of icy water. Contortions of sweating lead pipes held with shiny brass clips to the white tiled walls. The gurgling laughter, pushes and shoves. And threats of revenge.

"You just wait tonight. You'll feel something you won't like."

Balthazar in uniform, waiting by his bed. Beefy striding back from the wash room with his morning smile. As Balthazar enquires gently as to the way in this world.

"What will happen tonight."

"Masterdon's a big bully. He has foot rot between the toes. He'll put his larger snakes in Duffer's bed. They don't bite hard. They sometimes only give a little sting. His are only grass snakes but I am collecting adders."

Beefy over the days steering Balthazar from the lurking harms. The priest hole where they put you in up to your neck and kicked your face. The mud bath by the river where older boys commanded young boys to wrestle. Beefy said never cry

34

or show you are afraid, the dumbest and weakest boys get the worst and they are especially horrid to princes and lords.

And this Saturday evening at the assembly room to see a tattered film on the delights of Guatemala and splendors of Veracruz. Boys chattering at the door waiting with their pillows. While Beefy below in the basement made a raid on the kitchen and stole away to a little stray dog he sheltered in the woods and called Soandso. Sunday afternoon convened to sit and copy from the blackboard the weekly letter to parents and guardians.

Dear Mother,
     Yesterday was Founder's Birthday and we saw an exciting film all about Central America made by the Founder's father who explored there. On Tuesday we played golf. It was a jolly good caper. Soon we will be playing rugger. For dessert we had peaches and fresh cream. I am very happy here and very much enjoy the new friends I have made.
                                                      Balthazar

Evening prayers in a candle lit chapel this Sunday. High voices in song. Smell of wax and autumn winds bleeding through cracks of doors and windows and crevices of stone. Balthazar staring down at this hymn as the words grew faint then blurred and dimmed. Until he woke on his bed, matron bent over him, a cold compress on his forehead. Then lights out and Beefy kneeling close at his bedside.

"Are you still poorly Balthazar."

"No."

"You fainted. You must be frightened and sad."

"I want to write a letter to my nannie. And master said I can't."

"You shall. Tomorrow after golf. And then give it to me."

A stretch of blue in a bleak sky. Across the gently folding lawns the sun would speed. And sheltered south west, hidden by a canvas awning on the porch of the golf pavilion, Balthazar wrote his small scrawl.

35

Dear Nannie,

Today we are playing golf. The stick is too big for me and I cannot hit the ball. I now have a friend called Beefy. And his real name is Balthazar too. He is not afraid of anything and has gone far out of his way to protect me. On Founder's Birthday we had toast and dripping for tea. The big boys have torture chamber after lights out and they take their pleasure to bang the bottoms of the littler boys. They call it botty bashing and it hurts very much. Honourables get the worst thumping of all. They are the sons of lords. Nothing else is happening here. Tonight is private dormitory feast. My friend and I eat cheese he has stolen from the kitchen. There is starvation here and I am glad my friend is good at thieving. I hope you find a nice husband for yourself soon. I am sorry the man who saw the good mend in your skirt on the boat did not make your acquaintance as he would have found you awfully nice.

Balthazar

The envelope handed across to Beefy. Who tucked it beneath his sweater and set out at a trot to disappear with a wave at the edge of the wood. The trees laying great long shadows in the reddening setting sun. And a week later a letter came for Balthazar which he opened under the smile of Beefy.

My dearest Balthazar,

I did so much appreciate your very wonderful letter. And I am so glad you have made a nice friend. He sounds quite capable. When I left you to school I came to visit my mother and father who live just outside of this town by the Grand Junction Canal. Which is not awfully grand but there is some nice countryside all round. I take long walks by the canal and I carry a bag of bread to feed the swans. I can also see the trains go by and often I think of you. I too hope I find a nice husband soon. And when he is the man in my life, you will always be the other.

It will be so nice to see you at Christmas.

Nannie

36

To sleep that night this letter tucked away under the pillow. And carried each day next to his flesh until the weeks went by and the writing grew faint and blurred and the paper curled and split. To open it again and again until finally it fell to pieces. And one whole line was left.

When he
Is the man
In my life
You will always
Be
The other.

7

The day following the great night storm in the wild year of weather which sent tiles clattering from rooftops and the belfry from the village church, Beefy made his usual speedy mission through the woods to post uncensored letters to the outside world. Balthazar running behind the heels of this chunky stalwart engine puffing the way over fallen branches, threading through bramble patches and looking back to smile encouragement to Balthazar.

And they came to the rustic shelter of pine boughs round a tree. There was a whimper and happy bark and wagging tail of little black and white Soandso. Tethered to the tree trunk jumping and licking in the piles of straw. Beefy with his jar of water, cheese and bread. And great grin as he withdrew from beneath his sweater and shirt two thick lamb chops.

"These are choice loin. They were for Crunch's supper. He will be most annoyed."

Beefy patting Soandso on the head as he growled over his dinner. He said goodbye be a good dog, and waved back as they crossed into a haunted plantation of great ancient oaks. Black shadows of ravens high in the tree tops. Their low throated cries, strange cocking of heads and gleaming eyes. Through a thicket of rhododendrons. Until suddenly they stepped out on the village road near a cozy thatched cottage buried in roses and bramble.

"That's where Mrs. Twinkle lives. She's very nice. When I'm away on holidays she takes in Soandso. Makes him awfully fat. He gets healthy quickly again when he's back in the woods. We're invited to tea. Hers are the yummiest of scones in all of England."

With a grin Beefy pushed his letters into the red post box set in the wall. Ducking back off the road they crossed a field and entered a gate and along a grassy path through rows of moisture silvered cabbage leaves. Beefy knocking at the rose bowered door. The bright orange seeds against the crumbling stone.

Inside this low roofed room a fire crackling, Mrs. Twinkle's moist eyes as she scurried about setting tea. Balthazar scooping up spoons of jam and biting through white fluffy hot scones to taste the sweet melting butter. Beefy went to the piano. His stubby little fingers rippling across the keys, his light voice raising slender music as he sang O For The Wings Of A Dove. And what nannie told in all the little evening whisperings or when we watched out or walked along the Channel shore. She said in the grey heavens over England it rains on a quiet and contented land.

"Mrs. Twinkle thank you so much for having us."

Outside warmed with late sunlight red and gold through the trees. Mrs. Twinkle, grey head and black garments at her back door. The thin white hand raised to wave. The two little friends set off again through the woods. Gaily crossing a grassy valley and along the river. Beefy putting his finger on the small paw prints in the mud round a badger hole on the side of a hill. Through the beech wood and crouching along the edge of the golf course. They swung hands and whooped. And Beefy announced.

"I do believe Balthazar that I know how to butter up old ladies."

Ahead stood the high wall of the kitchen garden. And at the giant yew tree Beefy scrambled up the twisting trunk pulling Balthazar behind. On top of the garden wall balancing. A hole in the branches of spreading boxwood tree below. Together hand in hand they jumped. Into this brief darkness. And to get up from their knees into the clutching waiting arms of Crunch and Slouch.

Light quick hearts and ashen faces. Led between the lettuce and onion beds carefully tended for masters' evening salads. Up the back stairs in the awful silence. To the dormitory to wash. Back down the great staircase. Where the strange blood red spilled from the stained glass window. Their feet making this terrible noise on the boards. Of doom and disaster. Of God nowhere to be seen. Of nannie and her soft hair to let me rest my cheek when I weep.

"Don't be frightened Balthazar. I will do the talking."

"Stop that whispering number sixty four."

In this dim panelled waiting room at the end of the long hall. Sofa seats and tables stacked with the school magazine. Famous old boys on the wall. The cricket and rugby elevens. Voices behind the dark oak door. Opening now. And the grim face of Slouch.

"All right sixty four and fifty seven, come in. Beefy hands out of your pockets."

In the big room windows facing east and south. An oar high up across the wall above white shelves of bookcases. Framed parchments and degrees. Silver framed photographs on the desk of thin dark figures at a Palace Garden Party.

"Stand there. Hands behind backs. Well now this is a pretty little pitch isn't it. I said hands behind the back sixty four. Now then we have some items. Item one. You recognise this Beefy, sixty four."

"I think so sir."

"Do you or don't you."

"I think I do. Sir."

"It would appear to be your diary. Is it."

"Could you hold it a little aside sir, the sun's in my eyes."

"Is it."

"I could be mistaken sir."

"O you could, could you. Trifle with me, will you. It is your diary. Let that fact be clearly established. And it's utterly despicable and odious."

"It is the truth."

"Quiet sixty four, answer when spoken to and not before."

"Sir I should be allowed an answer to your slander."

"Shut up. How dare you. We're only at the beginning of this interrogation. Slander indeed. How would you know the meaning of such a word."

40

"I do sir."

"Shut up."

"You are being uncommonly rude sir."

"I said shut up you little devil. Six strokes of the cane for every uncalled for remark. Now then. Mr. Crunch, let us proceed, you are a witness. And sixty four I wouldn't try the tricky if I were you. Upon his return from Swindon, the headmaster shall have this matter put before him for action. I shudder to think all this is taking place during the funeral of the headmaster's mother. Now then. This is your diary. Answer me, you are a masturbator."

"Yes indeed sir."

"You admit it."

"Yes sir."

"When did you begin this foul practice."

"As soon as I was able sir."

"When was that."

"I don't know sir, ever since I can remember. It has been spontaneous with me sir. It has always felt nice to pull upon sir."

"Take that down verbatim, Mr. Crunch. Now then. Do you deny it was you who chalked up the legend I am the vast masturbator on the blackboards of this school."

"Not me sir."

"Ha, not me sir, yet, page fourteen of your diary. Let me refresh your memory a bit. September 27th. Tonight successfully succeeded in the deed. What did you mean by that. On the next morning following that entry each classroom blackboard had the said legend writ upon it."

"Sir you would allow there are many masturbators at large in this school who may have wanted to give utterance to their feelings."

"Pretty speech sixty four. Very pretty. Cunning and eloquence combined. But we're only beginning here. And you fifty seven. Shame on you to seek out such a bad companion. Of course you are a foreigner. What have you got to say for yourself."

"Nothing sir."

"Just as well. Now then. It has been established here. Firstly, that you are the author of the legend I am the vast masturbator."

"Begging your pardon sir. The legend to which you refer as having been written on the blackboards of this school was I am the magnificent masturbator."

"Magnificent, vast, what difference does it make. Pure pornography all of it."

"I would respectfully explain sir that there is a large difference between a vast and a magnificent masturbator. And it would be prudent if you got your facts correct."

"Six strokes of the best for that daring piece of insolence. Now then. Secondly. Stealing from the kitchen."

"I deny it sir."

"Liar. You are a liar. Mr. Crunch's two lamb chops are missing. Their disappearance not unremarkably coinciding with your absence. Your brazen effrontery is almost beyond belief. What is the motto of this school sixty four."

"Clean hands, candor and godliness sir."

"And what would you say your slippery shabby little hands have been up to."

"Perhaps no good sir."

"Quite. For once we have the truth. Too late of course to outweigh the numerous lies. Mr. Crunch have you any questions you'd like to put before I go on."

Crunch sat in his leather chair. His shoulders slumping about him. The four corners of his gold silk handkerchief drooping from his jacket pocket. Hands folded gently in his lap. And with a strange tremor to see moisture collecting over his eyes as he slowly shook his head back and forth.

"Very well. Now then. Masterdon, eighty four, claims to have seen you, sixty four, abroad outside the grounds of this school. Which is absolutely forbidden."

"What was Masterdon doing outside sir."

"You may ask that question. He had leave to purchase his weekly fruit from the greengrocer, that's what he was doing."

"It would appear sir you have me dead to rights."

"Appear. We have indeed got you dead to rights sixty four. I understand your grandmother is your guardian and you are an orphan. What happened to your parents may I ask. I think these are questions quite pertinent under the circumstances. Speak up."

"My mother was killed in a hunting accident sir. My father took to drink as he loved her very much. He drank his estate sir and died from an onslaught of creditors."

"You don't die of creditors."

"Yes you do sir. My granny refused to help him and she is very rich sir. I put the shilling in the gas meter sir."

"What are you talking about."

"My father sir. He gassed himself in an oven in a room in Glasgow. Overlooking the traintracks to Edinburgh, sir. I was but a mite then. He gave me the shilling to put in the meter in the hall. My father locked me out of the room. And he was dead when the police came."

"Are these lies sixty four, are you having us on."

Crunch put his head down into his open hand propped by an elbow on the leather arm rest. He made a long sigh. Slouch removed his spectacles and pulled a nose cloth from his sleeve and ran it back and forth on the glass. Crunch's flat voice.

"He speaks the truth, Mr. Slouch."

"I see. All right. Both of you can stand at ease. Of course it is very sad. There is no question about that. None. But if we were to let sentiment intrude upon justice where would we be. Where would we be sixty four."

"I guess up to our necks in injustice sir."

"Yes, well that's one way of putting it. Let's get on. Your granny, sixty four, is she your father's mother."

"No sir, she is the mother of my mother."

"In short then, your father's mother in law."

"Yes sir and she was most cruel to him sir."

"That may be. Our concern now is that your grandmother will be taking up this matter."

"No sir. She will not. As she has little to do with me. She

43

lives very north in Scotland where the Romans never con-
quered. My trustees will. They are in London. And they will
be alarmed sir."

"And so they should be. And pray what are they trustees
for."

"My mother's father sir built ships. And his ancestors before him. They built many of the ships sir, which defeated the
Spanish Armada."

"To be sure. I think we may be getting slightly off the point
here."

"No we're not sir."

"What do you mean."

"I mean sir, my trustees who administrate my fortune were
going to leave a packet to the school."

"What. Mr. Crunch, what do you know about this."

"I'm afraid not very much Mr. Slouch. I do know of sixty
four's trustees however. Two of them visited the school a year
ago."

"They were sir to hold the sum in escrow pending my passing out successfully from the school."

"Escrow, escrow. Do you even know what the word means."

"It's from the old French sir, escroe. A bond or roll of
writings."

Balthazar with half lifted right hand moistening his lips
and leaning into the hollow late sunlight.

"That is true."

"You keep quiet fifty seven. One of you talking is quite
enough. Of course we all know sixty four you're head of your
form. It would appear we have two little budding barristers
here. What. But I am quite satisfied sixty four that you are at
the moment seizing upon an opportunity to weave a new web
of lies. And when this little matter is res judicata you can
reflect upon it when pleading someone's case in Chancery."

"Upon my word of honour sir, my trustees are very powerful sir."

"Word of honour. O we are foxy aren't we sixty four. Very
very foxy. Do we think we are foxy sixty four."

44

"I am not foxy sir. I have merely stated that should I be sent down it would make my trustees look with displeasure upon the school."

"Threats, eh. This school has long been quite nearly a living facsimile of Debrett. And such as you, bragging about and tabulating your vile pollutions. And most inglorious of all, two commoners breaching the school rules, its very codes, thieving."

"Pray sir, my friend Balthazar has never thieved and it was I who led him off the school grounds and he did not know he was out of bounds."

"Well now we finally have a confession. One wonders where I'd be without a witness here. Two commoners indeed."

"Nobility sir has never prevented an Englishman from ratting. And pray sir, I am listed in Debrett."

"Are you indeed. Sixty four you will be amused to know that it so happens that we possess a copy of Debrett. What about that. Just behind you there, Mr. Crunch, at the end of the shelf. O I don't think we have quite finished here, not by a long chalk. Trustees. Armada. Packet. Packet of lies. That's your packet. Ah thank you, Mr. Crunch. Now sixty four under whose nobility do we enquire for you."

"Sir if it is the most recent edition."

"It is."

"I am listed fourth line from the bottom page 362 sir."

Sound of groaning horsehairs unflexing as Mr. Crunch shifted position. The long trailing whistle of a curlew out across the grasses. Now the month when the last of all the swooping swallows are gone. And Beefy through the night times said hear Balthazar, that hoot is the little owl and that shriek is the barn owl and they'll be grabbing up the rats and forest mice.

"Hmmmm. I see. Well. One hesitates to think what you will do should you ever get the title. Being that we have it already that you are an inveterate masturbator. And do tell us, the entry is missing for last week. How many times."

45

"Twenty one. Twenty three if we include up to lunch time today. Sir."

"Are you treating it as some distinction, flaunting it at us. A low habit that saps the energy of life, the spirit of the soul."

"Sir last year my average was only eighteen a week."

"I suppose we enter that little score as mitigation."

"Sir in the military manual it provides that troops must masturbate to prevent undue familiarity developing."

"Who the bloody hell has filled you with all this nonsense. I've served eleven years in the Thirty Fourth Poona Horse. That's simply not on. You are grossly impertinent."

"My tutor sir, told me so. He served in the Indore Mounted Escort, sir."

"And what else did he tell you. That gross indecency was the order of the day. He's bogus, tell him that for me, your tutor indeed. Impertinent, I think evil is the word for you. Forgive my shouting Mr. Crunch, one doesn't take slander of one's regiment lightly."

"Do you think we should adjourn for tea Mr. Slouch."

"I'm not quite finished yet with these two."

"Sir I may not be the most splendid person in the kingdom. But I am not evil. Nor am I impertinent. My granny's butler Swithins said that a bit of irreverent cheekiness was becoming in boys under ten sir, whereas the same behaviour might be perfectly insulting in one older. I have some fine qualities sir. Which you may not recognise as worthy. But I shall grow up and serve England and do my duty to the best of my abilities sir. I have the finest voice in the school choir. My ancestors have hewn and used the adze. And one day sir, when I am of age and come into my fortune I will buy up this whole area and blow up this school with dynamite."

"Pretty speech. Quite nervy. Very nervy."

"Into smithereens, sir."

"Smithereens. Well you might use such an Irish word. Typical of idle talk. You bumptious little boy. You don't dare stand there thinking for a second that you intimidate myself and Mr. Crunch who, if my memory serves me, has ridden

46

horse, Third Dragoon Guards. Eh Mr. Crunch. Blow us all up. Bit of military megalomania. Only thing can be said in your favour is you possess such a blatant disregard for caution in your remarks that you give amusement. You little rascal. Who put the eels down the bath drains. And let loose the toads in the faculty room. As per your diary, you threatening little rogue. Well we've got it all down here. A nice little interrogatory. And you French boy. Fifty seven. What have you got to say for yourself."

"I am Beefy's friend."

"Are you indeed. And you want to be sent down with him I suppose."

"Yes sir."

"And what do we know about you. An orphan too, perhaps."

"I do not have a father, sir."

"No father. Strange. How did you get here."

"I am here sir."

"With no father. Slow of mind. You don't follow me. And I'm not about to argue concerning your immaculate conception, dear boy."

"Mr. Slouch, should we not adjourn. It's time for the boys' tea."

"Indeed. A little solitary on bread and water would seem more appropriate. But I think we can wind this up. Yes. Sixty four, you're down for eighteen strokes of the cane. A further six of the very best to be added to the original twelve for threatening to blow us to smithereens. And don't think sixty four you'll be sent down before this justice is administered. Six strokes every other day, with a day's reflection between. That'll keep your bottom busy. And fifty seven pray tell what's your past."

"I am a Catholic sir."

"Good God, that bunch. Romish doctrine. Purgatory, pardons, reliques. Surely you realize it's not grounded upon any warranty in scripture. Whole thing is repugnant to the word of God. There is no popery here. Although we shall respect your beliefs. Well we know Mr. Crunch has striven to keep discipline in our midst. And we shall have gone a long way along the road when sixty four departs. But you, fifty seven shall not be let off so easily. Your mother shall be informed and we shall suggest keeping you here. To make an Englishman of you. Sixty four, prepare to pack your things. Be ready to vacate. The headmaster upon this report will decree your further presence in this school as no longer desirable. Smithereens. No wonder there are no dart boards in Irish pubs. And sixty four just let me conclude by telling you yours is the most remarkable exhibition of brazenness and insolence it has ever been my unpleasant duty to witness in this school in the seven years I've been here. Shirtyness is simply not in it. It's been cavalier villany all the way."

"Pray sir, forgive me."

"Forgive you."

"Sir, and allow me another chance."

"You have the barbaric effrontery to stand there and beg for mercy."

"Sir. Thou hast given me the defences of thy salvation, thy right hand also shall hold me up, and thy loving correction shall make me great. Psalm Eighteen sir."

"I damn well know what psalm. And they shall cry, but there shall be none to help them, yea even unto the Lord shall they cry, but he shall not hear them. Also Psalm Eighteen."

"By every indication sir, I am therefore completely buggered."

"I should not use that word if I were you."

"May I interrupt Mr. Slouch and say something."

"Do by all means."

"Beefy. Please remember, although you are sent down from this school, I am sure headmaster will give you the benefit of certain discretions which will not unduly reflect upon your future and you can make a fresh start."

"But sir if I'm flung out, my trustees will blow a gasket."

48

"You are not yet nine, your trustees surely will consider your age."

"Sir I am nine years, eight months, two weeks, one day, four hours and twenty two minutes."

Slouch tapping his pencil on his paper. The sun a great ball of red sinking and lighting up the edge of clouds in pink. All the lonely corridors, the bleak classrooms, the morning and evening dormitories now threatened to be taken away can suddenly become like home.

"One would think, sixty four, you were twelve to listen to you. I wonder do you know that your redeemer liveth."

"Yes sir, I know that my redeemer liveth. I know it."

"And you fifty seven."

"Sir I think that he may too, liveth. My ancestor was the author of the catechism, the christian doctrine by way of question and answer drawn chiefly from the express word of God and other pure sources."

"Good Lord, one constant stream of surprises."

Slouch raising eyebrows high and Crunch reaching into his pocket to withdraw a small rosewood silver embellished casket. Opening it with a click. Pinching out snuff and putting it up into each nostril. Sniffing and fanning his gold silk hanky beneath his nose. The sun blotted away and the sky darker, tumbling great grey clouds over the deep thickening blue. A bell clanging. And another gently off in the distance from the village church. How so much fear treads where all for miles is moist grass meadows, river and woods.

"Well Mr. Slouch, perhaps, if there's nothing further. I have a bell ringing engagement at village church, and some essays to correct before dinner."

"Yes. Well I think we've concluded this matter. By the way you have traipsed mud in upon headmaster's carpet. Now both of you get out. And after prayers, sixty four, you know where to be."

"Before I leave sir, I ask you give back my diary."

"It's evidence."

"It's mine sir. And you must give it back to me."

"O we will be keeping this little document. As an example to other boys who may be like minded. And after your trustees have given it sufficient and adequate perusal."

"You can't keep it, it's mine sir."

"I most certainly can keep it. School property."

"I bought it with my own pocket money. You cannot keep it."

"Don't you raise your voice to me."

"It is my copyright property sir."

"O we are a clever little boy aren't we."

"Common law sir. My trustees will sue you, sir."

"More threats eh. More uncalled for cleverness. We've come upon a very large cuckoo as is sometimes hatched in a poor little tom tit's nest. I'm so glad to have Mr. Crunch here to witness your display of legal knowledge, I'm sure no one would believe it. I think perhaps I'd better ring for Mr. Newt the school secretary. Get this all down on paper."

"You are afraid of me sir."

"How dare you assume that. Certainly not."

"Respectfully sir, it would be as well if you were. Because previously you have had me dead to rights. But upon my word sir I will tell my trustees to sue you to return my diary. And they are, two of them, solicitors."

"Mr. Crunch, go immediately and fetch Mr. Newt please."

"Mr. Slouch surely we're letting this matter get out of hand. Can't we take a sporting view. I think as a matter of fact that Beefy indeed is within his rights to demand the return of his diary. It is a personal document."

"And I am sadly apt to feel the ruddy little book is unlawful."

"No Mr. Slouch."

"What. Gross indecency with others is not unlawful. Come come."

"I think that is a bit extreme of you Mr. Slouch, his diary does not say others."

"I'm sure there've been others. Frivolities, invitations to bed with bigger boys. Things I hardly yet dare speak of. Unnecessary handling about each other in the rugger scrum. And in the baths."

"Mr. Slouch I can't feel we should pursue this melancholy line. There is no one in this school who takes a poorer view of smutty talk and behaviour than I do. And indeed I have campaigned vigorously to wipe out any evidence of it. But it is a question of the boy's property. I mean we must not get into a lather of hysterics here."

"I'm in no lather I assure you Mr. Crunch. I also happen to be deputy headmaster."

"O dear no one is usurping your authority Mr. Slouch."

"I should hope not."

"But if you shoot off a chap's kneecaps I hardly think there is point in putting bullets in his liver."

"What on earth do you mean Mr. Crunch."

"I think you're being unnecessarily harsh. And somewhat unfair. Indeed they were my lamb chops and had Beefy asked I would have given them to him with the greatest of pleasure. The boy's been punished quite sufficiently. And damn it, if you want the truth I think you're being a bully."

"That's quite enough from you Mr. Crunch."

"And I may add a blackmailer. By threatening to keep this boy's diary."

"Do I hear you correctly Mr. Crunch."

"You most certainly do, Mr. Slouch. This boy Beefy here, and I don't know the other boy sufficiently well, but Beefy is one of the most brilliant boys ever to set foot in this school. Indeed I should not be at all surprised if one day this school were remembered only for the fact that he was briefly here."

"Good Lord I won't believe my ears."

"Well you'd better believe this then. Unless the boy's diary is returned to him prior to his leaving this school, I personally will get in touch with his trustees. Good day."

This tall thin elegant man. His sad face hardened with knotted muscles across his cheeks. Standing glaring at Slouch. And reaching to grasp up the great thick red volume of Debrett and banging it closed between his hands. With a

51

sudden gigantic heave sending the noble tome crashing across the room against the shelves. The oar above clattering down. Slouch raising his arms to shield his face from the descending trophies. And one last, an ancient cricket bat, hanging askew by a shredded crimson thread, fell at the slam of the door.

Beefy with a pump of elbow into Balthazar's ribs. Brief grins and eyebrow twitching on the faces of the wide eyed little boys. Slouch slowly stands. Smiles fade. And Beefy, his mouth open drawing in his breath and raising a hand slowly to point at Mr. Slouch as he leans forward on arms pressed astride on the desk.

"Sir. Your flies are open."

Slouch with a shiver straightening up. Quick nervous fingers tugging and pulling and buttoning. A red rage steaming at his temples. Beefy clutching Balthazar by the hand. Retreating backward towards the door. As the words come hissing out of Slouch's teeth.

"You two get out of here before I kill you."

Balthazar turned the crystal handled knob and pulled open the heavy door. Beefy glancing behind and pushing Balthazar forward. The door slamming. And they ran pounding down the wax gleaming hall.

It is
The random
Accumulation
Of triumphs
Which is
So nice.

8

Across Berkshire, Hampshire and Surrey, the headmaster returned from Swindon. His little grey roadster pulling to a halt at three this Thursday afternoon. This early December. Rumours whispered. And two mysterious days went gloomily by.

On a damp Saturday they marched down across the pebbled path to the sports pavilion. Carrying their towels, striped stockings and boots. The crash and crunch of muddy bodies. Ear pulling, shin kicking. A wet rugby ball sliding from hands. And Beefy plunging his tough little figure past monster Masterdon for the winning goal.

To the strange postponement of beatings Beefy said they were finding out if my trustees are leaving a packet to the school. And then Sunday after prayers in chapel as cocoa was being given, numbers were called to report at Mr. Slouch's room. Twenty two, fourteen and sixty four. And as Beefy tugged on trousers over his pyjamas he said to Balthazar, they have found out that my trustees are not leaving them a fig.

Masterdon came grinning near slurping cocoa down his cheeks.

"Slouch nearly captained England Beefy. Scored one hundred and twenty runs. Your botty will surely be poorly."

"Shut up Masterdon or I will punch you in the eye."

"Just try it. Anytime."

Balthazar watched as Beefy walked out the aisle between the beds. And disappeared into the hall and up the stairs. And down to doom. The minutes went by. And then the first screams.

"Hey Balthazar, that's your friend Beefy."

"It's not. That's Duffer. Beefy will never cry out."

Above, at the end of each sound of heavy running footsteps. A loud scream. Six times. And six more times. And then the footsteps running and followed by silence.

53

"That's Beefy, Masterdon."

And the dormitory figures stood on their beds waiting. Beefy strode back in neither sad nor glad. Followed by whimpering Duffer and Jones. Who ducked and cowered between the beds as they were made run the gauntlet of knots and wet tips of snapping towels. When lights out to snuggle up to one's knees in darkness. Ahead a cold grey Monday. Of Latin cases, isosceles triangles, and the triumph of England at Waterloo.

At the evil sad time of four o'clock Balthazar and Beefy were summoned to headmaster's office. The oar and cricket bat back up on the wall. Debrett safely on the shelf, a wide crack down its spine.

"All right boys. Stand there. Would you kindly take a seat over there Mr. Crunch and you there, please Mr. Slouch. Now I'm not going to waste time explaining the enormity of the offences and why they merit the measures they do. We know that without rules chaps would be waltzing naked in Piccadilly. But before proceeding I would like to ask you number sixty four to recite the canons of this school. Indeed if you know them."

"Be respectful at all times to masters. Do not tease younger playfellows. Be kind and attentive to elderly people. Do no mean or sneaking thing. Be always open, cordial, honest, manly. Be at all times clean of ear, teeth and heels."

"Yes. Quite. But you have forgotten something."

"O. Don't spit bone or other substances caught in the teeth back on to the plate."

"Well that's certainly not done but it is not in fact a canon of this school."

"Pure thoughts and deeds sir."

"Good."

"Sir I feel sick. And am about to disgorge."

"Get out of here this instant then and come back."

"Thank you sir."

Beefy quickly exiting out the door. Slouch grunting. Headmaster taking his pince nez from his nose and pursing his lips.

54

"Well now fifty seven, your little princeling friend seems suddenly to have got a weak stomach. From what we hear of him it's certainly not his normal condition. I think we are all a little excited and bewildered. With this rather disquieting situation. I don't like much of what I've been hearing. But it would appear that you are being led by a boy much advanced in chicanery. The fact that he is to be sent down and you are to stay should be of no encouragement, let me assure you of that. Have you anything to say."

"Sir he is my friend. And I do not care to listen to what you might say about him."

"Noble of you, I'm sure. Cheeky too. We of course would not expect you to rat on your friend. But we want straight answers. Have you engaged with number sixty four or others in activities which might involve your being in the same bed with another."

The door suddenly opening. Beefy reappearing.

"Don't answer that Balthazar."

"How dare you come in like that without knocking. Stand right there and be quiet. I repeat to you fifty seven, have you engaged with sixty four or others in activities in the same bed."

"I refuse to answer, sir."

"Do you realize I may have you sent down for refusing to answer."

"Yes sir."

"Well are you going to answer then."

"No sir."

"Very well. We'll take up that matter later. Sixty four. I have here your diary. Is that correct."

"Yes sir."

"What is the meaning then of these smutty homosexual poems."

"What poems sir."

"Do you wish me to read them."

"Yes sir."

"I would eschew such a tricky little pose as you are attempting here sixty four. Don't try it on with me. Have you engaged in smutty behaviour."

"I have sir. I frolic at request with the big boys sir."

"It's clear then that what Mr. Slouch says is true, you are completely without conscience."

"I have always enjoyed sexual activities sir, my tutor said one must always uphold freedom of the flesh."

"That's quite enough out of you. Needless to say your guardian has been written to. And your trustees. And your removal from this school at the earliest has been requested. Do you understand what I'm saying."

"I do sir."

"However, Mr. Crunch here has pleaded upon your behalf and not without my listening with some sympathy. Also that matters in your past were not everything to be desired. And it is upon his pleading that I do not mark your record. You will go from this school able to make a clean start at another. We are aware of your considerable talents it would seem. That's perhaps the greatest pity. One allows for your exceptional abilities but that does not give you licence to attempt to make fools of us. Or that this school is run for the amusement and benefit of one or two boys. And now we come to the matter of the ownership of this diary. I am not satisfied that the opinion given on either side in argument concerning this is the correct one. But for the time being I personally feel the diary is best kept with us."

"Sir."

"Now I'll do the talking sixty four, you keep quiet. And when you have settled in somewhere else we may take up the matter of this diary again. Now who takes care of you in the holidays."

"I go to Sutherland to my granny's sir."

"O yes I know it up there, bit north but good shooting. Don't suppose you include shooting among your other more unhappy proclivities."

"Yes I do sir."

"Hmmmm. That so. Well I know it well up there. Yes. I

hear birds are plentiful on the moors this season. Last year, August, sixty two brace of grouse by seven guns in abominable and atrocious weather. North wind very adverse. So you shoot."

"Yes sir."

"Hmmmm. Good to start young. Keep your eye down the barrel on the bird. Where is your guardian located then."

"Ruppinton sir. Ruppinton House."

"Jolly fine shoot. If the day is not spoiled by mist and downpour. Very high rent for a season."

"My granny is a tartar sir. She has been known to charge for drinking water sir."

"Is that so. Well we won't go into that now. Mr. Crunch, Mr. Slouch, I think this sad little occasion is over then. Anything to say. What. I think we have dealt with the matter fairly. What. Can't let the school down. We raise boys to be leaders in all walks of life. And not so they are found some day waltzing in a state of undress around Piccadilly. Both of you are therefore dismissed now. And sixty four, take a bit of luck with you."

"Thank you sir. Goodbye sir."

A bright crisp sunny day. This Friday afternoon. Beefy on Tuesday went to the village and bought dog food for So-andso. Selected meats, liver, vitamins and minerals. And delivered him freshly bathed from the river to the care of Mrs. Twinkle. He went to a last choir practice. And his solo voice could be heard out across the fields. He said he would be going north to Scotland and knew what he would do on the train. He would look up in the dictionary many foul words and say them in memory of Slouch who was a tadpole and a bicycle seat sniffer.

Balthazar was given all the precious little treasures. Hidden behind a loose brick near the boilers where Masterdon kept his grass snakes. There was a hunting knife. A catapult and a pea shooter. A secret shoe box with two poisonous adders. And an obscene photograph.

Beefy bundled up with a long black scarf said goodbye at

the top of the great stair. The blood red of the window lighting up his ruddy cheeks and carrot hair. And Balthazar went to the room where his elephant Tillie was torn to shreds. His face pressed to the glass as those grinning ones that day. And out on the gravel a bowler hatted gentleman held open the door of a long black car. Beefy stopping and looking back at the window. He reached into his coat. A great grin on his face. Smilingly he withdrew a small black book. Held it up and waved his diary.

The car turned up the little hill of the drive. Tires crunching on the gravel. White exhaust in the cold air. And at the rear window the face of Beefy. Throwing a kiss from his fingertips. The naked trees. And now the car vanishing beyond the rhododendron. A last wave too late because he was gone. Towards the steeple tip of the village church, as it poked sharply into the sinking sun.

> And
> The bell
> Rang once
> To say
> Goodbye
> To
> Sixty four.

9

In the empty dormitory Balthazar turned himself upon his face and laid out his arms on the cold pillow of his bed. If only one knew how to die. And go away from this lonely friendless world. Rise by one of Uncle Edouard's balloons attached around the bed. And there floating high in the sky cast down much merde upon this school.

At evening table no glad tidings, nor bold moments. Of catapulting cheese lumps at the grey bearded founder's portrait. Or rolling a drinking glass to get crushed under a servant's foot. Nor at night hear his kind thoughts to comfort one through till dawn. You mustn't worry now. Tomorrow we are having margarine with breakfast and marmite. And I have put much salt in the masters' coffee grindings and they will screw up their faces and find the taste most awfully horrid.

And now to lie tired cold and shivery. To hold hands down between my legs. And knees up to my chin. When Beefy would tap his chest and say, let the magnificent masturbator speak. I am the king of masturbators and have a bent for botty bashing too. And somewhere sometimes another lonely boy would whimper, cry for mommie and in his tears fall to sleep.

This last week before Christmas holidays. To play rugger. Face, knees and elbows deep in the dark thick mud. Bruised and sorry. To drop the ball from slippery hands. Amid the shoves, screams and shouts. Beefy said always be gentlemanly and honest, except with masters, bullies and enemies and defend against them by all means at hand. And do the indecent thing to do, if possible.

Until this cold damp evening after rugger the dormitory windows black with night. Masterdon promenading in his soiled underwear strolling with his grinning big lips past Balthazar's bed.

"Frenchy. You're going to be in for it something shocking. They are clearing the foreigners out of this school. Frenchy. Those with dirty pictures hidden in the walls. Maybe you are not so spunky now your little piggish friend Beefy is gone."

Balthazar rushed forward and sent a looping fist into Masterdon's eye. The big boy reeled and reached out to grab at Balthazar's hair. Who ducked and ran towards the door. Followed by Masterdon's heavy slippered feet. Down the main stair. To the darkened entrance hall and into a door and down another stairs winding into the vast haunted cellars. Through the blackness into the warm dry air of the boiler room. Followed by Masterdon. Balthazar hugging close running round the boiler. Masterdon behind tripping over a box in the dark. Balthazar rushing out slamming and bolting the metal encased door shut. The heavy breathing of Masterdon the other side. Then his voice.

"I will kill you number fifty seven when I get out of here."

"You may never get out."

"I'll shout for Slouch."

"Do. He will never hear you. He is sniffing bicycle seats."

"You think you're clever fifty seven."

"Yes I do. Watch out, your snakes may turn on you and eat you."

"Shut up that talk."

"If your snakes don't bite you Masterdon, Beefy's adders will. I put them in there yesterday. Two adders."

"Shut up you."

"Adders Masterdon. Adders. They are able to strike in the dark. They can tell where there is warm flesh and strike. They are moving now towards you."

"Shut up, when I get out of here I will kill you just remember that."

"Masterdon. Adders. Masterdon adders."

"Shut up shut up. You'll be sorry."

"You'll be dead of poison from the adders Masterdon."

"You never put an adder in here."

"I did yesterday. Two adders in the white shoe box. And you knocked it over just now."

"Where were they then."

"They are there Masterdon. Coming near your ankles. It won't be long now before they strike."

"Let me out of here."

"No not till you are well bitten."

"Let me out I say."

"Apologise. And vow never to bully again. For I am not joking, there are adders in there, caught by sixty four."

"Please let me out now."

"Vow."

"All right, I vow."

"Vow to never bully again."

"I vow."

"Say it."

"I vow to never bully again. Now let me out."

"All right, but Masterdon, you better know I will fight you. And it will be worse for you because you are big and it will be awful for you if someone smaller gives you a thrashing."

Balthazar unbolting the boiler room door. To hear Masterdon's heavy breathing an arm away in the dark. Waiting for the grab of his hand. "Are there adders in there, fifty seven, turn on the light. I don't want to fight."

"Yes, there are. In the shoe box."

"God they could have got me. If they've escaped. You must be mad. I think you are thoroughly mad like sixty four."

"I am not mad Masterdon. But you are a bully. And you do not find fear so amusing when it is you who is afraid."

"You won't tell anyone about this."

"I am not a tattle tale Masterdon."

With the light on Masterdon searched and held down the adders with the furry end of a broom. Balthazar picked them up by the back of the neck and dropped them back in the box. The light brown slit eye and zig zagged yellow brown body and hissing little head as they curled to strike. And that night before lights out. Masterdon came padding across to Balthazar's bed. And handed him one of his tangerines.

The day before the headmaster's speech and the next day's Christmas holiday departure, there was a letter placed upon

Balthazar's bed. School trunks were being packed. A last fever-ish trading of uncherished treasures. And Balthazar sat and tore open the blue envelope postmarked Leighton Buzzard.

My dearest Balthazar,
    I have the sorriest thing, for me at least, to have to write to you. My father who has not been well for some time has been taking a slow turn for the worse. My mother who has arthritis cannot look after him alone. And so I have written your mother that here I must stay. I did so much want to look after you again during the Christmas holidays in Paris. A new nannie, your mother tells me, has been engaged and I am sure she will be very nice. She will collect you from school and bring you back to Paris on the train.
    With all my dearest love always.

Nannie

The blue paper stretched between his fingers. And her large curled writing that leaned forward so that it might fall. As a drop went plop and another drop went plop and the ink lines went furry under the tears. Nannie's cool hand on warm nights on the English Channel shore where there were the shooting stars. And she said that when you die some people say you go down in the ground and others say you go up into the dark and blue. And if they do, go up into the dark and blue, that's why there is so much shoving and pushing be-tween the stars.

In the assembly room, the squealing of shifting chairs and gabbing voices that raised the roof. Seated along a side row the masters, each looking out in directions of their own worlds. And suddenly the assembly called to stand. At the entrance of Mr. Slouch. As a whisper went through the boys.

"I am today, sadly, boys, deputising for the headmaster. Who sadly, has been called back again to Swindon, where I much regret to say, his father has now died. Let us all join here together now and say a short prayer. O Lord, we beseech thee mercifully to receive the prayers of thy people which call upon thee, and grant that they may both perceive and know what things they ought to do, and also may have grace and power faithfully to fulfill the same, through Jesus Christ our Lord Amen."

Slouch slowly rising on his toes and rocking back carefully on his heels. As he now bends forward casting a glance down his person, across his flies to his shoes and up again to the treacherous little lake of faces. His left hand rose to touch the red carnation in the buttonhole of his dark grey suit.

"Your royal highnesses, my lords, commoners, and other boys from other lands. You all know the holy season approaches. Good will towards men. And in view of the perils our Monarch and our country face, on land, on sea, and in the market place, that sentiment is not lightly spoken. Our colonies, upon which the sun never sets. India, Africa, not to mention Hong Kong, Suez, Mauritius, Tonga. To these places, one day, some of you here may go to rule in the interests of our Majesty's government. We must, therefore, send you forth with strong bodies, agile spirits, and not least of all, fair minds. Let us be quite clear on that score. Never, in this day and age, has fair mindedness been needed so much by so many. Often it is too easy to grab the quick profit and shun the long term prize. When the indecent thing to do seems the most attractive. I mean, it should never be done, the indecent thing. Now then to those of you who may be called to govern your country upon the death of a father or uncle. Let your decisions be guided by canons and codes you have found here at your school. In short, play the game. And let those among you, by whom this concept may be thought old fashioned, take heed. Those before us a hundred years did not think so, and those after us a hundred years, will not think so. That concept is as modern as it is ancient. Take fair play then firmly in your grasp. Hold it tightly. Let no foreign land, person, shake it from you. No jungle, no glacier, or desert weaken your resolve or fibre. And against all, especially the whisper that England is in a sorry mess, we declare aloud, England shall triumph, England shall overcome, England shall win."

A ripple of hear hear down the row of masters. Who briefly looked down at their knees and back up again with chins raised. A dapple of bright sun spreading across the wall. An impatient shuffle of feet and coughs and nose blowing in the audience of little boys.

"And now to those of you who leave us this term, to take the next step on the pathway to honours, we wish you God's speed. And lastly, a sad note. I should like to make quite clear, and say once again, that our efforts shall be unrelenting to stamp out practices in this school which are steeped in smut and defilement. There has been he among you found, corrupt and dissolute and who would spread a plague of vileness. We all know who he was who swam in the odious depth of putrescence. But I would not end on that unfortunate note. Our school has been cleansed of that lamentable catalogue of infamy. And so I now say with loud voice. When the wicked man turneth away from his wickedness that he hath committed, and doeth that which is lawful and right, he shall save his soul alive. Amen. Do not eat too much Christmas pudding boys. Now rise. Dismissed."

The long stream of cars next day made their slow descent to turn and park and wait on the wide gravel apron. As the heads peered out the windows, said goodbye to other heads and stepped forth with their little bags sometimes to kisses, others to bows and some to nothing at all.

Balthazar waiting searching among the opening and closing doors of automobiles. From a small blue motor, the village taxi, stepped a tall woman in a grey long flowing coat. And long soft light brown hair. She looked across the windows. She waited and Balthazar watched. And next him he felt the large arm of Masterdon.

"Fifty seven, do you see that long car which has just stopped. Watch. The gentlemen getting out are Beefy's trustees. Come to sue the school for a packet."

"How do you know."

"I heard Slouch say they were on their way. He was in a most awful tizzy outside the assembly room, rubbing his hands, he was saying what shall I do, the headmaster is away. I say, who's fetching you."

A shout up the stairs. For number fifty seven. Crunch smiling at the door towards this tall woman.

"Ah here you are fifty seven. Here he is. Not the worse for wear, it would seem. You managed through. Got your case, everything with you. Have a good holiday. Be off with you now."

The tall woman smiled and asked may I carry something. And Balthazar said no politely and lugged his two cases to the little blue car. Turning to watch the two stout, puffing and wheezing gentlemen. One in a black bowler and ecclesiastic gaiters, the other in grey homburg, black overcoat and striped trousers. Both white haired, wing collared and each with a cane. The blue little car was pumped with a handle, started, and moved slowly by the three figures meeting on the school steps. Slouch spinning his fingers round each other over his waistcoat buttons. The ecclesiastic gaitered gentleman raising his red tasselled cane in the air and barking out a deep throbbing voice.

"Sir you are an uncommonly mournful man and I would take my stick to you were it not an offence."

The taxi man wore a black cap which he touched to all questions asked by Miss Hortense. As they drove through the afternoon towards Dover Marine. Between the still milky green wintering fields. Through shadowy woods. And past a great marvellous windmill turning its slow slatted sails over the rooftops of a little town. The taxi man said aye Miss there is much hop picking during the summer, and there be gypsies everywhere.

Past the village greens, churches and clock towers. And cottages, some white, some thatched and all as cozy as Mrs. Twinkle's. To take afternoon tea in a hamlet on the flat lands of Romney Marsh. And that night to supper at an inn. Pigeon pie and sprouts and wondrous trifle. Nannie smiled and said do have some more. And we shook hands goodnight at my bedroom door. To climb snug between cool gleaming clean

65

sheets and to warm toes against a clay hot water bottle and make as Beefy said, little botty booms and pull gently on my penis till sleep.

Morning came bright, early and fresh. Horses and carts clip clopping below in the street. A taste of salt on the chill air. Waves on a grey pebbly shore. The harbour alive with masts. Fishing boats, a sail up, moving out between the breakwaters towards France and a rising sun.

New nannie at breakfast wore a short sleeved frilly lacy shirt tucked in tightly at the top of her grey long skirt. A gent across the room over his kippers waved and grinned. Beefy said the big white things on the chest were called breasts and they had ends on them called nipples, because his granny had a maid who sometimes in the hot summer attic let him play with hers. This new nannie had very large ones that pressed out tight against her shirt. And gentlemen seemed everywhere rushing round her in a crazy manner.

"Miss Hortense where do you come from."

"Huddersfield."

"Where is that."

"It's in Yorkshire where they make cloth."

"Is it nice."

"No. It's all foggy, smoky, but I liked it well enough."

"Is your father in good health."

"Yes."

"What does your father do."

"He is an impoverished clergyman."

"What is impoverished."

"It's when you make fires in the sitting room only in the evenings and on Sundays."

The waiter bowed over Miss Hortense and she quickly put her hand up to the frilly neck of her blouse. What Beefy said about them was true, they were white swellings and made you stare. And made the waiter bend his neck and the gent across the room missed his cup with the pot of tea and now the waiter was running with a cloth to mop it up.

Balthazar dug and cut into his toast, bacon and egg. And

66

filled his cup from a big brown pot under a thick cloth cover which nannie lifted up and said was very much like a bishop's hat. Her eyes are smiling and the world is so bright and cheerful. Bend the wafer of bread and sweep it into the red broken yolk and through the white sweet bacon fat. Tip upon it tiny specks of salt and lift it up between the lips, the yummiest thing for weeks. And chew with bulging cheeks the rich warm goodness washed down with splendid tea.

The gent bowing up to nannie as we left the dining room. He took a little book from his pocket and wrote in it. And crossed it out when nannie laughed and shrugged her shoulders as he grinned unhappily. Again he waved his hands, crinkled up his eyes and held his pencil to his book. And when nannie wasn't looking while she held her hand for change he lifted one of his shoe tips to shine it on the back of his trouser leg.

"Miss Hortense, what is wrong with that man."

"He fancies himself."

"Why do you say that."

"He invited us to Le Touquet."

Balthazar and nannie came out of the large green breezy shed, stepping across tracks. A white hull stood high along the quay and on the bow it said Invicta. Cranes hoisting great nets of luggage and mail bags. Stewards crowding at the top of the gangway. Tickets ready, please. This way to first class. All first class this way. Second class that way please. A porter packed their luggage on a shelf in the front lounge. White table cloths, green wicker chairs and potted palms.

A sailor said the sea was fresh to moderate. The ship's whistle blew. Coffee and refreshments would be served in ten minutes. Nannie's eyebrows curved like big rainbows above her eyes. And they were grey like the sea. She spoke with lips apple bright and gently soft. Her skin was smooth and nose upturned. And I wanted to lean over and touch her on her soft silky elbow.

"I hope you will be quite content to take care of me for the

67

holidays. I am really able to take care of myself so you won't have much to do. Are you looking for a husband."

"O dear what kind of question is that."

"My last nannie was looking for one. And a gentleman admired her. On this very boat. But she vomited. She was very good at mending. But now she will never get married. Because she must care for her father."

"That's very sad."

"Yes. But all the gentlemen look at you."

"Do they now."

"My Uncle Edouard will too."

"My goodness."

"He is very hairy and big and strong. I think that he can bend an iron bar. He kills animals with his bare hands. But now I must be very quiet all the way to Calais. To memorise my Latin verbs."

The ship's engines rumbled. The hatch doors banged closed. Sailors hammering wooden wedges under iron clips. The wind gathering up and blowing down the decks. And inside the lounge a peace descended. Nannie smiled and cast her eyes gently down under the gaze of a French gentleman with a monocle who swung up the edge of his grey cape with a swagger stick. He too came and bowed. Presenting a white little card upon which he wrote and nannie tucked it in her bag. His suit was checked and two of his teeth were gold when he smiled.

A tall tower above the town of Calais. The seaweedy smell from the shore. The dressing huts along the beach showed summer colours faded and cold on the lonely sand. Fishermen at the end of the pier. They all looked like peeing. Their serious faces. The ship crushed up against the wired bundles of sticks and the stout ribs of oak along the quay. Miss Hortense holding him by the shoulder at the railing. With a shiver to suddenly feel a touch of her lips warmly on top of my ear.

A stream of porters rushing up the gangway. A smell of garlic, cigarette, wine and onions. Officials' lower lips protruding looking up as they held hands folded behind the back of

their neatly pressed uniforms. A red pompon on top of a
sailor's blue beret as he casts a line up from the pier. This
squat brown eyed porter rushing up to Miss Hortense, as a
breeze billowed open her grey coat. The swell of one of her
bosoms tightly against her poplin shirting. The porter making
a quick sign of the cross. As he whispered to another porter
behind him, I say hello to the women and to hell with the
men. And to Miss Hortense he said, madam may I carry even
your handkerchief. Down to the gay shore of France.

> Where each
> Little fellow
> Is a
> Citizen.

10

Balthazar's mother moved from the big house off Avenue Foch to a sprawling apartment overlooking the gardens of the Palais Royal. Miss Hortense with her tall flowing gay willing way came each Christmas, Easter and summer holiday. Taking Balthazar back and forth to Paris by taxi ship and train. While his mother went hither and thither to Baden Baden, Liechtenstein and Biarritz, to one for a cure, to the next for taxes and to the last to swim.

And this summer now hot and dry. A white dust rising to whiten leaves in the Tuilleries. Balthazar's mother asleep till late afternoons. At nights to dinners and balls and weekends away from Gare St. Lazare to the country. A Czechoslovakian woman came to cook and a Russian to clean. They had their lunch in the big kitchen with the high walls hung with pots and pans.

Mornings Miss Hortense would sit doing the English paper crossword puzzle and play dominoes between the plates with Balthazar. And in the warm cool at night, hand in hand they sat on the balcony above the garden. The shadowy stone urns with upturned seventeen spears, and four fish hook prongs to keep out intruders. And one year ago Miss Hortense said I think it's time you called me Bella.

Each day to laugh down the steps and out across the gardens. To sit a while where the solemn little children played under the thick chestnut trees. Or watch the marionettes in the Tuilleries. And the favourite hours to quietly read away an afternoon on the sentinel pale green chairs. Miss Hortense to be seated with her pillow, her elegant long legs crossed in the hot sunshine. By a bed of pink roses while the sparrows pecked and scratched and bathed.

The mornings at dawn Balthazar heard the keeper open the

gates. And sometimes alone and dressed, Bella asleep, to go down and skip along the brown and black tiles of the arcade and pirouette on each four leaved shamrock. Bella said it was good for Irish luck. Then pause to read the garden rules which said no writing on the walls, no sound instruments and no games which can bring trouble to the tranquillity of the pedestrian.

And on this soft summer Saturday night. As Balthazar and Bella walked hand in hand past the black fence bars topped with golden spears. By the stamp shop and where the old strange watches stood in the window with coloured pictures on their faces. And near to me was Bella. The close up of her grey eyes was green. And her breath as sweet as roses. When she told her secrets in wide eyed words. And whispered dreams. And laughed when she lost at chess.

"Balthazar."

"Yes my Bella."

"You know something."

"What."

"I am going away."

"Where. What do you mean."

"I am going away from you."

"Why."

"It is too complicated to explain."

"Has my mother told you to."

"No not yet."

"Then why. Don't you enjoy coming to Paris anymore."

"Yes."

"Then why."

"Because this is all very foolish."

"What is foolish."

"You are growing up. You're getting tall. A full inch above my shoulder last year. And now, see. You come right to the top of my ear. When first we met you were only up to here. Soon you will be thirteen. You don't need me anymore."

"That's rather an unfortunate thing for you to say Bella. I don't understand why you've chosen to discuss this at all."

71

"Because it is ruining my life coming here three times a year."

Passing the windows of the red carpeted theatre. And into the peristyle courtyard. Crossing between the stone pillars, they stood near the restaurant with the golden walls and carved and painted ceilings and the mirror you could look up at from the courtyard and see down from the restaurant ceiling on to tables where customers were leisurely lavishly eating. To see now this moment a gentleman's hand with gold rings, his fingers opening and closing upon a glass stem which he raised to swirl a wine beneath his nose. On the restaurant window it said Sherry, Goblers and Lemon Squash. Miss Hortense took a deep breath and raised her eyebrows and bent forward as she walked.

"Bella, I did not know I was ruining your life."

"It was unfair of me to say."

"You told me it was nice these holidays like this. And you could give all the gentlemen about Kensington a merry dance. And you had your nice little change of situations."

"O God what a mess. Don't you see I love you. And you are far too old to be loved like that."

A strange shiver comes upon the back of the head and goes down the spine and lingers between the legs. The sound of our slow feet passing over the waves worn in the tiles. The lace shop. Rooms alight behind curved shiny windows above under the roof of the arcade. And through all the black muddy months there loomed her middle parted brown long hair. And how she bent each thumb backwards on her wrist and could spin her skirt high up over her knees and always forgot to castle her king.

To come now through to the empty street and back to the little bell and great dark green enamel door. Yesterday so bright and sunny. Shopping at Corcellet, where Miss Hortense smiled to rub her shoe on the brass letters of the entrance floor under the iron bunch of grapes. And she laughed and laughed as she sewed on her bedroom chaise longue. Of the story about Uncle Edouard. When a month ago he dined at a terrace on the Champs Elysées. When a gust of wind exploded upon the cafe, tore off the awning, and carried away the umbrellas over the tables. Le Baron the balloonist extraordinaire remained calm, giving instructions to the waiters to stand back from the cyclone. And as he held to his own table umbrella, it rose with a bang. Uncle Edouard clinging tightly as it pulled him off his feet and down the boulevard. Shouting. I am in control, I am in control.

Now climbing up these dark stairs. And the big brown doors. The incense smelling vestibule.

"Bella I am fond of you too."

"Don't you see that is the trouble."

Feeling a tender trembling and shaking. Her summer tanned back and the cool brown across her shoulders. The white skin under the straps of her light blue summer frock. My breath seems pushing up against the back of my eyes. And the first time off the train at Paris when I gave the address and opened the door for her into the taxi she smiled and took my hand and said your manners make you such a little gentleman and if only you were bigger I would have you for my man.

Miss Hortense swept into the salon and went quickly from table to table to turn on all the blazing lights.

"Why have you done that, Bella."

"I don't know. I think it's as well. Your mother is away. There's no one here the whole weekend. I've turned on the lights that's all."

"You're awfully upset."

"The fact of the matter is I'm twenty four and should be married."

"But every man will have you."

"That does not mean I want one of them. There's little to choose between a cunning solicitor and a rich dunce, except my choice would be neither of them."

"If you marry the cunning solicitor he's sure to be very rich one day."

"And his heart and soul completely poor."

73

"But Bella you said yourself that only money matters, and for a woman it's better even to have her own."

"Yes. I said that and it's true. I'll be cured next week when I buy a new hat."

"Shall we play chess."

"I don't feel like it tonight."

"It is not too late to go to the theatre."

"No."

"Do you want me to go away and leave you alone."

"For heaven's sake no."

"I am awfully sorry that I have made you so unhappy."

Miss Hortense against the edge of the high grey marble table where she put back her arms and pressed the heels of her hands. And her fingers whitening as they tightened around the cold hard stone.

"O God it's crazy. It's crazy. In fact it's far too funny. Here I am, good Lord, in love with a twelve year old boy."

Miss Hortense turned from where she leaned and slowly rolled herself over the arm rest and fell deep into the green brocaded sofa of eiderdown. This still night the end of June. Faint horns honking along Rue St. Honoré and the memory of an afternoon three years ago when I went down into the Métro of the Palais Royal, past the blue smocked woman at a desk with her plateful of centimes and stood to wee wee elbow high to a nearby man. Upon whose gleaming patent leather shoe I peed. And he reared backwards stamping his foot, his own pee crazily sprinkling his trousers and tiled floor. I quickly buttoned up and ran. Out past the phalanx of dark brown cubicles and up into the street into Miss Hortense's arms. And when she asked what did you do I said I peed on a man and there he is now with his black briefcase shaking his umbrella. And Miss Hortense turned and smiled and made him a fluttering curtsy.

"Bella why do you say this when I have told you that I love you too."

"Balthazar it's not your fault. I can't expect you to understand. What could you ever know about women."

74

"I want to learn. I have read some most unseemly books."

"God you're so sweet. And I mustn't say I could kiss you."

The tinkling eight thirty chime of the gold mantel clock. Miss Hortense's brown long legs shooting akimbo on the gleaming parquet. Her big toes upturned from her sandals. A great heaving sigh whispering out her lips. And back now these years. For all the hushed little nights when Beefy said across bedsides. Of what girls were for, and what you could do to them. More than botty bashing. More than pulling or playing put it in the ring. That his granny's maid said she had a hole like a penny slot and one day he would have hair there too. And out of his horn a white hot syrup could come. And Beefy would whisper as each urgent piece of news arrived about girls. That they had their own little knob upon which you could play. That nipples could get big and hard but he was not positively sure of this yet. And girls were of two types. One to whom you did the vile and odious thing and whom you would not love. She would be a servant, a waitress or a maid or be in a back alley of the town. But girls you loved were cousins at the race meetings or partners at dancing school or at aunts' and uncles' houses in their pretty dresses. You married them and always and always they had their own bed and dressing room and you would not go in there unless it was desperately necessary. Beefy never said what he knew about nannies for each one he had departed after a few days.

"I don't like you staring at me like that Balthazar. Do you think you should go and find something to do."

"Why."

"Because I think it would be proper."

"Why."

"Don't ask me why."

"Then I will not go and find something to do."

"Don't."

"I won't."

"I don't care if you don't."

"And I don't care that you don't care that I don't."

"Then don't."

"I'm not."

"Then I am going to go and sew."

Miss Hortense standing. Her sandals making a flapping noise on the floor. Passing by Balthazar as he stood near the door. His blue jacket closed and his flannel trousers long and white. Miss Hortense went by the fruit basket on the dining table and snatched out a pear. The strong muscles in the backs of her legs. And the thin tapering ankle and tendon down into her heels. Her bedroom door closing. I tremble and my heart thumps. Tight and hot in my head above the eyes. When I made a squeaking noise on a leaf between my palms, Bella laughed and said I can do that. I said beware my spit, I'll find a new leaf. O no I like your spit. On a bench near the Trocadero after I showed Bella my father's tomb. And I said I would not want a germ to harm you. She laughed and suddenly threw her arms about my shoulders and squeezed me tight and said I could eat you all up.

Balthazar turned off the lights of the salon, save one by the window and bookcase where he knelt and pulled volumes from the shelves. A faded green spine which faintly read The Neighbourhood of Dublin. His father's large scrawled signature inside the cover. Tales Uncle Edouard told. Of the noble and splendid blood of the Celt flowing through our veins. After the battle of the Boyne our ancestor fled in the Flight of the Wild Geese from Ireland to France. They were brave men of unquenchable principle. And he was one brilliant fellow, a Royal Astronomer of Ireland. He knew much of ether and even electricity. And from this great house he watched by telescope out into the solar system. It was only because of the clouds that he did not get much chance to see the stars. Remember always you are of Irish kings as well as of France, and all Irishmen are kings but not all kings are Irishmen.

With four tomes under arm and Paris bells tolling eleven o'clock Balthazar passed along the dark hallway to his room. The dry creaking of the boards beneath the feet. Miss Hortense's door with a bright dot of keyhole. To pause to knock. And no. She may never like me anymore. And tomorrow we were going to go to Sevres. To see the porcelain in the museum. All our splendid days we wandered here and there. Along the banks and book stalls of the Seine. In and out the alley darkened streets, Huchette, Suger, St. André des Arts, passing under grey peeling walls, buildings like full old bellies, buttons bursting and washerwomen's eyes staring sullenly down. Often they stopped at St. Germain des Près for citron pressé and all the young gentlemen giggled at Miss Hortense's horsey elegant beauty, twitching their shoulders as they went by and laughing in their little groups to catch Bella's cool grey green eye. She would rise up tall between the cafe tables. Her white beaded summer bag tucked neatly beneath a breast. And with the other cool hand to throw her hair back upon her shoulder and putting aloft her head, the tiniest smile across her lips, she stepped out on the boulevard, her hips gently shifting to and fro. A grin on her face as a cry went up from the cafe table, long live mademoiselle so magnificently callipyge.

Balthazar bent an eye to the keyhole. A yellow light and golden drapes at the end of the room. To be shut out from all her warmth and love. Across the polished floor and persian carpet hangs her light blue dressing gown from a chair. And a night three summers ago I awoke to rumbling thunder to stumble afeared out into the corridor. To say outside this door. Nannie, o dear I am most frightened. But not loud enough for her to hear. Too shy to knock and too shy to show my fear. And suddenly her door opened and lightning whitened her window and flashed behind her. Her body so long and slender and outlined against the light through her sleeping gown. She held me there and then said come, get into bed with me, put your head on my pillow and I will tell you why there is no need to be afraid. Because they are playing skittles in the sky and when they want to throw a ball, it's only that God puts on the lightning so that they can see. And then there's the big boom and the rain comes down to wash away all the mess. And in sleep I snuggled and clutched to her and dreamt I flew on a white horse up steps right into the sky and jumped over clouds and put my fingers into soft crushed berries and cream. And at morn to wake and see her brown long hair streaming across the pillow. As the triangle of sunlight rose up the green wall. And the clutch of deep dark small freckles on her back and I put a finger there to rub one away and she rolled over and smiled, her eyes so gaily alight and sparkling and she slowly withdrew one of her long long arms from under the covers and reached out and pushed me on the nose and said hey you, you must get out of here now.

"Balthazar. Is that you out there."

"Yes."

"What are you doing there."

"Looking through your keyhole."

"What can you see."

"Nothing."

"Come in then."

Balthazar turning down the handle on the door. Opening it into the soft light and blinking his eyes. Miss Hortense in her bed. The blue linen counterpane drawn to the bottom and up into the soft peach blanket stuck her knees and toes. The pillows piled high, a book clipped open by her elbow and shiny needle in her hand.

"Goodness Balthazar what are you doing with that awful pile of books."

"Reading."

"Sit down. Reading what."

"This one is about tunnels and railways. And this, it's a book about Dublin. Have you ever been there."

"No. My father has, he was born in Belfast."

"What is that."

"That's a city in the north of Ireland. Where they march and beat great drums and say they are up to their knees in catholic blood and up to their necks in slaughter."

"That's not awfully nice."

"No. It's not."

"Did he ever talk of Dublin."

"Yes he liked it there. And the pints of stout and chunks of cheese that he had in the mornings in a pub. He read Divinity at Trinity College. He said it was the happiest time of his life. And he always said, that there in Dublin, the sun shone in on our lives."

"Bella, you're not cross at me are you."

"No. Of course not, why should I be."

"I don't know. I feel awfully badly when I think you're cross with me. And now I feel much worse that perhaps you might be going to go away."

"You're such a silly boy."

"You know I'm not silly."

"Yes I know you're not silly. I'm silly I suppose. And really you're old enough to know. That I am going to have to go. Aren't you. But it's not that I want to. It is nice to be with you. And we do like so many things together. And so you know don't you that it's not that I want to. And that it has been the happiest time of my whole life. That I've ever had. Don't hang your face down like that."

"I'm not."

"You are. Come sit over here on the bed."

Balthazar put his tomes on the floor. And crossed to Miss Hortense's bed. Where the light shone down on the white folded sheet and her slender arms sat in cushioned little white cloth valleys. She lifted up an embroidery frame. Its streaming blue and green and yellow threads.

"Do you think this is nice."

"It looks such a bore to do."

"After all my work that's what you say. Anyway this is what I want to tell you. That this is not good for either of us. Soon you will want to be with girls your own age. And God knows I ought to be putting a rope around some gentleman and tying his ankle to my stove. You see Balthazar when I'm not with you. Well I don't know what I'm going to say. Many men have asked me to marry. It may be me or my little money. They all seem to get to know rather too quickly for my liking that I have a small income. But each time something always goes wrong and either I hate them or they hate me."

"I want to marry you."

"Balthazar."

"You mustn't laugh. You are only twelve years older."

"But your whole life, what you are going to do, where you are going to go."

"I think I am going to go to Dublin."

"Ah, that is something nice."

Miss Hortense's arm fell slowly and her hand touched Balthazar's blue serge sleeve. As she always did when she was pleased, reach out and touch me gently. With a closed mouth smile.

"And you know Bella how awfully rich I am. And when I am of age I can go where I want and you can come too."

"Yes."

"To go on big ships. To Africa and America. Will you wait for me to grow up. Will you please, Bella."

"That is the most wonderful proposal I have ever had."

"Will you then. Will you please. When I finish school before I go to college we could be married."

"You're so serious aren't you. And I will then be over thirty."

"I would not care."

"Yes you would. Your eye would be seeking out the young ladies."

"I would never want anyone else."

"Heavens, heavens. And what am I to do then from now till you become of age."

"Three times a year you would be here with me in Paris. We could go to Bucharest and from there to St. Petersburgh. We could go to Dublin. And have cheese like your father did and the sun would shine in on us."

"You rascal. You are. You have more daring than on a trapeze. God how girls are going to waste their tears on you."

Balthazar slowly stood up from the bed. Miss Hortense laid her embroidery away at her side. Her dressing table with her ivory brush and mirror and comb. The crimson lining of her open pigskin writing case with envelopes blue and pink. A lone bottle of scent and toilet water. Where his mother's bath was shelved high with colognes and sweet essences of faint colours and perfumes in all their tall fat crystal bottles. To bend now to pick up these tomes.

"O please don't go away like that."

"I will. Because at least I have told you of what is in my heart."

"Don't go away like this Balthazar."

"I am. Why should I not."

"No. Don't. Come back here."

Balthazar turned and laid the books on the chair. He walked back to the bed. And as his knees touched the edge, Bella's hand reached out and switched off the table light. And her hand felt and took his hand and she pulled him gently down. Her fingers up through the short hairs on the back of my head, and cool they touch in behind my ear. Tumbling down into her arms she whispers out o God come to me. Her kisses over my mouth. On the cheeks and eyes. Her tongue along the side of my neck and deep into my ringing ear. All the bells of Paris. And stormy choirs sing when it is not yet mass or Sunday but her silky long slender arms, smooth wrists, and soft slim hands. She breathed her breath catching in her lungs. And I can hardly breathe at all. Her hard teeth as she bites into my mouth. Her hand at my throat to undo my tie. Pulling herself up out of the sheets. Hair strings of shadow hanging round her head. I watched in the gardens once her fingernails as she sat and scratched her thigh and they made big long white marks on her sunny skin. Distant fingers unbuttoning my shirt one by one. And close by lips kissing me upon the breasts. Bella tell me what to do. Nothing nothing. Just take off your clothes. And so strange to wonder. Of all these years of dreams. To reach one day in the laundry room to secretly touch her drying underthings more close to her than I ever hoped to be. And now lay side by side all along her body and feel it pressed to mine, like two bodies all of your own. One here and one you reach around. Bella is what we're doing love. Yes yes. Hurry tell me how. You'll see you'll see. And I see. Bella on top of my mind chewing a cashew nut. Bella what do I do. Nothing nothing now. Like that flush of jealous courage two days ago. Waiting for a seat on the back of the bus to Place du Pont Neuf. When the conductor pinched her on the bottom and Miss Hortense widened her eyes, squared her shoulders, raised her brows and parasol and said in English keep your hands to yourself you miserable little man and the conductor laughed and as they returned once more to alight, he reached to pinch again and her parasol came slashing down across his wrist. It was an unfriendly time. To reach and gouge out his grinning eyes. Or wait one day till I was big enough to slap his cheek and shake his molars. For now I touch. All of this most precious prize. Here from the top of her head to the tip of her big toes. Can I touch and put my hand running over you you're so smooth. Yes you can you can and come on top of me. Bella Bella it's coming out of me. It won't stop. All over you. O darling you mustn't mind, sweetest and dearest, let it come out over me, you must not mind. Bella tell me what did I do. It's all right now. It should have been inside you. Yes but it's all right, you mustn't mind. I know it means you'll never marry me. And I hope I haven't been vile. Balthazar it's really all right, really it is. I feel all ashamed and all awful inside. You must tell me, Balthazar, tell me if you do. All around in me it's going very strange indeed, you're not a servant or a town girl in the street but if I've done this I can't be in love. O God what are you talking about, love is for everybody wherever it may be no matter what you are. You're so young you see, full of all those tall tales of all those little boys. It's not vile, it's not that at all, but what I'm doing to you is so wrong. Why do you say it's wrong. Because it's my duty to take care of you. But isn't this the best care there could be then. Balthazar you're asking such damn questions and knowing answers too damn fast, but nothing can be answered here, just lie now with your silly sad little face, and maybe a devil too, you know don't you that we should never do this again. If anyone found us I would be in an awful mess.

82

"But there's no one here but us. And if we never do it again you'll never teach me."

"You know enough already you little rabbit."

"What have you done with men Bella."

"And what have you done with girls Balthazar."

"Please Bella, what have you done."

"You mustn't ask me questions like that."

"I must know."

"Why must you know."

"Because if you did I may never speak to you again."

"O dear. Turn around your head. Come on. Turn around. You're quite spoiled you know. Look at me. Are you jealous. A little aren't you."

"I'm not discussing it. Do you do this. Without your clothes and be in bed with other men."

"And I'm not discussing it."

"If you've been like this with other men I will kill myself. With arsenic."

"O Lord."

"I will."

"Snuggle up close and comfy to me. Don't let me hear you say that again. Or I will be off to Bristol or something like that and go on a ship. To the south seas."

"Bella I love you so much. So awfully awfully much."

"There you mustn't cry. You really mustn't."

"And I never want you to go away for ever and ever."

"I'm here now. You crazy little rabbit. I'm here."

"If you don't stay with me I don't want to grow up at all."

"But you little rabbit you can't stop growing up. You'll know all sorts of girls. Through a whole bunch of years. Innocent and smiling ones who would make you think butter would not melt in their mouths."

"I don't care, if there isn't you I don't want anybody. No one could ever take your place."

"O God."

"Are you cross."

"No no I'm not cross. Just crosseyed. How are you to understand. I just feel I'm somehow sitting on my backside. In the middle of some very grand ball. And I can't get up off the floor. For months and months. I've wanted to just seize and hug you and hold you to me. And I knew, I knew this would happen. That we never should have been left alone. That all it needed was bumping into you at night in the hall or just the nosey moments in the evening when you get long faced when I tell you not to read my letters. And each time you sulked I had to do everything I could to stop myself hugging and kissing you. Don't you see how it's been for me. O but don't you get cross now."

"I'm not cross."

"You are."

"I'm not."

"O Balthazar. Don't you see. To you the world is just as you find it. Just as each day it's time to get up, to dress, to eat, to sleep. The trip to school. And to Paris. And here we kind of live in a little estate all of our own. Larking about in each other's hair. But the world is not like that. Like we are now. And if we were ever found. Really like we are now. God if we ever were. Did I lock the door."

"Yes. And you hung up the keys under the telephone."

"O God. I don't even know that I may be doing something criminal. I don't know but I might be."

"I am a criminal then too and we are still together."

"Yes. Till they cart us off to prison. And sling us into cells."

"Uncle Edouard would see that we were freed."

"Uncle Edouard, I wonder. Don't depend upon him."

"Why do you say that."

"I just do. He's nice. But don't depend upon anybody Balthazar."

"Did he attempt to entice you."

"O nothing. Three years ago."

"What did he do."

"Jealous jealous."

"I'm not. What did he try."

84

"Nothing. He invited me to the Bois. And so you came too. That's all. And once to Biarritz. And I said I went nowhere without my boyfriend. And he laughed and was quite nice. And probably he did want to take me to bed. You see how difficult you have made me for other men. And then one day you'll see a creature without whom you think you cannot live. And she'll throw her arms up and spin about and raise her skirt on her legs. And you'll like what you see. And she'll look beautiful and flutter her eyes. Put rouge on her cheeks. And tell you nice little lies. And squeal when you feel her breast. And as she shrinks away she'll say come hither come thither and do not dither dear blond beautiful Balthazar. O God she'll get her bloody hands into your hair. And you'll marry her. And she will be up to her elbows rummaging in your fortune when she isn't skipping down the Faubourg St. Honoré. For soap and saddles and suits and rose bouquets."

"I would never marry a girl like that. And who would put rouge on her cheeks."

"I hope when all the years have gone by. And I'm retired in my little country cottage somewhere in Devon. With all, I hope, my many emoluments. That you'll come and see me. And put your hat on a hook and a cane against the wall. You may even be tall and straight and grey. And bow as I sit in black and lace near my fire. With probably the same old embroidery frame. And you'll take up and kiss my hand. O God let me kiss you, kiss you. While you're still here here here."

The night hushed and still. Faint breeze out on the garden tree leaves. Paris cools in darkness. The slow slow sounds that transport over the city. A shout. And listen, a strange answer. Some night time philosopher advising himself. To avoid hunger perhaps and a treadmill day. Like the shadowy men standing inside the cathedral doors in all their silent poverty. Where do they go at night. And Bella said there they are on the benches and in winter they will lie on the Métro grating. To curl up in wait for another day. And the day Bella said let's, when I said why don't we go on a train. As we stood outside the building of the Légion d'Honneur as the sun

85

shone down the Rue de Bellechasse. She made big eyes on the street and made me laugh. And said maybe we should take a picnic and never come back again. We two. Go in search of the holy grail. And we go. Don't we go. Into the great Gare d'Orsay. And I looked up at her flowing hair as all the eyes watched her trotting by. Searching wide eyed between the wondering citizens. Under the darkened glass roof and monstrous tiled walls. First stop St. Michel and through Gare d'Austerlitz. And when we got off the train at a town, any town. Bretigny. There were kids with a flag marching through the street. Blowing bugles and workmen putting up coloured lights for a fete. When it started to rain. Houses shuttered up. And curtains elsewhere twitching. As we walked hand in hand down the street. And Bella said no holy grail I'm sure will be found, we are Balthazar in a most uninviting town. Would we ever live here. Yes with you. With you I would too. And back on the train in a carriage with three. Of gentlemen. Who stood and turned and sat and sniffed as Bella crossed her legs. And they said ah we are well fixed, I have just come out of the hospital and I am very well placed, to live just far enough outside Paris where it is country and close enough too. Each of them their eyes dropping on Bella's knees and looking when they could at her face. And when they left the carriage and in the corridor, one said my God if I were a young man what I wouldn't give to do what I could do to that one, and I Monsieur would not need to be young to do what I would do to that one. And we came back through the station and the urine smell. A man passed and said to Bella ah up there the unmarried employees live. And she said why tell me. Ah Mademoiselle because to have such beauty passing so close by I feel somehow that it is justice you should know. And we went to a restaurant up through the streets. Where she sat and I thought and thought of the men on the train what did they mean what they would do to that one. What would they do. And Bella let me have a full glass of wine. What would they do to you those men. O it's just talk, men never grow tired of flattering themselves. We raced and ran all the way

86

back up the stairs and into her room. And Bella is this what they do. When I put my hand here and feel your breast the way it swells up from the rest of you. And I don't know yet what you've got down there in your secret hair. Yes dearest it's what they would do. They would kiss me only I'm kissing you. They would grab me tight only I'm grabbing you. And they would do what I'm telling you. Come Balthazar on top of me. On top. Like that. And never would I want you to be them. You're sweet and sweet. And my own loveliest little man of mine. Get in between my legs. There. God it's so hard. I'll guide you in. Don't worry don't worry. O God there you are, there you are. O God Balthazar. You have it up in me. And all the thoughts you never knew you'd know. Of some strange miracle happening to it there. In that part of her. Was it her. Like her face and teeth and hair. These speaking lips so close. Just step out of my brain and into hers. And hello where's the holy grail. Like rolling down in grass in all the wet sweet smell of hay and stop and stare up into a sky of chestnut blossoms. White white planets everywhere. Bella. Have I done it right. Yes yes. O Bella o Bella please it's coming out of me, it's coming out of me, hold me please. Yes yes my dearest let it come. Bella don't let me die. O please. And bleed away all my blood. O Balthazar I won't let you die or bleed away all your blood and God I'm dying too. In all the nooks and crannies and shadows of the sheets. Torn back from bodies one wild one pale. Her hand bumping and counting on my spine. And put my fingers on the hard bone behind her tiny ear. Your face Bella has your eyes closed. And you smile all around your mouth. Everything now so still. Save another long cry from the street philosopher. In search of the holy grail. And you went back up on your shoulders and groaned and groaned. Bella it wasn't unhappy was it. No no not unhappy, you silly boy. I worried you were in pain, you went all so stiff and shook. Sweet that's the way it is when it happens, with happiness, happiness. Why then do you have tears in your eyes. I don't know why. Tell me why. Bella. You must. Tell me why you're crying and you are. And her elbows pointed out into the dark as she held up hands. Tips of fingers across her brows, palms flat on her cheeks showing just her lips and nose. I know I'm crying. And try to lift her fingers. O please what's the matter Bella, please tell me what's the matter. O Bella what has happened to you, what have I done. I love you so, I do I love you so dearly so and now I've done something, please speak and don't cry. Please speak. I can't I can't. The mattress trembling. Her stuttering sobs. Bella you're frightening me, please what's the matter. I won't be frightened if you tell me. O Balthazar I wish I were dead. I wish so desperately I were dead. O Bella you must not wish you were dead. You must be alive with me. Let me see under your hand. Bella. I always know what's in your eyes. Please let me see under your hand. No. Please and then I can make you better again and dry up your tears. Come you snuggle in Bella now, I'll take care of you and hold your head and make you nice again. Maybe you have a little stomach ache. Little men with hammers who jump around in your belly tinkering and banging on your pipes that's what you used to say to me when I had a tummy pain. You see Bella I make a cozy corral of arms for you to be in with me. Don't you feel safe. No harm will ever get you now. Balthazar I desperately wish it were so. I like you holding me and I know that everything you say is real and is true and what you believe, you must know that I do. But it just cannot be.

"Bella I love you and have told you everything in my heart."

"I know you have, I know you have."

"I will love you through all of my life."

"You can't Balthazar, you can't."

"I can I can."

"I've got to give my notice to your mother. I'm twenty four, twenty four."

"You'll not give it."

"I have to. We're sure to get caught at this."

"We won't we will go to hotels."

"O Christ."

88

"And I will go to my lawyers for the money. I like doing this to you."

"O Lord. But for God's sake Balthazar you must never never breathe a word of this. Never never no matter what happens."

"Why not if we're in love."

"Now listen to me, people just won't understand. You would never be that foolish would you."

"Yes."

"O God please now Balthazar I'm very serious. This is no joke. You would not want to see me ruined and that's what would happen if ever a word of this were breathed. To anyone."

"Promise then you'll stay."

"I can't."

"Yes you can."

"But what can we do together now. I mean you see it's all different now."

"You can teach me more about antiques."

"You know more than I do."

"Well then I'll teach you. Bella I won't tell anyone. But you must not go. I want everything to stay just like today."

"I know sweet but dearest, things change. Everything will be different in just a very few years. And you'll not care at all that I'm gone. Now hush. Listen. Balthazar, nothing stays the same. I won't and you won't. Even a day can come when I really will be dead. Yes. I will."

"If that day ever comes, all I will do as long as I live is remember you. I would build you a big monument too. In the Passy cemetery. I would have it have a big high roof. And it would be the grandest there was. With tall bronze doors. And inside I would have pictures of you and all your favourite flowers every day. I would come and sweep it out myself and polish the way all those old ladies do."

"Hey, you little devil. I'm not dead yet."

"Only if you were."

"I should hope so. Now maybe it's a good idea if you get out of here."

"It's only just rung half past twelve. I heard it."

"Gather up all your things now. Come on."

"No."

"Come on Balthazar."

"No."

"Now Balthazar you must. You can't stay here all night. There. Here's your tie. Heavens everything's everywhere. Out."

"No."

"Out."

"No."

"Out please."

"No."

"O come on Balthazar, don't be like that. Don't make me upset please. What if someone came."

"I should then depart in what is commonly called a jiffy."

"You mischief."

"Bella Bella I'm a mischief, that's what I am. A mischief."

"Push you out then."

"Push, push."

"Stop stop get your hands away. Stop it Balthazar. O stop. O you've got to stop. O you really really must stop. You must. But o not yet. O God Balthazar. Not yet not yet."

Miss Hortense with her hard little knuckled fists dug into Balthazar's sides. Opened out her hands. And reached his head to pull it smothering down upon her breasts. Cushion his silky blond face back and forth in all the milky softness. Her arms so tight around. And I press my sallow body to hers. To snake my own arms under and put them round her back. And I hold her now. More than she holds me. Why did God give her so much beauty and make her born before me. To give her years to flash teeth with love and laughter. And make me race and chase after her and feel before she should go, her warm soft tongue in my mouth and whisper of rabbit rabbit in my ear. I want to catch up. Ask you wait for me. The most nicest people are always taken away. And Bella I feel I have climbed up on a dark and strange tree. Flowering dewy wet and new. Beefy said there are more things in the world than jelly beans and lemon delights. Like your bottom Bella turns up as you roll over on top of me. Down there on your big spacious mounds I can put my fingers pressing softly. Where the conductor tried to pinch. On that white bright sunny day under all the trees' full greenery. And the hot silence against the stone walls along the Seine. Where we crossed the Pont Neuf and went down the dark stone steps to the Vert Galant and walked along the cobbles and sandy path. The barges throbbing by on the green grey river like your eyes. And we came to the point of this little island land. Dark figures grouped together by the park wall. I said look Bella. A man and woman clutching a greasy gathering of belongings, lay next each other in rags. The sun burned down on their dirt and dust encrusted faces dried and cracking. Toothless heads, lips drawn in over gums, strange purple swollen lips and mucous covered eyes. And before I could ask why. Were they so poor and why were they there. Bella said come along Balthazar we mustn't stay here. And I stood. Bella waiting. Three ragged men each with a bottle clutched in their blackened fists, came to stand over the sleeping couple. They began to kick them in the sides and head and bottom of their feet. And they awoke from sleep shielding their heads with raised tattered arms. And the kicks rained upon them and shouts, get out of our place. The man slowly struggled under the blows to his knees, his eyes blinking up into the sunshine. A foot smashed against his face and he fell forward as blood poured from both his eyes. The woman clawed screaming at the striking feet. The dark legs closed in on her. They struck sending dust from her ragged covered bosoms and she crumbled groaning to the ground. And as I stood there watching, the man and woman clutching at the sandy stony ground slowly began to crawl away. More blows raining on their backs and heads as they howled. Bella said you must not watch and pulled me by the arm. A day that grew grey and dark over

Paris. And cast shadows through the museums, on the boats, and along the boulevards. In the passing Paris eyes were cunning monsters brooding. To lift aside some shallow gaiety and see all the writhing sewer fears. To wish to be back in England. Upon a green unworried day. The crack of a cricket bat, the choir voices of evensong. Prayerful hands and glowing altars. Lay my head as it is now between Bella's soft neck and shoulder. Gone is my fever. I felt all these long days. And listen. Another shout out on the streets. He looks for his mother. On a golden most narrow day. To fit lips upon her breast. To lie quietly now on top of one another. She's mine. No one will ever take her from me.

The summer light comes up all over the sky. Bella it's morning. Yes dearest the sun came racing across the Ukraine over the Danube and valleys of the Rhone and Rhine. And it's coming in your window now. Yes. Up south over the Seine. And Bella northwards to Metz and Reims. And now across your naked golden legs. Do you hear the birds. I stayed with you the whole night. I'm glad you did. Hear the garden keeper singing. Yes I do. Bella promise me you'll never forget this night. Of course I won't, go away now and brush your teeth. And I'll bring you breakfast. Bella I want to shout and sing and go dancing down the street. Yes I know, now really you must must go. But it's nice, you were a boy when you came in last night. And I am happy for you.

For
Now
Out walks
A man.

11

And this waking and dying of all strange Sundays. Miss Hortense walking naked to the bath, barefoot on the parquet.

"Balthazar you're following me around like a little dog and you must not do that after today."

And in the afternoon they went to Sévres. Through all the rooms and gleaming cases of porcelain. And later by the Seine on a grassy hill. Where fishermen sat with sleeves rolled up and elbows on their knees. Factory chimneys away on the sky. And back in Paris they walked up the steps across Rue Beaujolais and through the streets behind the Bourse. They sat in a tiny Russian restaurant. And the wife cooked and the husband served and played the piano. And they had asparagus and steak tartar.

Pushing shoving and peeking in and out they waltzed back to the Palais Royal. And kissed behind the closed front door. And Bella lit a candle in her room and said you are getting your good innings indeed. And together they undressed. And danced and played. Bella did what she called the prismatic prance. And stood in front of her mirror as the candle light shone. And said I dare you try and catch me. And I did. After all the games. And we lay locked and moist in bed.

Until the sound of an opening door. Just before the chimes rang ten. And Pierre's voice and the scrape of bags sliding on the foyer floor. Bella sat upright drawing in her breath.

"O my God I didn't bolt the door, get out of here. Pick up your clothes someone is coming."

The light faint and flickering, Balthazar ran grabbing and tripping across the floor to get out the door. Fingers clutching in a shoe, an arm squeezing together jacket and shirt. The click of his mother's heels in the foyer the end of the hall. To close Bella's door and get behind one's own. Leave the clothes strewn or be found skipping nude. To run with jacket and trousers clutched against the breast. And feel a faint sandy grit on the bottom of my feet. As a voice comes down from the dim light up the hall.

"Is that you Balthazar."

"No."

"What. Of course it is. Is it you Balthazar."

"I'm just going to my room."

"O. Well I'd thought I'd return and pack tonight and leave early tomorrow for Menton. Chantilly was such a bore. How are you getting on. Why don't you put on the light. That is you Balthazar."

"Yes."

"Switch on, I can't see you. Is something the matter."

"No."

"Would you help Pierre, he has to fetch four more bags. Put on the light for heaven's sake."

"No."

"I'll put it on. It's irritating to speak to someone in the dark. Good God. What are you doing standing in the hall clutching your clothes like that."

"Nothing, I have come from the bath."

"Well wear a robe. What's that stuck in Miss Hortense's door."

Balthazar slowly stepping backwards towards his door. His mother in a dark blue flowered dress, its silky sheen gleaming in the chandelier light. Her blond hair drawn tightly back on her head. The great diamonds on a finger flickering blue and pink as it pointed to the white cloth hanging from Miss Hortense's door.

"I think it would appear to be a curtain."

"A curtain. No it's not. Is she in there. Miss Hortense, are you in there."

In solemn dry history books Miss Hortense said. There are times of treaty and times of war. When no one is poor and there's nowhere to go and many guns to make. And people feel better because they don't always have to think of them-

94

selves. And love is sadder and stronger then. Because you might be killed.

"Yes Madam."

"Something is stuck in your door."

"Thank you Madam."

To stand so frozen here. Covering all this pain. Why doesn't she go away. Don't ever come close to me.

"Good God, your tie there Balthazar, and this. This is your shirt. What is it doing here. May I ask. In Miss Hortense's door. What is going on."

"Miss Hortense was sewing my sock."

"And you had to take off your shirt and trousers and underwear."

"I have been to the bath."

"Yes and I think it is time you should go to your room. If it is not a little nudist colony here. And I think I should have perhaps a word with Miss Hortense."

"Stay away from her."

"What did you say."

"I said to stay away from Bella."

"I will do what I choose in my flat, my dear boy."

"Do not open her door."

"And what if I do."

"I will not return here ever again."

"You are taking such a privilege away. What foolish talk. This is my house. Miss Hortense is my employee."

"She is paid with my money."

"To be sure. We are suddenly so aware of our rights. She is still my employee. And if I choose to speak to an employee I shall."

"You shan't refer to her in that fashion."

"And what fashion would you have me choose. To find your clothes strewn about. Stuck in Miss Hortense's door. You have some other term for Miss Hortense perhaps. I think so. Miss Hortense, may I have your attention a moment please."

"Just a moment."

"I can wait. It is no trouble. Yes I think perhaps I ought to know more of what is taking place while I am away. Why don't you go to your room, Balthazar."

Miss Hortense opening her door. The pale profile of her face.

"It is just to ask, my dear, that I should like to chat with you tomorrow morning. About nine thirty. Sharp, please. I think we may have some things to discuss."

"Very well madam."

His mother turning. Her eyes of cold blue steel. Her back stiff and straight. And legs long and elegant. Click click click like a soldier she walks away.

"Bella please don't worry."

"Balthazar please goodnight get your clothes and go to bed."

To fall down through white tumbling sheets in a night of dreaming. And wake wide eyed to remember last morning Sunday, as Bella sat with breakfast tray and read the black headlines across the newspapers and said o Balthazar I think there is going to be war. It comes like that with photographs of men in high white collars with briefcases stepping from grand trains. They sit at great tables with glasses of water. Never any trust with treaties and someone will wield the sword. And that awful war there was before. My father said the rats roamed and ate the bodies of the dead and the whole sky smelled for miles. Like a yellow suffocating dust. And those horrid men with their black ties, smiling with their pens signing papers. Dearest Balthazar if ever guns spit red and smoke and fire please be far away. Tears in Bella's eyes as she poured our coffee in our white cups and the sheet dropped down from her breasts. She clutched it up and let it drop again and smiled. Her bosoms so strange and big when she leaned that way and nipples bright and hard. And then so tall and slender like a reed in the candle light. I chased her and her breasts bounced up and down. I caught her round the waist. She laughed to push down my arms. Her thighs so long and strong and so much bigger than mine. Just to know and know I could touch them and feel a long straight muscle hardening there. And not be pushed away. Bully you without clothes she said and tickle. Everything's unfair in this game. Now Balthazar stand still. I want to see you. Like a little statue so white and thin. You are a fountain and water should come out of here. And now, o now, I turn it on. With her open palm to reach and touch me, stay still, so stiff, you tremble. Fingers touching so lightly there. All along this funny little line underneath. Balthazar my beauty. Your splendid flower, its pink rose tip. And white blue veined stem. And all its tiny blond new leaves of hair. Bella am I brave to stand still. Yes. And beautiful. And I closed my eyes. O Bella it's coming out of me. Let it. And see where it lies. Like white melted pearls in my hand. And you are. A little fountain. And this is my gift in our unfair game. And yes I can pick you up and carry you. O gosh Balthazar, you know. What I shall do. What I wish perhaps. To marry a white haired man with so much money with whom I would not sleep and do the things I do with you and he should die within the year. And I would come and be your mistress. All dressed in black. And maybe just a light blue ribbon in my hair. Would you treat me well and take me on boats up and down the Rhine. I would say you were my son. You would keep your head down and walk around on your knees and squeak out when people asked, that you were Master Hortense and this was your big great old mother. We would sneak around the watering places. Sipping up the minerals. And go as you said from Bucharest to St. Petersburgh through all the towns and places you showed me on the map. Along green valleys and around white mountains. To Budapest and Prague, and whoops, I nearly missed Vienna. Then east to Warsaw across Poland all flat and lonely. No one would ever know us if we went wading in the Baltic Sea. We would be lost together and hold hands on an ice floe on the Gulf of Finland. And somewhere it's always black in sleep at night. And Bella faded away from shore. She stood in a long white lacy gown and waved back to the little boy. Further and further she floated. Out on the grey icy sea.

Licked by salty cold waves. Then I was the little boy. Running back through my life asking dark shadows the way to go. And they stood and looked down at me with jelly fish eyes and said we don't know. On I ran. Towards the arms of God. When first a country summer I was an altar boy. And carried a candle high. And in the rose garden stood the holiest Slouch. I shouted don't devour me you bloodthirsty priest. He was looking rather awkward in long winter underwear. Muttering that he was delegated to cast out the indecent apparelled. And put to shame all those suddenly found nose deep in smut. And the bicycle seat sniffers' band paraded by. As Masterdon swaggered across the cricket pitch saying in his loud boasting voice that he had quite fairly rogered his father's gardener's daughter right down between the green house tomato plants. And two footed gavotting Slouch said as he waved his tennis racket on high, I know that my redeemer liveth you damn devious boys, I know that he liveth and delivereth us from fleshy tomfoolery. Here spoken, my villainish boys, from verse nine of erotica. And Masterdon was waving his small penis in saucy applause and Beefy sat in a nearby tree eating an apple, and singing O For The Wings Of A Dove. And awake. Dark and the ticking clock. Bella. Don't leave me and are you gone. Run to you out of my bed now. Clutch you. Bury my face in your soft welcoming breasts. Hold me away from all that darkness. Like the narrow Rue Allent. The notice up on the wall. Urinators Will Be Prosecuted. And that day we went to the church of St. Louis where I was baptised. Nearly thirteen years ago from this morning of dismay.

Miss Hortense came in with breakfast. Her eyes red and cheeks blotched. And put the tray on my bed. Opened my window and lowered the awning on a rising sun. In her white frilly blouse, grey skirt and black shoes. A locket round her neck. I reach to kiss her. And she pulls my arms from around her neck. And holds my face between her hands and let me please cut a strand of your hair. It curled round her finger. And she tied it tight with a long strand of her own brown hair. And put it in the locket on top of my picture when I was six years old and standing by the sea.

"Bella what does it mean."

"Balthazar listen to me. Listen. I am going to have to go away. Just as I always knew I would. This evening on the train. I am packed. No listen to me. I must. I love you. A war is coming. And I somehow know it is when they say it isn't. You'll be gone to your new school."

"Will you visit me."

"I will try."

"O Bella say you will."

"I will."

"And write to me."

"Yes."

"I don't want you to go. Or ever leave me. I love you so dearly."

"Then you would do one thing for me wouldn't you."

"Yes, what is it."

"Let me speak to your mother alone. There are things I would like to say. That I would not like you to hear. And you mustn't mind too much when I go. We've had some awfully happy times. True love is always sure disaster."

"O please Bella, don't say such a harsh thing."

"I must go."

At nine thirty the salon doors closed. And Balthazar tip toes there. He waved away the cook who lurked in the pantry hall. She wiped her hands in her apron and scurried when Balthazar said shoo. And on the silk soft carpet he stood in his bare feet and robe and peeked through the keyhole.

His mother sat on a golden legged chair. In a white linen suit. String of pearls at her tan neck and her blond hair brushed back from her temples. A great diamond pin stuck from the bun gently golden at the back of her head. And she tapped a small silver pencil on her engagement book.

To see only Bella's legs and hands folded in her lap. And wish that my penis would not go hard and stiff. When anyone can look at you and say you are a naughty boy.

"Miss Hortense. I am a woman. It will be less painful if I do not beat around the bush. I will say what I have to say. I am, perhaps, not a good mother. I have no wish to make anyone unhappy. But I could not do otherwise than what I am doing now. I must give you your notice. That is understood."

"Madam I love your son and want to marry him."

"What. Do you want me to go and jump off the balcony. He is a child."

"He is a man."

"Come come my dear girl, what do you take me for. We are grown people and he is but a boy. You should know what you are doing, Miss Hortense. It is far too easy to seduce such a sheltered little creature as Balthazar. I would like to know before you leave that you shall not have contact with him again. That is clear."

"Yes."

"And very wise of you. You are of good family. And I do not blame you or Balthazar as I should have seen what was happening myself. It is a troublesome world. One does as one likes, if one can. There are rules. Be discreet and do not get caught. But believe me Miss Hortense you were lucky to get caught. A beautiful girl like you should have better things to do. Balthazar will be a bit lovesick but he will get over it."

Miss Hortense standing. A white handkerchief clutched in her hand.

"You awful awful woman. I love him. I love him."

"Your envelope Miss Hortense has been put under your door. Do not forget it."

"You're evil."

"You are wrong but also how sad you are my dear. How sad. Some thoughts are best unsaid. I don't suppose you will be foolish enough to try any tricks. I leave in half an hour. And you may stay till it is time for your train."

Miss Hortense pulled open the salon door as Balthazar stepped quietly back against the wall. He followed her along the hall to her room. She said you mustn't come in. And he went to the bath, and came back and came in. Her case packed and open on her bed.

"Balthazar you shouldn't have listened. That was a mean thing to do."

"Bella you said you wanted to marry me."

"Yes. But it wasn't for you to hear."

"Why."

"Because we could never marry. O God I'm going out of my mind."

"I have a cold cloth here for your eyes."

"You're sweet. I don't mean to be angry at you. But your mother thinks I've corrupted you. That I want to get you in my clutches. Get your money and get your life. That's what she thinks. Maybe it's true. But I love you too."

"Bella, don't be sad and cry."

"I want to leave and go right away now."

"Please wait till it's time for your train."

"No."

"Then I shall get dressed and go with you."

"No."

"Yes. I should be at your side. And please do not wear your hat and cover up your hair."

Miss Hortense stood, her knees against the blue linen counterpane. Her hands hang down and the veins are long and swollen blue. Her lips are open and her eyelids hang gently down. Where under lurk her eyes with just their touch of laughter left in their gallant green. And she takes off her hat.

"God what have you done to me Balthazar. What have you done to me."

At Gare St. Lazare. Out on the train quay at nearly six o'clock. They went that afternoon up to Sacré Coeur, climbing all the steps. And sat in the church while a procession moved around the aisles. Sacristans with crosses held high in their dark blue and red robes. Followed by women with empty married eyes. Their white pasty skins that held in their fat. And as they left the Palais Royal, his mother stood in the foyer and waved her wrists and sniffed and shook her head slowly back and forth.

The train doors slamming. Heads sticking farewell from windows. A whistle blowing. A green flag waving. A chug of steam. And the tall green carriage begins to move. I look up. The last thing we did together was to sit each with a sandwich jambon in a cafe across the street. To say little and then nothing at all. We were two lonely persons. Like we had never been before. And she put her hand across the table to me and bent her head. And the tears poured from her eyes. And I knew it was time just to touch her. And not say we will meet again or write. Because she would never walk out of my mind. While there was a glowing light. I knew because I could see her sitting there. Just crossing her knees. Where my lamp was lit and other lamps were out. And up in this window now. Her teeth over her lip. Her hand touching the blue ribbon she put in her hair. Choo choo choo. I cannot move or run. I stand. The train is gathering speed. Taking with it so many years. Dragging them away. Faces staring out the big glass windows. Wheels turning. Hard white steel on steel. Goodbye Miss Hortense, goodbye.

> And when
> The Channel
> Comes
> And you slip out
> On the
> Grey and greeny
> White
> Whisper to it
> And say
> God love you
> Tonight.

12

In that last Paris summer Balthazar B stood in the evening Tuilleries gardens near the big pond with his solitary love held in empty hands.

Alone in September he headed to his new school across the Channel and a short train ride from London. With autumn came the war rumbling east spitting cannon across the plains, rivers and valleys all the way between St. Petersburgh and Bucharest. And one afternoon on a hillside overlooking London he wept when France fell. The summers, autumns and winters turned all Latin and Greek, all grey and drab and Miss Hortense neither came nor wrote.

His mother fled across Spain and by tramp steamer to Argentina. She settled grandly in a suburb of Buenos Aires. And went horse riding every day. Uncle Edouard joined the Free French and in Easter holiday Balthazar came to visit. At a tiny London house where Uncle Edouard nearly filled each room with his big chest and stretched out legs. And then he was gone. His housekeeper whispered at the beginning of summer holiday that the Baron had been parachuted into France. And eight months later in February came news. The Baron had been shot against a white stone wall in the sixteenth district.

And through Uncle Edouard Balthazar B had appointed new lawyers, Bother, Writson, Horn, Pleader and Hoot in the Temple, and a firm of accountants up a dark stairway and street in the City of London. In May he was called to hear something to his advantage. Uncle Edouard bequeathed to him the big stuffed bear in Paris and his town house in London with all chattels. And Mrs. Bottle was given a three year contract to remain as housekeeper.

Quarterly Balthazar B was invited to lunch by these elderly

legal gentlemen. Until his school was evacuated north to Yorkshire near the Ilkley Moor. And there often he wandered through the wintry heathers and spoke to the lonely posted men of the home guard with cups of tea nestled in their hands. And one weekend the first month of spring he went to Huddersfield. Climbed a gentle hill. Between the sooty broken buildings across the town. And came to a low wall around a large stone house set in a lawn cold and grey. A woman in an apron answered the door and said politely Miss Hortense was in the military and lived here no more.

Standing at the stove in the small basement kitchen of the little house in Brompton between the quiet reaches of Hyde Park and Knightsbridge, Balthazar B cooked a kipper. When one month ago were said all the fond farewells from school. The wireless announced that the war was over. And there was dancing cheering and kissing through all the streets. One night huddled alone in bed I had a dream. That all were dead in France. And Uncle Edouard's big stuffed bear was standing against a sun rising high in the sky on a mild moist wind-blown day. The bear held great open arms out to where there were hills that were green. And brooks that flowed silver. There was a wide wide street and a great big park. And awake the next morning Balthazar B sat at the little oak desk facing out on the narrow back yards and wrote to Trinity College Dublin.

An end of September came when he took two trunks and an evening taxi across the bridge of the Serpentine through Tyburnia and along Marylebone Road to Euston. With a quickened heart and life lightly on the fingertips. The great granite pillars of the station. And then this moment. Amid the uniforms brown and blue. I saw a face hurrying by. Only an arm away. A woman who looked small. Perhaps because I've grown so tall. Her hair swept up under her cap, her legs in black stockings. I held two newspapers in my hand. And a voice called after me that I'd left my change. I shouted Bella. Under the great arching blackened roof. And the figure began to run. And I ran. Shouting Bella Bella Bella. And stopped. It could not be. And I hoped so much that it wasn't. If she would flee. Across the grey concrete platforms all grit and dust and wrappings. Where she went. Towards the train to Liverpool.

In the darkening night the clicking clacking wheels sped across England through Crew and Chester and into Wales. And out across the lonely land to Holyhead. On this breezy Saturday clear night I sailed to Dublin. With a heart hollow with so little hope. To read a letter again and again. And each time it was true. The words said we look forward to seeing you here. And in the upper left hand corner was a seal and a shield with a lion, harp, and book over a castle, and a gate and two turrets flying flags. In the saloon high amidships at a smooth brown table a waiter poured out a dark liquid which foamed and swallowed bitter sweet down the throat. The way now so grey. Miss Hortense said once that when she was glad she felt like a drop of dew on a blade of grass and when she was sad she rolled down and got sucked up in the ground. And ahead on a black shore were the flickering coastal lights of Ireland.

Tuesday, on the first day of October, Balthazar B removed in a handsome cab from the Shelbourne Hotel to go prancing down Kildare Street towards the wall and fence and trees of Trinity College. To smile suddenly at this city. The red faces of the men and white faces of the women. The missing door handles of the cab kept closed by string. And the unsmiling scattering begging bare footed little children. Last night to peer out a window across the top of trees in St. Stephen's Green. Other windows set in granite and blue grey rooftops wet with rain. Purple little mountains rising in the distance, set gently beyond the wispy fragrant smoke. And to walk the city as I did, down the dim lit streets and by the great walls and green railings behind which I would go to live. In one street past a cinema I walked. A girl on the other side of the road. She stared at me and I stared back at her. And both of us walked into obstructions. Me into a wall and she into a post. I laughed, she laughed. I bowed and she ran. And now this windy morning. Low sky of tumbling clouds. The curving fence of Trinity. The horse cab crossing College Green and down Dame Street to come back again and head straight at the grey stone front. A clock, hands at ten, the row of top square windows, the arched gate, and pillars. All this strange cold nobility. A toy green tram squealing by. And floods of bicycles. The tall red faced policeman stopping traffic and giving the horseman a violent wave forward across this open apron of street and in between the iron gates to stop before this great wooden door.

Two dark blue peak hatted porters, pulling back the great doors. They looked in the horse cab window. And I said with nothing else to say that I am Balthazar. They saluted and said very good sir. And I thought I had done terribly well. Clip clopping we went across this cobbled square. Groups of students in dark gowns standing at the open doorways and dotted on the paths between the velvet grass.

Down by a grey grand building and into a large square. Gnarled ancient trees fading yellow. A man in a battered brown hat stood on the granite steps. His hands on his hips, bicycle clips on his trouser legs. And as the horse cab stopped, he looked and frowned. Balthazar alighted. The man looked at the entrance wall upon a newly painted name.

"Begging your pardon sir. But are you the gentleman as is expected at number seventy six."

"Yes."

"The name is Balthazar is it sir."

"Yes."

"I'm Horace sir, your servant. Will I be giving you a little help now with your luggage sir."

The two big cases lifted from the cab. Horace giving little commands to the horseman. As they backed away into the dark hall. Stand here now on this step. The grass so greeny green beyond the iron fluted pointed posts holding a suspended chain. The air fresh and fragrant. A boot scraper here on the step. Take off my hat and let it blow my hair.

Along a shadowy stone paved hall. Up steps to a landing and up more stairs to another. And behind a thick big black door. There was a crash. Balthazar B stepping quickly forward. Into a large high ceilinged sitting room. Where one trunk lay on the floor on top of the pieces of a chair.

"Ah sir that chair was long in need of repair. Weak in the knees. Tired of being sat on. We'll send it straight to purgatory right there in the fire. Sure it will never see the sight of God."

Outside the clip clop of the horse cab went under the window and faded away. A pale glass shade over a weighted pulley light hung from the ceiling. A brown table and three more chairs. A light tan tiled fireplace. A turf fire glowing.

"With a little turf left over from the gentleman leaving I thought I'd air out a bit hearing as you were coming. Now sir, my duties are to keep the rooms well dusted out. Do the washing up. Get in the water. Lay a fire and will you be wanting breakfast sir of a morning."

"Please."

"Very good sir. And will you be requiring any of the fundamentals of living sir. Such as a mattress."

"Yes please."

"Very good sir. I can see to that very thing for you. Ah we've been having some shocking weather. Shocking. We'll have it right here sir in short order. And you'll be needing the odd blanket. I'm suggesting now that Henry Street is your man. Quality for the price, wool for the warmth. Is nine your time of rising sir, of a morning."

"That will do fine."

"There'll be a good big pitcher of hot water for you on the washstand there. Should I knock to wake you sir. Some of the professors are ones for the waking. Have to tear the covers back from the bed before they stir at all."

"Just a knock will do."

"Very good sir. Now I wouldn't be not minding my own business sir but sometimes it's handy to know. May I enquire what you are reading sir."

"Natural science."

"That's a dandy subject. I have meself many unnatural

matters on my mind, ah we'll have plenty of time to discuss that, eh, heh heh sir. The last gentleman here sir was an engineer. Ah he was a one for cylinders and motor bike parts all over the place. A devil to keep tidy. Didn't I see him once having his breakfast out of a hubcap. Well now we'll be getting on a bit. A good sweeping out while you settle in. Ah I had to laugh sir, as you came down the square in the cab. I says to meself who's this gentleman now, he has the notion to do it right. The only sure way to travel. Why the streets are blocked outside there with these yokes gasping for the petrol. Sure a horse you throw a fork full a hay to in the night and while you're sleeping isn't he being refuelled. Ah you wouldn't know what the world was coming to and that's a fact. Before you know it they'll be trying to put wings on a donkey and him only trying to graze."

Opening tall cupboard doors in the bedroom. Laying out on these empty shelves shirts, socks and the last remnants of Uncle Edouard's silk underwear. The yellowing thick masonry walls. The iron bedstead and naked springs. Tall cream shutters folded back at the sides of the windows. Look out across these trees and falling leaves. A solitary lamp post at the corner of the square. The lip of lawn and cobble stone gutter. Tiny flashes of dark blue in the sky. And a wind rattles the big window.

Balthazar B opened his bedroom door into the sitting room and fell back again and closed it shut.

"Is there something amiss sir."

"No."

Balthazar B bracing himself and taking in a great lungful of air. Opening the door again and setting forth across the room, Horace vaguely outlined crouched behind his broom plunging it forward as it curled rolling volumes of dust up against the ceiling. Horace paused and held a shielding hand above his eyes.

"Ah you're on your way out sir."

"Yes."

"Ah we'll have it spic and span on your return sir. And I'll be knocking you up at nine sharp sir."

"Splendid. Thank you."

Across the cobbles between these scatterings of eager faces. Through the mild and soft air. To go in under the portico and past the porter's little cozy room. Hung with keys, piled with parcels. A fire blazing in the grate. And out now into the bustling city. A phalanx of bicycles released by the tall policeman's white gloved hand as he urgently beckoned them on. And last night asleep. High up over St. Stephen's Green. The early morning coming down with its blue white light from the hills beyond the city. And revelries far below. Went to my window to look down. Saw figures in long flowing dresses and men in evening clothes. A casual gladness in the voices and their laughing shouts. And one voice which nearly seemed a voice I knew. Singing out above the others. On the distant hills the sun was rising. Full of an orange tickling and the last of an autumn's warmth. To go spreading redly down over this stone built city.

Out now to flow along with these pedestrians. Alive this gay afternoon on the great slabs of granite. Past giant green gates of the Provost's house. Green and yellow trams grinding and clanging by. Citizens as they nod and cock their heads in silent passing greeting. Sometimes stopping to give urgent earward whispers. Tiny scurrying white faced children, the wind blowing through their rags. Begging as one passed. Give us a penny mister. And an open shirted black curly headed man said to an open shirted burning eyed man, how's your hammer hanging Sean.

Through an aroma of roasted coffee and a glass mahogany swing door. By light eyed ladies with packages and gloves and sparkling eyes. In grey flannel suits and silken voices who let the breeze of passing people blow their cigarette smoke away. Everywhere, faces. And ahead past counters of cakes and breads and sweet smelling loaves, a great high ceilinged room of glass topped tables.

Balthazar B sat down on a crimson seat beneath a stained

glass window and perused this oriental menu. The black dressed waitress brought a large cup of coffee and plate of glistening brown topped currant buns. A dish of gold balls of butter. A woman with a priest. Two red coated girls with refined small fingers sticking out from their cups of tea. Little clanks of cutlery on the glass. Heaped pots of sugar pieces. Warm fragrant coffee in the mouth. To open an evening newspaper and read that a cow escaped onto a road and gave the garda a wild chase into a village where the beast entered a public house and set the occupants to holding their pints high over their heads so as not to have them spilled. A wondrous simple peace. Without years of lonely grey. And upturned rafters in brick debris. With bombs and cannons chattering up against the night and searchlights waving over a terror torn sky.

To walk back down again this bustling street. The shop lights go on. A sweet smoky air descends. My drop of dew on a blade of grass. Is my gladness. Hovering above the ground.

> High and still
> And
> Sparkling so
> In Dublin
> Town.

13

Balthazar B stood in slippers and the lower half of pink pyjamas at his marble washstand and slapped up water to rinse his soapy face. A time to look out across the square as students collect for classes in the arts. And the plane trees hang out wild writhing winter branches.

To go to this large garage out in the back mews reaches of south Dublin. For the purchase of a motor car. The proprietor wiping his hands in a petrol soaked rag. And with a quick little nod of the head, he smiled and was willing to please.

"Now what did you have in mind sir."

"I am not quite sure."

"Is it for the touring. Or town. Or the back and forth."

"Back and forth."

"Now let me ask you one question. Would you ever be wanting to be out on the road and in an awful need to get somewhere fast without much let or hindrance. Answer me that. And I may be able to help you. Without putting your mind through the torture of a lot of choices."

"That's quite possible."

"Now I can't promise a thing, but you know I think that you're the man I've been waiting for. A gentleman who's ready and able for them wide open spaces. And who's got the glint of the sportsman in the eye. Am I right."

"I'm not quite sure."

"O I'm right, I know I'm right. I know a keen man when I see one. Can't I tell by the cut of your cloth there, aren't you a man for the wide open spaces."

"I really want a motor to reach the race courses."

"Ah, now, am I glad you said that. Baldoyle, Leopardstown, the Curragh. I knew it. And you'll make the twenty four miles to Punchestown in twenty minutes flat. I'm telling you that. Just let me show you something now. Come along here this way. Of course I should have known you were a racing gentleman. It's written all over you. Now here we are."

"My God."

"O now just you wait till you see this. Just you wait. Just swing back these covers. Ah, I want you to take a long look at this now. What about that. It's the greatest four wheeler ever seen in Dublin. It would pull two hundred protestant donkeys backwards from Glasnevin to Rathgar and they desperate to get to Belfast away from the pope. Just have a look now will you, under the bonnet. Have a look at this now. Twelve of your cylinders. Ready and willing. Each the size of a man's thigh. With sparkplugs to match. Climb a hill as steep as the back of your head there and it be only in neutral gear. Commodious."

"It's awfully big."

"Let that be no deterrent. What would a keen racing man such as yourself do out on the highway without the little extra room for the lady perhaps. Heh heh. And sure you wouldn't want to be shouldered off the road. There's a bunch of them now, shopkeepers and publicans, motorists they call themselves if you please, out on the roadway of a Sunday. Let me tell you, they'll give you no trouble when they see this man here coming at them I assure you."

"Does it go."

"Does it go. You're asking me. Does it go. Get up there now. Ah that's a good one. Does it go. That's it now, are you right. Get yourself steady. Does it go. Sure do you see this little black button here now."

A deep growling whirring and a sudden explosion. A great white cloud of exhaust. As the massive machine rumbled and throbbed and slowly moved forward.

"Goodness."

"Does it go. It wasn't called a Landship for nothing. You out there Mick, clear the doors and make way in the road outside, we're coming out. Sure I'll give you a little tour right round Merrion Square north east south and west. Are you right."

The Landship securely moored now below the window. The great long black chassis on the tall wooden spoked wheels. Horace each morning cheerful standing at the water pump filling his bucket quietly contemplating the Landship. Stopping by it and slowly wagging his head.

"Ah sir, I can't get over it. I measured it three times meself and was telling the lads it was twenty two and a half feet in length as the crow flies and not a man of them would believe me. Ah it must be a grand powerful feeling to be rolling along in that yoke. Sure you'd need your own petrol station to keep it fed."

With breakfast laid out. A pint of cow's milk in a bottle. A fire smouldering in the grate. The chill wind comes whistling in round the tall windows. One sits rubbing bluish hands. And cupping tightly the warm green bowls of tea.

And always to have to get up from one's chair and cross to the fireplace and stand pushing knees into the smoke. And pumping the bellows to bring a red glow to the silvered ends of turf. Feet damp and cold. Then try to remain calm as the intestines will not. To grab one's long motoring coat from the door. And copy of last night's Evening Mail and head for the bog.

Each step along the cold street. Must hold on till I get there. Past the college Printing House. A pile of leaves blown up against a corner of its steps. Its blackened empty alcoves. In there the mystery of the exams turning over on the presses.

Through this broken three quarter door. Walk down the row of crappers. Seats torn off. Newspapers flying. Cold stone cubicles. The wind blows. As all of one's white body cries out for warmth. And count each day how many steps. All the way here. One hundred and thirty eight of them. To bravely now. Undo a buckle, open flies. Lower garments and unleash the backside to the shivering breeze and icy seat. Take a deep breath. And hope that after all the many mornings one could not budge the spirit to move out in the rains, that on this less inclement day the soul will shift the burden. Or surely simply break the arse.

But two more days till this one desperate morning. Six A.M. in the cold bed. A great churning through the intestines. Of an evening's reverie over sea foods and stout. One rushed for motoring coat and down the stone steps to mount the Land-ship. And set the monstrous engine throbbing. To get me to the bog on time. Waking up the college. As one sailed around the square and screeched to a halt outside the long wall of water closets. The following afternoon a letter came.

Dear Mr. B,

It is not allowed for an undergraduate to park a motor in College Square. Nor is it advised to set such motor running at an ungodly hour and wake those sleeping. Ample parking facilities are at the back gate of College.

I should be pleased if you could come and have tea at four this Tuesday coming.

Yours sincerely,
The College Authority

It was easier to stay irregular. And saunter down the square and through College Park to the Zoology Building. Go through the vestibule and into the centrally heated warmth. A momentary peek at the great room of museum animals. And when no one was looking quietly make for a neat mahogany water closet tucked away beyond the skulls and heads of beasts. And here with zoology notes on the knee pray again to shift the burden. Which earthworms do so easily.

Each day to sit at these high planks with their thin gently curving taps of running water. One's fellow classmates come in. Three always together, bundled up in great tweeds, Tuffy, Hinds and Byrne. They come happily larking into the room. I try so to show I'm friendly. And wished the girl in the thick grey sweater over amply nice bosoms who says, look at those three ruddy handsome fellows. Would say the same about me. With my pale silence as I wait quietly hoping someone will ask that I go for cakes and coffee out the back gate. And sit as they do gaily laughing and chatting under the great skylight of Johnston, Mooney & O'Brien's.

On this Saturday zoology practical dissection kits were slapped closed. Wait among these fellow students as we file out through the doors and down the granite steps. The cold greyness lays hold of me. They talk of a ball. A college hop. I go yes with my eyes and smile with my lips and plan to make some comment and never can. Out here now as I always am. Heading for the leviathan Landship waiting on the cinders at the back gate. To roar out past the porter's grey little lodge and towards the races.

Flags over the stand. Bookmakers wagging hands. Out here on the grassy slopes tip toeing over the churned up turf. Air moist and soft near the smell of the sea. Elbows on the paddock fence. The tight trousered figures in cavalry twill. Passing glistening haunches and snorting horses' heads blowing out twin clouds of steam. A girl in her heavy green tweed suit. A black silk scarf drawn tightly round her head. Goodness. Miss Fitzdare who has sat in class in front of me. She has dazzling blue gay eyes and leads a rather elegant chestnut mare. And she holds reins as the jockey mounts and pats the horse's neck. I could rush and say hello but can't. What would I say next.

Balthazar B put a pound on this seven to one outsider. And it won. Under purple pink and yellow colours. Pounding and steaming down the stretch by three lengths. I went to the bar and smashed back a double brandy. To buoy up one's lonely hope of a friend. Instead of figuring out the phylum chordata. Miss Fitzdare sometimes pushed the end of her pencil into her peach white cheek. And never said a word. She sat with her blue stockinged legs tucked on the cross bar of her stool. Sometimes an ecclesiastic gentleman in a chauffeured car called for her. And one unbelievable day when I accidently brushed her scalpel to the floor and picked it up, she smiled at me.

From Baldoyle I went via the heathery windy hill of Howth. To drive by these precipitous lonely houses hanging out over the sea. And then back to Dublin to dine this night. Bringing the Landship to a safe halt in the Suffolk Street. I crossed the Grafton and went in the alley by the stained glass window. Gave my coat, shooting stick and binoculars to the nice man. And climbed the stairs of this sprawling restaurant, across rooms and down again to the white tables and gleaming glass and gentle solitude in a little corner by the fire. And settled to smoked salmon, wild duck and rice eased into the spirit with wine from the vine of the Infant Jesus. To thaw the heart. And look for love. And take part in college life.

Aglow and gently tipsy Balthazar B proceeded at speed to Dalkey and back. Giving many an evening motorist a ghostly scare. And taking the breezes against the face and through the hair. To draw the Landship to a halt in front of my rooms. Fold my map, collect my binoculars and shooting stick. Reach over to turn down the handle and open the door. And hear the crunch of feet. In the darkness over there on the pebbles approaching. The College Authority. To give me what for. And the figure loomed close into the gas light glow.

"That is one very fine motor you have there."

"Thank you."

"How many horses."

"I don't know."

"You are a very modest chap not knowing the number of horses of such a fine motor."

"It has twelve cylinders."

"Very sporty. Dare say it would take you over the hills and far away. In quick order."

"Yes."

"I don't suppose you know who I am."

"No, I don't think so."

"Well I know who you are."

"Do you."

"Yes. I don't suppose you remember a little boy. A most awfully naughty little boy. Who got you in heaps of trouble. Called Beefy."

Balthazar B looked down upon this chunky figure. Whose

hand reached up and took off a wide brimmed black chapeau. To see in the faint light a shock of carrot hair. And round smiling cheeks. This Saturday twelve o'clock midnight.

> Bells ring
> And seagulls
> Come diving through
> The dark.

14

One hour past noon this gently raining Sunday. In blue pin striped suit, stiff white collar and small knotted black and white dotted tie I set off for the green front lawns of Rathgar. Past the flower beds and subtropical trees. Where at one red brick semidetached house I go by arrangement with my trustees, for dinner.

To stand at the fire in the sky blue room. Served two sherries by this bubbling lady with her big long hysterical nose and three marriageable daughters. Who appear one by one to nod and smile and curtsy. I bow. They each hold a hand at their pearls. And silently sit on the cold pink damask couch. And sometimes a Belfast doctor would stay as a paying guest. And following the ladies we went in to dine.

The doctor and I broke off our lively chat on Fasciola and Entamoeba as the black uniformed servant girls carried in the steaming joint of lamb. A silver bowl of mint sauce and one of golden roast potatoes and another of steaming sprouts. The trifle came under mounds of cream and soaked in sherry. Plates passed down table amid the smiles of our hostess and the three alabaster daughters. With candles lit on the quartet stand we tipped port and the doctor puffed a rare cigar in the withdrawing room. When the youngest of three sat to the harp and another to the piano and accompanied the eldest to Lieder. While I was so desperate to get laid.

At sometimes six fifteen p.m. I suddenly jump up to take my leave. For if I don't, hours go by as I figure out words upon which to take a carefree pleasant departure. And reach the cold hallway. Prints of Dublin and Edinburgh on the wall. Malacca canes in the hall stand and her late husband's military medals under glass. Lieutenant Colonel, Poona Light Horse.

"So nice having you Balthazar. We do look forward you know. To next Sunday. O dear. It's quite about to be inclement once more. You must put up the roof of your motor."

"Goodbye, thank you for having me."

Back now down the empty Sunday evening roads. The pubs not open yet. Wet softness against the face. The leviathan Landship forging through the night. Cross over the stone bridge of the Grand Canal. Down Harcourt Street past the big doors of the station. And hope always to come upon some gentle lonely lovely female along the ghostly granite pavements of the west of St. Stephen's Green. To motor with me. See only chasing barefoot children, their hands clutching each other. They shout and jeer and point. As I sail by the grim great pillars of the College of Surgeons. In there. Bodies propped up on tables all stiff and dry.

All these lonely Sunday evenings. Dublin shut. Odd lights here and there in College. To stare out the window. And wait for commons. Put on one's gown for warmth. The bell rings. Down the dark stairs. Gas lamps glowing along the dark squares. Figures on the steps of the dining hall and collecting in the foyer on the stone floor. In this great vestibule, two glowing fires with coals redly held against the bars of the grate. The blue uniformed man with gold buttons down his breast and his hair combed flat back on his head and parted in the middle. He watches the faces and marks his big book.

The great mahogany doors open. Into the vast room. The long tables. The huge portraits against the high panelled wall. The Senior Dean goes by, holding his big silver ear horn. And there was warmth from the night winterish air.

A tall scholar rushes up the steps to the lectern and Latins out grace. Beseated. A great clatter of shifting chairs. The carvers stand at their long tables sharpening knives. The great joints heaved up on their platters at the serving hatch. Thin harassed faces of these little women stared out across the dark gowned gathering. To catch their breath and go plunging back down again deep into the bowels of this dungeon kitchen. The clank of cutlery. The passing of the jug of beer. Light refreshing ale, a gift from a prosperous brewer.

And at another table I could hear a voice. Of elegant graceful quivering civility. Beefy. I look down on my plate of ham again. And hope someone will pass the salt. Bad manners everywhere. And tonight go back. Sit the evening out. Pretending some feeble joy at the remembered morphology of Annelida. Where the central nervous system consists of a pair of preoral ganglia connected by commissures to a postoral ventral ganglionated chain. When I am absolutely insane to be laid. Mind putting afloat one obscene thought after another.

And through this darkness after commons I returned lonely to rooms. Pumped the bellows at the fire. Sharpened pencils, pulled on my ear lobes, shook my head and sat with elbows planted holding the palms of my hands against my face. When there was a knock. And I opened the door.

"You are a singular chap, Mr. B. Huddle yourself away at commons. You should have come to sit with me. Bloody awful evening. Come to pay my respects. May I come in."

"Of course, but yes."

"Saw your light. What is this awful stuff."

"Zoology."

"O very handy, that. I hope you don't think I'm barging in. Fact of the matter is, I've come to ask you along to a little soirée. Will you come."

"I'd be very pleased."

"You are a terrible shy man. You know you haven't changed one bit. I saw you several times. Crossing Front Square. My rooms are up in the corner. Overlooking the ladies who go to and fro in number four. I said that chap I know him. But one doesn't want to intrude. I wonder often what brought me here. And it's always that no one else would have me."

Beefy in black thick tweed sitting back in the hard worn wooden chair. Knees fallen widely apart. As rain tapped the great panes of glass. And spreading and streaking pressed by the wind. Wild shadows against a dark sky. The shaking branches of the old trees. To see this round and ruddy face that went jaunting fearlessly through the woods. Those years ago. His hands now gently folded across his waistcoat.

They walked together through a dark rainy college. At the front gate Beefy tipping water from his black chapeau hailed a taxi. To ask the driver to go down Fenian Street between the dark houses. Shadows behind the tattered candle lit broken windows. Newspapers pressed as patches and torn curtains over the glowing sacred hearts. The Grand Canal lock and past the yeasty smell of gas works. Till the evergreen thickets of Trinity College Botanic Gardens went streaking by. And the world widened to lawn and warm golden lights.

Turning down this Ailesbury Road. Under the winter branches of the trees. Walls and fences of large houses. Aloof and stately in the dark. They stopped before a gate and path up to a lighted entrance porch. And went up the steep granite steps. Beefy pulled down a great brass handle on the door and it opened. Inside was warmth and gaiety. A room with greeting eyes. When one doesn't know what to do with hands. Step forward or stay where you are. Say hello. Or how do you do.

And as each was introduced round this circle of college people. Faces I knew passing in the squares. So full of colour now. A supper laid out through the wide doors on a great mahogany. Pinks and blues and light laughter. And at a high mantel. Its cold marble level with her shoulders. In the blackest of shimmering satin. Her chin held high and a small smile upon her face. Miss Fitzdare.

Across the wide salon. Four musicians played. The little band of college people took partners and swept waltzing away to outer rooms. I stand and swallow and so try to remain still. Not trip flat on my face. To go across and say hello to her. Dear God tell me. Just some more words I can add. To hello. Yes. That's it. I saw you with your horse. No. That will never do. Approach with a blank mind. Out which something stunning must come.

121

"Hello. I saw you with your horse."

"My horse."

"Yes. I think it was your horse."

"Horse."

"Yes."

"Horse. Goodness."

"Yes. It was a horse."

"Dear me what are you trying to say."

"I don't know."

"O well you mustn't look all upset about it. Please let me get you a drink."

Miss Fitzdare with a steady sure hand around the neck of a decanter. Just as she held reins that day. To pass her perfume so near under my nose now and pour forth a nutty sherry. She smiles and seems to like me. So strange and precious. After all the bundling up in tweed, and her boots tramping through the mud. Now a glittering diamond bracelet on her wrist.

"There."

"Thank you."

"That will make you feel much better. I think. Now the word was horse. You said horse to me."

"Yes I did. I saw you with your horse. Or somebody's horse. At Baldoyle."

"You race."

"I hardly do anything else."

"O surely not."

"I won seven pounds on your horse."

"I'm so glad. That was good of you to put a bet on Fasciola. Let me pour you some more sherry."

"Thank you."

"You must go racing often."

"I go racing nearly every day there's racing."

"You have that enormous car. It's so enormous."

"O it's not really."

"You must give me a ride in it one time."

"I'd love to. If you would come."

"Certainly I'd come."

"Wednesday. After zoology practical."

"Yes. I'd love to."

"We could drive to Stepaside. And up the mountain."

"That would be wizard."

"Well I think it really would be too. Would it be all right if I helped myself to more sherry."

"Do. But let me."

"I haven't really been invited."

"O but you were."

"Was I."

"Your hostess asked Beefy to bring you. She thought your car darling. But you're not a rich rich prince, are you."

"Good Lord. Who said that."

"Rumour all over college."

"My God."

"You are then a rich rich prince."

"Would you mind if I just had another little bit of sherry. This news is very worrying."

"Why don't you ever talk. You just never talk to anyone."

"I don't know how."

"Nonsense. You're one of the most interesting people. I don't think anyone has been seen in college in knickerbockers for years. So nice to see, I don't think they flatter older men. You look so well. Your yellow gloves and cane."

"Miss Fitzdare. Will you dance with me."

"I'd love to."

To take her hand. And put mine on the soft satin of her back. The blazing log fire throws red shadows. So far away from all the rain. One wakes shivering with cold this Sunday morning. To find after a long drawn day such kind welcome. Glad to see me. Their eyes sparkled and shone. To chatter away all the emptiness. Lowering on the dark afternoons when the horses have run. And I stray into a country pub. By the cold eastern shore of the sea. And sit. And let the winter stay and stay in my mind. The dark clothed natives steal up near. Enquiring in French or German whether I speak either tongue. And as I replied that one did not, they plowed on darkly in tongues invented on the spot. Until I would ask them what they were drinking. Ah well since ye ask that question and I wouldn't want to confuse you with a foreign tongue I'll have a ball of malt. A world alive in the world. With all its own land and sky. And Mick here he's a friend of mine who has stood on Broadway and Forty Second Street I'm telling you that's a fact with all them lights blazing in his eyes. To smile and feel the gentle beauty. No mixed bathing in Ireland. Nakedness long banned from pubs. And here amid the chippendale. Faintest powder upon her face, reddish purple of her lips. This mixed evening of young ladies and gentlemen. Generous gladness. Some arms bared above the elbow. If at five in darkness I sat in my rooms. Horace said ah wait till you have the great doings in Trinity Week sir, then there'll be some great lookers about and you can take your pick.

"I know I shouldn't but I feel so silly not to. Use your christian name, may I. It's Balthazar."

"Yes."

"Funny isn't it, if one keeps very much to oneself and lets others think as they may, one can seem so mysterious and strange. I never would have thought you were lonely and didn't lead the gayest of lives. You dance beautifully too. And now I can't say your name. But I will. Yes. Balthazar. Beefy says you're from France."

"That was many years ago."

"Do you like Ireland."

"Yes except when they suddenly step out on the street and direct traffic."

"I'm not surprised. When you come along in your motor. But you do like it here."

"Miss Fitzdare I think it would really be better for me to admit right now to you that I am utterly and absolutely bewildered by this land. From the moment I stepped off the boat till now. I'm dazed. I'm frozen out of my wits in my rooms. And forgive me. I have been constipated for weeks. I haven't an idea what's being said by the professor in zoology.

When I see all of you just cutting open your dogfishes the way you do, and somehow I cut into mine, and in my dogfish it simply didn't have a ninth and fifth nerve. I looked all over. I'm absolutely positive."

"You are funny."

"Miss Fitzdare, I am, really I am, utterly bewildered."

"O dear."

"I can't learn. I keep thinking what good is it to know ontogeny repeats phylogeny. I am sometimes most discouraged."

"So you do know something."

"Only because those two words rhyme. I really do swear to that. It was the ogeny that made me remember the phylo and onto."

"You are not quite what I expected. Mr. B. I don't know whether to believe you or not. Or whether you're having me on."

"I swear I'm not having you on."

"You mustn't swear. I hope you don't think I am just a little innocent girl and you pity me. In some things I am innocent. God now you've got me all blushing. This is awful."

"I am sorry. I didn't mean to embarrass you. Do you play the harpsicord, Miss Fitzdare."

"How did you know that."

"I knew. I don't know how. I can hardly meet anyone in Dublin who doesn't."

"O God what a thing to say."

"I don't mean it in its cruelest sense. I in fact mean it from the heart. You see I often sit and wonder if my way of life is a true one. That I shall take my place in some sort of society. Not high or low. Not too low. Make comments on the wine. Tell my host or hostess that the ceiling plaster is divine."

"Mr. B. Hmmmn. Yes you are rather more than one bargained for. We don't seem to be dancing. Shall we go back to the mantelpiece. Where we first met."

"You're not meaning to leave me."

"No. Good gracious no."

"I'm in need of another sherry."

"And I'll get it for you."

"Miss Fitzdare. The way you cross your legs now on the chair."

"Chair. What chair."

"Sorry stool, at lecture. And you wear those blue woolly looking stockings. You know I have looked at you many times. From behind. I even thought of asking you to accompany me to the gramophone society. And then I thought, no I was just sure you wouldn't come."

"You should have asked."

"If I did. Would you have come."

"I would have adored to."

"Now that's what I mean Miss Fitzdare. You say you would adore to come. And the word adore. That troubles me. I almost feel that how can one really, deep down in one's heart, adore to go to the gramophone society. My first night was awful. I had paid my shilling, and four pence for tea. And on a cold black night five to eight on what I thought was a Friday evening I walked across the playing field. At the other side all was darkness. I nearly stopped and went back to my rooms. But I couldn't face just sitting there. And I went on. For the first time I knew what it was like for those chaps at the pole. And how it was only their will to forge on. Ever on. And that's what I felt when I stopped mid way across the playing field. I thought. No. Courage. You must go on. Even though one sees no light. Somehow remembering as it said about the society, anyone who is interested in music should get in touch. And I had straight off paid my five shillings membership. You mustn't laugh, Miss Fitzdare. I was quite really a very desperate man."

"I'm sorry. I just somehow don't know just how seriously to take you. I've not quite heard anyone talk like you before."

"Well you may not know it. But I burst into tears in the middle of, I think it's the rugby pitch as a matter of fact. Like a scimitar had struck a bag of water on my head. Tears came tumbling down all round me."

126

Miss Fitzdare looking slightly away. And suddenly reaching for the decanter she poured Balthazar's glass over full and sherry dripped from his wrist and went coolly along under his sleeve.

"O dear I'm most awfully sorry I did that. Here let me wipe your glass. And your hand. I mean, I must say, I think because you must be alarming me. But do say. Did you get there. To the gramophone society."

"Yes. I did. I got there. Feeling every inch of the way that they would not want me when I did. And it was all far worse than I imagined. I saw a light on. And I went close and looked in the window. In the room that has all the plants. There was a man sprinkling something on top of a fish tank. I knocked at the window and he was paralytic with terror. And I nearly fell over when a toad jumped up my trouser leg. I guess my waving arms out in the dark were disconcerting. He became awfully angry because I had given him such a fright. Kept trembling and shaking and asking who my tutor was. He said the gramophone society was in the Physics Building. And not the Botany Building. And when I got round there. It was all locked up. It was a Thursday night."

"O dear I am sorry. You seem to have had awfully bad luck. But why don't you join the Christian Student Movement. I'm on the council. Annual subscription only five shillings. You seem to me, I don't know, perhaps I'm prying a little, but you seem as if you hadn't found out where you want to go in life."

"Have you Miss Fitzdare."

"Yes I think I have."

"And where are you going."

"Well I feel that one should devote part of one's life for the benefit of others."

"And do you."

"Yes. I do. In a small way. I know it sounds rather self proud to say a thing like that. Not everyone feels as I do. I don't really mind. Callous and cynical views have never changed mine. There's an awful lot of suffering in Dublin. In a room like this, with people like us, I don't suppose it appears that such a thing could be. I guess it's awfully unmodern but I have tried to take a christian attitude to questions which confront man in his daily life."

Miss Fitzdare moved her sparkling bracelet lightly to and fro on her wrist. Balthazar B wavering slightly. To straighten and come to attention for Miss Fitzdare. Her sudden cool dark elegance. Strange silence in her eyes. All those hours of her back facing me. As I pondered, amid erotic images, the early stages of a mammal. All utter Gaelic to me. Then to look up and see Miss Fitzdare's legs refold themselves. I thought she was so aloof to life. With appointments up and down Grafton Street and all over Merrion and Fitzwilliam Squares. Where briefly she would appear and disappear beyond the bright lacquered doors, paying respects to dowagers. And here in all this twinkling splendour of candle light. She talks. And I can almost hear. Her fearless handling of a horse. Nibbling and nuzzling her. As her own nostrils flair. Fluttering out at the end of the narrow bridge of bone so delicately straight. And the question which confronts me much in my daily life. To sow, please, one's desperate bag of wild oats in this country. Somewhere there must be a fissure in this granite ground.

"Miss Fitzdare what do you feel one should do with one's problems."

"Well I can sound awfully prim I imagine but if there is no christian answer, then I should think to follow one's heart is best."

Miss Fitzdare bowed her head. She picked up her pearls and put them in her mouth. Can I ever say. May I take them, your reins, your pearls, hold them. A bit between your lips. Miss Fitzdare. And ride you. All your white galloping skin. Lord I mustn't think of such a thing. That could warm me in all these shivering months. To let us go dancing quite indelicately in the sky. Would she. Touching under her satin and my silk. Embrace me to taste all her splendid little bits of beauty. I've had an awful lot of sherry. Chaps. Surrounded by all of you. Glistening with your welcoming gentle smiles. Faces scrubbed and shining. I just somehow know there are no motives low. I know it just as I thought I knew so many years ago that my redeemer liveth. That each gentleman here will one day walk up the aisle in his freshly aired and pressed morning suit solemn and above board. Between the collected tinted relatives and friends, titles and all described. From one whisper to another. Some winking above their smiles. Marriage. The organ music. O God Fitzdare. Have I found you. Can I hold back my unspeakable desperations. Till a ring is put along your finger. As wedded we will be. All the friends waving and maybe hating for us to go. Hand in hand to a honeymoon. Where God help me I would want to ride you in the bed. Across all the good racing years. Looking out from windows of our country house. To the grey and winterish conditions. Sherry in inclemencies. Vintage port in storms. Of a time. In June. When the white and delicate wine flows. A sun beaming over England. Gentle breeze that blows tender puffs of sky. Westerly fair across Britain. Over Henley's quiet straight waters. Down upon Ascot's perfumed carpets of turf. All the hues. Gay lads and maidens. We newly wed. Wicker hampers. Early afternoon feasting upon one's lap. Chicken, asparagus and yummy plums. One noble day after another. And like. The pound sterling. How does it waft, how does it wane. As England's flag waves. Fitzdare. Fluttering high over its parliament. You will be nervous. Just like the pound. In all its foreign markets. And I will admire you for being so. As sterling tends lower. But tomorrow always nudges forward again. Like we in our marriage do. Or remain quiet. For so many years. To never be devalued. As we get old together. The pound looking strong. Sterling firming up. You have two faces now Miss Fitzdare. I see them there. I shall point to one of them now don't you move.

"Are you all right Mr. B. You're swaying."

"Am I. Whoops."

"Heavens."

"I'm a little elevated. I think. A little. But I know. O God I know that my redeemer liveth. I mean Miss Fitzdare he could lead me and you beside the still waters. You know."

"Mr. B I don't want to say. But really I do. I think I must say. I do hope you're not blaspheming."

"O God no. Really I'm not. Not blaspheming."

"Ought you to have any more sherry."

"Just a jot."

"Steady now. Dear me. Steady."

"Forgive me. I think. Yes. Put my elbow on the mantel here. Firm up matters."

"Do you always drink as much as this."

"O I'm an old roué Miss Fitzdare. Drink like a drain. Always did. Glug glug. I mean that's the sound of it going down. The hatch I think. But surely we were talking. Yes of the Irish. They always lapse into what they call Urdu. Miss Fitzdare. Can you explain that."

"O yes. The Irish never want to be what they are. It's why they so envy the black men. The three black men rumoured to be in Dublin and the two in Trinity are always followed by a little crowd wherever they go."

"O God if only I were black."

"Yes."

"You feel that way too Miss Fitzdare."

"Yes. It makes one's teeth so white."

"O God Fitzdare."

"Is something the matter."

"No. Nothing. I just have to say. O God Fitzdare. O God."

"You're not, are you, blaspheming."

"No no. You see. This somehow is like walking into heaven. Meeting you. Being here. Every Sunday I am in Rathgar for an arranged Sunday dinner. I speak boldly I know. But it must be said. I simply must find some outlet. Your frock looks black but it's really purple isn't it."

"Yes."

"And what rustles. When you move."

"Mr. B, now now."

"What rustles. Please. Tell me."

"My petticoats."

"O God."

"Mr. B. Really."

"You know Miss Fitzdare you hurt me to the quick a moment ago."

"O."

"Yes. You did. When you said steady. Steady now."

"O."

"Just as if you were talking to a horse."

"O I never meant, honestly, such a thing."

"Well. I did feel I might be being led back to the stables."

"Heavens I hope I didn't sound like that."

"I suppose it's all right, really."

"You baffle me. You do Mr. B."

"Stepaside Wednesday."

"Yes."

"We can look down on Dublin."

"I'd like that very much."

A hall door swung open. Faces slowly turning. The beatific grinning face. Of Beefy. Grey top hat on his head. Morning coat and striped trousers. An ivory cane held in his grey gloved hand. He cut a quick motion on the parquet. Lifted his hat. And choo choo choo. The locomotive shuffle he said.

"Mr. B, that's your friend Beefy, wherever did he get those clothes."

Beefy went choo choo choo. Out on to the drawing room dance floor and back again into the dining room. Followed by a flushed hostess. Who put her hands up to her eyes and face. As Beefy climbed up on the dining table. Hurrying hands clearing his way of drinks and saumon fumé. His boots carving swirling ruts on the dark red gleaming mahogany. Amid claps and laughter and our hostess's dismay.

"O poor Philippa, I fear her party is about to end on a rather expensive note."

Beefy capered. The gathering laughed. Some doubled up and clapped. And the band tippled. Miss Fitzdare on her pleasant slender legs, took her leave. Followed by me. Said

131

she had not far to go. Just down the road. I said no I must see you out and home. And with coats donned in the cool·hall. And the gay stamping noise left behind. Here with all the hats and canes. The silver salver for calling cards. Architectural prints of Dublin city. And our hostess. Face alarmed and creased with an ever friendly frown. Shaking hands goodbye.

Outside on the dark roadway covered over with arching trembling branches. Balthazar tripping down the steps. Between the white globes of light and on the pebbles underfoot. His arm held by Miss Fitzdare. Her warm understanding smile. The moisty night lies out around us. From Ailesbury Road all the way across a green Kildare. To the Curragh stretched flat as a moonlit land. Where horses apounding go. And with me. To England, perhaps, Miss Fitzdare might you come. To my little house there. Where we would be and no one else would know.

"Balthazar. Balthazar. Can you see."

"I think so."

"You'd better hold my arm."

To feel close to her. Through our respective thick woollen garments. All those weeks she sat so untouchable. Distantly far away. In her own world huddled over her drawing of plasmodium. I watched the tip top of her pencil moving back and forth on the drawing paper. And mine an empty whiteness. Save where my pencil had wandered. Making round faces of little men, some who smiled and others who were awfully sad with their ears very small.

"I never thought we would meet like this Mr. B."

"Nor I, Miss Fitzdare."

By a high iron fence Balthazar paused, swayed and leaned against the black spokes. Slowly he slid down and down. Miss Fitzdare holding him by the arm as he sank to his knees and looked up at her face and into her cool blue eyes. A gleam of silk flowing with colour between her black lapels. Balthazar shaking his head and pulling himself up again. Looking round at this large stone entrance.

"Balthazar you cannot be left alone."

"I'm absolutely tops. Down for a moment. But up now. Very tops."

"You're not tops. You're squiffy."

"I'm tops not squiffy."

"Dear you've no transport back."

"Never squiffy. Not that. Tops."

"I could put you up for the night."

"Miss Fitzdare I could never never impose. I mean I'm topping. You think it's shocking that I say I'm topping."

"No. But we should go back and find you a lift. Or I may be able to call a taxi out from Dublin. You'll catch your death on the road."

"Would you care Miss Fitzdare if I died."

"Of course I would."

"My uncle was a great explorer. At the drop of a barometer. He went immediately to one of the poles. It's in my family. I will make it back safely to my rooms."

"I hope so."

"Miss Fitzdare do you really know me. How can you be certain I am not some mustachioed man, with the ends waxed and twirled. And that now I have cut off my mustache. You don't know that."

"I know you're squiffy."

"How do you know I'm not a dashy dandy."

"You're anything but."

"I'm just so so ordinary."

"Mr. B are you fishing for compliments."

"But do you know me from within. Miss Fitzdare. My little shortcomings, my little heartfelt troubles, my yearnings."

"No but I know you're a very nice person."

"How can you know that Miss Fitzdare."

"I do. From your eyes. You are a nice person."

"Where Miss Fitzdare have you been all these months. Why haven't we spoken before."

"You never troubled to look at me I fear."

"You must not say that Miss—"

"My God don't fall."

"Ah I am down."

"O dear. I've got you. Up up you come."

"Down and down. I go. But I love you Miss Fitzdare. I have no friends in Ireland. Nowhere to go. Sit at my fireside night after night."

"But I thought you were so very popular Mr. B. I'm sorry I had no idea."

"No I am not popular. I am down for the count."

"Dear me. You must not fall again. The grass is wet. You'll catch cold."

"I want to catch you Miss Fitzdare."

Miss Fitzdare shyly turning away. Her black gloved hand reaching to tuck upon the silk at her throat. A wind casting a lock of her dark hair in gleaming stray strands across her so white temples. Somewhere behind the hurrying cloud a moon basks. And it feels that my fingers clutch and haul me on the sands from an eastern chilly sea.

"Is this where you live Miss Fitzdare."

"Yes. It's my uncle's house."

"It's very nice what I can see of it."

"You know I'm really worried to let you go."

"Can I tell you Miss Fitzdare that I don't know what I'm doing in this country at all. They wrote in such a friendly welcoming fashion. That I just packed up. Got on the train to be here by October first. They never told me I would be cold and lonely and friendless all these months."

"You know you say this. And each time I wonder if you're having me on. Dear you're sliding down again. You must get up. There's a couch you could sleep on over the stable."

"Ah once more you think I am your horse, Miss Fitzdare."

"Heavens. Really I don't."

"Ah Miss Fitzdare why not. Saddle me up. Hear me I'm munching the grass."

"Please get up."

"I have been too careful for too long. It is only this evening, the first time I have ever stepped forth from my rooms and went in public without my gloves. I make my servant laugh.

We have chats. Ah no Miss Fitzdare, I have been careful far too long. I will not take advantage of your extreme kindness. By the stars I will find a way through these raging suburban jungles back to Dublin."

"There are no stars."

"I will feel my way through the laurels. Please don't let me keep you from your bed you have already been far too kind to me. I am not popular. That is certain. Today I dined with a mother, her three daughters and a doctor guest in Rathgar. Refined members of society. I a poor Frenchman who does not know what it's all about. They sit and I sit. We make remarks about the weather, the races. I am asked will I have more trifle. I say that is most kind of you. But then I say whoops that perhaps my remark that it is most kind, is wrong, that I have trodden too heavily in the etiquette, should have just said please and thank you. And not that I should be too delighted to have more trifle. In such dilemmas I perspire heavily. Sometimes I am so nervous that I cannot take my leave till midnight, all of us sitting and beginning to shiver around a dying fire. I never know what to say to get myself out of the house. I never know how to refuse when they say do please, come next Sunday. I am to put it mildly Miss Fitzdare in an awful rut."

"O but that's awful for you."

"Yes, I know."

"Can't you refuse."

"There is something wrong with me Miss Fitzdare. I do not know how to be unkind. I can suffer unkindnesses but I cannot be unkind. Again and again each Sunday I go back to Rathgar and we all sit on the settee. And the daughters change their frocks, one wears the frock the other wore the week before."

"How awful for you."

"But tonight. Beefy has taken me from all that. It is why I have had too much to drink. It is so kind of you to listen Miss Fitzdare to all my troubles like this. I must not keep you

135

longer. I must take leave of you. I don't want to go. But already I've been far too much of an imposition."

"You mustn't feel that, please."

"What way do I go."

"If you proceed down to the end of this road and turn right it will take you straight to Dublin. But I really shouldn't let you go."

"Have faith in me Miss Fitzdare. I am really related to explorers. It's the absolute truth. Just give me some natural phenomenon to head for and my instincts will do the rest."

"Tell me you'll take every care."

"Yes."

"There's a river. Walk straight as far as you can go. The River Dodder. Then turn right along Donnybrook Road straight into Leeson Street and St. Stephen's Green."

Balthazar B bowing. Slowly stepping backwards. Miss Fitzdare wore a silver jumping horse pinned to her coat. And she walks away between the high iron railings. Through a gate which creaks closed. A cement path to looming wide stone steps. A big shadowy house standing on dark lawns. Can see a stone porch and beyond looks like gardens. The fat upturned limbs of a monkey tree and others thick and tropical in the passing bits of moonlight. Door opening. She stands a silhouette. Her hand raised to wave goodbye.

> My finger
> Dips
> Into the cold
> Indelicacy
> Of
> Dublin.

15

Balthazar B raised his head from the wet grassy darkness. Moist patches of his clothes sticking to his skin. To remember forging bravely on some detour which seemed so quicker north west to Dublin town. Over a stone wall. To land in a ditch and field. Looking up at the sky for a guiding star. And then keeling over into empty darkness. And the steamy nostrils munching near. The ripping and tearing of grass. And sound of bone grinding jaws. To rise in terror as a cow reared and trotted away.

Miss Fitzdare's dancing blue eyes back there somewhere. In a white white skin and lips of redness that glowed. Must get up and back upon my strategic way. The bark of a dog. A cross. A convent. Nuns in nightgowns maybe. I'm utterly lost. Which way over these fields. Goodness, windows ahead with bars. And human anguished noises somewhere behind those walls. Civilization can not be far away. Must steer past this building of incarceration. Nothing now to do but flip a coin. Tell me which way is north. Uncle Edouard said always forge on. That way is north. Across there the faint shadows of a rooftop. In the wagging shrubberies and trees. Trudge muddily on.

Ah underfoot the firm feel of gravel. Will take me somewhere. A fence I see. And hear an owl hoot. Never had so much fresh air. Nor as much cold feet. Chilling me back to life. I am so lost any direction now will do. Should have stayed in her stable. Eating hay. Miss Fitzdare come out and give me a cube of sugar in the morning, and take me cantering round the lawn for exercise. Sitting up on me, moleskin riding breeches tightly clutched against my ribs. Could easily be an indecent thought. Good heavens, I'm wading through someone's flower beds, maybe azaleas ahead. Someone lives here

137

quite comfortably. Beefy said an area of embassies, and bank directors, salubrious and subtropical.

Balthazar B stopping before the shadowy outline of a house. Gabled roof over faint squares of cozy windows. No question now. I am on private property. How utterly awful. I must tip toe away. Casually. Into the dark. Over there is a garage tucked into this secluded house. With panes of stained glass I can make out. That way must be north. Uncle Edouard says to tramp steadily in one continuous direction is better than wandering in discontinuous circles. He was in my dreams when I woke back there on the grass. Gave me some rather amusing advice. At least I've struck out for Dublin when all odds were against me. Without stars. Just a momentary moon. O my God what's this. A birdbath. I hope. Hands out now to touch carefully as I go. Perhaps a vegetable garden to be crossed. There's got to be a field. And maybe a river upon whose banks I can guide my way back. Or swim this time of night. No nerve to knock and enquire. As Beefy could do all plausible and winning. Make my heart resolute now. Onward chaps. Get around the side of this house. Make a dash before there is a flash of moonlight again. I have a horror of trespass.

Balthazar B moved swiftly in the moist soft darkness. Guiding his way. And suddenly smashing into an obstacle. Something falling. And crashing to the ground. An infernal thump. Be heard for miles. Must run. Around this back corner of the house. Make exit. O my God something has me tight across the throat. They've got me already. Never did I have a chance. Please I'm only a lost natural science student from Trinity. Wait. What's this. Wet cloth. Clothes. A washing line. Lord a giant foundation garment. Fit for an amazon. Must get disentangled at all costs. And quietly run like mad away from here.

A light switching on in the house. Balthazar tugging at the line. As it stiffens and the garments rise up from the lawn. Yanking harder. A rip and crash of cement from the wall of the stuccoed house. Just below an open and ablaze window. To be back in Rathgar now to say push me the pudding will you. Instead of here helplessly damaging property. After all the bomb escapes. To be befallen this perfectly disenchanting exploration. Out of one's wits in someone's private garden. I wanted so much to guide myself homeward by the stars. To test my instincts alone with nature. And tell Miss Fitzdare. That I just followed the bent of ancestors. And now goodness someone is shouting.

"Who is that down there."

Make for that shrubbery. Crouching now in under this thick rhododendron. In the pin drop silence. And pull in this washing line.

"O Lord God Jimmie wake up there's something down in the garden."

"What is it now."

"Wake up I'm telling you."

Balthazar B hauled in the vague pegged white cloths lying out across the lawn. Which will lead straight to me. Slowly. So indeed indelicate. A brassiere. More female undergarments. All of them. Whalebone corsets. Pink silk pantaloons. Outsize. The woman who fits these garments upon her person is not to be trifled with.

"Jimmy Jimmy wake up out of the bed I'm telling you. There's a long snake moving across the lawn so help me God Jimmy do you hear me."

O my God what does one do now. I've been spotted pulling in the washline. People so easily disbelieve St. Patrick. Uncle Edouard can you hear me. At this most ignoble moment. In which I've not meant to cause such upset. Honestly madam I've only been trying to find my way back to my rooms. Somewhere north there beyond your garage. I would recognise the grey walls and high green fence in an instant. Just beyond Merrion Square. Thump the nail once or twice on the big thick door and a porter will come from his curled up sleep at the fire. To let me in. To go abed within my thick walled rooms, so safe and cold. Dear St. Basil the Great deliver me from this shrubbery garden.

"Jimmy ah God, you'd sleep would you, and I'm being

raped within an inch of me life, while you're snoring there, I'm being defiled. Wake up I'm telling you."

To have quietly trotted to Miss Fitzdare's stables. And munched sweet hay there through the night. She said such kind things to me. Opened out a whole world of heathery flowers. In rain they sparkle down among their browny twigs even when the whole winter world is grey. Just as all this green is so dark and hopeless. Got to shift position now I've dragged in this suspicious line. Just nip over across there to the thicker bushes. And the washing line will follow.

"Ah God Jimmy there he goes. I'm calling the garda. I've seen him now. Trampling my best roses. Down there in the garden. With a length of snaky thing coming out of him so long he's dragging it. I'm telling you. Jimmy. Get up, get up. If it's ever rape with a thing like that he's dragging after him. I couldn't stomach it, the little fig stem you've got is bad enough. He must be crazed by sex to have the likes of that on him. Jimmy wake up I'm telling you. Jesus Mary and Joseph, he could be a Mohammedan. It's been in the Irish Times that a horde could be coming any time from the East. That Islam is on the march. It's shock enough to know you're in the minority without them running loose in your garden."

"Will you shut up now about the yellow peril while I'm trying to sleep. Sure not a man of them cares two hoots about Ireland."

"Sleep is it, while defilement is but a hair's breadth away. And me raped following seventeen years of marriage."

"Shut up now about rape. There hasn't been such a thing in Ireland since the Danes and they were welcomed with open arms. Will you get back to bed."

"Jimmy for the last time."

"Shut up."

"I'm telling you Jimmy, not a bit of me will I let the rascal have."

"Too much of you anyway for him to want you all. Put out the light. And batten your gob."

"Abandon me is it. To men with the corkscrew things on them."

140

"Abandon you. I'm sleeping that's all."

"Batten your gob is it."

Balthazar crouched in the thicket of laurel and sinuous boughs of rhododendron. When trapped across the chippendale on a light note of conversation, an opera seen, a recital at the Music Hall in Fishamble Street, and one never knows that there are conditions and positions worse. Agony to ask to pass a sauce boat. Now, my God, the fear of running through unknown darkness. Just trying to get home madam, I'm no Moslem. Her shadow is at the window. She carries two portly breasts. By the feel of this brassiere.

"He's still there with the big long thing he's dragging. You lie there like that while your wife is raped out of her wits. I'm going to give you something to remember the occasion by. O Jesus Mary and Joseph what heinous new trials have you sent me to bear."

Damp and dripping in the rhododendrons. To know which way to run. Wait till the action dies down. Between this woman and the Far East. What was that. Bloodcurdling scream. And sound of broken glass.

"That'll teach you to lie there snoring and making dirty filthy remarks to your wife while a heinous rapist wanders in the garden. That'll teach you. Till the garda get here. To leave me panic stricken and defenceless against an immoral intruder."

A light bursting on, flooding yellow rays across the grass and gravel. A fallen ladder. Jimmy what did she do to you. I do apologise for all the needless upset. Crawled away here to cover. Just to wait now for the all clear. And the light out to give me a chance to run. Too late to offer one's card. By the silence ensued. The witty husband from whom there seems now no sound. Better advised to withhold a social overture. If I had my Landship now. I could suddenly emerge from the shrubbery. And twelve cylinders pumping, would get me back to college. Where I am but a harmless student of science.

Irish bugs fluttering at the glowing porch light. The grass pale white green. Crouch stiffly. O please, it's not the sound of tires on the road. It is. And twin beams of light through the branches. O God. Let it be some milk man and not the police. Tires sliding to a stop in the gravel. Car doors slamming. Flashes of torchlight. Three garda in their thick blue uniforms, yawning and rubbing their sleepy eyes.

"Can you see anything Milo."

"Nothing suspicious."

"Ah it's what I thought, what would a good Mohammedan be wanting wandering nowhere on a soft night such as this. Give the Mrs. a knock. And we'll put her mind at rest. It's a nice place they've got here."

The front door opening. Gentlemen of the Garda Schicona standing on the gravel. Helmets held in the crooks of their arms.

"Nothing so far madam, where last did you see the culprit complained of, described as Mohammedan."

"He was right over there with this long thing hanging from him."

"I must caution you now madam, we're three members of the Legion of Mary present here. Let that be understood. And I have to tell you to be careful in talk like that."

"Sure I'll have you know then that I'm a member of the Royal Dublin Society. Roses have been named after me. Only last year I exhibited myself."

"Ah now, madam, none of that. I must caution you again."

"You oaf."

"Now now. That's a matter neither here nor there. It's decency first. I'm ready to take down particulars."

"And let the scurrilous intruder escape."

"Now if your man, madam, was as desperate as you say, he'd be as far now as the Kilcool, in the County Wicklow. After waving goodbye to the protestants in Greystones."

"Eegit, eegit."

"Calm yourself madam, and be a decent lady."

"Didn't I see him five minutes ago."

"Describe his dress and distinguishing features."

"How many times do I have to tell you he was a Moham-medan."

"Ah well we'll have no trouble then, catching the likes of him, but sure madam he's as likely to be a prince travelling with, forgive the expression, his harem. There's one of them lives in the Rathgar. But from what we know of him he's a jolly gentleman. And it's the women we've got to protect him from. They're banging on his door, poor man, all times of the day and night. The gentleman can't get a moment's rest. I'm sure he thinks we're not civilized."

"How dare you, when Ireland preserved culture through the dark ages of mankind."

"Ah now madam what's a few old trinkets and pages of a book compared to the refrigerators some of these gentle-men have in their very cars."

"I'm going to faint."

"Boys catch her now. I've got holt of her. She's no light-weight, I'm telling you, any Mohammedan gentleman would have his hands full with the likes of her. In the door now. She'll come round. Milo you make a search there through the shrubbery for footprints."

Flash of garda torches approaching across the lawn shoot-ing between the branches and leaves of rhododendrons. Bal-thazar crouching low. A weary wave of sleeping chill across my head. How did I ever wake up into this. Out of dreams of a white bull goring a man in a brown suit. And of Uncle Edouard who stood in a pulpit preaching. About the routes to follow through life. Lighthearted on the boulevard, gay in the cafe, a good shot at the shoot. A flower delivered each morning to the door for the buttonhole. Put a smile on the face. Keep the collar worn loose at the throat. Be skittish laughing and droll. Wear the garter always for the sock. And Balthazar my dear little one. As the prickly problems of life assail, or get dumped on you all at once, then. Ah. Take the walking stick, put back the shoulders, chest out, emerge into the world, stare up at the sky, watch where you're walking and show them what you are made of. Move the bowel in the morning like the roar of a lion. Hum a lullaby while you pee. That is my dear boy, joy. Soar up in the heavens in the balloon. When you come down again and you find that your mistress has had a little on the side. Give her a small slap and say do not again be naughty. You hope that it was not with a rogue or swindler. That it was a gentleman of stature. Who knows his wine. And would always know his women. If he is black so much the better, and you then become completely white. For a change of pace. And last of all, let me say my dear boy. A little something about baldness. If you want to wear the toupee, which I do not suggest, always carry two. One for the white wine and one for the red. And when you drink the brandy you must of course be completely bald. And ah. For the great frisson. To press the top of the head against the breasts. It is perhaps one of the noblest of man's pleasures. The brain feels the breast right through the follicles. Undisturbed by the useless hair. You are not perhaps bald yet but there is hope. And then. You spin like a top upon madam's precious matters. After which death has no fear.

"Ah come out of there with your hands up. I've got him. I've got him. There he is. Up now. We've got the black Mohammedan for sure. Come out of there youse. Attempting rape on a good catholic woman and running around your own country without so much as a farthing piece shielding you from shame."

Balthazar rising to his knees. The drops of moisture falling from the leaves. Stumbling forward into the torch light. Eyes blinking.

"Ah. Sure your man is dressed like a gentleman. He's the whitest thing I ever saw. Ah now wait a moment now. He's got ladies undergarments dragging after him. That's lawlessness enough for me I can tell you."

"Milo don't let that fool you. Mind now. We have caught a dangerous desperado here. Easy boys."

"Look of the way he's bending over double to avoid presenting too large a target, sure he's learned that trying to escape from the Federal Bureau of Investigation in America.

Get the handcuffs now will you Sean from the car. He's no local criminal. I know the stance when I see it I'm telling you."

"Enough of your Yank folklore Milo. I'm in command of this arrest and will give the orders. Sean get the handcuffs from the car and me note book. Youse now. Let me caution you before you speak that what I think and see here will be used against you."

"That's not correct Seamus."

"Never you mind what's correct. Your man is a jewel thief, sure he's a jewel thief. And that's that."

"Sean write down jewel thief."

The madam of the house stepping forth on the gravel in a long green kimono. Hair pinched close to her head in curlers. Arms crossed over her huge breasts. Woolly red slippers on her feet. The garda stepping back and Seamus nodding.

"Is this your man madam, would you now positively identify him beyond any shadow of doubt as the Mohammedan."

"Didn't I tell you. The spitting image. Do you believe me now the rapist was loose."

"It appears to be established fact, madam."

"Fact is it, heinous rape that's what it is."

"Did you get that down Sean. And now you, speak up, what have you got to say. Get it down Sean, the rapist remains silent in face of the questions put to him by his interrogators. It is now five five A.M. in the vicinity of Herbert Park. The culprit although shivering appears not to speak. At approximately five A.M. we surrounded the accused, closed with him at five one A.M., the culprit was outmanoeuvred and after a brief struggle was overpowered and apprehended at approximately five three A.M. The clothes accused is wearing give the appearance of expensive quality and high class tailoring but it is evident that he has been sleeping rough recently. Search him Milo."

"He raped me. That's him. Hanging is too good."

"Will you be quiet madam. We have that fact down already. He'll be charged accordingly and hanged later."

Balthazar B trousers with muddy patches in the torchlight. The pin stripe in my suit has gone wavy. My scarf lost. Best to utter nothing in these circumstances. One could never explain lurking in the rhododendrons. Give a mute grunt in my defence.

"What's that you're saying. Get that down Milo, accused makes a high pitched noise following questioning. But due to the unidentified nature of the sound, we must surmise its meaning. I think the culprit means Milo he's guilty as charged. He would be off a ship maybe. Youse. You speakum English. Ah just as well he doesn't or he'd be incriminating himself every word out of his mouth. Caught as he is dead to rights. Hold him Milo while I get madam's statement in her own words. Are you right Sean. Now madam what are the facts."

"I was fast asleep with my husband Jimmy snoring up there in the pink bedroom. I heard something fall. It was the ladder there. Then came a rip at the side of the house. Which I now see to be my washing line."

"Sean make a note of exhibit A and B. Go on madam."

"I gave Jimmy an elbow in the ribs I was so terrified and said there is a Mohammedan in the garden."

"Ah now madam wait one minute please, you had not yet looked out the window. How did you know it was a Mohammedan."

"Didn't I read in the Irish Times that they are streaming over the earth in their hordes."

"Good enough reasoning, madam. Get that Sean, the victim was fully awake to the threat from the East. And what did your husband do."

"He groaned."

"Did he make for the window at a later stage after groaning."

"He did not. He turned over and began snoring again and I was abandoned to the hands of the rapist you see before you. I knew he was foreign. No Irish man would lay hands to a woman and take a liberty."

"Ah now madam we must confine ourselves to the facts. Was there any gesticulation of a moral nature or interference with your person now. I must ask these questions in the line of duty."

"Didn't I feel the scoundrel's hands around my throat making unwanted heavy breathing advances."

"Get that down Sean. Accused between the times of knocking the ladder over and pulling the clothesline off the side of the house with attendant plaster made a savage advance with menacing interference upon the victim's person. Now madam. What was the manner of the interference. Asked in the line of duty."

"Never you mind what manner. It was heinous. Isn't that manner enough."

"Sean's put down manner was heinous in nature. And madam I remind you once again I'm only doing me duty here seeking the facts."

"Well you'll get none of that kind of facts from me, I'm a respectably married woman and my husband is a business executive of twenty years duration."

"It was pure and simple rape then."

"Haven't I been telling you it was rape for the last half hour."

"Did the accused leave mud from his boots in the house."

"What do you mean. Are you not trusting me in my testimony. I'll have you degraded in rank. I have a brother a Jesuit and two more are Christian Brothers."

"I am a Knight of Columbus madam. But all the same isn't one Jesuit worth two of the Christian Brothers so you might as well say you have four brothers all Christian Brothers."

"This is not a joke."

"To be sure madam. Milo throw a cover over the accused, sure the poor man is shivering badly now."

"Shivering is good enough for him. Here I am nearly without a stitch on me. Hang him."

"Now be quiet madam, if you please. Rape is one thing. But inhumanity to man is another. Where did the interfer-

147

ence with the person of madam occur and were there attendant obscene grunts or gestures madam, having in mind of
course that if the accused voiced an obscenity in an unknown
tongue it might not give you immediate offence until it was
later translated, am I right, Milo on that point of law if you
please."

"Right captain."

"You are making a mockery of the victim of rape you eegit.
Sure that needs no translation."

"I am not, madam, making a mockery, what would I want
to make a mockery for this time of the morning with it
getting on for dawn and God fearing people asleep in their
beds. And if you leave us to the legal points, sure you can
supply the facts madam. It's as clear as the day I was born
that the accused will plead nolo contendere. Am I right on
that Milo if you please."

"Right captain."

"Thank you Milo. Now to what height of indecency did
the interference with you madam extend."

"You filthy minded cur. I could slap your face. Height is
it. Up me you're insinuating is it. I'll have you reported to the
superintendent."

"I resent that madam. And don't you raise your hand to
me. You report what you like to whom you like but I'm only
doing my duty. Sure your man here on the lawn could be
innocent. And you are not forthcoming with the facts. Close
the notebook Sean. The time is now five thirteen to the
minute."

"I am behooved."

"You may be behooved madam, I wouldn't know what you
were meaning."

"I am behooved. The Bishop will hear of this. The lot of
you will get your come uppance. Remove yourselves. Go on.
Take that rapist with you. Get your big hooves out of my
lawn."

"Ah Milo would you say now we were only behooving."

148

"Insults is it. The Bishop will fix your waggon. Jimmy, come down here. Bring the gun."

"Ah now none of that madam. Being behooved is one thing. But being violent is another. Are you pressing charges concerning the alleged interference with your person."

"I'll get the likes of you fixed fast. Just wait."

Sucking in her breath. Turning her stout build in its own tracks madam of the rape ran back into the house. The sound of her feet pounding up the stairs. Her voice coming out the open window from the lighted bedroom. Her shadow on the ceiling. Down in the damp dark silent greenness the accused mute and numb. The three waiting Garda Schicona staring at the stucco suburban house.

"Ah Jimmy, Jimmy me dear what did I do to you at all. Speak to me. Speak. O Lord God what have I done at all. Saints I have him kilt. O God what is he doing dying and he's not due for pension yet."

"I don't like the sound of that one bit Milo. I'd better get up there and investigate. Sure this is beginning to sound more like a war than a Mohammedan loose in Donnybrook. Take the accused and wait for me in the car. Don't panic. If not back in two minutes come in after me."

Balthazar B marched between the two garda. They fell into step one in front and one behind. Left right, left right over the gravel. Milo first opening the door, giving a salute and bow as Balthazar crouched into the small black vehicle. A rug pulled up over his knees. Milo taking out a packet of Woodbines and putting them to Balthazar. Refuse the nearest.

"Ah now Sean what do you make of this at all. Sure your woman has done something to your man up there in the bedroom. By the sound of it a blow upon some part of the higher learning delivered with the maximum from behind while the innocent gent was dancing in his sleep with a Hollywood movie star."

"Ah I wouldn't want to be on the wrong side of that one meself."

"What do you make of your mute man here Sean. He seems decent enough when you get a good look at him in the light. I mean you'd have to put him down as a member of the gentleman classes dressed as he is. Sure that woman's out of her mind, how would this slender dignified gent here rape the likes of her. He'd have more chance strangling the Loch Ness monster. He may be lost on the highway or something. Isn't the Ailesbury road full of embassies with foreign gentlemen dining there of an evening. I think your woman is out of the asylum over beyond if you want my shilling of information."

"Ah you may be right Milo. You may be right. She'll be giving Seamus the swipe of her tongue in any event. And that tongue of hers is the size of an ironing board. O Jesus what's that."

"It's Seamus, the poor man is running for his life, with that one after him. Ah God hasn't she got a hurling stick aimed at your man's head. This is an awful night for the Garda Schicona I'm telling you. Jump to now helmets on and give your man some aid."

"What about the prisoner."

"He's content enough. Sure he's safer in here than outside be the look of things."

Milo and Sean jumping from the car. Seamus running from the building. Out of a cloud of pillow feathers the lady of Donnybrook environs emerged swinging a long stick round her head. Seamus ducked and side stepped. Madam's kimono flying open. Heaving rolls of breasts and bellies.

"Men make back for the car your woman's the maddest thing on three wheels. She has the husband nearly kilt. Quick now."

The huge bulk of Seamus as he bent to squeeze into the front seat of the car. Two handed blows of the hurling stick raining on his shoulders. Milo slipping in beside him and Sean getting in the back. The slam of car doors. Revving the engine. Backwards towards Dublin.

"What kind of woman is this at all."

"Sure let's get the hell out of here and find that out later."

"Watch it Seamus, watch it, she's coming at the windscreen. Sure God help us we'd need all the Mohammedans we could muster to save us from that one."

"Eegits. Eegits. Buffoons. Get that rapist out of my life."

"Sure I think your woman is mental if you ask me."

"Ah Jesus I'm not asking anything but to get the hell out of here fast. Would you put the accelerator to the floor. She'd hit the pope in the haggis, that one would."

The vehicle reversing along the curving gravel drive. Sean with the torches shining rearwards out the back window. Your woman in the headlights. Smashing blows on the bonnet with the hurling stick. A palm tree passing calmly. A sign on the gate. Happiness. The little car backing now out on to the road. Back in the shadows madam stands. Her eyes looking wild. Her last gesture suggestive.

"Now what would your man have married a one like that, would you tell me Seamus."

"Sure the heart does a lot of strange things. Who knows he might have married her for her beauty. She would have been a stout heifer in her time."

"Ah now, none of that."

"Sure praise God there's got to be some kind of amenability between man and woman, as between a bull and heifer, or none of us would be here at all."

"Your woman back there was verging on the obscenity. It's been a hard enough night. How's your man Sean, is he bearing up. Poor chap. We got there in the nick of time. The likes of her would have killed us all. Try the Gaelic on him Sean."

"Mise le mas."

"Sola juvat virtus."

"Ah that's grand, he's talking, your fearsome woman must have struck him dumb. And isn't he speaking the language of the pope. He's a white Italian gentleman, sure as your foot."

The light of a grey dawn. The moist air blowing in the open

151

window. The police car passing along a river. Dear me the Dodder was not so far away. Just down those green banks. Over there, walls of a flour mill. These cross roads and they say Ballsbridge.

"How do you like that Seamus, the woman says she's a member now of the Royal Dublin Society. Why the place would be a wasteland by now if your woman was let loose in there."

A clanging bell. The sound of the tram. There it is. All lighted and yellow and warm. Squealing on its tracks. Stopping for its little group of passengers. To take peacefully into town. The toy city awakes. As I sit here apprehended by police. Jail bars ahead. Uncle Edouard said, be always handsome witty and brave. To police and lawyers and many others too, my dear boy, make no sound that can be used against you. Try never to teach the world a lesson, for they will forget it within the week. Be honest till the temptation comes to tell the truth. Then dear boy it is time, believe me, to say nothing. Keep your wine cellar cool. The bowel clear. The foreskin clean. Use soap perfumed of the fern.

Merrion Square. Odd windows lit. Past Lincoln Place. The back lonely gate of Trinity. Down there just a little bit. The Landship moored. I am far too young to start a criminal career. Hold back my voice. Through the wet streets of Dublin. Just some little time more. Kneeling so many years ago. On a carefree carpet of the Palais Royal. When all Dublin and Ireland came as sunshine to me. Through the little green windows of Bella's eyes. Her soft hand touching my face. And Bella you ran from me. On my way here when all I found was rain. Crossing college squares huddled in one's gown. The moisture dripping dropping down. The chill creeping across the floors. Seeping out of walls. I screamed once a dark lonely Sunday in Grafton Street to stop it, stop it. I can't stand more. I prayed in college chapel with others cold and shivering. Singing out against the mortal cold. I hoped that candle light would help. No hell is under Ireland. Of that they're surely right. They say instead, a dark daughter. The country at the end of the earth. The oldest place.

> Of the great
> Long hair
> That hangs
> To cover up
> All shame.

16

Past the safe walls and fence of Trinity. A grey stone building. The car stopped. Balthazar B led up the steps shivering.
Wrapped in a blanket. Early nosed newsboys asking what's
your man's crime. Did he do in his mother.

A sallow dusty room. Notices tacked to walls and scarred
bulletin boards. Hungry shouts from corridors within. A pure
voice singing like a bird. And words, would you live on
woman's earnings, would you give up work for good. By a fire
glowing Balthazar B sat on a worn bench and hung his silky
blond head. A cup of tea was brought. And a man who sat
away behind a long counter asked over and over in his sundry
languages. What's your name.

"Sure tell us something, you're not to come to any harm.
Seamus did you try the Dutch with him at all."

"We did."

"Ah your man is Urdu or Icelandic."

"We'll give him the Danish then. God morgen, ja, tak. Ah
it's no use. Sure if he was a Dane he'd be feeling right at
home."

"He must speak something."

"We got the Latin out of him when we tried the Gaelic.
But Milo just came in with the translation a minute ago. And
your man says in the Latin virtue alone assists one."

"Is that a fact now."

"That's a fact."

"Well I wouldn't want to depend upon that one in me
wanderings through life, I can tell you. We're sending over to
Trinity for a professor of languages."

Balthazar looking up. One can delay no longer. Time to give
an inkling. The police faces turning. Waiting. As Balthazar
reaches into his pocket. Withdrawing a notebook and tearing
out a piece of paper. And writing.

Ich bin Balthazar B. Ich bin ein Student an der Trinitas Universitas. Mein Tutor ist Professor Elegant.

"Ah will you look at that now. That's a relief. It's German. I'd recognise it anywhere. Shouldn't we have known by the blond hair he was from beyond the Rhine. Driven westwards by the war. Thank God we didn't have to use the Serbo Croat. We've your man's fixed address at last."

"It was the Lettish I was afraid of meself."

"Go on Milo now. Nip and get your Professor Elegant. We'll clear up this mystery. Not a moment to waste. Your man there looks like catching his death."

"Right captain. I am this second gone so fast that I am back now and ready to go again."

The telephone ringing. The sergeant picking it up. Looking out across the dusty sallow walled room. Cigarette burnings on counters and benches. Sergeant's eyes looking from face to face. As he puts the phone back on its hook.

"That was the raped herself on the phone. She has no marks of violence about her person but she's been on to the newspapers with the story all the same. It's been some night. We have a man back there singing in the cells. He was at the gates of Trinity, making an unholy fuss. Going to fight the whole college. Didn't we get over to him and he was going to fight the lot of us as well. We closed with him. Just a touch of a stick across the backside did he feel and he lay down on the roadway. Wouldn't get up. He was going to take the North by storm. And we had to take him by the arms and legs back here. The lad has a fine singing voice. Sure he could be kicking a gateway in an opera and be getting paid for it."

The door opening to the smoky room. The early morning sounds of the city. Ding ding. The bells of passing bicycles. Buses pulling away to go out along a southern coast. And in grey herringbone overcoat. Black silk tie against cream silk shirt. His early morning face scrubbed and new. Entered Balthazar B's tutor.

"Good grief, it's you Mr. B. I'm afraid I thought it some kind of joke."

"I do apologise sir, I'm most awfully sorry. I haven't said a word. I've just been too terrified and thought it best to pretend I did not speak English."

"Ah glory be to God will you listen to your man, as fluent as you please. Hasn't he heard everything we've been talking of all the way from Donnybrook. Couldn't he be charged with wandering abroad without due care and attention to a language. Ah I don't like that at all. Sure if he knew the lingo he could have told us he was keeping mum."

"All right officer. Mr. B say nothing now. I'll deal with matters. What is the charge."

"Rape."

"Good Lord. Where. Whom. How."

"Ah it was a stout lady in Donnybrook. As to how. I would be the first to say it was a mystery."

"Very serious. Of course penetration will have to be proved. And corroboration. We'll have to serve writs for slander this instant. False arrest. Mandamus. Of course Mr. B there's nothing to this charge. Answer yes or no will do."

"Sir I got lost and was merely hiding in the bushes when I accidently found myself in someone's garden having knocked over a ladder."

"Simple innocent trespass. We'll serve writs. Do that straight off. Can't have a Trinity student accused of rape. Simply will not do. We will fight this to the last drop of ink. I'm sure this whole matter is strewn with irregularities. O I think there's much improper conduct. Habeas corpus. We'll have this res judicata in a hurry. And substantial damages. O yes I think they will be very substantial."

"Ah sir, now not so fast. Sure it's been a friendly matter all the way. Your woman is a wild heretic. She walloped her own husband insensible."

"Wild eh. O we can commit her along the way then. We'll commit her right off. Can't have people running around slandering and damaging. Mr. B here is from a fine family. Obviously this heretic's property was not properly fenced causing Mr. B here to wander without warning off the public

156

highway to founder in dangerous gardens in fear of his life. And then to place Mr. B in false arrest. Simply preposterous, unethical and inhuman gentlemen."

"Ah now sir, we've not arrested the gentleman. Merely gave him a ride to town."

"That's true sir, they've been most kindly to me and treated me awfully well, in fact they saved my life."

"It's a fact sir. Not a hand of apprehension was laid upon him."

"Leave this to me Mr. B please. We must protect your interests in every wise. But if you've been treated well then we will see to it that recommendations go out for the deserving. No fear about that. Now Mr. B I think the college baths for you. Then come directly to my rooms. And we'll give you a good breakfast. For the moment here, you must have some of this."

Professor Elegant unscrewing the top of his cane and pouring a silver cup of liquid.

"Put that in you Mr. B. You'll feel much better. Anyone else need a little back stiffener."

"Ah it would be very welcome sir, but we're on duty."

"Another time then."

"Thank you sir."

"The charges then sergeant. There are none."

"None sir."

"I take it then that the matter is closed."

"Like a book sir, not a breath of air between the pages it's slammed so tightly shut. The gentleman is as free as the breeze."

"And I hope not blown constantly."

"What was that sir, I didn't catch that."

"Just a little prayer."

"Ah so."

"Come along Mr. B. This way. Get you bathed and back to normal. In quick order. You did well to keep silent. One must never admit to anything you know. Never never. Then you go in clanging with your own writs, cross complaints, reserve actions, mandamuses, the lot. Set up one awful stink. Amazing what one very loud shout in the beginning can save one in the end."

"I'm most awfully grateful to you sir. For coming to my aid in this manner."

"Nothing Mr. B, nothing. On the contrary rather enjoyed it. You come to me any time. Anything you need. That's what I'm for you know. I had been expecting you to call on me. Give you an hour. See you for breakfast. You know where I am."

On the black and white tiles of the bath house. Beyond the dark panelled wall the attendant drew the emergency bath of steaming waters. Into which under the skylight Balthazar slipped. Down into the welcome warmth. To close one's eyes. Out of harm's way. To turn the big brass taps and out comes hot. To gather up fortitude. Conquer irregularity, chills and ills. Uncle Edouard said for the best results plunge the cure up the rear so as not to ruin the stomach with the pills. Ah Balthazar you were born a nice fat little fellow, I saw you not long after your birth, the nurse, she had you by your legs and she held you up to stand you on your head as you went waaaaaa waa and she pulled back the foreskin, ah you had a big prick for such a little boy. Your mother would not circumcise you. It was sad for hygiene but good for the frisson. She fought bitterly with your father for your foreskin. Under which you should wash well my boy. The prick is the palate of the soul.

Balthazar B lathered himself with a cake of oatmeal soap. A red colour coming back into cheeks. Stare up at this roof. The university silence. When one could now go to sleep. Saved soothed and salvaged. Rest quietly till I see Miss Fitzdare again. Take her up away on the windy heather. Wednesday. Larks fluttering in lighted skies. To want so much to press me deep upon her dark blossom. And blue down there. Is it Miss Fitzdare. As all the wet grass was green. As I lay. Nearly nibbled by a cow. Could have been some fresh breakfast milk. I dreamt we walked through flower gardens, breathing scented

158

air. Down a long aisle of roses and forget me nots, an altar. High and thronged with lilies of the valley. I put my hand in yours. Cannons boomed salute. Flashes of fire, puffs of smoke. And not far away another vision. Continentals in grey thick overcoats clutched each other, holding tight. And I said as the minister pronounced us wed. I said what are you chaps doing. And I shuddered and shivered on that Donnybrook field. They said we are transplanting souls.

Balthazar B stepping from the bath house. Like a private little bank. Deposit your dirt. Emporium of waters. Each bather with his own little vault. The roadway gleaming wet. Past the grey stone. Of this shadowy square they call Botany Bay. Out now to the open spreading elegance. A little tree grows near the doorway of the Modern Language Building. Where one supposes the linguistic garda rush in and out. Mastering tongues. To tempt confessions from foreigners. I go up my steps again. Name still on the wall.

Balthazar pushing through his door. The clanking loose floorboards. To think in horror you'll find the whole world changed. The choking dust. The world's still the same. Horace sticking his head round from the sitting room, battered trilby hat jauntily forward on his head.

"It's only me Horace."

"Ah I wondered sir."

"I'm having breakfast out."

"Very good sir. I'll just get along here now with me cleaning. It's shocking weather."

"Yes. I'm just coming in to change."

"Ah no trouble. I'll be out of your way. Sir I can't help noticing have you been caught out in the weather."

"Just a late night stroll. Ran into some rough country, heh heh."

"Ah you need boots for that sort of thing. A good heavy mac is handy."

"Yes."

"Are you fond of the countryside sir."

159

"Quite fond."

"Sure meself I'd thought of doing a bit of the farming in me younger days. Me brother has a little farm in Monaghan. But I couldn't stick the country. The moaning sheep and goats were enough for me. Sure it's better to have four pint bottles of milk standing at your door of a morning than having to go through cold and wet to callus your fingers getting it out of an udder."

"Quite right."

"Rumour has it that some Americans are arrived at college sir. Have you heard that. It's been creating some misunderstanding. And there was this one of them in high boots marching across Front Square with a sign Modernise Ireland. They want the water flowing instead of out of pails. Sure you get a cup of water quicker out of a pail than a tap. And you can empty a bowl faster than a sink. I can see you're in a hurry sir, if there's anything now I can do, say the word."

"Thank you Horace."

Balthazar B in Manx checked tweed. Cream silk shirted and dark tied as one's tutor. With the antique links of one diamond set in mother of pearl laid in gold to join cuffs. Hold the socks out against the turf embers. The steam rises. And warmed socks slipped on cold feet. For a moment. No matter what you do the moist chill comes again.

On this college day in a sprawling low ceilinged room. Balthazar B sat at his tutor's table. The walls covered with tomes of law. Tort. Statutes. Contract. Trusts. Linen napkins. Plates of fried egg between pink rashers. Grilled tomatoes. Toast and tea. Servant pouring the dark tinted liquid. Turned pale with milk. Warming and comforting all down one's throat.

Out the window the spidery branches of the trees. Students passing darkly. Those who tarry and turn in laughter. Others cycling at breakarse speed. Professor Elegant leaning back in his quiet book lined life. Rush of air up the chimney after the licking flames.

"I think you had a very close scrape there Mr. B."

160

"Yes."

"Whole thing has blown over quite nicely though. Have some more marmalade, my wife's, the best in Dublin."

"Thank you. It is awfully good."

"Tell me have you decided on a career."

"No."

"Hobbies."

"I go racing."

"O yes. That's not going to be your career."

"O no. I hadn't much thought what I would do. I would like I suppose to work at a fishing station. Classifying flora and fauna."

"Good show."

"Yes I might rather like it."

"Well Mr. B. We must see more of you. You haven't really entered into college activities. We haven't seen you at college hops, or meetings, or societies."

"I've been taking my racing rather seriously."

"Quite. But we want to see more of you. Get what you can out of your university days. They tend to be very short ones after they are gone. And any little trouble or big trouble for that matter. You come straight to me. I'll take care of it. These can be very worrying years. But thing is stand on two feet, two fisted and give better than you get. There's pomposity here in the college just as anywhere else and it must be diminished when possible. Good to see you. Don't think your detour in Donnybrook did you any harm. But try to keep on public footpaths."

"Yes sir."

"Good. Come see us in the country. We do want to see more of you."

"Thank you and thanks awfully much for breakfast sir. It really has made me feel very able again. And splendidly refreshed."

"Good."

Professor Elegant smiled a firm goodbye at his door. From these cozy comfortable rooms. His wavy greying hair. He has seven children. Scurrying about a country house. His wife all dressed in tweeds. Blue eyed and radiant. Kids on ponies. Cantering through meadows in sunny lives. Sitting evenings at fires overlooking their busy days. From Howth to Kiliney, and out across Kildare with all their fluffy haired children romping over the grass and outcrops of granite.

Balthazar B weak of stomach went back and lay on his bed in his room. Pulling back the washstand from the window and closing over the tall great shutters. Hold out the wild hair of the trees. To wake again in gloomy darkness. One's mind areel with pounding horses. Hooves flicking clods up against the sky. What will ever happen in my future life. When I step out and say to the world I'm here. Foreskin saved. They'll say you're just like the others yesterday. What is that pounding and pounding. Dark outside. And late. After sleeping. And still so often I chase her. Bella. And each time I stop. Bend my head and feel tears fall down on my folded fists. And turn back for wherever is home. When now at this grey ancient university. I can't bear to put any knowledge in my brain. That I'll never use again. Still hear pounding. It's my door.

Balthazar B pulling back the heavy blue wool blanket and stumbling to switch on the light. Shuffling in slippers across his sitting room and into the hall. The door shaking on its hinges. Open up. Some mayhem all over again. Or arrest. Draw the bolt. It's Beefy.

"My God Balthazar."

"What's the matter."

"This."

"O no."

"O yes. Headlines. All over Dublin."

ISLAM PERIL
STUDENT LOST IN LAURELS

At five A.M. this morning in the exclusive district of Donnybrook, the demesne of many prominent business people, an unusual confrontation resulting in misunderstanding took place in the grounds of a Dublin assurance executive's home. Garda were called and a squad car, the first of its kind to be used to stamp out crime, was dispatched from Dublin. The lady of the misunderstanding, who has been sleeping lightly recently because of current newspaper reports regarding the spread of Islam across the earth, heard a noise in her garden, where there are many rare roses of which she is a fancier. Having jumped to a certain conclusion at the further aggressive sounds, she roused her husband who immediately challenged the dark complexioned people thought to be aswarm in the garden and who had already pulled off half the stucco plaster the east side of the house, the damage being effected by a yank on the clothes line. As he rushed forward attired lightly in pyjamas to grapple with the Moslem mob thought to be reforming ranks beneath the window he shouted "Up the Republic" and told his wife to raise the tricolor immediately on the roof, that Irishmen everywhere would give a good account of themselves this night and once again put the invader to flight. His wife however thinking he would stand no chance against an emotional dusky skinned horde, telephoned the garda and gave thanks along the way to Blessed Oliver Plunket that the communication lines had not already been cut.

Her husband meanwhile with no regard for his own safety and armed only with a hurling stick ran out into the night against the protests of his wife. Although finding nothing he concluded the adversary would be adept at blending with the darkness. Upon his return from this reconnoitre the lady of the house screamed at the sight of blood pouring from her husband's head who in his rush down the stairs had hit it on the ceiling. He said that the first wave had obviously passed and that the Islamites must have debarked from boats on the Dodder River and taken Donnybrook by surprise. And that they should lay low till the next wave and await army reinforcement.

The scene changed abruptly however upon the arrival of the garda who swiftly took control of the situation and upon issuing a challenge to a movement in the shrubbery came upon an elegant gentleman sheltering under an Aliantus

163

Grandulosa tree, identified by the garda in charge who is an amateur biologist and linguist.

The gentleman however remained unidentified as it appeared he knew no tongue spoken by the garda, who went painstakingly through his entire repertoire. Garda unraveled him from the householder's laundry line. And upon closer scrutiny the garda could see that the gentleman was hopelessly lost and suffering shock from exposure.

The entire misunderstanding came to a most happy conclusion when the garda assured the lady of the house that wherever it might be that Islam was on the march there was no trace of the said group that night in Donnybrook. The garda and the lost elegant gentleman, who later proved to be Mr. Balthazar B, a student of the natural sciences at Trinity College, were invited to clean up after the havoc and a hot cup of tea was served to all.

Upon further interview from this reporter, the lady of the misunderstanding said it was heinous to contemplate being at the mercy of Islam. She hoped that her husband, although in his early forties, would be an example to other Irishmen who sometimes left their wives in the lurch when violence was afoot. She attributed her husband's youthful agility to good toilet habits and grooming. But both of them had long been accustomed to doing eight deep knee bends at an open window each morning. She was especially glad that what had started as a hideous mystery could now be looked back upon as another incident where Irishmen, when oppression threatened, would rise up to take the cudgel or as in this case, hurling stick, to drive back the intruder. Her solicitors were looking into the question of damages.

Blackness gleaming on the large panes of glass. Soft lamplight below in the square and through the trees, the lighted windows in the Rubric. Balthazar sat slumped in his chair. Eyes closed. A strange terror seeping through one's veins. Defamed. Disgraced across the drawing rooms of Rathgar. Up and down the mahogany sideboards and in all the silver salvers. Balthazar B on my calling card. Caught in trespass lurking in the bushes. Who would ever believe I was but travelling north back to my abode. To see again this face of Beefy. Only friend I know.

"Dear boy. Dear boy. Don't take it like that. You're upset. Buck up. You crafty article. You got off with Miss Fitzdare. Good ankle. Ample about the chest. Slow to keep up with fashion. Bit of a blue stocking. But she has formidable connections with the Church of Ireland. Deep in with the ecclesiastics."

"I'm cast in a very poor light."

"It casts you in light dear boy that's all that matters."

"After such as this I'm not good enough for her."

"I am of course, Mr. B, not taking you seriously. Rash remark. If you look into it, you will always find, if not in the evening newspaper, something rather shoddy and shabby back in everyone's pedigree. Crafty frauds perpetrated upon poor old widows. Miss Fitzdare will have her little shabbinesses."

"Don't please speak ill of her."

Balthazar leaning forward to his table. Elbows up on the worn top and hands at his temples. Beefy sad and quiet and reaching across a hand to put on Balthazar's shoulder. Evening bells tolling six. Newsboy shouts on the streets not so far away. And Beefy's voice.

"I'm sorry, I had no idea. I do retract my rather hasty and uncalled for remarks. Certainly you must not listen to me. Miss Fitzdare's a fine girl. You're quite right to feel the way you do."

Balthazar B said yes with a nodding head. Beefy stepped backwards to the door. The evening paper spread on the table. All its black and white print. A day begins prostrate on a field of grass. With some joys held in a hazy head. The kind blue warmth of you Fitzdare. Your magic and strength as you patted your horse. I wanted so much for you to lead me out to graze. Hold my reins. Give me laughing lumps of sugar. Sweeten the sour look of me on this page. Where a world wags a finger. And if I run they will bite at my heels. And if I don't.

They'll
Want
To sink
My soul.

17

That late winter the snow lay for weeks across Ireland. Sheep buried in drifts. Roads and railways blocked and racing cancelled at the courses. The giant brown pyramids of wet turf stacked in Phoenix Park. And when the snows left, the rains came.

Balthazar B lay late abed. In sweaters, shirts and socks. Cold winds shaking the great window frames. And when shadows settled over college. He went discreetly across the squares. To take half pints of creamy topped porter from the marble bar of the Wicklow Hotel. To soak up the warmth from the gleaming mahogany panelling. And at the latening hour to devour sea food and steak. Tucked down this narrowing street.

The Landship, of the monstrous rumbling motor, after these months motionless, was sold to Beefy. He came in motoring cap and leather coat to take it through its paces. Fourteen members of the rugby team pushed to start it out the back gate and along Lincoln Place. In Merrion Square the motor faltered and failed when the transmission fell out on the road. A team of horses came to haul it away to a mews garage. Balthazar offered Beefy his money back. And he gallantly refused.

"A bargain my dear chap is a bargain although one of us may not be amused."

Miss Fitzdare sometimes passed in a little motor all of her own. With just room for two and a package on the back seat. Of all the embarrassed days. Unable to face her carefree smile. When once even she waved at me. And I could not lift my hand or grin but fled. Till this April afternoon. The days were softening now. There came a rap on my door.

Horace had put a pitcher of beef tea at my side. I lay back

on my chaise longue in a pose of indisposition. Which I often took. Through these days. Wearing purple ecclesiastic silk at my throat and a blue smoking jacket. To hold firmly the spine of a tome. The Morphology of Vertebrates. And Horace nipped his head in the door.

"Sir, there is a young lady calling upon you. A Miss Fitzdare. Shall I show her in."

"My God."

"Ah you're not receiving."

"O no no. Show her in please."

"Very good sir."

The sound of feet in the hall. Horace's voice may I take your coat miss. And a voice melodic. Like a thrush sitting first and fat in spring. Here in my chambers. In all the dust. Something I can't believe. She would call on me. Horace so anxious I should be happy. And not lie entrenched and enclosed all these weeks. Writing letters back and forth to my trustees. Who like to make me feel I am improvident.

The Temple.
London, E.C. 4

Dear Mr. B,

Your letter of the fourth instant to hand. We have acted upon your instruction to transfer the additional sum you request to your account with the Bank of Ireland. However, it is our duty to inform you, having regard for the magnitude of the additional monies, that we would be pleased if you would advise us of any not usual contingency which may have arisen unforeseen and with which perhaps we could assist in extending our advice. Do not hesitate to call upon us to be of any help. Meanwhile we continue to conduct settlement terms regarding the damage claimed with reference to your trespass and will keep you informed.

Yours faithfully,
Bother, Writson, Horn,
Pleader & Hoot

As my big black door opens. I stand to receive. Horace stiffly as he does coming to attention. She wears the black coat she wore that detouring night. Light silk on her legs and her shoes low heeled and gleaming with two flat little bows.

"Miss Fitzdare, sir."

"Hello."

"Miss Fitzdare. Do please, come in."

"Thank you."

"Would you bring another cup please Horace."

"Right you are sir."

"I do apologise for barging in like this. Walking along I couldn't help but see your light. You've not been at classes. You haven't been ill."

"No."

"O."

"Please, sit here Miss Fitzdare. I fear I've been rather flamboyant with this chaise longue. But during long afternoons it affords a simple calm comfort."

"O you mustn't move. Please don't. I'm fine right here. On the end. I don't really feel very, I don't know how to say it, but I shouldn't call on you like this, I know."

"I'm so glad you did. Really I am."

"I felt that perhaps there was something I did or said without realising and that I may have offended you."

"O no. You must never feel that. Here. Thank you Horace. Have some of Horace's beef tea. And could we have some more toast, Horace."

"Very good sir."

"You'll have some toast. And beef tea. And try this honey. Then we'll have china tea."

"I'd love to."

"Good. It's for me I suppose the most important wonderful part of my day. I have to hold myself back in the early afternoon. When four approaches I blurt out to Horace. Beef tea. I know it's awfully indulgent but then I have china tea and lemon to follow. Languorously sipping all the way to six o'clock."

"You're swotting too."

"O. The Morphology of Vertebrates. Not really. I think it's to do with these drawings. When one looks at the dorsal side of things. All so neatly laid out on the page. And absolutely nothing to do with the horrors of life. These dormant pisces and aves."

"You've been asked after. Professor said where has our elegant friend got to."

"O Lord not that night again."

"He didn't mean to pry. I'm sure. But you know the account in the paper did rather put you on the map. I felt awfully responsible. That's why I thought you were avoiding me. It was so much my fault. To let you just wander off in the night that way. And the least I could do was to come and put things right."

"Is that the only reason you came."

"No. I did want to see you again."

"I'm glad. You see I felt perhaps. Well as you say, it did rather put me on the map. But the ladder, the shrubbery. I thought people would think I was trying to look in their bedroom. And I suppose I just couldn't get myself to walk into class again."

"O but it was so little a matter."

"My lawyers haven't found so. I've been sued for enormous damages."

"O no."

"Yes. It doesn't matter. But it makes you feel people can be extremely unfriendly."

"O but that's awful. I had no idea."

"My tutor handled things marvellously and I suppose all would have blown over. But they heard rumours of my enormous car and riches. Totally unfounded, the riches that is. And that was that. Ah toast. You will have some."

"Love to."

"I put just this little extra touch of marmite on. Would you like extras too on yours."

"Yes thank you."

"Will there be anything else sir."

"No thank you Horace."

"I'll be pushing off then sir. Goodbye miss."

"Goodbye."

"Shall I shout you up in the morning sir. Eleven as usual."

"Eight please."

"Ah. Forgive me for commenting sir, but I'm glad to hear it. I think it's the effects of your call miss. And I hope you don't think I'm cheeky when I say we hope to see you again."

Late afternoon settling greyly. Somewhere west peeks a sinking sun. Fanning pink across the clouds. The stark chimneys of the Rubric and the tip top tower of the Campanile. When a spring stillness comes to the soft air. The world stops. And suddenly it goes on forever. Turning slowly round in its own tiny time. Click of the cricket bat and pop of tennis ball. The air comes down and breathes on you. When all the flowers know and rush to grow. Their fattest flowing leaves sent up. Their white bulbs secret and pleased in the moist black ground.

And Miss Fitzdare sits. One knee further up than another. The green plate on her grey wool skirt. I swallow my breath to look down and see her swell of thigh. Frightened of the world I'll always be. Never to stand up and shout. That that woman is mine. Sit instead to bow my head. And quake with loneliness when at last she's forever gone.

"That was an awfully nice thing for your servant to say. And I want to ask you something. You did say that time ago if you remember. That your Sundays were. O dear. What I'm asking is if you wouldn't like to come and lunch with us Sunday if you can. It's with my uncle where I stay. He's a nice old dear."

"I'd like to very much."

"And I think you do like horses. Don't you."

"Yes but I fear recently I've been visiting turf accountants. And haven't been out at the courses."

"Well I thought that if you had nothing better to do, you might like to come and visit where I live. But that can wait."

"O no don't let it wait."

"I thought before Trinity lectures began."

"Do please have more tea."

"And if you like the countryside."

"Yes I do."

"Do you shoot."

"Yes I do."

"Do you ride."

"Yes I do."

"O dear I feel I'm making you say yes unfairly to all these things."

"O no. Not at all."

A slow smile on the lips of Miss Fitzdare. Dare not look at the contours on her purple soft sweater. She wears two. A twin set I think they're called. Buttons mother of pearl. One turn back of the long sleeves and her small round gold watch and black band shows.

"O I am. I know I am."

"Well yes perhaps. I'm not really a crack shot. I mean I do try to get the bird. O Lord, Miss Fitzdare. I miss badly if the truth were to be known. Frankly I can't shoot at all. I'm mortally terrified of horses too. But I do love the countryside. I mean would that be enough."

"O goodness yes. I love everything to do with the country and I sometimes, I know, am unbearably enthusiastic. You mustn't feel you've got to shoot or ride. Honestly. I only asked because if you did shoot, we have a shoot. And if you rode we could ride. Or weekends, hunt. And O Lord, really, if only you would like to go for walks that would be awfully nice."

"That's what I would like to do. More tea."

"I must be going. I had only meant to pass a moment. It's been such a beautiful afternoon. Balmy and calm. And I'm so pleased you'll come for lunch Sunday. I did often think of you and your Sunday appointment in Rathgar. You mustn't mind uncle, he blusters a bit about the Empire. He is sweet. Horticulture and astronomy are his passions."

"That's interesting."

"O you know he potters about but he has the largest

private telescope in Ireland. I'd better warn you. You'll get a conducted tour."

"I'm awfully interested in the stars."

"Well then we have a date. I am glad I perked up my nerve. I thought you might be awfully busy or something and I'd be shooed away."

"O Lord Miss Fitzdare. What a thing to think."

"I've not ever been in rooms in this part of college before."

"Perhaps I could show you, I mean you wouldn't mind, would you, it's only my bedroom."

"Well yes, do. Show me."

"Well. Certainly. It's rather barren I fear. But there we are. Obviously that's my bed. Giving me permanent curvature of the spine. I rigged up that little lamp there. I'm not much of an electrician. I'm sure to be electrocuted."

"O you must be careful."

At the open door Balthazar B turning to Miss Fitzdare. She smiles. And turns away back into the drawing room. Glancing over the books in the case on the wall.

"Goodness. Etruscan pottery. O do you go to the London auctions."

"Yes."

"You have all their catalogues."

"A way of spending a not unpleasant afternoon. Tarrying around the galleries."

"I'm sure you're one of those people who stick to Meissen onion pattern."

"That's extraordinary. How did you know Miss Fitzdare."

"O I knew."

"Would you like to see my scullery."

"I'd adore to. O mustn't say that word you took me to task over once before."

"O no, do please adore. I mean I'm quite happy you said that word. I'm afraid things are rather a muddle in here. That's the larder. Where I keep my marmite and cornflakes."

"What's that."

"O it's my peanut butter. I have it sent from Boston."

"Is it nice."

"It's scrumptious with strawberry preserve and butter in a sandwich. And in here. My two burner stove with grill."

"That's rather elegant."

"Left by a rich American I believe. Who couldn't stand the bitter cold and fled back to New Orleans. He used to lie in that room I understand, covered in coats and blankets, surrounded by hot water bottles and an electric fire shining on him through the night and he'd wake frozen."

"O the poor man."

"Horace arranged to get most of these things he left. Horace has been awfully kind to me. That's my pail of water. That's my turf bin. Beefy has one with a false bottom. You can hide underneath, through a little secret door. But that's very hush hush."

"How is your friend Beefy. One hears so many stories and rumours about him. I don't know quite what to believe. He seems such a kindly person."

"He is."

"It's horrid that people don't mind their own business."

"What do you hear."

"Nothing. Not anything worth repeating. And what's in here."

"Well I made a little effort to use this room as an antechamber. It's where the American driven out by the bitter cold made his last stand. I use it for nothing in particular at all. That's a little print I bought."

"It's nice."

"And those are early editions of zoology texts."

"O aren't they lovely. How wonderful. Wherever did you get them."

"On the Quays."

"You are a strange one Mr. B. One never knows about people. I never would have thought you collected books. I don't mean that in any way derogatory. But when one saw you in your enormous car, I thought you were the complete sporting gent. And not bookish at all."

"Well, Miss Fitzdare, I fear you really still don't know me. Now. You see over here. Notice, all locked up out of sight. But there you are."

"Goodness, magazines."

"Movie magazines. That's really what I read."

"I won't believe it. O I think you're having me on."

"It's absolute gospel. That's how I while away my days."

"O you don't."

"I do."

"You're reading morphology."

"It's just one of my guilty days. I settled down to some morphology. Usually I'm engrossed with film stars. I like the reckless abandon with which they live."

"O Mr. B you do amaze me. Thank you for showing me your rooms."

"Thank you for coming to see me."

"I'm awfully glad I did."

"I'm glad you did."

"So till Sunday. If you can manage about one."

"Yes. That's splendid."

"My coat."

"O yes. Sorry."

"Thank you."

"I can never hold the sleeves in their proper place. Can you manage."

"Yes. Thank you."

"You're not wearing your little silver jumping horse."

"My you've got a vivid memory, Mr. B. You do notice things."

"Yes. I do."

"I'm warned. Must go. Thank you so much for tea. It was awfully good."

"Not at all. So nice having you."

"Well thank you."

"Thank you."

"Goodbye."

"Goodbye."

The door closing as Miss Fitzdare stepped out into the dimly lit hall. She'll go down the stone steps. And if I get to the scullery window. I can look out and watch her go. In her black coat. Under the lamp post. By the slung chains. She turns her head. O Lord. She waves. O heavens. I've got to give her everything in my smile. Caught watching. Perhaps I shouldn't have been. Then she shouldn't have turned. And she did. She likes me. I'm going to lunch. What about that. For joy. O God this is awfully good. On an otherwise doubtful day. Jolly and scrumptious. When least you expect something beautiful happens. She asked me. To lunch. She did. O God on that day. Please don't let me stray. Make me go and catch the tram. Go rolling along the tracks. As goes now the last sight of her. A black spot between the Rubric and all the converging perpendicular slabs of granite. On her silk stockinged legs. Her hair floating darkly behind. I may never have to be sad again. If we go cantering up over the hills and heather.

Balthazar dressed at seven in a double breasted black pin striped suit. Light blue shirt and black silk tie. To pass now outwards. Across the bumpitibump Front Square. Lanterns lit over the dining hall steps. And one over the big granite doorway. The sky morose and grey. The wind freshening. How will she look after all these years. And why did she come. How does one meet one's mother.

Climbing the steps of this hotel. Through the swing doors. And across the black and white floor. Stand here and look. The little groups. And there. That woman sitting in the corner. Her legs crossed. Large wide hat and can't see her hair. A long black cigarette holder. And next to her a dark man. About my age.

Balthazar crossing the faint brown carpet towards the beige settee. And glass topped table between the chairs. The two figures rising. My mother's hand touches me on the shoulder and her perfumed powder on the cheek.

"Balthazar."

"Hello mother."

"You're tall. And too thin. Otherwise you look as I expected. This is Georgie, Georgie my son Balthazar."

"How do you do."

"I am honoured to meet you Balthazar."

"Please sit down now both of you. What can I get you to drink."

"Sherry."

"Good. What we are having too."

Balthazar crossed his leg and uncrossed it at the sign of a drooping sock. Shaking his head up and down for a momentary yes to all the questions that did not come. Facing these two on the sofa. My mother's shadowy eyes under her shady hat. A slanting wisp of grey hair in the blond stretched gleamingly brushed over a tip top ear. Little webs of wrinkles around her eyes. Just now as she lifts her chin. Light suit of magnolia cavalry twill. Freckles big on her soft delicate hands. Two great gems one red one green on a right and left finger. And a flat slack bracelet of many many diamonds.

"Please will you have one."

A gold case of cigarettes offered to Balthazar. Who smiles a brief nod no. To Georgie sitting back to light the tobacco cylinder held at the distant tips of fingers. He wears a watch chain across his waistcoat. A stiff collar and small knotted polka dot tie. His tailor made his suit a trifle too tight. And his barber takes too much care with his black curly hair.

"How is university Balthazar. Do you like it."

"Yes."

"Are you comfortable."

"Yes. Some conditions are a little primitive. But otherwise quite satisfactory."

"This most curious country. I've never been in such a city as this before. Everyone is mumbling, scowling or smiling. And they say yes certainly in a minute to everything, and it takes an hour. They send you left if the way is right. One is shown to one's rooms and there is already someone there. You say but there is someone in this room and they giggle as if one

177

were crazy. But I suppose you have come to manage here. Are you eating enough."

"Yes."

White coated waiter lowering three sherry glasses to the table. One looks down at Georgie's rather too pointed shoes. He smiles too much. He looks for the ashtray. To tap his ash away. He blows the smoke too hard. Holds his hands resting and tired rummaging in my mother's fortune. The telegram came in its brown envelope. During a desperate moment of the afternoon. Fighting to read The Embryology of Rana. And Horace brought it when he brought tea. And saw the blood fall from my face and said ah sir I hope that that was not bad news.

"Balthazar had you liked you could have brought a friend."

"I do not know many people in Dublin to invite."

The silences get longer. The cigarette case of Georgie comes out again. Gleams with a monogram. He tap taps the tobacco down. Tilts his head. Puts it between his lips. The chain bracelet on his wrist shakes. My mother waves away a handful of his smoke.

"Georgie teaches skiing in the winter and swimming in the summer."

"O that's nice."

Georgie with an open handed slow flick of his wrist raising his chin carefully as he shows teeth to speak.

"Ah for me it is a little boring. I like to travel. To go places."

Balthazar's mother pulling a long pin and taking off her hat. She stands to beckon a waiter to take it to her room. And turns her long slender elegance to put one hand touching flesh at her throat.

"Well shall we go in to dinner."

Balthazar's mother led the way across the mirrored lounge and down steps to the long white dining room. Georgie bowing and ushering Balthazar ahead. Dark coated waiters sweeping back and forth. Hard red faced landowners from the country. Seated by slit eyed wives with lemony smiles for

178

waiters and silence for husbands.Georgie before coffee. Got up to bow and said I am sorry I have a headache I would like to go out in the air. Balthazar placed and replaced his spoon and fork. Pêche Melba was soon to come. And trolleys wheeled by to flash flame for crepe suzette.

"Well Balthazar. Here we are. After so many years."

"Yes."

"You are not very talkative."

"No. I'm sorry."

"Do not apologise. I understand. A little of what you must think and feel. I have my own life. I must live it. You will when older understand. However I do not want to cause embarrassment between us."

"You do not have to explain."

"No. I do not. Georgie insisted to come. But one should keep matters in good taste. There are times when I do not. I am returning to live in Paris. I have taken a flat in Avenue Foch. And you will always be welcome. But there is another reason why I am here and why I have come. It is to tell you something. That I should not like you to hear from other lips. Something which is perhaps very sad. Very tragic. And I think in fairness I must tell you. It is about that girl. Miss Hortense, you remember. She had a little boy. You were his father. He was adopted after his birth. Where he is and who he is we do not know. And will never know. It was part of the arrangement that that should be. Will you have some brandy with your coffee."

Balthazar B took leave of his mother in the lobby where she stood with her bedroom key. He bowed stiffly and she kissed him on the cheek. And watched him going out the door and down the steps. A soft fine silver rain fell through yellow lamplight in Duke Street. Crowds of pushing figures emptying out of the pubs. Bartenders ushering from the doors. Now come on gentlemen it's well after time please, now gentlemen please. Arms cradled high with grey bags of stout. Shouts and pointing the way by ringleaders to cars. Mid singing and laughters and jeers to gestures indecent. These throbbing jungle streets. The slamming and locking of pub doors. And to suddenly hear one's name called. And hurry one's steps away. Past this map seller, down the shadows of Grafton Street. Past the locked gated entrance of Mitchell's cafe. Up there once on the second floor I saw Miss Fitzdare having coffee. I watched her looking out the window and she smiled when a chap in glasses came. He selected cakes for her from the tray. I didn't know her then. But felt all the sad alarm of her beauty lost and living in someone else's life.

The bell in the grey high looming Campanile. Tolls as I go by. To get back to my bed. My feet walking beneath me. I held her hand all those years ago. And I know. The seed I planted then. Came out of all the love I knew. Down deep and spinning in a pool. With a little tail. Like a line thrown ashore. To anchor there. All round and red and blazing. For Bella was my bride. We had a son. And all these years a father. When only still a son. He goes somewhere out in the world. Awake in some city. Climbing up some steps. A little fellow now. Who might run frightened and afeared. And you walk along in darkness by these familiar chains. Across the cobbled square. Ahead my windows. In there I sleep. While nothing now stands still. To throw your arms around and say stay. Or a little boy who could pass his hand to me in summertimes. Something born nudges you gently to go and die. It all could be a flower you lifted once. Looked at. Held the stem. And then you turned your head away.

> To
> Weep
> The night
> Till
> Day.

18

Sunday this mild mellow week. Buds crashing out sappy green on the trees. Crocuses exploding yellow across suburban gardens. Balthazar B went through Ballsbridge on the Dalkey tram. To tug the bell chain hanging against the cold cut stone.

Miss Fitzdare stood smiling half way in the gleaming hall. Of this house rising greyly and ivy clad from great rhododendrons and sweeping lawns. A hushed raven haired maid in her fresh black frock and white lace collar to take my coat with her trembling hand. This massive hall of this big house. A fire flaming flanked by pink marble praying angels. Gilt framed mirrors. Two steely figures of armour, haunted slits for eyes. And Miss Fitzdare wears her purple twin set again. The thick tweed grey skirt and her string of pearls. Tall chiming clock rings one.

"You are awfully prompt. Do come this way. And meet uncle and aunt."

Brass knobbed heavy mahogany door ajar. Polished and glistening faintly red. Held open by the raven haired maid. Tints of blues and whites in this sprawling drawing room. Cabinets of porcelain. A harpsicord in a white arched alcove. This thin grey haired lady. Slowly twisting her lips between her smiles. Offering her long blue veined hand. A short round gentleman in thick rust tweeds. Purple silk hanky and gorse coloured tie.

"Aunt Miriam this is Balthazar."

"I've heard so much about you."

"My uncle Frederic. Everyone calls him General. Balthazar."

"How do you do General."

"I do splendidly when my gout doesn't play up. Do please sit. And what can we warm you up with. Whisky, gin, sherry."

"Well sherry if I may sir."

"You may by jove. Medium dry or that stuff they say is sherry that's very dry."

"Medium. Please."

"Ah, that's a good fellow, know your sherry. Miriam. Sherry."

"Yes today. We'll have a wee bit. Doctor Romney says I'm to leave off but I think today."

The General standing at a high sideboard of bottles, trays and decanters. Pouring the light brown liquid into thin crystal glasses. His brief smile as the silver tray passes to each. Between two facing long light green sofas. The raven haired girl peeks back into the room as she quietly closes the great door. This grey haired lady raises her chin and lowers eye lids to speak.

"Mr. B I understand you're new to Dublin. How do you find it. Our dear dirty city."

"Most charming."

"O good. Elizabeth tells us you race."

"Yes I do get to the courses now and again. Not much recently however."

"O. You'll be here for Horse Show week. You must not miss that."

"I sincerely hope so."

"Wonderful time of year. We're at our best then. Always brings one back to times when things were not as they are now. Very sad. So much has passed from us."

"Now Miriam, that's not the attitude. What does Mr. B want to know about that for. He's young. He wants to enjoy himself now. Of course we've had a lot of louts and rabble-rousers about but things have settled down. Let them blow up a telephone kiosk now and again and they're quite happy. Are you interested in the stars, Mr. B."

"Yes I am."

"Good. After lunch then. We'll show you about. Would you like to see my astronomical laboratory."

182

"Very much sir. I had an uncle who was very interested in the sky."

"Good. Ah. There we are. The gong. Brought that back from India. Served out there. When I was Brigadier. Bring in your sherry with you."

Two wide white doors folding back. A long dining table. A fire bursting with flaming black chunks of coal. Two tall windows. Look out across lawns and gardens. Pebbled paths. A stone wall and beyond the tops of blossoming apple trees. Little blue dishes of salt set in silver holders with birdlike paws.

"Sit you all down."

The General at the head of table, Miriam at the foot. Prawn cocktail and thin slices of brown bread. Faint tinge of green in white wine poured. A leg of steaming lamb carried in by a big chested girl of blue eyes and large pouting lips. The General carves. The whole silent afternoon outside. White plates with thin little weavings of gold handed down the table. Roasted potatoes. And sprouts moist in butter. A claret wine of gentle red.

"Elizabeth you ought to have Balthazar come when we're having ham. We feed our pigs on peaches you know. When you've tasted a chappie so fed, I think you'll agree you never realised what ham could be. What."

"I'd very much like that."

"We leave that then to you, Lizzie. Good larder is a man's salvation. People nowadays don't take any trouble. Not the way we used to. Of course then one gets on. Dashed cold winter, what. One of worst in memory. When you get to my age you feel it you know. Get a bit of damned deafness too, it's the wind. Gets up a pressure. You take port my boy."

"Yes sir."

"Good show. Got a bit there decanted. Laid down when I was a subaltern. Yes. A man's best years you know are the thirties. Plenty of polo, outdoors, that's the way of life. The end comes at fifty. You know then there's no going back. If you don't go forward you don't go damn anywhere. What. Yes after fifty it's all over, you know."

"O Frederic, really."

"Can't overlook the facts Miriam. A man's a man till fifty. You might stretch it a year this way or that but largely speaking, that's when a man puts away his gun. Takes out his port. Of course a lot of it is in the mind you know. Half the battle is keeping up appearances. And appearances be damned as well. A shrew for its weight is more fierce than a tiger. It will seize upon a worm and devour it in an instant."

"Frederic please, not while we're eating."

"Shrew of course will easily die of shock. Poor little fellows. Now I don't suppose either of you two zoologists knew that one."

"No sir, that's fascinating."

"Eat their own weight in food every three hours."

"Now Frederic that's not a pleasing subject."

"There you are my boy. Get your innings in while you're young. Ladyfolk have you later on you know. Hound you about a bit. O we'll wait till the reincarnation. Hope I get a good regiment. Cat's got your tongue Elizabeth."

"No uncle. I'm just amused as I always am at your chatter."

"O ravings of a poor old soldier. But when I was a boy we had to tow the line. Not like these days. My father lined us up as boys. Hair had to be properly combed. Hands clean both sides. Chores done at six fifteen A.M. None of your nonsense. Walk with a straight back. See your face in the tip of your shoes or my goodness you would soon get what for across your what you sit on. Where did you serve my boy."

"I was a friendly alien sir. French."

"Pity. The discipline, routine. Good for every lad you know. Not to be shunned. Have a good swallow more now of that wine. One of the lingering pleasures. If one leaves out bridge. We had an awfully funny situation out here not too long ago. Chaps were full of it at the club. Said the papers played it up marvellously. One of your fellow students. Went completely haywire. They thought it was the yellow men

184

from the East. When it was only a chap got lost in the gardens. Likely story. Caused quite a bit of stir."

The flowing blood up to Miss Fitzdare's pallid face. Her cheeks blossoming bright red. The General sawing across a grey slab of lamb, Miriam ringing the little bell at her place. And the vast breasted servant called Briget going round with the wine once more. Dripping a drop on Balthazar's silk cuff. Briget put her fingers to her lips.

"O excuse me sir."

A smile from Balthazar. As a golden clock on the mantel rings chimes. A portrait of a lady in scarlet robes and ermine. The General clears his throat in his napkin. Miss Fitzdare's face goes crimson again.

"Balthazar, do please say if you would like more lamb."

"Thank you I have had a sufficiency."

"Come come my boy. From my memory of rooms at Trinity it's damn chilly there. A person needs a good Sunday lunch. In my time scholars used to come charging through college on horseback waving sabres a propos of nothing at all. But a deuced good fright thrown into servants and porters. Junior Dean got killed, hit on the head with a grate. Some rough times indeed. Wasn't safe at night, college bloods armed with daggers. Just a little that was before my time. But the chaps left their mark."

Balthazar B remaining to light a cigar with the General at table. As they sampled port. The ladies lightfooted back to the withdrawing room. And there came the tinkle of the harpsicord. Purple shadows of the evening stretching out across the gardens. An old fading moon blunted in the sky.

"You know my boy, you'll pardon me I'm an interfering old rascal. Meddle in right where I have no business to. But our Elizabeth has taken a great interest in you. Took us long enough to get her to get you here. Fine girl. Miriam and I love having her with us. She has a wonderful nature that girl. How many of your women these days would spend three afternoons and evenings in the poor wards. Not many I can tell you. Yes, go down the aisles of some of them. Only way they know whether a wretched creature is dead is to smell them. Often said it's not the kind of work for a young lady. She won't listen, insists going right on. Can't say she's wrong to go her own way. Some of these people haven't been out of their garments all their lives. Come into hospital, can't get the clothes off them. Here, little more port for you."

"Thank you sir."

"They have to cut the clothes off. Put a sling around them and with a derrick they dip them in a vat. Sometimes the shock's too much. These old creatures get so frightened they die on the spot. Nothing as bad as it was in India but still pretty bad. Prostitutes in off the streets, when they get a cure they stay on as nurses to pay off their debt. You know about Elizabeth's work."

"No sir, I'm afraid I don't."

"O. Perhaps I've breached a confidence. Hope not. Strange girl our Elizabeth. Very rare girl."

"Yes she is sir."

"Looks like her mother. Mother died you know. Burned up in a fire. Quite awful. Elizabeth was only twelve. Poor little creature cried for weeks. We had her here. Beautiful woman her mother. Great horsewoman. Cost her her life. Saving horses in a burning stable. Brave woman. Elizabeth's the same. Well come now, that's been enough of this chitter chatter. Shall we join the ladies. Then we'll take you up. Might spot Mars on the horizon. Give it another hour or so."

The General rising. Neatly folding and rolling his napkin, pushing it in its silver ring. So strangely reminiscent of Beefy. There seems no end of Miss Fitzdare. And all explained, those times when I was rather bitter lipped. Hoping I would have nerve enough to ask her come for tea. Or join me at the Shelbourne Rooms for drinks. Thought there was some other man. Those afternoons she disappears. Like the one who gave her cakes in Mitchell's. And like another who stared at her during zoology practical. Rushing to give her sharpened pencils, to lend a scalpel or hold the door for her. Smiling

186

eagerly and remarking of the weather. And once as I was leaving he came pushing behind me, punching a fist into my back. I turned and he gave an unpleasant sneer and smirk. I suddenly wished I had muscles. Big fists to smite him one upon the intelligence. Instead I raised my eyebrow, and stood aside to let him pass if he pleased. And angered more he stood on the gravel, eyes smouldering. Then one Sunday Beefy said he had seen this ruffian in a cinema in O'Connell Street waiting with Miss Fitzdare.

Now I walk with her. And touch her hand. As we go about in the district. After lunch and harpsicord. Along Sydney Parade Avenue. To the strand of Dublin Bay. The tide out across the strange grey flatlands and scattering sea birds. We step down the granite steps to the sand. Make footprints there. A grey whiteness across the water to Howth. Night comes east. I want to say marry me.

And returning to the big house. To go up a spiral stair to a great room. Gleaming brass knobs and telescope. Copper domed roof. A shutter opened at the sky. The General twirling handles. Miss Fitzdare laughing at my surprise. At the craters in the moon and the orange sparkling light of Mars. At seven at the door. Her white slender fingers and gleaming nails. Leaning against the cut stone, Miss Fitzdare said goodbye.

"I hope it wasn't all too dull for you."

"I enjoyed every moment. Thank you so much for having me."

"Be careful how you go now."

"Heh heh. I shall keep to the tram tracks. See you tomorrow. At lectures. I'm feeling academic again. Do thank your uncle for showing me his stars. And I should be delighted if you would come and have tea at my rooms."

"I'd love to."

Waving from the gate. This high iron fence set in the stone. Goodbye grey house back in the shadows somewhere. Up there on the first floor will be your bedroom, Fitzdare. At night do you stand and look out over the gardens. And see

187

dreams in the branches of the trees. Dying old men to whom you give your pale hand. Listen to their tales of life. Of wives long dead. Of scattering many children. And they see your splendid blue white beauty with a last gratefulness in their dim eyes. Wrap up their scrawny bones from bed. Pack them away in the ground.

Balthazar B this night rode the roaring tram back to Dublin. In mild darkness and an eastern breeze from sea. Along the Merrion Road. To go lighted and merry on this iron wheeled vehicle. And at the bridge to alight down the steps from the greeny upholstered seats. As the father of one child.

Balthazar strolled along the Grand Canal Dock. By dark pouring waters and shimmering light. Past the bridge into Rings End and Irishtown. It says Shelbourne on that pub. The pleasure of being all alone with the air gently on the face. Her mother burned to death in fire. Across that waste ground, ships setting sail for sea. Lighted portholes. Never know which is red for port or green for starboard. Just see the blue eyes and black hair of you Fitzdare. Sparkle of your teeth. All your grace. Now I walk back again. To look at these great walls of blackened bricks. The gas works. Sooty grime and fire in there through these bars. Dark shadows. Men moving with their lighted ends of cigarettes. Fitzdare. Will ever we wed. All flowing veils. Trumpets blow out across England to our country house in Somerset. Away in the soft green peace Fitzdare. You will touch the stems of flowers every day. On hall stands through the house. Bring your horses with you. We'll fox them all at Ascot.

Misery Hill. A name down these black streets. And a walk along here by the water on a narrow edge of granite by this plank wall of a coal bunker. And suddenly a shadow is looming up above my head. A figure with an arm raised and in a hand a lump of coal. Good God. Someone to kill me. Knock me on the head. That I would fall to this granite, to take my money and roll me into the greasy water.

Balthazar raised up a shielding arm. And the figure high in

the bunker teetered and fell from sight. An old grey bewhisk-
ered face. Staring and mad. And all I can do is run. Away
from here. To the Liffey. By all the long rusting sides of ships.
And rats nipping over the wet gleaming cobble stones.

Balthazar B chased along the Quay, chest choked with a
beating heart. Detouring from walls, shadowy cranes and dark
doorways. Heading west for the life and lights of the city. Past
gangways up to merchant ships. White shirted figures in the
portholes. Others leaning with lighted cigarettes looking
down from the ship's railings. A warehouse ahead. Keep out
on the clear road. Away from harm.

At the corner of the shed Balthazar B gasped as he bumped
into and confronted a figure. Of strange lighted eyes. And a
round suddenly smiling face, so unsurprised.

"Beefy."

"Balthazar."

"Beefy what are you doing here, you frightened the life out
of me, I was nearly murdered a few minutes ago."

"I am looking for sin."

Balthazar staring at these two unflickering globes. Jacket
askew on his shoulders. Tie loosened from his collar. All the
strange rumours. About this man. Who reads divinity. That
Fitzdare would never say. To find him here. As he finds me.

"I was nearly hit on the head with a lump of coal."

"Dear boy. There are no rules down here on the Quay. No
rules. Do you understand. I have come for sin. I know where
to find it. Come with me."

"Beefy what do you mean."

"Deepest most sordid sin. I have been to the latrines. But I
am randy again. I have other places too. Come. The deepest
and most sordid sin purifies. I bugger old men. I lay old ladies.
Some of them are dying when I do it."

Balthazar looking into these burning eyes. A tremor of fear
takes a fluttering hold of the heart. The lips smile. A ship
hoots.

"My God Beefy, I don't know what to say."

"My pleasures are utterly beautiful Balthazar. Sacred. I mingle my elegance with their wretchedness. This city is a sewer flowing with rancor and decomposed flesh, rotting through all these streets. Disease eats out these hearts. Bodies full of poison. I come with my beauty. I bugger them. And do appalling things. And I invite you to come too."

"I was rather planning an early evening."

"I shock you."

"You terrify me out of my wits, Beefy."

"Ah. I thought so. But I will introduce you slowly to the pleasurings. Very slowly. You will thank me. When you get into the grisliness. That you can savour such things as I can show you. The sin. I love the sin. That's what I most desire. You look so left out of it all Balthazar."

"Would you care to come back to my rooms with me and have some cocoa Beefy."

Along the Liffey quays this night, puddles of water on the cobble stoned street. Lonely lamplights. Coal dust and barrels, crates and bundles of wire. Great shadow of the gas tank rearing in the sky. A whiff and sniff and smell of pine timber. Beefy reaching up his arm to put a hand on Balthazar's shoulder. To look with easy warm eyes on this pale blond apprehensive face.

"Balthazar, my dear man. I am most awfully sorry. I could not resist to shock you. Do you know you are a most handsome fellow. You are in fact very beautiful. Your beauty would lend so well to my planned defilement. Look at you. I've never seen anything like your saintliness. Have you been seeing Miss Fitzdare."

"I had lunch with Miss Fitzdare and her aunt and uncle."

"O my God how charming. Did you sit poised on the settee."

"Yes."

"Did Miss Fitzdare tinkle the wires of her harpsicord."

"Yes."

"I knew it. For joy. I knew it. She is a lovely creature. But think what wonderful defilement you could lend your spirit to tonight. Sunday. After all the prayers are said. But I think it's so splendid. You and Fitzdare. It crucifies me, your blond and her black beauty. O my God."

"Please come and have cocoa, Beefy."

Wild shadows against a sky faintly purple. Clouds rolling with moonlit edges. The blast of a ship's whistle. A hawser splashing in the water. Up in the crystal night the ship's red light. Trembling engines as the great black silhouette moves out on the flowing river.

"Ah but I must go. Upon my appointed rounds."

"I have cream to go on top of the cocoa."

"I must not be distracted from my mission. Sinful desire consumes me. The most malodorous and desecrated defilement is waiting. Only fifteen steps away. Come. Please. Just along here. Let me show you. You see nothing. But wait. We go now up into this doorway. It will amaze you. You will thrill to this creature."

An opening broken door up wide greasy granite steps. A stench of death. The choking wail and sob of a child. A lurking face. A girl. Half her face in the light. A tiny bow of ribbon tied in her hair. Her hands clutching a broken black shiny bag.

"Ah Balthazar this is my queen. She waits for me here. Her name is Rebecca. Isn't she beautiful. But she does not think so herself. But Rebecca, you are."

"Go on now I'm not."

"Rebecca, I want you to meet my friend. He is beautiful too, isn't he."

"Ah he is."

"But it is I who have a horn on me this evil night. Rebecca you have the most splendid eyes to gaze upon this horn of mine."

"O go on with you I think you're crazy."

"And you have limbs. Fine limbs. I could eat up your white beauty Rebecca you know that I could, don't you. Wait Balthazar, don't go. You must not leave. Rebecca will fetch her sister for you."

"Ah sure you've got the gentleman upset, can't you see he's upset."

"Balthazar you're not upset. I would never want that. Isn't it marvellous here."

"I think I must go Beefy."

"Come. With us. Rebecca too will come. And so will her sister. We'll go over the fence at the back gate. Even though needs be a spear up the rear. And I will take Rebecca and her sister to my rooms. We will all like it there. Come now, Rebecca. Let us get your sister. And I beg you Balthazar don't desert me now."

Their feet sounding up the broken stairs. Past a great tall window on the landing, its frame buckled, string and bits of rag blowing in the breezes. A three legged dog hobbling down between their legs. Bits of bicycles and broken prams along a wall. The dim slit of light under doors. Where dark Dublin lies sleeping.

On the attic landing Rebecca pushed through a door into a great darkened room. Rags and bones and suitcases in a corner, hunks of plaster hanging from the ceiling. A man sitting hunched forward on a chair staring silently into the red dying embers of a fire who slowly turns a head to nod at Beefy and Beefy nodding a smile to Balthazar.

A table covered in newspaper, cups and crusts of bread. By a red candle burning on a cardboard altar near a window a thin dark girl sits huddled reading in the flickering light. Rebecca whispers in her ear. And they both look at seven heads sticking from the covers of a great mattress on the floor. The dark girl steps behind a torn curtain and emerges with a handbag. Pulling a sweater over her shoulders as she turns towards the sleeping figures under a picture of a bleeding heart encased in thorns.

Balthazar B descended last out of this broken gutted building, taking deep breaths as they walked under a black railway trestle towards Trinity down an empty desolate lane. By locked up shops and closed pubs. Along Fenian Street taken that night with Beefy when I first met Fitzdare. The heads of

192

death lurk in all the black skulls of houses. The girl dark and small with beady black eyes. A gold cross upon her throat. Blue dress, blue sweater, her elbows poking out the sleeves. And I feel so bereft of Fitzdare. So alien to this wisp of girl.

"What's your name."

"My name is Breda. What is your name."

"My name is Balthazar."

"Are you a student."

"Yes. What are you."

"I work in a pub out towards Howth. I'm a barmaid. I'm not her sister. She enjoys a lie. I come from Cavan. I was just into Dublin to help take care of her little brothers and sisters. She's the oldest, she's twenty three. Her mother died three months ago. I know of your friend. He's been good to her family but he's a holy terror in other ways. You don't look the sort as would be down the Quays associating with strange women. Are you afraid of me."

"No."

"You won't say much. I don't mind. You're English, that's the way you all are. Never say what's on your mind. How will he ever get us over that big fence."

Beefy high up balanced between the fence spears. A hand held down to Rebecca. She reached up, one foot on Balthazar's shoulder. Beefy with a great grunt and heave lifted her and their hands parted to drop her back down again into the arms of Balthazar. As Beefy lowered himself into Trinity and grinned through the fence bars.

"Come now."

"Ah no. I'm not climbing up that again."

"You must make her Balthazar, grab her arm and twist it."

"Ah you're not to twist me arm."

"Chuck her in the gutter Balthazar, this is no time for niceties."

"I'll give him one in the jewels if he does."

"We must get them over Balthazar. Put them through the most amazing antics you have ever seen. Here let's try to squeeze them between the bars."

"Beefy the porter's lodge is just there. We'll be seen."

"You'll squeeze neither of us between the bars I'm telling you."

"Just look at them. The two of them. Think of the defilement."

"Come on Breda, let's go on out of this now."

"Stop them Balthazar, stop them, I'm coming over. We must never let the two beauties go. It will be as splendid as running wild through a hospital of incurables. Get them back."

Balthazar stood and watched Beefy chase the girls down Lincoln Place into Westland Row. Where they have an Academy of Music and where Miss Fitzdare may have learned the harpsicord. They returned hand in hand in the darkness. Beefy's eyes coming near, alight with pleasure. So strange he treats them with such soft grace. Between the threats of violence. So brilliant in scholarship. So fearless at sport.

"I have it Balthazar. I have it. We shall enter by taxi. It is all agreed. Grandly through the front gates. Under the noses of porters. And be in my rooms in Botany Bay in due course and defilement."

In the shadows of Wicklow Street just past a window display of spring fashions in Switzers a taxi was loaded with the women. A white five pound note passed by Beefy to the taxi man. The girls covered in a rug squeezed down between the knees of the gentlemen. Beefy handed his silver flask to Balthazar to take brandy at this delicate moment. Poised for fluent entrance without the flicker of a lid, or murmur of lie. To present at the great wooden gates. And safely pass.

The taxi proceeding around these bleak corners of commerce. Down an incline between pubs and banking houses. And out on the broad stretch of Dame Street. Leads west to the Atlantic. East to the black high arched portal of this ancient seat of learning. The massive grey pillars and porches of the Bank of Ireland. The taxi heading across the tram tracks. Over a bump. Under that blue gold clock high above.

And Beefy is giggling as Rebecca's head is rather burrowing where it shouldn't be.

"Stop it Rebecca. This is a tender moment when one's countenance must wear a bland look of ecclesiastic purity. Demanding of a salute from those who serve."

Beefy rearing in his seat eyes widening in horror as the taxi fails to decrease speed. And slams to a stop against the wooden barricade. Two porters come out. Slowly inspecting the dent in the timber they come to the window and peer at a motionless Beefy. They go to pull up the iron pins and lift back the main door. We move forward. Porters lean over ever so slightly. Beefy nods. They touch their caps. And now we trundle across the cobble stones.

"By God we've done it Balthazar. By God we've done as nice a piece of elemental underhandedness as could be expected in a vehicle which should not be allowed out on the roads. Just lie low now girls until big uncle Beefy gets you safely into his randy quarters. Who's for brandy. Ah Balthazar. You know I'm enjoying your company. You give me a sense of destiny. I rather mean to say my character is all shot to hell. I'm skidding along now on infamy. Heading for my holy orders. With my trustees screaming. My granny stony hearted. My vile despicable propensities raging. Of course I shall take my holy orders. But not before I've had my fill of the diabolical."

"Beefy I don't like the look of things. I have a strange feeling we got by the porters too easily. Can't we have cocoa and go out again."

"Balthazar you are an awfully polite man you know. But not one for filling in the silences in conversation, are you. Taxi man, apply your brakes now, that doorway right there. Get close in. That's a good man."

Beefy debarking with rug. Holding it aloft between car door and the dark stony entrance. To let the damsels discreetly pass. Into chill darkness and move up three landings guiding with hands on the smooth banisters and creaking stairs. Beefy whispering close.

"Ah Balthazar aren't you excited tonight. With these two lasses. You can engage in any proclivity you fancy."

"I heard what you said and don't be thinking I don't know all them big words mean the same thing."

"I love you Rebecca. I love you."

"You love yourself."

"You see Balthazar these girls are clever. Far above the ordinary. You know, this isn't a time to bring this up, but I rather funked it in the military. Could never organise an assault. Would say to the chaps. This is your captain speaking, can you hear me chappies, there are the buggers beyond the ridge, let them have it by God, mortar them good and proper. Forsooth I set off a barrage to give them what for beyond the ridge. After the preliminary softening up I told the chappies to rush them. I put my umbrella up to march out setting a good example, through the rain of shells. Men didn't like it at all. Thought I was putting on the dog. But the enemy were so stunned to see me marching at them under my snake skin handled umbrella that they ceased firing. Just as well. The unhappy thing was, I was attacking my own men. I was an absolutely dead loss at war. Soon as they got rid of me they started winning like mad. But you know, let me say confidentially, I tried to soldier well. Even now when I pass Horse Guards' Parade in London, hear the band, the crunch of heels on the gravel, a reverberation goes through me and I thrill to an instant erection. I mean some chaps express their loyalties in other ways. But that little signal, that pure salute. One's private little pole. Standing outright and quivering. Has always made me feel that my love of regiment, my loyalty to the Monarch, was a swelling splendour of heartfelt salutation. Wait girls, for your captain. This fearful trip is not yet done. Until we are safely inside."

Beefy opening the door. Ushering in his guests. He goes from room to room announcing an all clear and switching on a light. Breda staring around these booklined walls. Hung with risqué tapestries and silver ornaments. Crossed sabres over the mantel. Four shotguns locked against a wall. A great carpet

196

woven with the facial and saucy aspects of a Persian gentleman in all expressions from sadness to outright laughter. In every nook and cranny, crystal splendours. Bound volumes. Ecclesiastical Policy. Eucharistic Faith and Practice. A Short History of the Doctrine of Atonement.

"That woman there on the wall is my granny. Who has made much of what you see here possible. Often I kneel of an evening, light a candle and look up to her and pray my thanks. She is as flint hearted as she looks. But do help yourselves to the bowl of raisins one and all. And allow me to pour. Rebecca, whisky."

"Ah you're a cod. Sure this place is like one of them black gentlemen have."

"I have my dear woman not been blessed by a dark complexion but I am a man of the divinity, do not forget that. Must satisfy the Archbishop King's Professor that I am an habitual communicant of the Church of Ireland. Nor forget that before ordaining a candidate for the ministry you must have your medical certificate of health. Leave no doubt as to physical soundness in the performance of ministerial duties. There Rebecca read that tome, The Problem of the Pastoral Epistles."

"What would I want with such protestant rubbish. Sure you'll burn to a crisp in hell, you will."

"Ah Rebecca you take the pope to heart. Did you know he was a share holder in your breweries."

"What kind of talk is that."

"Ah Rebecca, Rome is finished as a power. The pope is in voluntary liquidation and is making for Zurich but I thirst for a glance of your naked person, your fleshy realizable assets."

"You'll roast for centuries."

"But tonight let us not be squeamish. Blessed is the man who puts his pole into the ungodly and spits mighty spurts. O God I'm so painfully horny. Step lightly forward now in a rhythmic manner my dear. Off with your garments. Let us have some balletic expertise."

"I will in a tinker's tit, in front of everyone."

"Ah no vile language here, girl. British territorial prerogatives prevail within these Trinity walls. Be not base low mean and shabby. Strip off."

"Will you listen to him. Strip off he says."

"Ah Rebecca can't you see I'm agog for your nude form. Breathlessly impatient for visiting vile humiliations upon you. Blessed are they who lay down their garments one by one in a manner of teasing dalliance for they will have a pole of plenty eight miles up them. In due ruddy course. Of course."

"You're a Presbyterian."

"Ah you've uttered the one thing that provokes me Rebecca and calls for, of course, rape. I must rape you. Don't try to struggle it will be useless."

"Sure I can scream the bricks down of this building."

"We must employ the gags. Can't have outcry when Beefy is scintillating through his magic mire of shame. Just here inside this cabinet, here we are, the gags, the silk pyjama cords. For trussing up. For the vile proddings."

Balthazar hands joined entwined, his back pressing against a series of volumes in the book case, A Theological Introduction and Texts to Religious Experience and Divine Diverticula. Breda looking from face to face. Beefy dropping his trousers. Rebecca pulling off her dress. Not to know what was funny or what was sad. Or what was rape and what was mad. But only to tremble in terror. Visions of porters and authorities marching eighty abreast across Front Square. Crowbars held high. For breaking and entering. Hangman's nooses for stretching throats. And to dangle, one's university career at a dismal end.

Beefy raging with considerable nudity holding up his silk pyjama cords. Breda covering her eyes with well spaced fingers. Rebecca in a wild peal of laughter seizing this unforgettable instrument asway upon Beefy's chunky person. As I good heavens, feel constrained to look out the window. And Breda gasps.

"Ah God I've never seen the likes of a thing like that before. It's as big as a donkey's. Sure your man is a mule."

"Good God your toenails Rebecca, need cutting, I'll report you to the Society of Chiropodists. Ah but otherwise, isn't she my Rebecca, the most splendid creature. Pirouette my dear. Ah that raised some fine points. Of divinity if not law. But we're losing the sense of rape here. Cringe back a little my dear. If the Provost could only see us. Keeping up the fine traditions of the college. Numini et patriae asto. And now. For rape."

Beefy charging across the floor. Hands raised in a pose horrid and menacing. Pyjama cords draped in a priestly manner about his neck. Seizing Rebecca by the wrists, her legs buckling beneath her as a smile broke across her face and laughter trembled her knees.

"Rebecca you're ruining this deadly serious act. I am about to rape you. This won't do."

Rebecca doubling up with her hands held across her belly. Beefy bent pulling them apart. Shaking her into resistant action. As she went limp on the floor. Breda wide eyed and pushing back her sweater sleeves.

"You're getting awfully dusty Rebecca. It's not fair of you to behave this way. Resist. For God's sake. O dear what can I do, my charm melts all hearts, and everyone, men women and children open their legs to me. Into the bedroom, Rebecca. I will lash you to the bed. And in my best secular manner I will have at you like a beast bounding straight out of the bible. Numini et patriae asto. And don't spare the jujubes."

Balthazar swallowing constant lumps of air. Wiping his brow with handkerchief. The crumpled giggling figure of Rebecca carried into the bedroom. Jubilant jouncing coming out the half open door. To reach and pass the bowl of raisins across to Breda. To select of these dried grapes.

"What was that he was saying in that funny language."

"I stand on the side of God and my country."

"Sure in the condition he's in what God or country would have him."

"Would you have tea if I can find the kettle and leaves."

"Aren't you about to try anything with me."

"No."

"I'll have a cup then if you're making one. Can you tell me if your friend is completely round the bend."

"He's the most brilliant brain of the university."

"Is that a fact. Well if you ever knew what was on another person's mind you wouldn't know what to put on your own at all. He's one for devilment."

The door crashing open. Beefy, trousers down around his ankles, shuffling and hobbling in his socks. His private signal tied with a bow of pyjama cord waving in circumcised salute, poking out beyond the floating tails of his shirt. Breda shrinking back from this bullish grinning ruddy face.

"Balthazar. Where are you. See for yourself. Rebecca trussed up. Ready to give treats. My dear girl show some shame, how dare you stare at my instrument in that manner. We shall rape Rebecca. Then it shall be your turn. While you rape Rebecca Balthazar I shall truss this truculent lass to the other bed. And by God we'll rape you."

"I'm making tea for us, Beefy."

"O my gawd. You'd let such opportunities as I've prepared slip. For the sake of Empire dear man. For Monarch. We must on with the felony. You lass you're next, make no mistake about that."

"I'm not with you I'm with your friend here who's a well behaved gentleman."

"Stop. Do I sense here the shirty and utterly shabby nuance of criminal impertinence. And take your eyes off my instrument this instant."

"Sure it's not my fault if it's there put in front of me eyes."

"You are a saucy lass. I'm putting you down in my notebook. Needy of corrective measures."

"You fancy yourself. Standing around like that. You should be ashamed of yourself."

Beefy, eyes so brown ablaze with merry evil, moving forward towards Breda. As she rose from her chair and slowly stepped backwards around the room. Past the shotguns, past foils stuck in an umbrella stand. Till she fell on the brass studded gleaming leather couch. Beefy's great instrument pressing at Breda's face as she waved it away. Balthazar scratching his head in the scullery doorway. This can't be college. An evening such as this. A hidden world never seen before. Until you think that this is the way it must really be. The carefree frolics of undergraduate years. That we grow up to live in steadier and sterner ways. Look back and say I was a naughty fellow in my younger days.

"Come my dear girl, it's as hard as a baby avocado, don't push it away, it likes you. Give the boy a treat."

"I will in me witless ways. Go on before I give you a bite of your balls and they'll be through bouncing anymore I can tell you."

"Blessed my dear are the non violent girls who blow. A sound from this horn delivereth me up to the heights of ecstasy. With such elevation I could spit on Mars. The explosive grandeur of tickling your tonsils would make this poor boy so happy. And also clear your complexion of any blotches. You pretty girl. Come put a ring of lipstick round it. Leave a marvellous stain. And we'll both get to Mars."

"You'll get away with that thing or I'll stain you with the back of me hand. You're out of your mind."

As Beefy disappears to the bedroom. A sound. A sharp crack. Balthazar turning to look back in the scullery. The steaming spout of the kettle aimed against the window. The parted white and blue checked curtains. A busted pane of glass. Misted and streaked. To touch where it split and look out into the thickets of the new leaves. Something strange up in the tree. Strain one's eyes to see. A shadow entwined about a bough. And down there. O my God. Passing by the shed of cycles and motor bikes. A lantern swinging. Spreading light across the hard grey ground. Three figures approaching this way. One in dressing gown and slippers between two porters. They stop. They look up at this window.

"Beefy Beefy."

"I'm lingering. In the most spooky pleasuring."

"The Proctor. Coming."

"Nearly."

"O God. I mean it Beefy."

"Nonsense. I'm in elemental ecstasy."

"Please Beefy."

"Dear boy how can you, how can you, call, o my goodness, at such a time, o Lord that's nice, awfully nice. Tell my trustees of your trouble. They deal with all my debts and tribulations. So that I may pursue without hinder. Divinity, first ranking of the professions. Followed sadly by law, medicine and literature. The rear taken up by science and music. First you get baptised, grow up and get sued. Life goes on till they saw off your leg. If you survive you can read a good book. My advice in life is to proceed in a blaze of contradictory remarks, and send one's trustees each year a valentine. Rome is finished as a power. The ecclesiastical tom tom says so. Church of Ireland is taking over everywhere. We are winning souls left right and evil. Right down the coast to Greystones. And doing awfully well in Dalkey. We must kick the indulgences and plastic relics out of this isle. Give them a nine first Fridays of my Lutheran horn up the hole instead. Tear back the camouflage of emerald purity. Thou art Beefy and upon your arse I shall build my bank. No one gives a damn about the organic unity of Christ. Or the ecclesiastical jurisdiction. Rebecca, darling, the cardboard crucifixion is crumbling."

"You're mental."

Balthazar at the open crack of the door. As the gospel according to Beefy drones on. One's two hands held tightly together. If not altogether wringing. Certainly drained of blood. To tip toe into someone else's intimacy.

"Beefy, I think this is urgent, can you hear me."

"Single handedly I shall bring down Rome. Rebecca. Severe ideas are called for. Ukase. Deliver up delinquent attitudes. Papists will cower. Liberty loving protestants will march elbowing harlots out of the way, on to Belfast. Very militant. The Divine Founder will scream out the Coptic Rite and screw the eastern schisms."

"You're mental."

202

"Beefy they're coming. The porters."

"Really Balthazar. Can't you hear I'm in the middle of my outloud meditation. Kicking evil little bugs out of the conscience. After one has defiled numerous orphans, widows and motor mechanics. My God what did you say."

"I said the porters are coming."

"Pull that sash cord. That's the general alarm. Quickly Rebecca up. Keep all mouths closed and fast come with me. Gather up your garments. Into the scullery. No time for moderation. One grasps at a moral morsel and sinks promptly in a vast sea of human betrayal. And new rattings from every side. One sings loudly protestant praises. And porters get it into their heads to do their duty. No panic, quite safe. This way through the dust. Old Beefy knows how to disport. And retreat with a gusto unknown to modern man. Just when I was going to ask you to take down your trousers, Balthazar, and present your particulars to the pleasurings. God I'm going to soon show my age beyond my years. I'm such a young vital chappie. This way. Girls obey now to the letter. Not a murmur. Just do as you are told. And the whole misunderstanding will pass shortly. Been a slight breach of security. Soon patch it up. Keep an eye out Balthazar."

Beefy pulling on underwear with one hand, leading his two female guests with the other. Into the scullery. A scrabbling and scuffling. A banging. On the door. Beefy putting his finger to his lips for silence, as he tip toes back into the drawing room. And across to his bedroom. Emerging again in dressing gown. Locking the bedroom door. Dropping his key into the pocket of a long flowing black silk robe. Satiny slippers embellished with gold threaded crossed cues on his feet. And he looks down upon his person and smiles at the ashen faced Balthazar.

"Believe in me. Trust in me. I'll do all the talking. Make believe you are merely playing bezique at your London club. And the world lies around you sublime. See, I'm in my billiard slippers, means we are quite safe. You mustn't shake like that Balthazar. I've been through this before. Just a very ordinary nightmare. Shush. Now. Wait. They are at the door. Listening. O very crafty. But what they hear is silence. We are engrossed in a tutorial."

Three loud knocks on the door. Balthazar taking one deep breath after another. Beefy lighting up a large cigar. His eyes blinking in the smoke, slowly taking tomes from his shelves and opening them out on the table. All seems somehow to have happened before. Three more bangs on the door. And Beefy was on top of that girl. As her legs wagged in the air. A bare arse pumping up and down during his academic career. Of devious divinity. One must turn a blind eye to sacrilege. Uncle Edouard said it was always wise to kick up a disturbing row if one were tapped unwarningly upon the shoulder. Three more loud bangs. A voice of authority.

"Open up this door."

Beefy tip toeing around in a circle, raising his eyebrows up and down with each step. His elegant nerve. When I should be content somewhere in Siberia now. Or strolling the afternoon by ice age morains in the countryside. Tracing fossil ferns with a light thrilling finger. And the warm voice of Fitzdare. O Lord.

"Open up. I know you have women in there. I am not going to stand out here in the cold all night. If this door is not opened presently, I shall have the clerk of works summoned to knock it down."

Beefy advancing close to the door. Listening. Taking a great long puff on his cigar. Shaking his head slowly up and down. Two squash rackets leaning against the wall. Beefy taking one in hand and sweeping it in a strong forehand volley. As three more knocks land.

"Now please, be sensible in there and don't make this occasion more unpleasant than it already is."

Beefy smiling. Feinting deeply with a flexed right knee. A blurring back handed cross court three sided killing shot administered with a swish of breeze. And a gracefully slow follow through. While I tremble. With no way out. Save a window plummeting down three floors. With two broken legs one could not run. But better to stand by the window. Just in case. To look down. And see if it gets any nearer. Seemed so certain we were undetected through the front gate. My reputation of the rape of Donnybrook following after me. My God what is that out there in the tree.

"Beefy, come, look."

Beefy peering out into the night. The branches of the nearby tree. The tangled snaky boughs. Beefy taking his cigar out of his mouth. His eyes cold.

"That wretch. Out there spying in the tree. Betraying us. Thinks he's going to delight in our apprehension. The jealous Greek scholar, the bogman Muggins. He's laughing. By God wait till I get my hands on him."

"Beefy open the door please. They're beginning to use force."

"An innocent man is never in a hurry Balthazar."

"But we're not innocent."

"In spirit and heart, yes. We are. That's why I wear this look of permanent bewilderment. Whoops, yes, that was rather a loud bang. Thought they might give up."

"I know you have women in there. I will not ask again that this door be opened. I am not going to stand out here all night."

Beefy advancing to the door. Drawing back the bolts. One high one low. Lifting his eyebrows as he turned the lock and pulled open the big black door. The Proctor in a brown ankle length bathrobe. Designed perhaps for such evening missions. Pair of red skiing socks and scuffed pair of leather slippers. A sky blue scarf wrapped high up round his throat and flowing over a shoulder. Rowed stroke or bow or something for Cambridge. A year when Oxford sank with all hands in the river. These two small porters look from under their blue bulging hard hats. Peering out from the college secrets piled up over the years. And one steps forward to put his lantern atop the turf cupboard.

"All right Beefy, where are the women."

"Sir, women."

"Yes, the women. Don't play games with me. Where are the women. I want this over without delay. You may as well come clean. Where are they."

"Sir, you do know I'm reading divinity."

"I should not attempt, if I were you, to start clouding the issue. Which is quite grave."

"Sir I'm afraid I don't have the faintest idea what you're talking about. With all respect, really sir. I do not."

"Don't try my patience."

"Honestly, Balthazar B here. Why we came back this evening to college, having missed vespers and taken a walk about Stephen's Green, and we set about slogging. Quite above board. Books there on the table. Mr. B's Littlego exam. Latin is giving him a good bit of trouble. Thought it would polish him up nicely if I took him through some of—"

"That's quite enough. I'm not going to stand here all night listening to your explanations. Either you admit now to the women or I shall go into that room and expose them myself. As distasteful as that may be. But you've only yourself to blame if this cannot be dealt with in a civil manner. I have not got all night. Come on. Don't trifle with me longer. I see. Very well. Let us have that door there opened."

A nod from the Proctor. A pointing finger raised. To these dark uniformed porters in their peaked hunting hats. Who step forward. Across this ornamentaled tapestried room. They turn the knob and push shoulders against the locked door.

"All right, Beefy, the key. Let us have the key."

"Sir, what key."

"The key Beefy."

"Sir as you know."

"I know nothing except this is most tiresome. Give me that key."

"Upon my word, sir, one has desperately been pursuing the doctrine of atonement, christian ethics."

"You are really bringing me to the end of my endurance. I can see this little evening has all the appearances of a tutorial."

206

"Fructu non foliis arborem aestima, sir."

"Do not Latin me. There's quite sufficient fruit to be seen and judged here."

"Sir I think you should look out the window in the tree outside."

This tall handsome man, waves of quietly greying hair across his head. One hand tightly holding the wrist of the other. Stealing a frowning glance at the green ecclesiastic tomes. As he steps forward. Porter coughing into the hollow of his fist. A satin sash with bright red tassels round the Proctor's robe. To wake up again in one's own life. Delirious in this suicidal dilemma. Just as the golden moments are gone. Fading lighthearted elegances of a Sunday afternoon. As raindrops begin to hit the window panes.

"Beefy I'm warning you, either you produce these ladies instantly or something much worse will happen to you than you think will happen."

"Sir upon my crossed squash rackets I swear and with all due respect, you are barking up the wrong tulip tree. I mean really, how can I otherwise consider that you are not, without malice perhaps, but persistently, making unintentional slanderous accusations here. In front of witnesses."

"Are you daring to try me. Are you."

"Sir there is no need to shout."

"You do try me."

"No sir. I am distinctly not doing. Nor trying."

"All right break down that door."

"Please sir no."

"Break it in."

"O sir, you really shouldn't. This is awful."

"Quite."

"I don't think I can bear to watch. I am cut to the quick that my word should not be believed. What am I anyway but a mere student. Giving of my best. And getting back the worst."

"Keep quiet."

"Yes sir."

The two porters taking up positions. A signal and the dark shoulders crashed upon the door. A groan and raised eyebrows as the black portal refused to budge. A stepping back of three paces, another onslaught. Beefy covering his eyes. A splintering. Two panels cracked through. One porter down. Holding his shoulder in pain.

"Sir please, allow me, I can't bear to watch anymore. I've got the key here. I'll open the door. It's the principle of the thing. It really is. Not to be believed. To have had a command in a regiment with which, sir, I know you are acquainted. There. It's open. Get them. Eighty ladies. Twenty of them dusky. Before they get out the window."

The two porters rushing into the room. Pulling back the deep blue satin window drapes. Opening the clothing cupboard. Tearing blankets from the bed. Beefy giving a nervous start as something clatters on the floor. The pushing aside of stacks of towels and shirts. And finally standing hesitating over a great iron deed box. Room enough for two well packed midgets. The Proctor thin lipped, white faced. Stepping forward. Pointing with a finger.

"Open up that box."

"Sir, that is confidential."

"I said open it."

"Sir you have no warrant."

"I can tell you Beefy, that my anger shall be sufficient warrant at this moment."

"But sir there is no room for ladies in there. Not nice ladies anyway."

The porters triumphantly holding up the foot long key fallen from the bedcovers. Smiles as they plunge it into the top of the great box. Four hands turning it. A click inside. Lifting the heavy lid open, propping it back. The great locking teeth round the lid rim. And the porters standing staring silently down.

"Yes, what is it."

"I don't know sir. It must be thousands and thousands."

"Thousands of what."

208

"Pounds sir. Five pound notes. Hundreds of them."

"O dear. I'm not ready for more jokes."

"It's not joking sir. See for yourself."

"Good Lord. What's the meaning of this Beefy."

"Nothing is the meaning of it sir, except that you have searched my apartments, opened my confidential strong box and failed to find any crumpet, fluff or frill."

"How did this come to be here. All this money."

"I put it there sir."

"Are you completely out of your senses. You have no right to keep money in this quantity in a college room."

Beefy crossing to close down the great iron lid with a crunching bang. Turning the huge key. Lifting it out again and slipping the iron circle over his wrist. Making an about face. A clatter of slipper. A slow march back to the sitting room. Plumping into his leather sofa, Beefy crossed his carrot haired legs and opened a tome across his lap. Book One of Aristotle's Nicomachean Ethics. Balthazar B reflecting apostate, down hearted and sad, raising his chin momentarily as the Proctor stepped back into the sitting room.

"Stand up Beefy."

"Sorry sir, just keeping up with my ethics."

"This is not over yet."

"O."

"I will get to the bottom of this. Meanwhile that money is to be put properly where it belongs, in a bank."

"I don't trust banks sir."

"I don't care whom you trust. Get that money out of here. Who is your tutor."

"Professor Elegant sir."

"And yours, Mr. B."

"Professor Elegant sir."

"Professor Elegant has his work cut out. Be at my office tomorrow at three o'clock, both of you."

"Sir are you going."

"What I do is not of your concern."

"I just thought sir that you should know there is something

awfully strange out there up in a tree. If you look out the window sir."

The Proctor pushing apart the drapes. Peering out into the night. Taking a torch from under arm and shining it out the window. Turning back to these two attending porters awaiting their further instruction. To keep the college clear of misdemeanour. To track down abductors. Rout out the harbourers of females laid liberally on for riotous and indecent behaviour.

"Porters, go fetch that man out of that tree. Who seems to find matters in here so amusing. I should not smile Beefy, I'm not by any means finished with you. I am not satisfied that there is not something quite fishy here."

"I understand sir, completely."

"This university is not some kind of brothel."

"I quite agree sir. No brothel here. And I want you to know sir, that although it might not at this moment seem very evident to you, I know that my redeemer liveth. Sir."

"O quite. You're going to need him. Be assured of that."

Beefy joyfully leaping to the door. To put to the bolts once more. And a finger up to his lips. At the departing sound of steps down the wooden stairs. To the window now, they could see down to the foot of the tree. In the lightly descending rain the Proctor and porters waiting. In torch light and lantern glow. A student scrabbling down to the ground with long flowing hair. Brushing bark from his person. Turning to point up at this window. As one and all nip back.

"That evil snooping scoundrel. Been scrounging around me for months. One doesn't mind his constantly shitting and pissing out his window after dark. But as a leech on my life. Never."

"Let us out of here."

"O my God, the girls. Please stay right where you are and don't move till I tell you."

"We want to come out of here."

"Not yet. You must lie low for just a while longer. Ah Balthazar you are quite a person under fire. However, be

210

ready, the last tribulation is about to unfold. An old college tradition. In circumstances such as this. They go away. For a few minutes. And then when one is up to one's neck again in lewd gymnastic indecency. They come crashing in the door. Not nice. So we'll just sit here at the table. Take up the tutoring where last left. Ah here we are, a little something on the constitution of Athens."

The door came asunder. With splintering door jambs and plaster. Three porters pouring through. Balthazar jumping to his feet emitting a slight shriek. Beefy relighting his cigar gone out in the former festivities. The third porter new to matters rushing the bedroom. Reappearing vacant faced and bemused. Beefy blowing a large smoke ring across the room. Which wreathed his granny's portrait and smashed out in wavering billows against the wall. Balthazar B with his hand held against his lower throat sat down again.

"Are you porters done. Dark beadles of injustice. How dare you burst in in this manner. Bringing plaster with you. Causing nuisance to a man who will one day follow quite closely upon the heels of Christ. He was an awfully good walker before they tacked him up."

"We are under orders sir."

"Well then. New orders. Vamoose. Take your lot out into the night. O yes, the Provost will hear of this. My trustees will certainly be assembling in front of the Bank of England over there in the land of fair play. And by God when the drummer begins to strike a cadence, they will march to the Holyhead, stepping of course right over Wales. Do you hear me. Put down that crowbar. Quite untoward. My trustees will be on the night boat soon and by God they will be scribbling out writs and the like, as well as many other beribboned documents."

"Very well sir, very well."

"You know I happen to be a scholar."

"Yes sir."

"Ranking of the fifth rank in this college. And a gentleman of the choir."

"We do sir know this."

"Scholar in classics, as well as a man who is to take holy orders. And you chaps break down doors and visit indiscriminate injury to the sensibilities of myself and Prince B. Your Highness my profound apologies. As your host one wants so much to blot out horrendous spiritual bruises which smite one in one's chambers. Quite odious."

"We are quite sorry sir to have incommoded you."

"All right. We all, here present, know our redeemer liveth. Let that suffice. I am tired."

"Goodnight sir."

Porters departing silent and open mouthed. Beefy examining his busted door. Sad bolts and latches hanging, screws twisted out of the splintered wood.

"Don't you find this all terribly unrefreshing Balthazar. Look what they've done to my poor door. What a waste of their broken shoulders to think they could outwit Beefy. Infantry captain extraordinary. I think cannibalism is next on my calendar of lusts."

"Let us out of here."

"Right with you girls now."

Beefy at the turf bin. Lifting up the lid top. Displaying the brown piles of turf. His hand choosing a crumbling piece.

"Quite real. You see Balthazar. Now. We close this up. And here, come watch, undo this and we draw back a little secret door. And the two morsels of our delight. Good evening girls."

In the shadows, sitting upon a low bench. Breda and Rebecca grim faced and unglad. Shuffling out sideways. Pitter patter of the rain. And the wind rising. The scullery window ashake. Helping the ladies back into the little game. Beefy so gallantly plays. With rules writ. For black bliss. Oblique and naughty. Smiling he bows. This boy of all those years ago. Whose purest voice raised such sweet threnody to sound across meadows blending the lightest green with daisies and buttercups. Taken by his friendly hand through woodlands gently away from fear. He made my Tillie well again.

"Get us out of here, I want to be gone out of here altogether."

"Girls I myself would dearly like to be lost at this moment. Amid the gaieties of the London season if possible. After all the recent rattings. Buggering up the stylish sauciness I had so hoped was to be our lot. And still can be."

"I'll not be arrested in this college you chancer."

"Rebecca that's not an awfully nice thing to say. After risking all to keep you safe from harm. Allow me to take this strap from your tempting shoulder."

"You're the devil himself, you are."

"Please. Both of you are my honoured guests. Good grief. Abandon ship. The windows."

A woeful crash. The door falling flat into Beefy's chambers. Over it tramping three porters. A wave of dust rising. The Proctor rigid at the disembowelled entrance. All triumph buried unseen in the sad face. The sound of doors opening on the staircase landings below. To see what the earthquake is about. Windows squeaking, and others slamming shut. A college awake this night. For an awarding of a degree. In harlotry.

"Very well. I apologise to both of you young ladies. I'm sure you've been misled here. You Beefy, and you Mr. B. Attend tomorrow at three. My office. I shall appreciate your escorting these young ladies, again with my apologies, out of the university. A taxi has been summoned. That is all. Goodnight."

A roll of drums beating. Cannons firing salvos. In a coffin two blank parchments. Of ungranted degrees. Drawn on a gun carriage. Hooves echoing their clatter up and down Dublin streets. Sorrowing people wave their little flags and tap their tears. The wind awakes and blows. Bends and flattens highland grass. The bagpipes play. A purple music across the heather. Go down to death bravely. When you go. Neither to weep nor smile. Tomorrow will be a yesterday when nothing mattered at all. It rains tonight. This bishop born Beefy. Anointed with his own gracious infamies. A high stepper in

213

all doggish demeanours. We both are led by the scruff of the
neck. To the black long taxi. A light lit inside. To reload the
girls. In this college square they call Botany Bay.

> Under
> The wild
> Hair
> Of the trees.

19

Across empty midnight cobbles of Dublin. Past the time tolling up in a tower clock. Down a steep street and by an ancient church. Beefy told the taxi to stop. He helped Rebecca alight. And said goodbye.

Balthazar B looking out the back window as the motor drew away. Four caravans on a wasteland site. Tinkers bundled up in sleep. Near an edge of lamplight Beefy stood, his arm around Rebecca. And there he seems to stay.

The taxi crossed the Liffey. White swans floating. Rolling now past the shuttered shops of Capel Street and out along an empty northern strand by a flat deserted park. Clontarf where so many times I sped through, hurrying by Landship to the races at Baldoyle. While little kiddies waved and shouted at me with joy. A flashing beacon of a lighthouse beyond the shadowy floating bumpiness of North Bull Island. Played a cold day of golf out there on those sandy hills. Dreaming far less sporty things as I struck the ball. Of a female I could call my own. To send tulips to. Have somewhere to put my pleasure as I lay my heart down against hers. Breda with her dark little eyes and bony narrow wrists.

"What will they be after doing to you at college."

"Rustication."

"What's that."

"They banish you. Send you down."

"Is that worse than up."

"Yes down's worse than up."

"I guess it doesn't make any difference to that Beefy. With his millions of pounds. Sure he could just laugh."

"Sometimes it's not that easy."

"I can't see what's hard about having all that money."

"Well someone like Beefy has trustees. And they can be troublesome."

"If money's there what's trouble about that. You could give me all the trustees you like. He's some fellow the likes of him. That I've not come across before. Not that I've been anywhere in my life. I'm just ordinary working class. I've never been in a room like that before. It was like something you'd see on the films. With the carpets on the wall. And shiny things jumping out at you from the plaster. I guess I'm not what you might call educated."

"Education is learning only what you don't have to know."

"Is that a fact."

"I think so."

"You're a very funny person. Not like your friend. You're the quiet type. I guess you don't think much of me."

"Why do you say that."

"Well I won't say now but Rebecca she's my oldest friend because we were reared together down over in Irishtown. We're not exactly princesses. Are we. I don't live far now. You don't have to have the driver go any further. I can walk from here by a short cut. If you stop by the shop on the corner. Ahead there."

"We'll take you all the way."

"No I want to get out now."

"It's raining."

"I don't mind."

"Driver stop. There. By the post."

"Very good sir."

"How much do I owe you."

"Ah let's see now. Forty bob. This time of night. Been a lot of wear and tear on the tires. With the grain of cement lying the wrong way on the road if you understand me sir."

"All right."

"Now if it was another kind of road sir with the surface giving less trouble."

"Goodbye driver."

Balthazar B standing on this grey wet pavement. The rain falling through a halo of lamplight. A post office, butcher, grocer and newsagent. Lonely houses behind high hedges.

The wind with a seaweed smell off the sea. This girl thinly standing, clutching her handbag. The rear red light of the taxi still seen after all its sound is gone.

"Sure you're stranded now."

"I'll walk with you home if I may."

"Sure you may and I'm glad of company. But it's an awful wet way and how will you ever get back."

"I'll manage."

"Ah God you'll catch your death of cold just in your suit."

"I'll be alright. You've only got a sweater."

"Ah don't worry about me, I'm used to it but the kind of life you're accustomed to leading. It wouldn't suit you to be wandering out here in the rain."

"You won't mind my coming with you."

"Sure you're welcome. Sure you know that. That you're welcome."

"Thank you."

"That taxi man has made himself a fortune this night, cheating like that after your friend gave him five pounds. That makes me angry."

"You musn't worry."

"It's a fortnight's wages to me."

Out into darkness. The lamplight left behind at the cross roads. All familiar just a short time ago. An afternoon expedition, a class outing looking for fossils. Students standing about in their belted up macintoshes, some in mountain climbing kit, with rucksacks strapped to backs. And I came roaring through in the Landship. Heading for the nags at Baldoyle. To stop awhile in the little gathering. I had not an acid bottle nor hammer, just the racing form. I thought I would be welcomed. That perhaps they had missed me. And all I seemed to see was a laughing Miss Fitzdare as she pedaled someone's bicycle around in a little circle on the road. Then she leaned back on the handle bars. I saw her stretched out legs in her blue stockings and they looked long and handsome. And I was so surprised.

"This is the short cut I'm taking. Up back here. That's the

North Bull lighthouse in the bay and the other is the Poolbeg. Rebecca and I when we were only little would ride her bike down the wall all the way to the end. Where the lighthouse is. It was like being out on a ship with water on both sides of you. She's a bit of a wild one. She'd throw rocks at old men. Her father before he got sick himself beat her within an inch of her life night after night. Take her things and throw them out the window down on to the road when she'd try to run away. Sure all she owned was an old chocolate box full of bits of old pens and her Sunday hat for church. She was trying to write a book. She got no further than the title. You might say the book was commercial romantic. It was called The Price Paid For The Pearl of Purity."

"That's a rather good title."

"She scratched it out and wrote another one later, which wouldn't be proper for me to tell you. But she didn't go on long paying the price for purity. She was paid a price is more like it. O God look at you. Rain dripping off your hair. It's very nice of you to walk like this with me. I could have managed on my own. But it's nice. I like walking. I don't ever have much time but when I do there's no one to walk with. I go along the beach out there. And collect shells. Give me your hand now, across through here, it's awfully slippy in the wet and you can't see the path through the bracken. It's only a little ways now."

Mists against the face. A faint fog horn. Her hand small and strong, to feel strangely delicate and warm. Brown slapping fern wetting the knees. A pouring sound of water against the ground.

"What's that noise."

"Ah it's nothing, the sheep, they hear something passing in the night. I don't want to be bold or fresh, but they are peeing in the grass in fear. Now that's where I am. The little bit of extension out on the back. Sure you've got an awful long trip ahead of you."

"I've done this before. Try my luck again. I'll be guided back by the lighthouses."

"You look chilled. Ah God it's not right. You coming all this way."

"It's fine."

"You look to me of delicate constitution. I'm small looking but as strong as an ox. Sure you're just but very wispy. It becomes you, like a saint starved you might say. You know a thing I want to ask you. About your friend. Is it true or all made up what he goes on saying. We're taught a poor opinion of the protestants. But myself I've always found them honest and decent. And my own kind I found would cheat you out of your sight. I've never known the likes of Church of Ireland people to get up to the devil and mischief of your friend. I'm broadminded but Rebecca allows him shocking awful liberties. Then if a fellow can give you a laugh he doesn't cheapen you. We're nearly here. Mind now this fence. There's broken bottle and barbed wire. Listen to that. The wind is getting fierce. North westerly. Always makes me homesick. I know it's blowing across Cavan. Many a night it makes me cry to sleep. I can't think of you out in the likes of this."

"I'll be alright."

"Ah God look at you. You won't be. You're shivering."

"I always do that."

"Ah don't cod me."

"No really."

"I don't know what to say. But. But I don't want you to get the wrong idea. That I'm being bold. It's two by now in the morning. I could be murthered for it."

"What's that."

"You would say in English now, murder. In Ireland we say murthered because it takes us so much longer to do it. And I could be murthered but I mustn't let you go."

"I'm fine."

"Ah I'm no good. No good at all."

"Why."

"I'm just not that's all. What I'm really trying to say to you is I don't want you to go back. But stay. Go ahead you can say no, it won't be then for lack of me trying. Goodnight. If you go out the alley now and be careful of the barrels it will take you into the road and you go left then and keep to the sea."

"I want to say yes."

"O."

"If you're asking me to stay, and it won't be any inconvenience to you."

"It's yes then."

"Yes."

"O."

"What's the matter."

"I don't know. I didn't think you would say yes and now I don't know what to do."

"Do you want me to say no."

"No."

"But if it's upset you."

"No. I'm glad you said yes."

"Yes I said yes."

"I'm scared out of my wits. I could use a bit of your friend Beefy's nerve. O but it's not to worry. That's my room up there."

"I don't want to cause you distress. It's no trouble for me to go. If it's difficult for you."

"You're the most beautiful man I've ever seen in my life. O God. Just give me a moment. I'll collect myself now. I'll be giving you an awful swell head. And mine I may get knocked off me. Now I have got to go in and when I get up to my room. I only have to open the window and you get on that barrel and step to the roof of the gents and it's easy to pull you in off there. You won't mind, my quarters are not grand."

Balthazar B stood in the yard, a cold shadow under the eaves. Fat raindrops landing to flow down between the roots of hair and drip from eyebrows, ear lobes and nose. Water gushing from a broken gutter pipe. Shadows of crates stacked. My wet silk shirt sticking to my ribs. A smell of hay. Somewhere warm and dry. In the sheltered opening of this old cow shed. An unending night. If Miss Fitzdare ever hears. I'll never see her again. Mid fingerbowls, linen and lace. Here now in mud, manure and rain.

"Hey there."

"Hello."

"Mind now very quiet as you go. On to the barrel first. That's it. Put a foot there and I will catch holt of your hand. Grand, there now. Don't be worried, get one hand on the sill. O God hold it there. Hold it."

"I'm sorry I'm not awfully good at this."

"You're doing fine, it's only some old pebbles and bits of cement. Ah now, a little more. This way. There. In you come now."

Balthazar B scrambling across the sill. The sound of pebbles and lumps of cement falling to the yard below. Clattering above the whistling wind. Years since one was in out of inclemency. Or not pulling plaster out of walls. Safe a moment. Up here in this tiny room. Her narrow little bed along the wall under a crazy quilt. In the red electric fire light. Shadows of a tall cupboard, varnished brown. A light green plastic handle to pull it open. Two suitcases bound with belts stacked on top. A dressing table with a dish and broken brush and comb. Two jars of sea shells and a bottle of perfume throw shadows across a cloth in the candle light.

"It won't be long to heat the room. With a bit of the electric fire. Landlords raise a holy terror. Watching the electricity get to me with a microscope over the wire. God love you you're wet through you poor man, a raindrop on your nose. You're the most beautiful man I've ever seen. What kind of mother and father did you have at all. Take this jacket off you now. Put it here over the back of the chair and let the fire shine on it."

Balthazar B sneezing. Bending double as he held hands up to his face. Hair wet. Head dizzy and tight. The room goes round in circles under a naked bulb hanging from the ceiling. Now black and red and light. All those voices are calling me. Locked away in this room. I'm going down now and down.

Balthazar B swayed in his wet shirt sleeves and slumped with a sigh unconscious into Breda's arms. Catching him under the shoulders and lugging him onto the bed. She kissed him on the eyes and lips and put her ear over his heart. To hear. Who goes there with footsteps. Where are you in the world. Walked here through bracken along a little path of slippery clay. Her hair is black. Combed with a broken comb. I saw a movie magazine. An issue I'd read cover to cover. It lay on her bedside box. We've the same taste for stars. Who come and go. As surely as trustees are not supposed to die. London streets turning upside down through all these recent hours. Where I walked swinging with a lightfooted stride. Out my little house. Along Brompton Road. Past the Hyde Park Hotel. Turreted, red bricked and tall. To make down the incline of Piccadilly and up again. A light breeze in the air passing the Ritz. To tea with lemon, squeezed under my tip of spoon. Feel so faint and feverish. Cold moments in school chapel so many years ago. To keel over and wake in bed. And just hear the distant singing. White owls fluttering overhead. A little girl friend looked at me on a Paris street and smiled in her white high shoes and gloves. She told me later in dancing class as I stepped on her toes. You should be ugly and I should be beautiful. My eyes are open. I'm not in Knightsbridge. It hardly matters now. A black head of hair on the pillow. Right by my side.

"You're alright now. You're here."

"What happened."

"You just went down in a heap. I caught you falling. You feel any better."

"O God."

"You're alright now. You've got a bad chill. You won't think it's a liberty I took of removing off your suit. I hope you don't mind my boldness. I left the socks on you."

"I'm sorry to be of so much trouble."

"Sure it's nothing. No trouble. As easy as handling a child. I don't mean like now you were a child. Undressing a gentleman in decency is a funny enough thing. Your ribs show. You don't mind being in bed with me. My ribs show too. But tell me. Is your will power sapped."

"What."

"O God I don't know what I'm asking you at all now you're awake. But would you kiss me."

Take this black haired head. Rolling over on top of me. My own head throbbing. Wind whining around the window. Her mouth strangely sweet. On the eve, the end of my university career. Rain like pebbles against the window. Her breasts round and hard. Sinewy muscles in her arms lock tight in tiny bulges. All these weeks and months dreaming of a naked female body. Staring out silent from my evening rooms. Down on a college street glistening always glistening in the rain.

"Ah God you kiss like a demon. I have to pinch myself I've got you here in bed. It wasn't to save you dying out on the road. That I brought you in. It was to save me dying of loneliness. Your shirt is real silk. And here you are with the likes of me."

"You mustn't say things like that."

"Sure the contrast is fun. I know where I'm at. I'm from Cavan originally. Where I should have stayed. Well out of the allurements of the world. They tell you to keep your tabernacle of purity. The fearful toll you can pay for a moment's thrill. And I can tell you one I paid. In holidays I went back to Cavan. I used to sit thinking at the cottage door looking out to the road. It was my uncle's was the farm. Ah God I'd do chores, sitting on the milking stool pulling away on the teats. When the neighbour's son comes in and says give this here thing a yank. I thought what harm can it be. An innocent lass in my poor flowered shift. Only frock I had from age twelve to sixteen. I yanked it for him like I'd milk any of the cows. And wasn't I later reported to this priest. Up there in the pulpit every Sunday. Shovelling his loads of misery out on the heads of the poor parishioners. Ah God I thought, listen to him and dropping his bits of flattery to the shop keepers before the collection is taken. They washed my

223

mouth out for weeks with soap. Beat me black and blue. Sure this is all Greek to you. It must be a wonderful thing to be an atheist. Or like your friend combining lechery and religion. Do I seem a stranger. I wanted to get you into bed. From the moment I clapped eyes on you back there in Dublin. Standing you were, so nervous. With your long blond silky hair just visible in the light. Then I thought you'd never speak to me walking along the street. I was itching just to put my arms around you. Like this. Listen to the wind. It's getting up a gale."

"What do I do in the morning."

"Don't worry. We'll get you out the same way you came. Take a bite of this now. It's the last bit of a bar of chocolate. It was me midnight dinner. When I can't sleep I read and have a piece of chocolate. Do you think purity is a joke. You're a quiet one. What does it all matter. I never thought I'd ever set foot in Trinity. Moving in real society. I did a funny thing. I stood up there at the mirror after I got you to bed. I hope you don't mind, I put your silk striped tie across me bosoms to make me look I was in Tahiti. I guess I'm out of my mind a lot. Keep dreaming I'll meet a sober serious gentleman with a drapery shop and set in his ways. I don't know what to say to you. You might think I'm daft. Would you love me. Before the beautiful likes of you are gone forever. Would you. I want you to love me. Say nothing now. While I put my hand over your mouth. I don't want you to speak. In case you want to tell me to get away. Ah God your thing is as good as that Beefy has any day. The feel of it. It stands up honest and protestant. Life is always travelling to a sorrow. On the way a taste of this will not lead immediately to tears. Warm like cattle we are in here. Ah God entwine me you prince."

Her strong thin arms. Red weals of shoulder straps marked across her skin. Two globes of arse like acorns. She climbs over and closes down on me in bed. Was there ever anywhere milky sunlight. Where great almighty poets sing. To warm her soul and parts of her too cold to touch. Other little weals. Stained on her stone white skin. She breathes and licks with kisses. Wet little lips on my chilled nippled breasts. To-morrow at three. Can't count the hours away. My brain so tired. Be in the afternoon. Just as it was when we were little boys. Dragged both before Crunch and Slouch. And all grown up now as a woman rides on my pole. Gripping like a hand. That pushed Beefy's away. Who said to Rebecca as he pointed it again I give thee darling this big prick in all its jolly frivolity, amplified by hand, pulled by night through my tender years. When now I think of London so far away. Of women, wan and white faced, sewing over benches in lofts from Whitechapel to Hornchurch. In broken buildings. By weed green bomb sites. Where I'll soon stand and look, chucked out of college. And all will be finished with Fitzdare.

Wind outside dying down. A cow coughs across the fields. Her belly is on my belly. And never left my calling card. Dress her up in finery, bring her back to Paris. Dine on the favoured boulevards. Soften her working hands. Let her smiles blow up in delight. Away from all her tortured harm. But I am not a pushy man. Too shy to say more than hello. We lie together and Breda says we are over the bottling room. Where the stout comes out of barrels. And corked and kept cool till it grows sweet. And foams a brownish cream. You screamed she said. I could feel it shooting into me. Never mind there's no one to hear. Not this time of night when they're snoring.

Now a fog horn mournful. Rain turned to mist and mist to dawn. World grown white and silent out the window. I hold her body as she sleeps. A spider's web in the corner of the ceiling. Her head covered in all its black hair. Without a face. Buried breathing in there. My white skin as white as hers. My temples burning and my eyes hot.

A clip clop of a horse somewhere on a road. In her sleep she moans. Grinds her teeth. Said you don't know anything about me. Then she tosses and turns. Out of sleep and back to sleep. Must get to Trinity at three o'clock. My joints ache and feet shiver down near the window. Reach for my watch. Across her head. To anywhere else in the world. Squeezed for space.

With lips to kiss and breasts to feel. And the honey running between her legs.

"What's that, who's that."

"Just me, I'm trying to see the time on my watch."

"Lord save us. A sergeant major in the Legion of Mary was beating me with a thong. The cruelty. Making me give a public confession. Thank God it's only you and morning I have to contend with."

"You were talking in your sleep."

"Ah God what did I say. Don't tell me. Just what's the time by your watch."

"Five minutes to six."

"It's fog out the window. Poor man how are you feeling this morning."

"Not so very well."

"Let's feel your forehead. God you're burned to death with the fever."

"I don't feel terribly good."

"O you poor lad you might be dying. What are we going to do for you at all. God I'm in for it now. We can't have the doctor come to you here."

"I'll go."

"You couldn't go out into the fog, you wouldn't get a hundred steps before you'd be lost."

"O no I'm alright, I'll go."

"Your eyes are awful red. Poor lad you could be breathing your last."

"Do you really think so."

"God you could. By the look of you."

"I've not made my will."

"Sure that won't get you well. But I have an old notebook there. Would it do for writing your last wishes."

"Yes. But do you think I should. Do I look that bad."

"Maybe a bit like a man at his wedding. Ah my heart goes out to you. Wait now while I brush back your hair."

"May I call you Breda."

226

"Sure you better after what's gone between us. We're not exactly strangers now."

"Breda, do you really think I'm dying."

"I can't be sure. But you don't look good."

"I don't have heirs."

"No sure you don't have airs. Who ever said a thing like that. You're a charming humble gentleman."

"I don't mean that kind of airs. I mean heirs who inherit money."

"Ah I know what you mean now, ha ha, that's good gas. I'm sorry to laugh. But you mean you don't have anyone to leave your money to."

"No."

"Don't you have anyone belonging to you."

"No. Except a mother."

"Sure you could leave her a bit of your ready."

"What's ready."

"Ah the ready is money. Wherever you go or whatever you do you've got to have something ready. And it's always money."

"I could leave you some."

"Ah God you don't have to. I wouldn't want a thing. Only maybe to see you again. But sure you'll go on living."

"If you could get me a taxi or something. Have it stop down the road. I'll get back to my rooms."

"God love you now, I couldn't let you go as you are. Your pair of blue eyes in their balls of red. Would you be able to make love to me again. God I fancy you. The fever has brought such colour to your cheeks. If you aren't the most beautiful creature God ever made."

"You mustn't say things like that."

"Why not. God gave me the luck of this night with you. And I want to say it out loud so he can hear it. And this other thing he gave you. I can feel it. Hard as a stone. Would you be able for a frolic. Before the fever kills you."

"I think so."

"Like one of Finn MacCool's Fingers it is."

"What."

"Ah in Cavan there's a row of stone pillars sticking up out of the ground. Near where Myles the Slasher is buried. My landlord here is called Myles but he's no slasher poor man. His wife's the slasher. Ah you boyo. I'll sit up on it. First take me breast in your mouth. Poor lad your lips are hot with the fever. Sure I'm killing you. I'm wild. You've no idea how exciting this is. Been months and months since I had a man."

Winey smell. The mists creep by. Ships sail and hoot. The mail boat arriving from Liverpool. As she tightens tighter round me. Dark headed white bodied. Filling her womb. As she keeps wanting more. Where will I go when I'm well again. Far away from college squares. To walk in tweed with yellow gloves swinging a stick. Part forever from books and rooms, stone halls, and ivied buildings. The black gowns gone. And the carving of fish and frogs. To feel like the midnight homeless. Newsboys wandering empty streets, shouting out Herald and Mail. On their blue ankled bare feet clutching their last papers for sale. By the blind drunk lurching figures reaching out for something to read. I lie here so weary. Yet calmed with sweet ripples of wandering pleasure up my legs. Breda. Nails dig in my neck and scratch down my back and teeth biting blood from my lips. You lie in your linen sheets Fitzdare. I know you do and this could be your head and these your breasts and this I hold your hard pumping twisting little arse. But yours is bigger and you are taller and we may never see each other again. The daylight has come. I'm going to be dead soon. Pulled in a coffin through the streets. By black high prancing horses. Laid in a grave. And while I'm dying. All I have are fears. Golden eyes of Bella. Please look down on me. For years and years and years. Took away your slender fingered hand. You touched me with. Purring laughters broke your lips. You crossed my life on long tanned legs in a Paris sun. Running and running. Hair resting on the wind. Across beaches down dunes. You fly. Our little fellow. Came out of you. Taken from between your legs. He had little hands and cheeks. Ears small like yours. To hear the puffing and whistling trains. Where everywhere across a station I see you. Passing hurried in your dark clothes. Why never did you say. Or tell me I am a father. Of our little son. For both of you to have everything I own. And take you safely to the end of life. Started down in you that night. Where does he walk. That little fellow. Full of fear like me. Stare up at big high faces. All goggle eyed little boy. Shut behind these gates. Which open with a whole flood of tears. I can't stop pouring out of me. Wiped away by this girl of poverty I hardly know.

"O God my lad. What makes you cry."

"I'm dying."

"Ah surely you are."

"And that's so terribly sad."

"Ah not so in the land where everybody does it. The only thing they're good at at all. Come lie now with your head here. A woman's breast is the best place for you feeling like that. What's troubling you."

"I don't know."

"There's something deep is troubling you. The way the tears come welling up. Otherwise dying would be your only worry. I've spent years terrified of my last moments. With the hand of God waiting up there to slap me across the face. And me ready to give back to him a kick in the shins he wouldn't soon forget. One day soon enough my time will come. I won't have energy left to care. Cuddle in close to me. You're like the little boy I had once. In my arms but three short days. My father was a cobbler. Drank us out of hearth and home. When he wasn't doing that he was beating my mother with his fists and us little kids with a razor strop. Or screaming round with the pain of hammering his thumb. There was howling all day long. My uncle kept the farm in Cavan. I was sent out there to fatten up they thought I was going to die. I'd be back and forth to Irishtown. I liked Cavan and the country ways. The little beauties. Tadpoles and toads. Catching eels in the grass. Gave me a fright when I first saw one of them. I was frightened it was a snake. My uncle got me a situation in a hotel away in Kerry. A beautiful young priest on

his holidays stopped me in the hall. I was carrying an armful
of sheets. He said was I behaving myself. Had I been yet to
Lourdes. I said I had not. He says did I hear tell of the talk of
the scandal up the coast. A bunch of Americans in a castle
raising cain. He says to me was I sure I wasn't up there.
Where poor innocents had already been impurely enslaved. I
looked at him. He was as serious as they come. Wanted to
know of my company keeping, whether I was thinking of
getting married or did I think I had a vocation. I said yes,
carrying sheets like I am doing this minute. O he was a
smarmer. He said how is your immortal soul. I said fine
thanks. He asked if my room where I slept was of a hygienic
standard. I laughed in his face. But God it wasn't long before
he was up there hearing my confession as we sat on the side of
the bed. I am telling you my life's story. And maybe you're
dying in my arms."

"I'm feeling a little better thank you."

"It's a woman's breast every time. To put a little comfort in
a man. A woman's dream, you are. I had my dream ruined
soon enough. Dominic was the priest's name. He says to me
he says blessed are the clean of heart, for they shall see God.
Carrying on like your friend Beefy. Giving out the religion
before taking out the other thing. I was daft enough. He said
have you had a holy familiarity with God my child. I said who
do you think you're talking to I said. He said don't be boastful
to me. Imagine. Boastful. Says he, God's divine plan is that
one day you should be a mother, my child. I told him get out
of the room as the housekeeper was coming. That scared him
across to the window. He nearly went through only it was four
floors up. Left him time enough to tell me not to let self
abuse mar my immaculate purity. Or become a ruined temple
as he put it. Well he marred it three days later. Busted the
door of the temple. And a black car comes collects him away.
Leaving me pregnant. And hounded by nuns trying to lynch
me with rosary beads. I was away from there. Went by lane-
ways, fields and carts all the way to Dublin. Sleeping in the

hay at night. Milking a cow I'd catch in the morning. Munching an apple I'd find. Or a turnip out of a field. He put his religion into me. And I said to him to look me up on judgment day and mind not to trip on the last step to heaven. Ah you're cheering up now. That was a smile. For such a sad story. Maybe you're not dying."

"What happened to you in Dublin."

"Ah it was miserable enough. I found I had not a friend in the world. Went from door to door. For any kind of work. But before I left for Dublin at all I went by the castle the priest was telling me about. The scandal was unabated they said, raging within the walls. But the clergy had it watched. The Americans were in there, protected by insurgents. The whole countryside agog with the goings on. With me as scullery maid in a house in Fitzwilliam Square, sure I was destitute. Working seven in the morning till eight at night for twenty seven and six a week. I stole my fare out of the good lady's handbag on the evening I took the boat to England. Ah God I had a little boy. The sweetest little thing. Taken out of my arms. He was gone away from me to a better life I suppose. Missing the love of a mother. They said he was cursed, the son of a priest. I tore at the eyes of the first nun they let near me. Ripped her rosary out of her hands as she was at the bed praying to save my soul. Found a job as a barmaid up the Edgeware Road. Until one day my uncle from Cavan walked in. Nice as you please. Ah poor lad, are you going to sleep on me there."

"No. Listening."

"I couldn't tell a word of this to anyone before. Makes me laugh that I feel at home with a pagan."

"I'm not pagan."

"Ah it doesn't matter. Would you be able for a little breakfast in awhile."

"I think so."

"I'll go down there and use a few of their rashers of bacon and old hen's eggs before they, the two of them, know what hit them."

"What happened when your uncle found you in the Edge-ware Road."

"You're an interested one. The kind as might write a book. He came in, like I said. Did the uncle. Sat down at the bar and took off his cap and scratched his head. He put the cap back on again and wagged his head from side to side. Like a monkey in a zoo. I said to meself what's this now. Have they come from Cavan to string me up on the cross. I served him without a word, he could have been a wall in Jerusalem. He was having pints of cider. I'd put one before him and he would look straight up at the ceiling staring at one spot. Then he would say out loud with everyone looking at him. It's so. Four times and four pints till I couldn't stand it anymore. Staring up at the ceiling and saying, it's so. I came up to him across the bar and I says what's so. And he looks back up at the ceiling again. I left him to it. Every ten minutes till closing time, up at the ceiling he'd look and say it's so. Well he did that five nights running. I lost my appetite and thought I was dying. The bar was full of Irish like himself. Saying ah your man's behaviour is quite correct you know, what's wrong about saying it's so. If it isn't so, someone else can say so, they said. The stupid eegits. Well on the Saturday night he came in again. I said how would you like to see me selling myself down around the Piccadilly I said. I took the pint of cider and threw it in his face. I said there that's so. It was the first laugh I had for months. And that's exactly what I did, I went down to the Piccadilly. I nearly had my face cut open. And just as I was going to try the Bayswater Road instead, a nice gentleman from Pakistan came along. I was living in a filthy basement hovel in Paddington. He bought me presents and I got a good bed sitter. I nearly landed on my feet. Sure I had a radio bought. It was a miracle lying there listening to the music. I can play some of the programs over in my head now. But one morning I woke up and found myself answering questions to the police. Your man was an embezzler. Known in other circles as the Tricky Turk. Starting companies all over London. He was good to me and I didn't worry. If it wasn't for him I'd be ruined forever as a woman. The kindnesses he gave me brought back my self respect. He had an Irish accomplice educated at Clongowes Wood College. To give the whole fraud a style as you might say. He was a grand man was the accomplice, only decent Irishman I ever met. When he laughed the ceiling would shake. He went by the name of Percy. He had another name of Ferdinand. Ah God you're passing off to sleep. I'll get you breakfast. You poor darling, sure the fever is raging in you by the feel of your cheek."

"May I have some water please."

"I'll get you anything you need. I'll slip to make the fires below or there'll be murther. The two should be still asleep. Last Friday I had a little peek of them through a crack in the door. He was up on her. I was gripped with such fascination I couldn't tear my eyes from the sight. There he was going away strong and she has her arms out either side holding open the Evening Mail and reading it over his shoulder. I laughed so loud I was nearly caught. But the two of them have an awful way of leaping out at you in the morning. Snooping and looking for cigarettes they hide from each other around the house. Now don't do a thing if you hear any strange sounds. You poor lad. God love you lying there. Aren't you trembling now. Sure wait. I'll have the breakfast and water to you."

Knobs of vertebrae down her back. Phylum chordata. Two pointed pink tipped little breasts. The white slender legs that went twinkling from her dress. Blue veins behind her knees. She twists up her hair. And pins it high on her head.

"I feel no shame standing in front of you. Would never let the poor old Pakistani see my body. It would give him fits. He'd kick his turban round the room. If you really go for someone. You don't mind what they see."

"I have to relieve myself."

"Ah God now wait a minute I knew that must come. I can't let you out to the water closet. But wait now, a second."

Breda going out the door. From the bare walls of this barren room. A film star's face tucked in the corner of the

233

mirror. And death around me. My chest tight, throat sore. The light painful coming in my eyes. Squeezed the night with her on this bed. Escape away to the watering places. As Beefy came roaring out of the Dublin Quays. Wake one more damp morning. And hope as this door opens it's not my last.

"It's the best I could do. Two pint milk bottles."

Balthazar rising up from the bed. Putting legs down from the torn sheets. With each step all pain. Cool airs blow up on the soles of my feet through the cracks between the boards. Drop backwards out the window to the barrel below and crawl. Two feet. Found dead in bracken and broken glass. Student rusticated. Formerly sent fears of the Asian peril through Donnybrook. Take up the bottle. Can hardly hold my prick. Half hearted swollen. As she watches me wee wee all dark yellow and filling it to the top.

"God you're going to need the other."

"Yes."

"Here we're ready now for the flow. I've got you. Sure where does all of it come from. O God you're getting to the brim again. Holy murther it's going to overflow. Don't mind, let it go on the floor. It'll go below. Won't do the stout a mite of harm. I heard a woman out in Mayo was cured with a vial of the pope's pee. Like everything else you hear you wonder. But not long afterwards you could get a vial of pope's pee all over the West. His Holiness would have to be peeing his heart out, poor old gent, to keep up the supply. They'd sell an edge off a fart of Jesus if he were still around. But you're not to mind, get back to bed. That's the way. Ah you beauty sick as you are. Keep the blanket up snug."

Bottles of pee put on the dresser at the side of the door. Breda nodding a smile stepping out into the hall. Just through a corner of the window, a wet gleaming blue slate roof. Rubbed with leaves of a holly tree so oily green. Fog lifting. Patch of blue. Ridges of cloud. Sea gulls sliding down across the wind. And squawking as they do sitting high on college rooftops. Stepped out into life. Holding this naked kindly little creature. Upon whom I laid my head resting in the night. Felt her arm come across my ear and pressed my face against her breast. Teasing her nipple in my mouth. Suckle there and eat. Near black little tufts of hair. Smell her sweet and musky sweat. How much did I drink from my mother. When she was my milk. To splash away all the growing up fears and terrors. And sent my Bella away. That day under the high skies of France. White dust on lips. That will never go away. Mine so hot and dry. Breda in this black loose dress, a tear across the backside. Sunday best she said.

A creaking in the hallway. The door pushed open. A tray comes in.

"God I hope they are not on to me. She has every grain of sugar counted in the house. It's about time I had two eggs and a bit of bacon once in a blue moon and eat it by myself in the bedroom. Her with the hair up six feet high in curlers. Zombie slave driver. Now. See if that doesn't put life into you. Taken with a bit of sauce."

The tray laid across the bed. Balthazar propped up against the pillow. A brown tea pot. A plate covered with rashers and eggs. Two sausages and halves of two tomatoes. A stack of bread and butter. Warm tinted smells. A big fork curling up at the prongs. A knife with a melted ivory handle and blade from Sheffield.

"I didn't know if you wanted them sunny side up. Don't mind it's hard to find a plate not chipped or cracked. The good delft is locked away."

"This is very kind and it looks awfully good."

"You poor man you can hardly see at all. Here get the hot tea into you first. Sit up a bit more. We'll put this sweater of mine up here round your shoulders. You're not to worry about a thing. You look smashing sitting there in front of your feed."

A creak in the hall. Breda stiffening and turning. The door slowly pushed open. A head in curlers peering round the door.

"What's going on in here. I thought I heard voices and I did."

235

"Don't you come in here."

"What's this."

"It's my sick big brother from home, he arrived feverish in the night with nowhere to stay. He's not well at all. And I'd be pleased if you got your head out of the door."

"I'll do no such thing in me own house. A likely story. A man lying in the bed. I know your tricks. You dirty little slut. You won't be raising cain in this house I can tell you. Come down like that bare faced and go off with two eggs, six back rashers, half a loaf of bread and quarter pound of butter for breakfast. Whose food do you think it is. And you get whoever that is there out of here in a hurry. And I'll thank you to give that tray back to me now. Keep your dirty habits with your girl friend down there on the Quays. The filth of it."

Breda sprang like a cat from the side of the bed. One bounding swift leap across the room. Her two hands came down flashing across the woman's face. And reached up to plunge a grip in the mountain of curlers. Dragging the landlady's head downwards till she fell face forward on the floor. Her outstretched arms grabbing at Breda's ankles as she stepped backwards kicking at the clutching hands.

"Slut. She's trying to kill me, Myles. Myles. Kicking me is it. Scum. Soon deal with you."

Landlady scrabbling up to her feet. Curlers dangling from streaming hair. Large breasts heaving. A red patch at her throat. She rubs her hands off on her bosoms and belly showing through her dress. As she plunges forward grabbing at Breda's white thin shoulders, pushing her back against the dresser. Bottles of pee falling and crashing and breaking on the floor.

"Filth. It's piss. Drown me in piss will you. Slut."

"Pope's piss you hag."

"Vermin. Godless vermin. Time to remedy you for good."

"I'll rip you to shreds you maggoty old bitch."

Sound of tearing garments, a flashing hand cutting across the woman's huge bosom. The landlady's hands clutching downwards at Breda's throat. And sharp little knees kicking up

236

into the fat belly. They clinch together, spin round, and brushing by the bed, plunge crashing to the floor. Breda buried beneath the great grey bulk. Landlady's mousey scattered hair as her fists pound up and down and suddenly reach upwards spreading fingers as she gives out a blood curdling scream of agony.

"I'm bit. O Myles I'm bit. Myles. Get her chained the dirty thing. Myles hurry. Get her off me. The cat. I'm clawed and bit. Get her off me before I'm kilt. Myles."

Feet pounding up stairs and running down a hall. Dark curly haired man, sleeves rolled to his elbows stopping in the doorway. Blinks his eyes. Surveys the scene. Gives a nod of greeting to Balthazar sitting up thin and feverish in the bed. The two figures on the floor panting, grunting, and their clutching hands buried in each other's hair.

"Myles can't you see I'm kilt by this one, get her off."

Myles putting his hand to his chin and rubbing back and forth. He leans left and leans right. He looks down close. And puts out a finger to tap Breda gently on the shoulder.

"Ah now, what have we here. Have we here a little misunderstanding. Sure we have now. Nothing more. Some cross purposes. Nothing more than that sure. Just a little bit of involvement every house has in its good time. Breda now. That's a good girl now. Let's have a calm analysis. Sure the cock's crowed twice now and we all know it's morning, don't we now. Know it's morning. Sure we do. As why wouldn't it be morning if the cock himself knows it and is crowing. And start the day now afresh. Ah let's go easy here now."

"Myles she has the teeth in me."

"Breda now. Enough now."

"Get her hair will you Myles of this fucking tart. And pull her mouth out of me."

"Ah now I'll hear none of that bad language, if you don't mind. Enough Breda is enough now. And why wouldn't it be. Let go a holt there. Sure if it isn't enough the term has no meaning at all. The language would fall of a sudden into disuse. Let's be decent people here now. It would be war

237

everywhere. Without decency. Why wouldn't we be decent now nearly eight o'clock of a Monday morning. Decent starts the week there now. That's the way. Keep bodies away from fighting with the souls."

Myles holding back the arms of Breda, raising her gently to her feet. Hair down over her face. As she flings back her head and shows two burning dark eyes. The landlady rolling over slowly on her side. Vast belly and breasts shifting fatly. Her face turning upwards towards Breda and hissing coming out between her bared gums.

"I've lost me dentures Myles. That creature's lost me dentures. There. Don't step on them Myles, back of you there. Scum. Do your whoring down on the Quays where you belong. In the pestilence. Dirty filthy priest corrupter, I know all about you. Take in scum off the street and it will go out as garbage."

Breda's sharp toed high heeled foot shooting out. Kicking the landlady's upraised arm. Myles pulling her backwards as she twisted and squirmed. The muscles all tight and white in her arms. A bulging pulsing great blue vein down her thin neck. The strange momentary reflex to tip one's trilby one is not wearing to this civil landlord as he entered the bedroom nodding greeting. Henley Regatta will be soon. The Boatrace on the River. The lawns mowed and rolled smooth for Wimbledon. Strawberries and cream under the parasols. And sit in the big high backed chair between the mirrors and curling balustrades of the Ritz. To take late tea on an April afternoon, quietly reading about country life. Till the menu comes with a bottle of champagne and order escargot, steak tartar and Gevrey Chambertin. While this landlady turns slowly over on her gargantuan side, drawing up her knees, her hand holding out her arm.

"Me wrist. O me wrist. It's broke. Broke it she did. I'm crippled from her. Get her away. As the changeless Christ stands before me, I'll take the kitchen knife to her if she's not out of this house before this day is done."

"Ah you're not hurt, wife, you're not hurt at all. Didn't I see it. It was a light tap of the foot."

"Dirty slut with him there in bed. Look at him will you without even a singlet on him. Myles I'm telling you now to get the garda. I'm in the urine. Pope's pee she says is it. They're both to be charged with indecent wounding and sacrilege."

"Sure all wounding is indecent but the gentleman in the bed is minding his own business. Get holt of yourself now wife. Charges are not in order now with his breakfast getting cold in front of him there on the bed."

"Them's my sheets he's lying in."

"Shut up you stupid old cow."

"Speak to me like that will you vermin. I'll have the knife to you."

"Now ladies please. Do away with the discomposure. The gentleman in the bed is red faced with embarrassment. Barging in here like this. Turning his breakfast into a tumult."

"Barging is it. That vixen tore open the door dragged me into the room by the hair and flew at me throat like a wild animal. With the piss everywhere."

"Ah Breda sure meant no harm."

"You say that when your wife lies here kilt before you."

"Nonsense now. A wee little tumble. Sure we can put a lid on this perplexing drama with a good cup of tea."

"Blood, you see the blood Myles. Me dentures wet in the disgusting urine."

"Ah to be sure, to be sure."

"Her teeth did that. Blood."

"Sure blood is no worry if there's plenty more where that came from."

"You listen to me. If she's not out of this house lock stock and barrel, by noon this day. She'll be in the courts and prison where the likes of her belong. Selling herself on the street, showing her wagging backside around this house. Enticement. And him there too in the bed. Who are you."

"Now woman enough. Sure the gentleman in the bed will think we have no manners at all."

"What do I care what he thinks. Rolling in lust with that trollop."

"Now for the sake of peace and didactics. Have a bit of control of your conversation. Can't you hold your tongue and have some charity. Breda take no mind. A most unfortunate discomposure have we here. Best soon forgotten by all. Wouldn't we be the better for it. In God's holy name. We learn by our mistakes. And who hasn't made a mistake in his time. Sure sometimes the whole of our lives are mistakes. Aren't we trying to mend them. To get from day to day. Can't we now in this room take a page out of the book of Matt Talbot, that saintly man."

Myles imploring his eyes up and down to heaven. The wife struggling to her feet. And suddenly charging like a bull. Breda twisting from Myles' arms. As the lowered head of the wife hit Myles himself mid on in the stomach. Driving him backwards into the corner of the room. Breda leaping on the landlady's back.

"I'm being savaged Myles."

"Ah God you've taken the breath out of me, woman."

Breda's hands tearing open the back of the landlady's dress. Foundation apparel somewhere snapped. Or was it the crushing of plastic teeth. As the cupboard door swung open. And divers garments mixed in the mêlée. The landlady turned leading with her left hand and in one clawing sweep tore off Breda's dress. And the latter's small fist came crashing smack between the landlady's eyes. She went backwards landing on the breakfast tray, her ample arse spread across the cold greasy eggs and rashers. The pot of tea knocked over. The spout pouring somewhere. The little leaves drying on the blanket. And Balthazar B hiding a withdrawn head against the bed board under his white long arms and long fingered hands pressed up to his face. The landlady's shout near his ears.

"I'm scalded with the tea."

"Didn't I tell you to put a lid on this perplexing drama, didn't I tell you that woman."

"I'll cut her throat, I'll get this fork into her."

Breda one hand up across her breasts. The other holding out the broken top of a milk bottle. The women crouched. Moving forward and back. Bumping the dresser, bumping the bed. A black cat flitted by through their legs and stopped to shake its paws of pee.

"Sure let them men see your tits, go ahead now Myles there you are, there they are to be seen, you've been wanting to see them scrawny things on her long enough and there they are now. See them. Have a good look."

Myles making a swift sign of the cross. And holding up his two hands in the air. The landlady inching a left foot forward. Breda shaking the jagged glass up and down. Balthazar lowering his fingertips beneath his eyes.

"Come and get it you sow. Just take one step. Just one and I'll rip this glass across your throat."

"Myles. Myles. Just keep your eye on the man in the bed behind me. Frightened she is of the knife. Look at her. She's not so sweet and pretty now is she."

"Ah God in God's holy name now stop. It's gone far enough. Before you're both slaughtered. The man's breakfast is ruined. Sure isn't he trying to hide his eyes from this impudicity. As a professional publican I urge a settlement between the two parties. Now sir, in the bed. What do you suggest to that now. A settlement, what."

"I'm sorry, I'm just awfully ill."

"Did you hear that now. Your man here is awfully ill. Have respect now. For a man ill with his breakfast smashed all over him. It's a sickening enough scene already. Now neither of you make a move. I've had enough of this murther. Just stand as you are. Give us the cutlery woman."

"I'll give her the cutlery. In her guts. I'm dripping blood."

"Sure we all are."

"Myles there you. Don't let her get out the door. You taking her side while I'm wounded."

"Ah no one denies duplicity but there's lots of iodine for everybody. I'm moving around here now to bring a halt to hostilities. While any of us are still alive at all."

Myles pushing past the open cupboard door, moving across and slowly down by the side of the bed. His nervous hands opening and closing. A white fleshline around his throat. Groping and feeling. His eyes on the silent antagonists. My God he's hooked somehow into the bedclothes. Pulling down from me. One clings desperately in fever. And like Beefy. To the hope of sunny tinkling terraces of the London season.

"Excuse me."

"What's that sir."

"You're caught in my covers."

"Ah I beg your pardon, sure I didn't know I was pulling the bedcovers off you. I'm so distracted with the trouble. I'm sorry. It's a confused moment we have here. Sure stay there safe now on the sidelines. It's a bit cramped for manoeuvering. But I'll have this over. Please God. Give me the didactics. And we'll have a suitable settlement here. It's the use of weapons has me bothered. What harm a fingernail or a fist but cutlery and jagged glass. There'll be malicious murther. Women will you listen. Neither of you move now. And we'll see if we can't fit some sense in between you. Sure the panic is over. I can't give the infallible remedy here. But it's time for a temporary composure. We've shook ourselves free of hatred now."

"I'll dig this one's eyes out."

"O God woman hasn't enough goodwill been squandered by this reckless hate."

"Look at her. Take your last look of her. Let that excite you now. As it's been over the weeks. Don't think I'm not wise. And then plaguing me to put your thing in."

"That's improper, wife. I'll not allow that talk. In front of a stranger now. Sure lay down the arms and come to a settlement of the grievances."

242

The two females eye to eye. Weapons held aloft. Breda holding over herself a garment grabbed from the floor. The landlady suddenly quaking. Dropping her knife and pressing her hands up to her face. She turns and rushes out the door with a howling wail. The landlord going to Breda to take the bottle from her hand. She pulls away and flings it crashing through the window.

"Ah that's satisfactory enough. Opens the window a bit. Dry things out. A breath of fresh air coming in will cool it off. Will anyone have a smoke now."

Myles looking from face to face. The packet of Woodbines held out. A cool sweet sea air filling the room. As Breda and Balthazar shook their heads no.

"Do you mind if I have a puff. I'm sorry you've suffered the present interference and interruption. It's the missis' way to get things out of her system."

A crash from downstairs, sound of breaking glass. The watery plop of bottles exploding. Myles putting his head back and perking his ears.

"Ah let the situation run itself out now. Again apologies. I better get down there. From the sound of that last one, it's valuable stock being destroyed. Ah God, there they are. On the floor. Smashed so's you wouldn't know they were teeth at all."

Myles bending and reaching under the cupboard. Picking up the membrane pink and ivory white dentures. Holding them between his hands as he clacked the twisted uppers against the crushed lowers.

"Ah these have had their day. Wouldn't be able to chew the cream off the top of a bottle of milk. And you know, it shows you now. Just to give you folk an example of a case of come uppance. Your woman when she married me had an awful resentment as I was with a full set of me own natural teeth. And she couldn't abide it as she was without real ones of her own. She wasn't satisfied till I went to the dentist down there over the way and had every last one of mine torn out of my head and a set like her own put in. Here are hers

now. Just look at that. Sure you never know where justice will
strike next."

                         To bring
                         A good
                         Laugh
                         Where there
                         Was so much
                         Maim.

20

Four thirty o'clock Monday following Trinity Sunday the summery month of June. After embattled weeks of waiting. A somber Professor Elegant came down the steps of the Examination Hall. Crossing the clean knobs of cobbles to the two figures leaning against the granite stone of the Campanile. The air all perfumed with the new mown green smell of grass. Laughter of students peddling by. Professor Elegant looked at the two sad faces and said he was sorry, the appeal had failed.

All these days of hope. Sitting through the golden afternoons the window open of one's room. To hear the glad carefree voices passing below. The white pop of a tennis ball. Students calling out college gaieties through this week of June. Taken away from a leafy square that I've come to know. The beds of flowers. Daisies twinkling in the sun. And a forgiving Fitzdare. Who said please, please, you must still come. And stay with me in the countryside as we planned.

Rumours all over college. Snickering behind some hands. Little huddles as one goes by. And faces whisper turning to watch as one was past. Breda came riding on a bicycle. I smiled. I saw her from my window looking as she passed each doorway reading up and down the names. Until she came to my entrance and I heard her little knock on the door. She found a situation in Cabra. And wanted to see me now to know I was cured.

Horace brought us tea. And she had a new black coat. And stared around the rooms. And looked in books. And I gave her an armful of movie magazines. And as she sat there was another knock on the door. And in came Miss Fitzdare. Who stood and smiled to say she only stopped a minute. And Breda said she was going now. They each left quickly after the other.

And Breda said ah God how money can make you beautiful, and if you're beautiful already money can make you supreme.

I bought Breda a jewel. Flown from London and sent her by messenger in a blue velvet box. A flawless emerald big as a cashew nut, cut like a heart, on a platinum chain. She wrote a neatly printed two penny postcard in reply.

Thursday
June
Cabra

Dear Balthazar,

No one has ever given me anything like jewels before. Or even anything else I could ever call a present. This is to let you know that I would rather have you than this gem, just in case you didn't know. But as we are of opposite ends of society it wouldn't do to prolong the agony I feel. You didn't have to give me anything. This situation here is worse than my last. And I would as soon be out of here and suffering instead in pagan England.

Always yours if you ever wanted me.

Breda

Beefy disported back and forth. Unmindful he said of worldly shames. I asked of the great deed box stuffed with money. He smiled and said you'd never believe. And he introduced me to a blue black complexioned man in Front Square. Who read silently his Greek and Latin to bring them back to Africa. And had never been known to speak one word in all his time at college.

"A very shy chap is this black fellow. Sat next me for months. Would only grunt or squeak. But we became awfully good friends. And then one day he handed me a bit of paper. On it written a word, sometimes two, sometimes three. One day it would be Sure Footed. Another time The Bug, Fire and Ashes, Mr. Motto, or Dandelion. I always smiled thankfully just thinking poor chap had his brain fried too long by the African sun. And next day I'd meet him grinning and shaking his head up and down. And I'd do the same. Until one day I saw an evening headline, Blue Danube Wins Thirty To One. There it was on my little piece of paper Blue Danube neatly printed out that morning by my friend Zutu. From then on I've put two fivers on every horse he's tipped."

Through these last days. The university cricket match. College races in College Park. Trinity Week Dance. Fitzdare asked me to go. Instead I got drunk and incapable. Hammering on Breda's door in Cabra where they said she'd left the day before. All across college, smiles on all the faces and sorrow on my own. Horace came that last morning as I was packing.

"Sir it's been a privilege and pleasure to be your servant. I just thought I'd let you know. You can't help getting kind of used to someone over the months. And I'm sorry now to see you go."

Two great steamer trunks packed and locked. Standing in the middle of my empty sitting room all addressed to London. A lorry came and four men carried the heavy weights down the dark stone stairs on their backs. And with a suitcase I went to the hotel up on Stephen's Green. Paying my last college bill on the way. Eighteen pounds eight shillings and eleven pence. For servant, milk, gas and electricity consumed, chamber rent, and commons fund. The amount increased by seven and six, a tardy fine due.

To watch as I have before out across these green trees, the distant slated rooftops and reddish chimney pots, to the purple mountains in the morning sun. All the mirroring windows and doorways around the square. And a letter from my trustees.

The Temple,
London, E.C. 4

Dear Mr. B,

Your letter of the twenty third instant to hand in which we are informed of your decision to follow a career in the breeding and racing of horses and further that a suitable property is urgently required for the pursuit of same. We do not at this time wish to set obstacles in your way but it is incumbent upon us to advise you to continue your studies at university. Also, having regard for the long experience necessary to successfully pursue the above occupation we would be remiss in not pointing out the grave and expensive risks in such undertaking. Furthermore, a castle and five thousand acres with deer park, having regard for outlay for stock as well as the high upkeep and considerable wage bill involved to maintain such premises in a good state of repair, could be crippling and therefore we are duty bound to take a position in the matter of advising in the strongest manner against. And we would look forward to a further and different word from you in respect to your plans.

Regarding the incident of your trespass, a settlement has been reached for the payment of two hundred pounds, fifteen shillings and four pence (£200.15. 4) damages and costs and the matter is now at an end.

> Yours faithfully,
> Bother, Writson, Horn,
> Pleader & Hoot

Beefy waved the letter gently in the air. He stood in my long narrow sitting room as ducks from the pond of Stephen's Green flew past the window as they did at ten fifteen every morning.

"My dear boy, but of course you must rear and race horses. You must. What a jolly fine outdoor idea. Newmarket. Good hunting country. Everyone randy for miles around. Eminently sensible. Profoundly suitable. Fitzdare. I mean a great horsewoman. Two of you. Set up together. She's a good mare, would foal a few little ones. Plus, my dear boy, her stallion Dingle. Every time that chappie covers a mare you can spend a fortnight in Nice. Of course my own trustees are being very shirty. You know how one gives one's acquaintances a friendly goose up the arse as they mount or dismount horse or motor. My trustees are vastly and continuously goosing me. Not nice. I am steady in morals, elegant in manners. No peeing in bedroom basins. And still they doubt me."

And the door opened with a knock. A tray and ice bucket of champagne. A dish of tongue and smoked salmon. Put on a low round mahogany table. A silver haired waiter in his long tails. Tearing off the grey gold foil, gently lifting the wire cap away. And with a neat quiet twist, a discreet pop and a little white froth he poured two glasses, bowed and smiled and was gone. Beefy sitting back in checked cap, plus twos, orange tie and yellow shirt.

"One is now launched in life. Pick up a little London town house cheap. Throw in a few silk rugs. Little leather work around the place. With a marble hallway and staircase nothing can ever fault one's dignity. Asprey's nearby where one is able to rush to cure one's pale spirit. Me old granny has taken the news of my being sent down rather amiss. Usual old threats. Cut off the allowance, disinheritance, and the shoving of one's person into residential furnished chambers a shadowy end of Mayfair. Not nice. So much unhappiness and misunderstanding these days. I gave that rough who was pursuing Miss Fitzdare some what for. There was a whistle for a set scrum and the chap elbowed me in the ribs. Finally had to say, please don't do that. Had to settle his hash with a bolo to the haggis. And bundle him into the mud. One knows his type well. Fortune hunter. You mustn't worry. But of course you know you must propose to the precious Fitzdare immediately. Matchmaker Beefy knows the time to strike."

At eleven the phone rang. The taxi was arrived. To go out northwards from Dublin. On the Swords Road through Santry. All my shoes shined by Horace to last for years. A final cold crap done in college bog. A moment remembered by an elm tree, one day passing the playing park. Miss Fitzdare giving of her all on the ladies hockey team. Showing her splendid knees. I was just in time to see her slam the white ball when grossly fouled by a fat creature. And Fitzdare ran on to score a goal, to walk back midfield most unperturbed her hair hanging in a pony tail.

Beefy motored with me to the airdrome, his legs crossed and cap lowered over his eyes. Out past the green fields. Grey gateways to haunted houses back in the trees. He stood out on the balcony of the airport building. I walked with my gladstone bag over the lonely concrete to the waiting grey plane. Beefy said good luck dear boy and take your tea like a man, and see you back for my monster party. I climbed up the little ladder. Beefy blew a kiss goodbye, his hair waving in the breeze. Two engines humming under the wing, its nose pointed up at the sky as we rolled along. I sat mid ships near a tiny window looking out past the strut. And we bumped down the runway and slowly up into the air.

Rising in the western sky. Dublin to the south a grey pincers biting a blue sea. As cows jumped scattering across the grass below. Hedges grow small. And beyond, the fields stretch to the heavens. Turning north now over Drogheda, the coast and Irish Sea. During the awful weeks of waiting. Fitzdare came and said but you jolly well must cheer up. I've come to take you out to Greystones. The train is in twenty minutes from Westland Row. Out by the sea you'll feel so much better. Do come please come with me. It was a Saturday. Together we went down and out my steps. Across by the lawns, out the back gate and along Westland Row. Yes that's where I learned to play harp, piano and harpsicord. She wore a light grey sweater, moss green suit, a purple line making big squares. Her string of pearls and a black silk scarf tied under her chin. A smile and laughing teeth. I think you'll like this uncle too. He's nice. The great train came pounding and throbbing into the lonely red brick station. Two round trip tickets travelling first class. Past the rusty stone of Blackrock between walls bursting with shrubs and flowers. The sorrow of these grey gravel platform stops. Carrying all my sadness further out to Sandycove. Glenageary with pink flowers in the grass. Out of a dark tunnel we came. Our hands touching on the seat. She turned and said please, before you go away to London do come to Fermanagh. And down below the tracks, grey waves of the sea on a wintry looking beach. Past green hills to Greystones. In a summer house under yew trees we sat with her uncle sipping gins and tonics. A whispering wind in that pine scented garden. A gentle rain sometimes falling. There she was. She sits. Her laughter flowing sweet. Eyes always adance. And later walking back to the station we saw nuns standing silent and dark at open windows reading in their black prayer books. She said as we passed the big house and high hedge they're all alone with their hearts and it must be calm and not unhappy. Fitzdare said when she was a little girl on holidays here she borrowed books from that public library. Tied her horse to the railing and he drank water from the trough. There across the road against the wall. My desecrated life. Up here in an airplane through these purest clouds. I fly to see her. From my beery shenanigans. Rocking in the air. Alone on this plane. Bumping over the purple grasses far below. Ponds and rivers. Blue mountains, silver streams. Gone now my rooms in Trinity. The grey expanse of college. And those terribly sad moments walking up my granite steps, haunted on the stone slabs. The afternoon the college authorities handed down their verdict. I stood at the bars of the half landing looking out back at the rugby pitch of College Park. Heard a train puffing over the tracks towards Westland Row. I held myself together. Wrapped in my arms. Climbed quickly up and entered my rooms in case anyone would come and see me there. I never wanted to be sent away. From the bootscrapers at the doorway entrance. From all the knobbly trees in the square. Where the sharp iron spears hold up the chains and one could hang from the cross bars up on the lamp posts. Horace stood by and asked if there was anything he could do. I thanked him and he left, away on his bicycle under his battered hat. I stood at my scullery window. The shattering loneliness makes the spirit well up and grieve. All this now is gone. To leave the green peace and beauty. The lovely walled silence safely away from the hurrying world. Look and see it all for the last time. The morning rescued out of Donnybrook. I lay in the warm waters. In the bath house which squats before the Dining Hall windows in Botany Bay. Under the skylight, within cubicles on the smooth tiled floor. Big hooks for clothes and I dreamt of Fitzdare lying there. All of her long white alabaster body. The tip of my pole poking above the waters. To be in you Fitzdare.

251

Give you joy without pain or heartbreak. One knows of other college sorrows. Of only two weeks ago. A man jumped from his window and splashed his brains on the cobbles of Front Square. A scholar passing in the midnight found him there. When other night times Beefy stole pears out of the Provost's garden. And daytimes the sun did shine in on my life. To let grow up such strange dreams before the verdict was handed down. Of glowing golden cities to the east, waiting for the step of my foot when my moment would come to travel at the close of the academic year. After the last postings of white sheets of paper on the boards. Final meetings of unions and societies. I was glad through the days of Advent and Epiphany. And watched as a scroll was handed to Fitzdare. On a grey cold Wednesday. The awarding of the Diploma for Women in Religious Knowledge. And I could not sleep that night and awoke early in the chill for my one and only religious moment. I washed staring out across the empty square. With combed wet hair and sniffling nose I hurried along the gleaming street. Cold out and cold within. Briskly on frigid feet in damp socks to chapel. Eight thirty o'clock. Hoping for some little warmth from one's gown. Black light fabric sweeping aside with the breeze of walking. All the tiny warmths escape. The chapel smelling of its timber. The engines tremble this airplane. Make these moments always keep. Take them with me wherever I go. As I did that morning to hear the voices singing. The cheeks of Beefy's face puffed in song. After a night of sin. He goes all better all beautiful. About his ways. Under the stained glass eyes of God up there at the end of the chapel. And behind him College Street, a yeast company, and wandering citizens. God has such big shoulders and long flowing white hair. Please look down on me now. Dry away the helpless sips I took of friendly impurity. Make me good and worthy of Fitzdare. I seem so unclean. Only one charge put down for baths on my college account. The curtain fallen. On university years. Ireland down below. Where waits Fitzdare. Able to recite all Chordate characteristics. A ventral heart. Blood contained in vessels. And saucy minded, all I can

252

recall is the tail extended beyond the anus. For which I would listen for her lips to say. Anus. She said it bravely and abrupt. Her cheeks slightly coloured. In all my zoological knowledge anus always stood four letters alight on the wasteland blank of my mind. O Balthazar it's so easy to remember. A dorsal hollow nerve cord. In Amphipoda, the carapace is absent, the eyes are sessile and the uropods styliform. And upon that academic instant I struck out. We sat across our afternoon coffee in the stained glass no smoking room up Grafton Street. I said come to Paris. Her face went beet red. I panicked holding my hand over my heart, fingers perusing the embroidery of my linen hanky. I stumbled on in a broken hoarse voice unable to stop. We could go spooking around my father's country house all shuttered up for years. Inside the big brooding walls and iron gate. Or go to the races at Chantilly. Separate suites at the Raphael. She looked down at her folded fingers. And said yes, she'd come anywhere with me. I sat stunned in this long silence. Our bodies together between the sheets. Tears came hopelessly carefree out my eyes. I had to turn my face away. And found all the afternoon dowagers staring. I got up and hurried out. My God what's wrong with me. So afeared and frightened by her courage. To ask her come away with me. And she says yes. I told Beefy. He said my God marry her before you get corrupted in evil ways. Take her not to Paris but in marriage, dear boy. She will look splendid in mountain climbing gear. Two of you. Out there on the crags, fussing over outcroppings. Sighing in ravines. Dear boy the two of you have so much to learn. The foldings of the mountains. Follow her up the icy peaks and not me into hell. Each banging with your little hammer. And down there I see some rolling mountains. The pilot shouts out his little open door. Descending now. Fasten your seat belt please. Belfast is on the right. Loughs lie in a green flat gleam. Ragged coast. He says there is the River Lagan. Can't believe Fitzdare will be there. Just waiting. As Belfast sits in a valley, faint smoke hovering above. Light green the world once was. We go lower and lower now. To turn fluttering in over the rolling fields. Wind whistling by windows. Closer and closer. Farms and barns. Tilled brown acres and yellow ones. The hedgerows pass. The wet runway. Hares scattering across the grass. The bumping wheels. And one sits back again. Low cream coloured buildings. Like dead sun and sand. A summer sea so many years ago sucked in from beneath the soles of my feet. Waves washed around my ankles, my young skin white and blue. And once when nannie lay in foam, the sea washed up between her legs. I said is that hair there, like sea weed and she rolled over on her face. And the water came up around my knees. Now past all those years, from the summers sprang blond autumn trees. As this aircraft stops. And the pilot smiles. A little bumpy coming in but we're safely here.

Balthazar in rust brown tweed suit. His walking stick and yellow gloves. Crossing towards the barracks buildings. Flat roofed on this flat land. Bereft and lonely. A soft mist. And no one here. Only the hares out on the flying field swivelling their ears as the plane taxied past. And clouds of starlings and flocks of plover. The endless green flat countryside beyond.

A little slope of lawn. In the center a ring of boulders. The flag of Britain flying there. O God she didn't come. Found out all about my saucy escapade. Call the pilot back. I want to leave at once. Take my bag to customs first. Through this door. Along this corridor. Customs man in blue, gold rings round his sleeves. This your only luggage sir. Are you out of that plane. Yes. On holiday. Yes. His smile and mark of chalk. And I go out these doors. And may have to come back through again.

Balthazar B passing out to this waiting room. His cane and his bag. Through these sprawling huts. Look here look there. And no Fitzdare. Maybe wait atop these steps. The rough may have lured her away. Let her wipe her feet in his hair. Now I'll go back in again. Eat this great bowl of emptiness. And suddenly turn. So much despair on my face. And see standing there. Watching me. Fitzdare. Like a whole blazing sun in this land so solemn, silent and bare.

A chauffeur in leather leggins, grey uniform and grey peaked cap. Took Balthazar's bag. And held open a door into this black leather topped limousine. An ancient long black car. Fitzdare in a pair of rubber boots. And a zipped up green jacket with folds of maps sticking from the pockets. Her teeth so white and lips so lively red.

"Gosh you've come. I just had to watch you. Looking so lost and strange. I saw you walking from the plane. I apologise for this great old crock of car. But it does get one there. I don't know what to say. Just to see you sitting here. O push those over. My weekly errands in Belfast. Will you have a grape."

"Thank you."

"So funny, you stepping out of that one little plane. Hello."

"Hello."

"I just want to say hello again. I hope you're not too hungry. We've fifty miles to drive. Terence will take us the quickest way. I've been trying to figure one on all my maps but give up. I've got a pocket full of walnuts. Have one."

Narrow empty winding roads. Horses and tractors cutting and raking meadows. White walled farms. Fields cocked with hay. Neat thatched roofs. The muck and mud at fence gates. Churns of milk waiting at the end of lanes. Wheels whirring on the black wet gleaming surface. Fitzdare said through there you can see Lough Neagh. Down across the sodden fields and scrubby trees a grey water haunted and lonely out to the horizon.

"I call it the eely eerie pond. Full of eels. There is an island where there are dangerous rabbits. They fought off the rats. And now the rabbits are so fierce they'll attack and bite a man. The flies are awful in summer. Keeps the shores very lonely. Lot of funny names to our towns. Tanderagee and Ballygawley. O dear I'm sure I sound enthralling as a guide."

Through little towns and villages. Castle ruins silhouetted on the hills. She gives each its name. I ride with an erection. One's hopefully imposing perpendicular. All my own. To cross into County Fermanagh just beyond Fivemiletown.

255

Fitzdare with a signal ability to crack her walnuts. She feeds
the meat to me. From the cool palm of her hand. Will confront her father. I've designs on your daughter dad. In the
musty upholstery smell of this car. As now Miss Fitzdare sits
up. And suddenly shy.

"It's only along here now beyond this bend. Up there on
that hill there's a sort of table land where one can get a
marvellous gallop in the wind."

A wall, stones sleeping all stacked up. Beech trees, their
smooth grey silver rising high in the sky. A white gate hanging
broken from an upper hinge. Bumping over a pot holed drive.
An umbrella of rhododendrons. Over a little bridge and
stream. The road turning through meadows and another
wood, haunted and strangled in vines. Chauffeur slowing to
an open gate. The wheels making a ringing noise bumping
over the rungs of a cattle trap. Parkland and grasses. Now
between two tall stone pillars mossy and green with ivy leaves
into a cobble stone courtyard. Fitzdare so still and silent.

The grey heavens opening to a stretch of blue. The sun shot
out. Rolling and spilling over lawns aflood with green. And a
rambling great slate roofed house. Could see a porch across
the front held up under high granite pillars. Gleaming tall
windows. Ivy covered grey blocks of stone. Chimneys and
chimney pots. And blue lake water sprawling in the distance,
against hills turning gold and purple.

"We're here. Everyone's going to mind I brought you in
the back door. We've got to get you boots. There's Dingle.
See his head sticking out of that stall. Show you him later.
I've put you in a room where you can see the lough."

Miss Fitzdare pushing open a brown door. Slamming closed
behind us. Cold paving stones. A chill air. Doors, halls and
kitchens. Past a shadowy scullery. A grey haired woman turning to look up from her table stacked with greens as we passed
by. Who smiled to Fitzdare's smile. A boy with his hair
plastered down and parted in the middle. In a tight grey coat,
his blue wrists and wrinkled nearly white collar. Carrying
Balthazar's bag. He said yes miss and no miss and I don't

256

know about that, miss. A flush of colour on Fitzdare's cheeks. Walking fast and certain on her way.

Through this rambling house. A high long corridor. A print of Trinity Dublin. And out now into a great front hall. Gilded mirrors. A wide staircase. And high up a round skylight. Yellow flowers on the mantels. Portraits watching down. Light blue carpet and marble balustrade up by these wide gentle white stone stairs. Just as Beefy said. Nothing can ever fault one's dignity. Can't believe I'm here. Just behind her. Seems so strange and far away. As she plods in her boots. Following this little boy. Who now lags behind. Haven't seen to that yet, miss. I'll be walking him about four miss. And he gives a little bow of the head and leaves us in this spacious room. A fire blazing. Great sills of the windows. And seats piled high with golden pillows.

"I hope you're going to be comfortable. I've been airing it out for three days. You're west and south. In the morning it's quite magic when the sun is shining on the hills and lake. This was my mother's room. Hope you won't mind the canopied bed. If there's anything you need. Just push the button there. Someone but not a footman will come. You laugh but it really works and someone comes. I know what you're thinking, well you look just as strange standing there to me as I must look to you. Neither one of us has hardly said a word."

"It's terribly beautiful. I'm rather speechless."

"Tea will be in twenty minutes. And your bath and dressing room's through there. Just come down. Whenever you're ready. Dear me. Can I just say. I'm so awfully glad you're here. I thought of it so much. And now you are. I'm at such a loss. Look at me. In my gum boots."

Miss Fitzdare a curl of her black hair fallen over her brow. Cool white face I could gather up in my hands and press my lips on her eyes. Grab her shoulders. Pull her down with me on the crimson counterpane. Amid these faint white white walls with drawings of little inky flowers. As she smiles and steps away out the door. To leave me now. And stare out the

257

window. A table under a folded fading awning. The grass so smooth and rolling down to the water's edge. Across a metallic glimmering grey to low pastures and higher hills beyond. Dreamt of her sitting somewhere out there so many times. That a breeze would come and flutter the page of her book as she read. Through the summer afternoons. And she would close it then, to look up at the sky. When life stops in the silence. With only racing buzzing bees and dancing white butterflies. A bird sings. Reach up to put a hand to some dream you kept awake. Now you take it like a red ripe apple and polish quietly up and down one's sleeve. Sent away from college. The sadness is I've left her there. With all the arthropoda. And phylums of polyzoa. And o God the subclass of crossopterygii. As this sky goes so quickly grey. Getting on for rain. A portrait there. Her mother. An elegant face of black hair and blue eyes. Will watch me pull on my knickerbockers. I so specially brought with my heather coloured stockings. To cut at least a sporting figure. Look everywhere here for signs of her. There she sits in this tiny photograph on a donkey and over here on a horse. Row of little leather books. The History of Armagh. My bath and dressing room. Oatmeal soap in this flower covered dish. Soft clear water runs and fills the bowl. Brush my hair. Take lint off the coat. Stocking seams straight. Put on my walking shoes. Cold crystal delicious water to drink. Goes down my throat and washes the soul. Seagulls over the lough. Great slow flapping wings of a heron. The rarest Fitzdare grew up out of this land. On the blackberries and cabbage. And behind those trees, her horses graze. Must rub a little across the toes. Uncle Edouard said a gentleman's shoes should never carry too much shine.

Balthazar B went down the hall. Past the double doors of all these rooms. By portraits of ancestors and stallions held by grooms. Under the great high skylight and step by step down so silently. She brought me in the back door. Means she likes me. Touch these porcelain and alabaster urns. Six candles in the gleaming glass octagonal chandelier. She sat all those months, blue stockinged legs twisted on the stool as she wrote out labels for her collection of marine and fresh water fauna. And now to see Fitzdare here. In all this palace splendour. Where does she sleep. And bathe and take off her clothes. Her back would be white. Lay my hands on her shoulder blades. Must pause. Let my swollen perpendicular die at the bottom of these stairs. So randy in the countryside. And by my watch it's time for tea.

From a soft green velvet sofa chair Miss Fitzdare's father stood up and smiled. Putting out his biggish hand to softly shake mine. His reddish hair, and neat tweed coat. Grey flannel trousers pointing out over thick brown well repaired shoes. A tie with twin white stripes. And freckles on his tan hands. Shorter than Fitzdare. Of a kindly saddish fleshy face. A gold watch chain across his waistcoat. Takes out a great round clock. We all want to know the time.

"Should be tea any moment now. Did you have a pleasant trip."

"Yes thank you."

"Do you like our sad green countryside."

"Yes, it's very beautiful."

"Things look good this time of year. Not so pleasant in the winter. You could have come via Dundalk on the train, a long but rewarding journey. Anyway you got here and I must apologise for my daughter bringing you in the back door."

"That's alright."

"She doesn't mean to be rude. Boodles scolds her the way she plods round the house in gum boots. Kicking off the mud. Not so funny if one has to do the cleaning. How is dear old Trinity."

"Fine."

"I lived up top there in Number Five, overlooking the Bank of Ireland. Used to be the old parliament. And so did my father and grandfather. When the horse cabs went bumping over the cobbles in College Green. Had to rough it then. Suppose things have changed."

"No sir, they haven't."

"Ah well a lot of other things have. Nothing stands still

these days. You young people like to rush things along. Natural enough. Get these old stogies out of the way. Do you play billiards."

"Not quite sir."

"Well perhaps you'd like to have a try. I'm sure Elizabeth has a lot of things for you to do. But when one is so far away from the bustle it's hard to get anyone to come over of an evening. People hate to stir. Do you shoot."

"Well not really."

"Ha ha, you mustn't get alarmed. I know how it feels when sporty people start their subtle examinations. But you do look very fit for the field. That's always nine tenths the battle. It's all mostly for the fresh air. Elizabeth's out back there. She has a steeplechaser with a lame hoof. Jumping a bit of wretched wire. Rather a worry for her poor girl. She very much loves and lives for her horses. And her pappy foots the bill. Never mind. It gets up some good mushrooms in the fields. Here's tea. Boodles, port tonight, please. Ah lots of Mary's scones I see. And her gooseberry jam. Thank you."

"Very good sir."

"Mr. B here is with us. At Trinity with Elizabeth."

"Welcome sir."

"Thank you."

"Boodles tell Elizabeth in the yard we're waiting. Just give her a shout."

Fitzdare came through the great wide door, wiping her hands across her tweed skirt. Neat little laced walking shoes on her feet. She smiles at us both and sits on the thick woolly rug before the hearth. Her face makes purring laughter float through me. Curling back her legs under her bottom. Never without her string of pearls. To watch her eat. And sip tea, cup and saucer neatly in hand. Put gooseberry jam between her lips. And chew. Where I would go and taste it there. Just to be that jam. Between her radiant teeth. My legs crossed here on the soft cushions of this chair. In the warmth of eiderdown. A whole moment beyond belief. A daughter and her father. Out the wide windows the blossoms and

260

blooms and over the velvet grass to the haunted dark vines weaving up through the trees. Whither goest that Beefy who said I should marry her. Take her as a wife. Climb up on your mare dear boy. Spend these splendid years ahead. Cantering over the table lands. Where westward all the dark hills lie out upon the blue. And sun goldened bracken between the boggy sharp pointed clumps of grass. How can I ever say, just to squeak out the words. I want to marry you. Take you as a beautiful wife as you will take me with all my hopeless sins. Caught in Donnybrook gardens. Trapped in college rooms. Watching helpless during turmoils crushing a landlady's false teeth. Another throbbing painful erection now. Untrained to keep its place. Gets up to antics in the country. All that green. As Uncle Edouard said a great vintage my boy you will feel between the legs. O God Fitzdare. Your knees. The muscle rising in your calf. You prostrate me. You do. All your black and flowing celtic hair.

The rooster cries. The sun shone on the purple hills just as she said it would in the morning. And last night we dined in candle light in a great long columned room. With high arched cathedral ceilings. Fitzdare in a long blue flowing dress. Diamonds sparkling on her bosom. I struggled with my black bow tie. Pounding my fist blue on the dressing table. Lost my studs and blackened my cuff. When desperately I wanted to look so nice. Saw all her stables. Her thin leathery faced jodhpured trainer. The boy brushing down the sleek sides of Dingle. And jumping like a cat as a hoof slammed out and splintered the stall. In my sudden fear I shied back and nearly ran. And again gathering up a sporting bravery I tip toed close. To this strange dark stallion with his red glinting eyes. Weaving his head back and forth beyond the bars. And nibbling with his lips and teeth at Fitzdare's hand as I nearly reached up to pull her arm away. And saw this stallion's organ from where I stood grow huge and stiffen long under his belly and my God so did mine and I trembled faint hearted that she might ever see and know the saucy racy thing happening there. And then to whisper a little prayer, please Miss Fitz-

261

dare don't tomorrow ask me to get up on a horse. With visions through the night of those hooves smashing down the great front door. And comes that Dingle pounding up the marble stairs and galloping wildly along the hall to break not through my door but come smashing out and down the whole wall of the room which fell in on me. And so encouraged, all the other horses came too. The whole giant pounding steaming lot of them. Pouring out across the rugs, hooves sliding on the floors. I woke shouting with my fists knotted and held high, grabbing at the halters and reins lashing everywhere. Saying they're coming they're coming right through the wall. Crashing out the stones. Making a storm on this moonlit night. With the heavens passing fast. And there standing over me. A lantern held in his hand. In tasseled night cap and long flowing gown, was Boodle. I said please where am I, turn on the light and he said I'm sorry the electricity is off for the night. And I remembered now. Flying in a plane through the clouds to come here and visit with Fitzdare. Neatly packed and spruce with my gladstone bag. And I said I'm afraid I had a nightmare. Horses came pounding through there out of that wall. And Boodles who slept in a room above said, here, this will help you sleep. I bolted back a whisky. And hoarsely said goodnight, wrapped tight in the blue silk warmth of my pyjamas and head buried in pillows, neck tucked up safely in linen sheet. To see the dawn at the window and thank God that now it's morning. Awake at cock crow. Hear footsteps pass down the hall. Soft rug on my bare feet. And slap water on my face. Look out a window, see if the world is still here just as it was last night. I walk down the stairs, and across the great hall. Lift up the latches. Pull back the heavy door. The air smells young and free. Blanket of sparkling dew out across the grass. And there. Caught in the morning sun. She goes. Galloping. Her hair flying from her head as Dingle's flows out from his mane. A gleaming black body rippling of muscle. Great long legs stretching out on the emerald turf. Please Elizabeth. Please Fitzdare. I feel for the time being a nervous wreck.

Balthazar B stepped across the gravel and up on the grass. Fitzdare gone now behind the trees and hear the hooves pounding as she turns and comes back racing along the lake. Crouching forward her head turned a little aside. Clods of earth thrown in the air. Closer and closer. The sound bigger and bigger coming up under me. As she reins up to the wall. Walk to her across this croquet lawn. And not show any fear. Nor run outright if she comes up close. Feel so utterly wrong now in my plus twos. Just a sham shy of beasts. With the world so fresh and sunny. Eight o'clock on this morn.

Miss Fitzdare her back straight and face asmile. A flowing pink bandana at her neck, black jacket, boots and hunting hat. See Dingle still charging across my room last night leading all the other quadrupeds. Scattering my cuff links. Sending me clutching up the wall. As he moves close upon me now. This seventeen hands of horse. Towering living pedestal for Fitzdare.

"My you're up already."

"Yes."

"Will you come a ride."

"Well really I'd rather just watch you. The splendid speed."

"Dingle's superbly trim. He's in excellent form. Aren't you Dingle, in excellent form. Specially when the going's firm. You big rascal. Say good morning to Balthazar."

"O no, he needn't do that."

"O you mustn't run. Dingle won't hurt you."

"O my God, hold him back Miss Fitzdare."

"O you awful man calling me Miss Fitzdare."

"I'm just a little shy of horses this morning. Elizabeth."

"Please, Lizzie."

"Lizzie."

"I don't really like the name. But at least it's friendly. Isn't that so Dingle. You wouldn't hurt Balthazar down there now would you. No you wouldn't. He lashes out now and again when he gets nerves. You just mustn't get in close behind him. And he only makes believe he bites."

"I see."

263

"Let's saddle you up a horse. Have you had breakfast."

"Not yet."

"Come on then. I have a good old hunter. We'll both have roaring appetites."

"I'm not really a riding man. Perhaps I should sit this one out. Here on the wall."

"Daisy's so mild she'll pick you up when you fall off."

"Well that would be awfully nice. Of Daisy. But."

"Yes come on. I'll take you up on the hills and then we'll have a marvellous breakfast."

Balthazar B walked back across the lawns by the gleaming windows of the house. In there we dined last night. Right in that noble room. Fitzdare's father poured out the port. All dark and splendid. Flowing down the crystal. An eternal sweetness buried deep in the somber ruby red. Under the antlers high up round the walls in the billiard room. Miss Fitzdare gave out with her purring laughter. As I tried so desperately to carom the balls. Giving great attention to chalking my cue. Meaning watch out for my next shot chaps. Send these spheres of elephant tusks dancing a rumba along the cushions. With full massé. But at last to be left deliberating lengthily. Lip pursing and the lot. And all to no avail. As both Fitzdares were gracious and each of unnerving calibre. Reach then for my glass and triumph at quaffing port.

A grey haired ancient groom helped Balthazar B into the saddle. Leading him by the bridle past the stable door. Ah you're right now sir, ready for the St. Leger. With droopy walk and two hanging heads, horse and man crossed out from the courtyard and clip clopped down the farm road and left through an opening into the fields. Fitzdare waiting there. Laughing gay encouragement and greeting. To lead them along a cypress avenue and steeply up a rocky path from these bottom fields climbing to the table land. This great wide animal beneath me. Female. A wafting breeze could bring a signal to a male. O my Lord, Dingle may try and jump her. Bite my ass right out of the saddle. Like last night. I wouldn't stand a chance.

264

Fitzdare racing ahead into the morning sunlight. Soft summer breeze blowing across the hills. And up at last now to see the great arching strides of Dingle stretching over the hard packed grass. Rising up like a great invincible ghost over walls without a change of stride. As I dismounted to go through the gates. Pulling and tugging to get back up on Daisy again. Until she leaned suddenly down to gobble up some succulent herb and I slid forward and spun clinging round her neck to land spreadeagled on the moist ground.

The curlews whistling and kestrels hovering against the wind. As I came walking back. To sit with her at the open breakfast room windows, a bow front jutting out in the rays of sun. A great painting along the wall "Coming Together Of The Meet By The Shores Of The Lough." Spotted leaping hounds and red coated gentlemen on long bodied horses. The sideboard of hot plates and silverware. Sausages, tomatoes, bacon and butters. Hen's eggs and gull's eggs, syrups and creams. Toast and urns of steaming tea and coffee. With most memorable and delectable of all. Gooseberry jam.

"I thought you did awfully well, I really did. A lot of people are shy of horses. I shouldn't have been mean and made you ride."

"Going up the hill was fine. But I got used to leaning forward so that when she leaned forward to eat the grass it turned awkward."

And we went off through the mornings and wandered along the lake. Strolling past a field of mares and foals. Another of milk cows. She was so good to me. Not to ask that I should ride again. We watched a blackbird wiping its orange beak on a green bronzed apple branch. All these avian creatures looking so proud sitting in the trees. And I said that really and most honestly I would tell the truth that I was a picnic man. To proceed so bravely now. With this wicker basket of picnic things. Build Fitzdare a fire. Pass her chunks of cucumber or biscuits sweet with chocolate specks. I could be a cave man too if only a cave could be found somewhere nice.

"Balthazar."

"What."

"O I just wanted to say your name."

"O."

"I like it. And also just today you know I'm so happy that you're here. Took all my courage to ask you to come. I wanted you to meet my father. He's nice isn't he."

"Yes. He's very nice."

"A lonely man. I don't think he's ever got over losing my mother. And it's so many years ago. I had a little brother too. He was drowned with his nannie in a boat out on the lough. Just a few yards from shore. Daddy has his two spinster sisters who come to visit. They spend nearly all their time weaving and making jam. The gooseberry you like. My skirt's their cloth. Daddy should have married again. I sometimes wish he did. At twelve one still needs a mother. Some nice woman. He has friends who come to shoot. But he's lost interest now. I suppose that this, this whole place will have to go. The ruined castle there on the little island. The land reeks with history. I often think what sorrows passed here. Long before one's own."

Gulls wheeling by under the greying heavens. And the far away moaning of a cow. The distant web of stone walls making little fields on the hill sides dotted with specks of sheep. The mountaintops purple. And east the sky a rusty tint. As Balthazar B stood, a hogskin gloved hand holding tightly the picnic basket and turning to see two blue eyes made bluer by the sky. The splendid laughing voice.

"O gosh come on, I'll race you to that dead tree."

Miss Fitzdare ran. In her strange and horsey way. Feet flying out to her sides. The thick green tweed she wore with all the tiny little bits of colour. The long coat belted round the middle with its big square pleated pockets. A golden scarf at her throat and her hair flying free. We stopped by a little stretch of sand by the lough shore. And I went finding stones and built a fireplace while Fitzdare gathered sticks and brush. I said watch it will only take me one match. And it took eighteen. To start the flames. She lay along her side in the

266

thick clumps of grass contemplating me. As I enacted so urgently one little catastrophe after another. Till finally I managed a stone slab bridged over the flames and put the sausages roasting there. She smiled and was pleased.

"They're really cooking aren't they. I think you're wonderful."

The tiny kettle placed to boil. A pot of tea was served. Light yellow little cups and saucers. Stirred with silver spoons. We were covered in great linen napkins, swallowing down slices of quince and orange chunks of Leicester cheese. Patches of light in the southern sky. Westwards there must sink a redless sun. And I remembered a strange moment which seems so long ago. In the chemistry laboratory. Fitzdare working at a titration. Turning the glass stirrer in her solution. As she does now the spoon in her tea. And I watched spellbound as she took a spatulate of sulfur and melted it on an iron ladle over her bunsen flame. While I stood blank minded and bemused with my own haphazard group of substances, staring at her beauty and I nearly died when I thought she glanced and winked at me.

The afternoon passing away. Adrift. As the tiny tints of darknesses push west out of the east. We sit on these boggy bunches of grass. With the warm mellow taste of tea. Chewing chunks of cucumber and these brown little spicy meats. Moved back from the fire's exploding stones in the heat. Watching the fading glow. Two great black ravens. Feather fingers of their wings squawking as they squeezed down against the air and passed overhead. To dive and sideslip over the water and disappear into a meadow ringed with trees. Their low deep throated calls. And Miss Fitzdare lies staring at me as my eyes turn to hers.

"Balthazar."

"Yes."

"Would you marry me."

She sits propped up on her elbows near enough to touch her hand. And smells all heathery and milky fresh. As I smell of smoke and burning sausage fat. Daisy flowers peeking white and yellow from the grass. I race a thousand miles away. Over oceans and up through glaciered valleys sliding on the ice, shouting out questions against the snowy mountains and cold blue sky. Give me back an answer. From all the centuries of thinking. And a voice whispers, my dear man the world was never different and all hearts love the same. And now I can't get my mouth to speak.

"I'm sorry, I shouldn't have asked you that. I guess it's taken you very much by surprise. And I suppose there's someone else in your life."

"No. There isn't anyone else."

"Please. I didn't mean to say what I did, I just blurted it out, I don't know why. I was saying it before I knew what I was saying. And I don't mean to pry."

"And you want to take it back."

"No not really I don't."

A blade of grass squashing green, rubbed back and forth between Fitzdare's fingers. Little splashing waves falling against the shore. To come very close to her. Put my arm out under her shoulders. For the first time. Waited all these months. I kiss her. Lips stretched hard across her teeth. Her hesitating hand on the back of my neck. My nose goes buried under her hair. Nudging against a soft tender lobe of ear with nothing I can say. Unbuckle her belt, open her coat, four horn buttons undone and feel her breasts under lamb's wool. Nipples hardening there. The muscles of her arms go soft. And now her mouth under my lips. Opens tasting sweet. Despite the scandal which raged through college. Would you marry me she said. Under a deep deep blue above. Where stars come out amany across a great hushed canopy. When wisps of wind veer in off the lough. Be a little family here. Away from all the rest of the world. Singled out and now embrace this strange Fitzdare. Far from the grasping hands of the ruffian. Who could threaten me with bloody noses and black eyes. And now she will marry me. Both of us so lonely to say come please. Just the one of you to be with the one of me. Not through duty or because you must. But come because

268

there is a breeze sprinkled with butterflies. And something in your heart says something to mine that neither can hear. But we know we must. We must. Stay close together. While cattle go mooing by. O God Fitzdare. My pole is shivering stiff between my legs. And my breath won't stay still. How can I tell you now. O God as the sperm spurts down my leg. A pearly liquid my Bella once held in her hand. And sown in her made a son. Wrap me tightly please as I hold you and softly cry. To tell you this. Love may be all the things you never know. As who sits beneath those slanting beams of sun. With little hammers under the rainbows counting crocks of gold. That's why I softly cry. And tell you. I have a son. I've not been married but I want you to know. It was with a woman when I was very young. And will it mean you don't want me now. And her arms squeezed me tight. She said. Nothing you say could make a difference but how sad for you. How very very sad. That it makes me cry too. Strange anyone would ever think you fast. And I know you're not. In spite of all the stories one can't help hearing at college. I want to say something to you now. That I'm happy you told me this. And I only want to hold you. And say your name. Balthazar.

A fish jumped and splashed out on the silvered water. In all the silence around us here. Lying tightly held in each other's arms. The fire glows out its last heat. A curlew goes high whistling from its long curved beak. Over evening deeps. Sleeping. A little boy. Some little fellow. His heart a brother's heart. Gone away too.

Where
Flowers
Live.

21

The days gently flew. Like all the birds passing over the rolling low hills and island dotted loughs of Fermanagh. When rain wet Miss Fitzdare's hair and made little white holly blossoms of moisture there.

On that picnic afternoon we kissed as we walked and walked and kissed again. Up and down meadows to go deep among the haunted trees. To see the gravestones of her mother and little brother. And nannie of nine years faithful service. Under thick yew branches. Where the chiseled words said their names. And here on this hillock and small walled clearing in the wood, her father would be buried. And if never she married she might rest too.

That evening we stood out under the sky when dinner port and billiards were done. A moonlight on the lough. And Miss Fitzdare cupped her hands to her mouth and blew hoots. Which came back answered by owls for miles around. And I watched her go down a candle lit hall, waving back and blowing kisses as I stood at my door. Would she ever tell me where she lived. In all this big house. What turning would I take in the night. In what wing and up what stair would I find her. Which door to open. And step in.

I lay awake for hours. Had brushed my teeth. Looked in the mirror. To see what love had done. It made my eyeballs the purest white. And when we walked by a clear little brook. She reached down and pulled up the green leaves, the trailing roots and stems of watercress. And gave me eat from her hand. As she ate. Without fear of tiny specks of dead leaves or bark debris.

I fell at last to sleep. Passing in a dream into a college dance. At the door a chaperoning member of the faculty asked me where I was going. I said to the college hop. He said are you a member of this university. I was shattered, taken aback and angered by this aspersion. I grabbed him by his black gown. Gathering the cloth tightly in my fist and slamming him back against the wall. He was such an absolutely tiny person, no bigger than a rather small midget. And I was immensely much encouraged. To wrap him up in his great long scarf around his neck and juggle him nicely in my hand. But I might break his very white thin little wrists. And that wouldn't do. I was so amazed when he remained calm. Can't even scare people in dreams. And so I put my fingers in his collar and turned my knuckles in against his throat. Still this professor remained unflappable. And indeed was uppish. So I clouted him a medium blow on the cheek. Really only a finger flick. For the first time a little fear came into his eyes. I was so pleased. I said if you breathe a word of this to anyone and I am sent down from this university I will come back and kill you. By a resounding blow by truncheon across the mandible. And if you're not here I will search you out over the ends of the earth. Including the tourist depths of Killarney. And jump upon you from the dark. I left him there quite a bit disturbed. And I proceeded back from the dance to my college rooms. I had a great white throne for a crapper with frilly tassels about the seat. And a bath steaming with scents shielded with a Chinese lacquered screen. Horace stood in red raiment and white leather gaitors sprinkling perfumed salts from a crystal ladle and then suddenly there stood someone in the rising steam. Seemed a father of some girl I had wronged. Then the figure turned white and faded again till the wronged daughter was standing there. Where her father stood. And the whole wall was moving. And I was sure now I was awake and sitting up. In the streaming moonlight. And there God help me was Fitzdare. Coming right out of the wall. And said across the darkness as I reared in fear. It's me. And that was before I knew it was anything at all. And the wall behind her closed again. And tip toeing now to turn the key and lock my door. Returning smiling to my bed in a black silk dressing gown opened over her lavender gentleman's pyjamas. Her teeth biting into her lower lip, eyes alight with mischief I'd never seen before. I was aghast that this was still a dream. And said tell me is it true. And she came out with a purring laughter. And said yes. And yes again when her cold foot touched mine. She was trembling now. Balthazar I didn't think you'd mind. That I would come to you. Because I knew you wanted to come to me. I said for God's sake are you real. Yes you can see and feel all you want. This was a king's room before my mother's centuries ago and he had his mistresses visit him. And I don't want to waste any time. So I came too. Before you go. And are gone to London. And may never come back. But now. In just that jiffy we were out of our pyjamas. Her breasts seemed so big and white in all this heartbeating utter reality that I was amazed. So much lay hidden under wool. The muscles of her belly and strength of her legs. I die to do what's expected. Not easy without practice. With someone you think you know becoming someone else all new again. Fitzdare grunted, groaned and growled. Grabbing me fiercely by the perpendicular and a too firm grasp by the balls. That I had to say out a little squeal of agony. And she drew back and said I'm sorry. Put your hand there again, just a little more softly now. To push and press my pole slowly down and down. On top of her here. Is her hole. Seems so small that there is nowhere to go. And now I'm there. Wrapped as she is all around me. And she said no, no one has ever been in me before. So hard to believe I am the first. But she said you are. And if I am. The first. How are you like you are. So unafraid. To give me your body. And just take off your clothes like that. In a jiffy. She said it's all because I wanted to. Over all these months at Trinity. I planned to get you just like this. Right here in this bed. Even on this day of the week and week of the month, with moonlight in the window. I planned it all. Right from the first day I winked at you if you can remember. At chemistry practical. I remember. And I thought if ever I got you here. I'd put you in my mother's room and come as I've come there through the secret door. It's dusty up and down the stairs and cobwebs all along through the walls. And

272

I can't tell you all the hundred nights I dreamt of this, to sneak here from my room. I knew I would never wait for marriage. And I guess my only weakness was. I just had to ask you. To marry me. First. I knew it might frighten you away. But then I'd never let you go. Were you frightened. No. Ha, I know you're not, because I've got you locked up here in my arms. And do you. Ever think you could marry me. Please don't say what you think I want to hear. Just tell me what you feel. Well I would have to consult my trustees. A little quiver in Fitzdare. At these words. Balthazar tell me. Are you awfully rich. Lizzie it seems so funny. But I don't honestly know. Each time I've ever asked, my trustees, all of them to a man, turn slowly and look out the window. So I've always just gone on requesting drafts and signing checks. And they write that they advise caution in my expenditure. God love me Balthazar. Push it all the way in. Like that. O God please give it to me. Ever inch and every drop. I pushed. To think I may be at stud. A gigantic fee paid for this nomination. In the paddock of Fitzdare. And how she got me here. To love. When all the time in my heart my tongue hung out to the edge of my heels. The blinding flashing explosion when it goes into someone you love. The whole world changes on nearly every turn. And dies in front of you and all the people run. To gather sticks and prayers to burn and pray because it all must start again. Little eyes, little lips, and maybe you can then say please, if all the others die, don't let me. Hold on to you Fitzdare through all the years to come. Till we stroll old and grey. Past perhaps your barn full of cows as we did one day when they turned to look wild eyed. Under the brown smoked rafters. Twitching big oval ears. Standing on nobby legs swishing tails. Their curly hair you rubbed between their horns. And you trod with such dignity in the cow flop on the golden straw. I saw you hug your new born calves. And show me their big long lashed eyes and the new white ivory hooves clean from the womb and you said they're so sweet and milky aren't they, their noses so moist and sniffing. Standing steamy in the hay, licked by a big long tongued mother. The sound of piss, and milk pinging

273

in pails. The barn clanking, cows shaking their chains, jaws full of munching hay. And when I asked could you milk a cow, you did. I was enthralled. With evil thoughts. As you sat there on the little stool so expert with your two handed pistol shots shooting out the white streams. And one which you sent right out on my boot. I laughed. And my perpendicular went down. And went up again motoring to see celtic crosses in your funny little car. And Fitzdare I ask you. Are you awfully rich. Yes, I think so. My father is in linen, ships and tea. I had an uncle who lived across the lough. When I was a little girl he had whipped cream on his porridge in the morning. He lost his fortune in America and came back to drink himself to death. And always used to tuck me under the chin and say be glad you're rich. And I never was. It always made me sad. So many are so poor. Their troubles come swarming. It gets so hopeless for them because they think the world can't stop. It sometimes helps to think it can. And the skeletons come dancing out of all our closets. As you did Lizzie out of the wall. Like the night air in the window. Then that sound. What was that. A death in the woods. A night time creature meeting doom. Makes one want to live before one dies. Dress up and look nice for the world. The two of us. I must fly to London. Tell my trustees. That we will wed. Have your white fine body always mine. And Beefy best man. To punch anyone who says they know cause or just impediment why we two persons should not be joined together in holy matrimony. Or not lie so happy like this. Third time of orgasm entwined. In the sight of God. Smelling your sweet sweat. In Fermanagh. Satisfied of lusts and appetites. So discreetly ordained by Fitzdare. She rolls her body all over mine. I lie unthinking and still. Hoping not to hear another creature meeting doom out in the wood. And be haunted. On this our honeymoon. She covers my back with her arms. Pushing her fingers through my hair behind my ears. The church bells will ring when we wed. The ruffian might come screaming at the last moment down the aisle. With a cause unjust. Stabbing an impediment between us. That we may not be joined together.

That I laid Breda out in the direction of Baldoyle. Not nice the bitter days of judgment. When the secrets of all hearts are dug up. And the stolen gold falls out. Balthazar, will we like each other always. I felt your seed come into me. Way way up inside. I know so much sadness lies outside in the world. And we could bring it something good. It's so honest the way we touch each other. I don't feel I'm sinning. Do you. If we love each other. As I do at least love you. I'll tell Pappy in the morning. Not what we did tonight, my goodness. But what we want to do for always and always. He'll be so pleased. He likes you. But if you've any doubt that you want to marry me, please say. It would be too painful, I know, if I felt because I love you so much that I trapped you. I think I did. But I'll wash and clean and scrub. And manicure your nails. I'll bring you breakfast. And go with you anywhere. Over the whole wide earth. And the tears I cry are tears of love.

I lay with Fitzdare till the dawn came up. And never slept a wink. She went to sleep buried under her dark hair. I was nervous and feared of the blood we left staining through the sheet. That someone else outside one's life will come and see and know. And it will go all whispered through the house. To servants and grooms and keepers out to other houses for miles around. I sneezed Fitzdare awake and she scrambled out and crossed to the window. Standing naked silhouetted against the satin drape. I looked at her back and bottom shining by the morning light. Then she went away and came back with clean bedding. And said I'll tell Pappy, maybe you both could meet at ten. And that morning in the little library beyond the drawing room. As I came in. Wiping a moisture from my brow. Eyes tired and limbs ashake. Would he see the desperate satisfaction on my face. And how and what do I ask. I think they say can I have your daughter's hand in marriage please. And he rises to shake mine.

"Good morning. I think I can call you Balthazar."

"Yes. Indeed. Sir."

"Sit down. I'm sure I can help us both a little. By saying I'm extremely pleased."

"Thank you sir. I've never done this before."

"Well, ha ha, I'm sure we both hope it's the first and last time. There's been good word of you from every quarter. You're young but you'll manage. The General particularly spoke highly. As did my brother in Greystones. Who are your principals."

"Bother, Writson, Horn, Pleader and Hoot, sir."

"Good show. I know Horn. I've served with Hoot. My chaps will be in touch. I don't think there's any more we need say. Except I hate to lose Elizabeth. And you may have this place on your head one day. Dry rot, fallen slates, drains, poachers and woodworm. But never mind. You're young. You'll prevail. And I know Lizzie will be very happy. And that's what matters."

The moment of dread. Like nothing at all. And suddenly with a smile and handshake one has the precious Fitzdare. And one rides with her now holding her hand and sitting close together all the way to Dundalk. To catch a train instead of my cancelled plane. And go south to Dublin town through Drogheda and out along the wintry looking shore. We kissed on the station. We would marry in the fall.

And riding on this train. Through Donabate and Malahide. Over the flat stretches and estuary waters. Fitzdare stood high on her toes as she waved goodbye. And last thing we shook hands. Seeing in each other's eyes. And suddenly she wouldn't let me go. And clung as my hand reached down from the window and she ran along the platform tears streaming from her eyes. And the sight of her when I looked back was her head bent down.

The houses grim and tinted red as we dip down into Dublin over the river Tolka. Breda, that little wisp of wiry fighting girl, gone from Cabra somewhere with her jewel. Click clack past buildings tall dark and tattered. Citizens in this summer time go greyly overcoated, black belted through the streets. How will I ever find Beefy to tell him the news. And at the hotel desk an envelope left. I opened it rising up in the lift cage past the crimson covered floors.

276

My dear Balthazar,

I have had a debacle. Had hoped to catch you back. Will call again this early eve. Believe me when I say a pox upon the elderly. But let us be goodish and deter distress.

Beefy

I bathed in pine scent. Nearly wafting off to sleep. Changed my somewhat seamy underthings. I ordered blue steak, mashed potatoes and peas and Gevrey Chambertin to be served in my room. And as my first succulent slice was put between my lips. Beefy knocked and came in.

"My dear boy, how are you. But let me tell you, before you tell me, how I am. Firstly I am in need of gripe water. Secondly I am bedazzled. Benumbed with befuddlement. Carted off bodily to Unthank. And there pissed on. From a dizzying height. And soon I shall be seen somewhere in Paddington light footed in the rooming house hall wearing sunglasses, wielding squash racket and utterly unclothed. Allow me please to have a spoon full of these peas."

"Beefy sit down."

"Thank you I actually will."

"I have the most wonderful news. I am betrothed to Fitzdare."

"O isn't that splendid. I'm quite cheered up. A solemn moment. O yes. Very solemn moment indeed. Ah. I am most happy for you. I mean that Balthazar. From the bottom of my heart. That is indeed such good news that mine I fear deserves not to be told. I have been utterly disinherited. Dispossessed. I have only my deed box full of fivers left. I know I shall raise rebuttals. But my God how. Aubergine's my colour. Nobility my demeanour. I am not yet stripped of all privilege. One's been to a good school and has the right if slightly tarnished background. And at least I have never stooped so low as to vulgarize myself with a carnation in the buttonhole. No matter whatever other humiliating deeds I was enthusiastically engaged in. There shall be fight. Count on it."

"I am awfully sorry to hear of this, Beefy."

"Sad. But not yet fatal. Never thought she'd do it. Granny.

277

These days folk play foul with their nearest and dearest. Without a murmur of conscience. A man came to my grandfather when he was in a hotel in China. To ask if he wanted any delectations of the flesh. A prudent as well as prudish man he said no. And your chap offered then the ultimate. Fished deep from his cubbyhole of delights and soothings of the spirit. He said does the honourable gentleman wish to see an execution. My grandfather said certainly not. The chappie said it was at the honourable gentleman's convenience and priced at twenty pounds. My grandfather who thought he was on to a splendid piece of magic went off with your man to a chamber to see the brilliant occult mystery unfold. He paid and watched. And a chap was beheaded. Blood everywhere. The spectacle of execution was real. Men offered themselves for execution and the money paid would go to their families. There was a long line of applicants my dear Balthazar. And the story has always impressed me. One man of a family would give his all for the rest. But not my dear old granny. She won't die. She won't budge from her flint hearted throne. And she's ninety one. Told my trustees I was a waster. Countenance that. What an awful thing to say about a man destined at one time to take holy orders. Who will not bet on nags not tipped by Zutu. Ah God that dear man, I miss him. Well my path is clear. I must marry a fortune with the utmost dispatch. Before my hair drops out and too much belly fat collects. You are a lucky one with your Fitzdare. She is a treasure. Of such tantalising beauties, it fair makes me weep. God speed you on your way into such dear arms."

"Beefy would you be my best man."

"Nothing in this world would give me more profound pleasure."

"Is there anything I can do for you Beefy."

"Yes. I should adore to quaff a bottle of champagne. In these testing times."

This cozy narrow sitting room. Drapes aflutter with a summer breeze. And Dublin lies out there. For all it's worth. It will speak to you when one is least ready to listen. The

278

champagne comes. A smallish boy enjoying this duty. Making a little cascade and popping the cork across the room.

"To you Balthazar. Fitzdare. And many little Balthazars."

"Thank you Beefy."

"And while my money lasts. I must disport in London. Clutch to my strong breast some moneyed morsel who can barely hobble with the burden of family jewels at Palace parties. First chukka of my life still to be lived. Second chukka shall be winningly played. But you know, with this saddening news came piles. A rather diabolically unfortunate case of same. Not nice. Balancing on one cheek of arse. Waiting always to move to the other. No. Not at all nice. One's income, once large and sure from granny. Will now be miniscule and uncertain. Ground rents, rates, gas and electricity will be paid for, and renewals of fuse wire for the lights. Food, drink, travel, servants, other rents and lecheries, all these have ceased forthwith to be reimbursed. Until such time as granny packs off to heaven. Which I hope is at any moment. Even then she may have done the dirty on me. Meanwhile I fear I may have to take on a mare with legs between which I cannot see the daylight. Having always deeply cherished that exquisite separation of the thighs. Deprived of that I should end up sweating on the upper lip through life. Chucked out of the Church of Ireland. Be banging soon at the doors of the Church of England. Those chaps are so selective. I'm bound to be debarred. Not owning any longer, as I once did, the Hyde Park grazing rights for escargot. Of course there is the piano department of Harrods, if the chaps will have me. Whacking great commissions on those whacking great pianos. And the analogy dear boy is. I am seated playing a soft delicate passage in my life and granny comes sneaking up behind with her pearl studded ebony cane and prises down the piano cover slamming on my fingers. Never mind. At least I can prior to the fifth request for payment still venture to the haberdasher, shout shirt. To the bootmaker, shout shoe. To the hatter, shout hat. And stride dignified up St. James. You know of course it is not done to walk down St. James. Approach always from Pall Mall. I'm drunk you know. Just in case you did not. Know. Still hope I have the temerity at my club to raise a finger for whisky and wipe out members at bridge and bezique."

"I do wish Beefy I could say something to cheer you."

"Make me your factor when you and Fitzdare are possessed of your delightfully situated period residence of great character and charm, sheltered from the north, approached by a long drive in a completely secluded setting, yet incorporating every modern amenity, crawling distance from a good hunt, stabling for forty and other useful outbuildings, deer park, o God to think I have come down into penury with piles. Me the purest voiced of all. Sorry to behave like this. But I have my little seizures of self pity. Invariably disappear in a few months. But you know when one talks with one's inner spirit, it's always up to giving rumblings of a sexual or financial nature. Disheartening for the goodishness I think I still retain. In my thumb tips and toes. I'll find some little detour around this nightmare. But for the moment I feel like a freelance archbishop to a group of Siberian atheists who are manufacturing religious artifacts with a word of mouth option for distribution inside the arctic circle. Destined as I may now be to do deeds foreign to my character. Unless I marry rich. And soon."

"I'm sure Beefy things will turn out quite properly for you."

"Civil of you to suggest. Really is. I suppose in London one shall spread it about that one is of the Dublin Social Register. One can hear it said already, is that agricultural dear boy, so nice to meet Irish who are not servants. The noiseless gouging will be on. Foreskins drawn back, knives out. Mommies will be delving into my pedigree like thieves into a Knightsbridge back garden. Looking for a sign of shipping lines. Or land grants in Oxfordshire. And to find I am dispossessed. Then they will be rude to me. Not nice. Where's the humanity. I am almost a disgracefully humble person. One's name unaccountably keeps looking smaller in Debrett. How does one explain the shifty eyed look of one's forebears. Direct descent from horse thieves from the days of cudgels and kicks up the arse. Century upon century of the most mischievous thievery you've ever heard. And when they weren't thieving people's horses they were thieving people's saucepans, codpieces, loose ecclesiastic attachments and turnips. God I have a volcanic erection. Would you believe it. Keep in line folks. Don't crowd around. It will stand up indefinitely. Eighty fourth wonder of the world. This way now. Folks. There it is. You'll get your chance. Don't shove. Yes, half crown a look, five bob to touch. O God Balthazar, there are knotty times ahead. And I must move to make preparations for the battle to be joined. I shall fight them up St. James as they come seething down, in and out Jermyn Street, along Piccadilly. I shall wage the struggle. Barricade myself in an attic room of the club till my dues are due. I have a porter, old chap who lays on a few lashes. I like to take a bit of the whipping now and again. But the doddering gent's arm isn't what it used to be. I'm driven from Ireland where the strange mysteries of the primitive lusts so easily flower. Many hybrid departures in sauciness. Just as there is too much cross breeding in roses these days. I mean my God where are the petals of strongly scented crimson sublime with the darkness of blood and wine. They're gone Balthazar, I tell you, gone. People like your folk in the back gardens of Donnybrook have done it. Rosy pink or pinkish roses mean nothing any more. The history of that elegant flower is full of people crowding to nail their names on the beautiful handiwork of God. Dear me. I am tight. Couldn't care less about roses in my sober moments but then I am mostly given to my doggish proclivities of pleasurings. Strange how in the morning and into early afternoon one prefers ladies of fulsome legs but as evening approaches I rather fancy space between the thighs. Granny o granny you have made little Beefy a sad chap. And he took a shivering ice cold bath this morning to stiffen up the character for the hard days ahead. And dislodge the little fats here on the belly. For the climb into early middle age. The sun set upon youth."

"But Beefy you've got a long way to go."

"Not if the Lord does not preserve one from lingering disorders. And deliver to his obedient servant a true, sure aid to regularity. Disinheritance has messed up my bowels. Feels like a bishop's mace been stirring there. Could I prevail upon your most cordial hospitality Balthazar and have another bottle of champagne. I'll pay. But I would like to have it here in this peace with you."

"Not at all, Beefy. We'll both have some. You'd be most welcome to stay in my little house in London."

"That's very good of you Balthazar. Very. But I must refuse. No time to cushion the spirit I feel. Time to fight. Always been my strong point. To answer the call, take up the cudgel and wade into the enemy, laying about me with much what for. My trustees of course think it's very funny. As they steam away in their suitable motors to Suningdale. You know Balthazar I'm beginning to detest people who go away on the weekend. And leave me behind. I suppose I would give anything to have a rose named after me. Years now of entertaining a vision of riding that fat ecclesiastical train into rural old age and face instead slanders of having attempted to shoulder aside the elderly. It's the rich Balthazar what gets the antiques and it's the poor what gets the tremors. Facing penury upsets my whole system. Takes so much steady emolument to traverse one's daily life unhindered. Able to say at the drop of a vowel I'll thank you not to fuck about with me you low cur. But you know Balthazar, unless one has a majesty about one's apartments, people will walk all over you, put ash on the carpet, kick the olive pips under the tallboys. As one stands there desperately besmirched. Trying that awkward laugh through the teeth. Giving the demeanour, o you chaps don't put me off my stride at all. As you face all the flashing out of smoking appurtenances, the cigarette lighters, the cases in beaten gold and silver. The English have no mercy. Out of their fat packed diaries they pick another appointment and leave you utterly alone."

"Beefy you mustn't get so upset."

"I know. But the deep dreadful fear of earning one's daily bread assailed me this afternoon. Could throw myself at the mercy of the theatrical world. Think of that. I can't act a damn. But it would be an excuse to go on living. While suffering my piles. I suppose the audience would notice wouldn't they, my hand held constantly to my arse. O dear, that won't do either. Had I taken holy orders dear boy, I was to have shooting rights on forty thousand acres. Two disused lead mines. A shipyard, two mills and three distilleries. The loss of the latter has hurt me most. But it's unforgivable of me to tumble these complaints upon your good natured head, Balthazar. And I owe you the very deepest apologies. Having got you sent down with me."

"You mustn't mind. But can't you appeal to your grandmother to reconsider."

"Alas my God Balthazar, what I did was. To threaten to sue my granny. I thought it would put wind up her enough to gently expire her last spark. It was heinous and ill advised. I mean one can shove a legal point up some cad's arse upon which he will chew for the rest of his life. However to threaten writs upon one's old granny I suppose is unforgivable. But she could simply leave the bullion to a cats' home. For unpleasant cats. In any case she just laughed and slammed down the phone. I'd been begging Smithers to put her on for half an hour. There used to be the day when light fingered hair surgeons danced about me in a fevered lather of attendance. To keep me beautiful for tea time. I was such a nice little boy of big cheeked arse and face. Had enormous curls in childhood. I did. Now all and everybody is going to go piggish."

"I won't Beefy."

"I know you won't Balthazar. And I won't go piggish just to suit other swine. Justice is decaying about me. I think my heart is liable to failure in pulsation. I rogered Rebecca last night glissando and then grosso molto. Poor girl couldn't really care. Said Breda just upped and disappeared I hear. And I go with vowels to cut a swath through London. Take the first hedge in the steeple chase. And be damned the mumpish miseries."

Another bottle of champagne. Comes through the door. With smiles and the hospitable genuflections. And the empty taken away. To see this man here before one. So sad. In need of solace. Of rich round friendly cheeks. When I was a small thin white complexioned boy. Frightened and feared of a new world. And first saw his small carefully sewing hands beneath his sunny face. On the blackest horizon of my life.

"Balthazar it's been heartening to spend this moment with you here. In the peace of these surrounds. But I must take my leave and go. Rebecca waits for me on Butt Bridge. Dear girl. I sneak her as my mother into my hotel. She is full of fight you know. Wants to come with me to London. When I take out my instrument she seizes it with a wild peal of laughter. Very unirish of her. But marvellously charming. Granny taught me at table not to ask for a second service of soup. She was always fond of saying haste was vulgar. Don't leave a door open you find closed or close a door you find open. And above all she said don't trouble people with your mishaps. As I've ignobly done tonight. Wish me well. I now go forth in search of a young lady whose endless pence can slide me over these bumpy times. Shall we meet in London. Seven weeks exactly from today. Waiting hall of Harrods. Are you on. Three o'clock. The course should be clear then, free of unpleasantries. Must go. Drain this last of wine. Blessed are the randy makers for they shall themselves be even more so. My hotel serves only tomato and oxtail soup. For breakfast lunch and dinner. Each time I ask for soap they say the girls will see to the soap. And my God I'm exhausted seeing to the girls. I must go."

"You'll overcome Beefy."

"I guiltily hope so."

Balthazar B watching as the lift cage descended with Beefy. To make sport with Rebecca. Uncle Edouard said you must take women as they are with perhaps a little Chablis and snail. I took Fitzdare bare arsed out of a hole in the wall and am still trembling with the memory. I'll go stand at the window. Look down. All just as it was when I first came to Dublin. And heard on an early morn. A voice. Singing down below. To hear it now again. And look. There on the pavement, hands resting on a pillar before him. He stands. Looking up here at my window. I wave. And the strains of O For The Wings Of A Dove. Go in my ears. That sunlit hearth of Mrs. Twinkle's cottage so many years ago. And as I will wake to look out on Dublin. I give a wish. For you Beefy. That a time will come. If just you wait. For one of those pure days of accident when everything turns to bliss.

> Then
> Pack away
> Pleasures
> All you can.

22

Balthazar B sailed from Dun Laoghaire back across the Irish
Sea. Arriving near midnight in the deserted town of Holyhead. High up in a hotel attic overlooking the harbour he
woke in a room with three beds and two other men. At breakfast he sent a seaside postcard to County Fermanagh and
Fitzdare.

> Dear Lizzy,
> Arrived now in England. Had, it would seem, to share a
> room with two gentlemen who arrived later in the night.
> There must be crowds here but they can't be seen. Upon
> finishing this kipper I now dine upon I am proceeding to
> London via various circuitous routes which may take my
> fancy. First stop Chester. I miss you and think of you much.
> Balthazar

By taxi and hired car Balthazar went from town to town.
Signing strange names in guest books taken from a volume on
the lives of the saints. Chester to Shrewsbury and heading
around the great white haze over Birmingham. Kidderminster
to Stratford. And by whim to Eatington, a place unfamed.
Until a final day at Oxford and a morning walk by the
meadows and along the towpath of the Thames to go south
east to the big smoke of London on the train. A photographic
portrait awaited, taken of Fitzdare. The days were all soft and
warm and sunny. Matters were proceeding rapidly between
the principals. And a marriage settlement was nearly reached
with Raphael Uryan Trusscutt Fitzdare.

Two chars came to clean and scour out the little house in
Brompton. It was painted and put up for sale. The convened
principals said it would not do for size nor dignity. And Lizzy
pleaded too late to keep the little place she said she wanted to

see. Bother, Writson, Horn, Pleader and Hoot had found a proper residence facing slightly north east near gardens, containing the usual and suitable appointments in this most favoured area deep in the heart of Knightsbridge. And one moved into the family elegance of the Hyde Park Hotel to wait. With no news of Beefy all these days.

Each morning to look for mail and await anew a letter from Fitzdare. But none did come. To stand there looking at the little cubby hole and hope for some sign of her pink stationery. Then go out and wander walking in Hyde Park along the Serpentine. And in the evening on the pebbly path feeding the black and white ducks on the still water. The faint glowing gas flame inside the big glass lamp globes. The great grey stretch of sky. Squawk of ducks, geese and swans as they made their way to nest for the night. In the darkness to sit on a bench in Rotten Row. Just to wait. Until a letter did arrive. From my trustees.

> The Temple
> London E.C.4

Dear Mr. B,

We are pleased to inform you that contracts have now been exchanged with the vendors for the purchase of 78 Crescent Curve, Knightsbridge. Steps are in hand to put the property in order and we would be pleased to hear from you concerning any particular wishes you may have in the matter.

Regarding the marriage settlement the principals of the other side have not yet returned to us papers and we are told that there has been some unforseen delay. Although there is no particular hurry in the matter we have advised them none the less that signatures would be appreciated within fourteen days. A country property meeting with your requirements has now come to hand, a survey is being presently conducted, and we will be counselling you of further particulars in due course.

> Yours faithfully,
> Bother, Writson, Horn,
> Pleader & Hoot

287

On the days of inclemency Balthazar B went to the Natural History Museum. Walking quietly there peeking in the antique shops along Brompton Road. And one afternoon he fell asleep in the Reptile Hall. And had a rather unpleasant dream. Of all the reptiles coming to life. The cobras, pythons and rattlesnakes. They writhed across the floors, pouring out of the glass cages they broke with lashing tails. To entwine, attack and poison, heads drawn back with deadly gleaming fangs to strike. To shout oneself awake and find me surrounded by blue uniformed museum attendants. Who were gently reassuring and brought me a glass of water. One smiled and said that sort of dream could happen to anyone.

I walked several times along Piccadilly. And down Regent Street to Pall Mall. Lurking by the doorways to listen. To find if one could hear distant screams from the attic rooms of clubs. Wondering always if Beefy were having me on. Balthazar my dear boy, of course we have scads of valuable tomes in the club library which are fulsomely documented treatises on the lash. The chaps of the old school, they sit there over whisky and soda and when the cries erupt and echo down the marble stairs, they say, hear hear, that's Roger, know his scream, George must be giving him his tonight. My dear boy Balthazar, one often lies there as the lash falls reading the personal column of The Times. Members select and reserve their fancied whip of an evening by appending thereto their racing colours. Always a fair crowd around the display cases in early afternoon. The whip chosen is entered in the whip log along with the lashes to be administered. These are checked of course daily to avoid members taking on too much at one go. Just after port is the best time for the lash to fall. There was a member expelled. He was distributing pictures of himself. Taken at moments when the lash was landed. That's simply not done. Chucked out he was. I think really it was his American style underwear that brought it about. But never think we're runaway masochists dear boy, the cat-o-nine tails is forbidden. And one is not to be caught using the Russian knout or oriental bastinado. And where was Beefy now. As one wanders and wishes to see him. And hear his lyric tales unfold.

On a Wednesday morning I came down after breakfast in my room. And passing out the lobby there was a letter. Not pink but white. And somehow opening it. There seemed a gathering perplexing doom. After all these days of waiting. Decorators daily urged to finish the scraping and painting at Crescent Curve. My mother expecting me in Nice. And tomorrow I go to meet Beefy at our appointed time.

The Temple
London E.C.4

Dear Mr. B,

We very much regret to inform you that the arrangement reached between the principals concerning your marriage to the Miss Elizabeth Astrid Benedicta Trusscutt Fitzdare has now been withdrawn by the other side without explanation. We are taking the liberty to write again this day to enquire if this decision admits of no further discussion or if the matter may be reopened at a later date. However, it is only fair to make known to you now that as far as our opposite colleagues are aware, the instruction given them is final and the agreement reached thus far between the parties is cancelled. Our own personal regrets in this matter are hereby extended to you.

Yours faithfully,

Bother, Writson, Horn,
Pleader & Hoot

Balthazar B on that Wednesday. Walked out down the steps and into the street. To stand there for moments staring across the heads of passing people and the traffic and buses moving by. Suddenly to be told you're not wanted anymore. A bleak black curtain brought down. To fly by airplane to ask. But if one is not wanted how can I ever go. Or know whatever went wrong.

Balthazar B motored by taxi to the Temple. Mr. Pleader sat at his wide desk with bundles of paper tied in pink ribbon. He said in his experience it was all quite strange. But there was nothing one could do. The young lady, how was one to know, could have changed her mind. For any one of many reasons. As sad as that may be. I stood there as one was leaving, unable to shake hands. And saw propped upon the mantel, caught in the window light, Mr. Pleader's wife and little children, a dog among them, all smiling on the steps of a country house.

That September Balthazar B sat a month in his mother's flat in Avenue Foch. In a sunny vestibule off the drawing room watching a tank of fish. Each day staring out across one's hands placed on the top of knees. Two Polish women came to cook and clean. My mother still away in Nice. And back at Harrods waiting hall that afternoon. I was sitting. Beefy came. On the dot of the appointed time. And saw what the world had done to me. That I could not speak. And wrote for him what had happened on a piece of paper. He came and saw me every day high up in my suite. We sat hours together playing chess. He had taken a job on the stock exchange. And I knew he was missing so many days he would be fired. I wrote on my little pad of paper that it would not do for him to lose his job. Next day I took the boat and train I knew so well to Paris.

October came. And the fish in the tank had babies. Balthazar B stood up. And for the first time in many weeks went out. Across Paris walking and walking for miles. To make the blank future lift its daily dread. Until his mother returned. In a sporty car piled with luggage, a young man at the wheel whose name was Mario. And Balthazar moved out and into a suite in a hotel on the Avenue Kléber.

Mornings to walk and afternoons to soak an hour in a hot bath. He attended the steeple chase at Auteuil but could not wager a bet. Often he visited Uncle Edouard's grave. Passing up that cobbled little road and by the great green iron box. Where I put all my coins for the poor of Paris. Atop the grey stone was a bronze balloon and gondola. And one day with a wetted handkerchief I washed away the grimy soot till it was shining smooth again. Over this balloonist and hero of France who roused a cause célèbre when he summoned the pompiers to put out his cigarette. And the only man who loved me when I was a little boy.

During a cold and bitter winter Balthazar took classes in comparative anatomy at the Sorbonne. And lying late at night abed, tomes open everywhere. Breakfast brought with the pretty portrait on the porcelain, touches of red blue and yellow. The warming deep crimson of these rooms. Ebony push buttons tipped with mother of pearl. The wall panels of pale golden satin brocades. The brass bedstead sitting on blobs of paws. The clock face I watch through all these months high on the wall with its wood cowl of grey and pale gold, each black numeral of every hour held in a little rainbow of roses. And the world did little to me here. As I sometimes watched out my window over the stone balcony and black railing. To walk out past the concierge each morning and there always seem to find a man urgently making arrangements to go to Istanbul.

Behind the grey stone of the Sorbonne was my other world. When one was staring so hard to take eyes desperately away from the sight of the cut open flesh of a dead man. Somehow seeing the same clochard, kicked and beaten, I saw that day when I was with Bella. So long ago on the green piece of land jutting out in the Seine. And then this one afternoon stepping from the great barren lecture hall, I stopped and looked down in the grey sunless courtyard of the medical school where the live dogs were kept. A strange thought went through my head. I live and draw a flow of gold. From a dead father's reservoir of riches. I retreat further and further back. Behind my own lonely elegance. Where no one will ever again get to know me. And speak less and less. And on that first day my voice came back when the little fishes in the tank were born. I wrote to Beefy. Care of his club and the stock exchange. Asked him please write to me. One wants so much to hear a word.

My dear Balthazar,

Needless to say I have not lassoed a mare galloping by
rotten rich. I abhor my occupation. Far too many chaps in
London whose cunning outstrips their charm. I play polo
when I can and poker when I shouldn't. The money fast
runs out. I met our old friend Breda. I promise you, purely
by accident. She was busy along the Bayswater Road. At the
mention of you she rather choked up. But once she smiled
and asked if still I was a Presbyterian. I told her that Arses
was king of Persia in 338 B.C. And that news seemed to cheer
her up. Nice lass and she wore a pendant which to my carefully trained eye was not paste and that I would estimate
cost a pretty piece of change. Do come back to London, at
least for a visit. As you well know I am to be not thrilled easily
but things are slowly gathering gaiety here and one quite
rightly gives the birds in the bed more seed. If they are heart-
less enough to find this insufficient one imparts the goose
capri followed in rapid succession by that of the goose volvo
and belair. I have many long tales to tell. Write soon to say
you're coming. I am glad to hear things cheer somewhat more
for you. Remember, blessed are they who are willing victims
of the whip for they will scream to high heaven.

> Mortally yours,
> with much eye ball movement,
>
> Beefy

And over the months we often wrote. And I had some tales
to tell. I left untold. Of wandering along Pigalle. To pick up a
rolling coin dropped by a passing girl in a tight orange dress,
with black straight shiny hair. I handed it back and she said
she would buy me a glass of wine. In a cafe we sat over two
vin rouge. Faintly sweet with preservative. She kept smiling
and looking at my eyes. And said they were the most beautiful
she had ever seen. She came from the countryside near Metz.
We twirled our little funnel shaped glasses of wine. Her dark
eyes and tan skin. From all the summers of picking grapes she
said. And you she also said are but my second client, I am

only new at the trade. It is because you are so beautiful I will do it free out of desire. We sat and sat and I didn't know what to do or say until she put her hand out on top of mine and smiled and said come, you are so shy. I had a cognac and I followed her up narrow stairs into her little room. My body stilled ever since Fitzdare. She said when she first came to Paris she lived across the canal from the abattoir and the smell always stayed on her skin. And she sniffed her arm and laughed. She took off her clothes. On her wall a little picture of Saint Agnes, a soldier taking a swing at her with a sword as she was tied to the stake. She inflated her chest and pushed out her breasts and said she did not know what age she was but thought she might be seventeen. With all the money she made she would buy a farm. She watched staring at me as I undressed and said you look like what I would think a prince would look like, so weak and white and thin. She was slippery and covered with sweat all through the Paris afternoon. I slept and dreamt and awoke again. To see her smiling and smiling at me and leaning over to push back my hair. I would close my eyes again. Uncle Edouard said no man was a man without a mistress. And also said there was something eternally macabre in Metz. But Balthazar if you travel in Italy label your luggage "beware poisonous reptiles" to be safe from thieves. We dined together in a cafe off the Avenue Trudaine. And walked through the streets to the Gare du Nord. We parted. She asked if I would ever see her again. I said yes. And she said you know my address and waved out the window of the taxi cab. Which I could see stop further along the Rue Dunkerque. Where she would now continue to ply her trade. And I walked back all the way to Avenue Kléber in bewildered despair.

But a week was spent cheered. With an erection rising on the Métro and often in the bath. Where Beefy said it was always nice to give it quietly a soft and soapy pull. My heart now came to slowly climb that last bit of cliff to the mountain top. And just as I could stand there and see. Outside again. The world all around. Noisy boulevards and the night hour as

293

cafe proprietors rub eyes and waiters count their francs at tables and counters across Paris. And I lay reading one morning the paper to see what new matter was afoot in Metz. I scratched an itch in my pubic hair. I took the autobus and scratched again on the way to class. At night I scrubbed and scratched. Through two days more. Whenever I decently could. And finally thought my God. Anoplura. As this word fell from a long closed closet of useless knowledge. After all these intemperate times. Shouted out as I lay in bed. Where I happened to be. Two jointed tarsi adapted for clinging to the host. Mouthparts used for biting or piercing and sucking.

And Balthazar B took a taxi to the public hospital. Walking in these dismal doors. Asked to wait and then what's your complaint Monsieur. Would Monsieur please remove his trousers and lower his drawers. A magnifying glass put near. Ah yes, ah ha, just what I thought. Please wait Monsieur, I shall be back in a moment. I stood waiting. Until I was ready to complain. And the man in his white coat came back, a pleased look across his face. He said I would be much obliged if you would come this way with me.

Balthazar walked trouserless in shoes and red unforgettable socks. The doctor opened a small door at the end of the room. He stepped aside and said pray proceed. I held my trousers over my arm and heard the strange murmur of voices beyond. The bare and dusty floor. A smell of paper and ink and familiar university sounds. Now become hushed. And I catch my breath as I suddenly stand facing the faces, a few black among the white, tier upon rising tier. Turning as the door slammed shut behind me. A white haired professor at a lectern. Smiling as he approached slapping a long pointer in his hand. Good day, Monsieur, thank you for coming. Now ladies and gentlemen, we have a rare case not too often encountered. Phthirus pubis, the infestations of which are less frequently seen. This good gentleman has been kind enough to help us today. That is enough, there will be no laughter please. Now. Monsieur. Would you lower your drawers please. Do not be alarmed, we have all seen what you shall show us many times before. And we would not trouble you but for your particular complaint. Yes. Please. Just lower a little more. Yes. And just a little more. Good. Thank you. The professor raising his eyebrows, touching his spectacles back on his nose and turning his voice to the class. Balthazar speechless, hands terrified at his hips, with nowhere to move or run, with the feel of blood burning on cheeks as bright as his socks. Catching his breath as the pointer comes back pointing again. The easy drone of the professor's voice. Now, it is a characteristic ladies and gentlemen, that while the body louse is never found on the head, the head louse may be found on the body. But the pubic louse may be found on other parts of the body including the head. Expect to find the louse wherever one finds man. If standards of hygiene are low they will be favourable to their multiplication. Stop that please. This is no laughing matter. This is a disease which can spread through an army and reduce it to a bunch of scratching idiots. I shall require complete silence while I continue please. In this case the pubic louse, sometimes more commonly known as the crabs, hooks into the skin near the roots of the hair. Here note the lightness and soft texture of Monsieur's skin which makes for an optimum host. The movement of the pubic louse is slow, crablike and deliberate. The professor turning. One moment if you please Monsieur. Balthazar B slowly pulling back up his drawers. Ah Monsieur, could I just ask that you keep them down for a few moments longer. Thank you. It is interesting to note that in the case of the body louse a louse free person lying in the same bed as a lousy person will begin to complain in six hours. Here now at the base of Monsieur's pubic hair, and you note it is thickest as it arches here over the penis. Here the eggs are attached when laid. Incubation eight days. The sensitive person reacts with scratching. The bite of the pubic louse, and this is most interesting. If you will permit me Monsieur, yes, to have a closer look. Now we shall see. Ah, yes, the characteristic blue spot is present. Thank you Monsieur. These spots are not found after the bites of the head or body louse. Typhus and trench fever are not transmitted. However, rarely but it is possible, blood poisoning and death can result from an infected scratch. Our patient here does not yet display any laceration. Treatment. As you can observe in this case, Monsieur's pubic hair covers the area about his private parts. These should be completely shaved. Silence please. And, ah pardon, the hair is to be shaved. And the area smeared with vaseline. Also. If you will turn around Monsieur please. Also, you should guard in treatment that the perianal area is accounted for. Oil treatment is to be avoided as it gives rise to smarting of the genitalia. The simplest and the best is the modern insecticide. Thank you Monsieur, you have been most helpful. If you go back by that door, I am sure the best treatment awaits you.

For the first three long seconds Balthazar B could not move at all. Staring as one was at the ball of paper nearby on the floor. Behind which one's whole being was desperately crouching. The professor's voice droning on in one's ears. Ladies and gentlemen, we may as well go on to the flea, the vector of the plague. As I now gather up my crushed soul and perambulate towards the grey door on my shoes hanging darkly from my red socks. To have a nurse behind curtains lather and shave me with idle heads peeking now and again and grinning. My penis would not stay down till I was nearly in tears. And jumped when the nurse flicked her fingers painfully hard on my poor pole end. Out of the hospital I ran two blocks, downed a cognac and changed to evening clothes to go that night carrying upon me a peculiar smell. I dined in solitary splendour off duck and Grand Echezeaux to gently gather up the shreds of me and avoid the Sorbonne forever.

All these months passing. I read Halsburg's laws of England until I got to the volume Malicious Prosecution to Mines, Minerals and Quarries. When you stop to look back and see all those days dreaming of a future. And say then, that was my life. And if any new days are to come it's now time to move. To go from this pleasant place. Of mahogany and tiles. Soft carpets and quiet grace. Where meals were amiably solemn. One's entrance and exit awaited by waiters smiling and the air anointed gently with towels. Uncle Edouard said my dear boy if ever you are financially incommoded. Go at once and stay at the best Paris hotel. Live elegantly and well till the bill is enormous. Then call your lawyers to come. For the time has arrived to throw the fake heart attack over a sudden fright from something in the closet. The ambulance comes. To take you of course to another hotel. Your lawyers surround you as one leaves on a stretcher. When the bill is waved in your departing face and the screams descend for payment, the lawyers will say Monsieur has had a woeful shock and they will be hearing further and better particulars of the spiritual and dietary damage soon.

And now this midday, sunshiny breezy and clear, Balthazar B walked out between the panelled walls and across the black and white tiled hall. All belongings sent the week before to 78 Crescent Curve, lain vacant over all these many many months. Courage now to go back at last, agrip of one's gladstone bag that went with me swaying in the moist clear breezes of Fermanagh. Soon to see Beefy. Whose last letter three days ago was amusingly brave and sadly grave.

The Club
London S.W.1

My dear Balthazar,

This city now abounds with matters many of which are very gay and others decidedly detrimental and dismayed. But London goes modern as fast as some others are slow to lose the indulgent splendours of the old days. Meanwhile I am so delighted that you are coming. And look forward to seeing you Harrods at one. Where alas some few days ago I was passing one of those plaster mannequins and as is my friendly wont, I administered a light fingered goose delux. It suddenly brought both its hands behind it. It also leaped in the air and screamed. My attire at the time did not afford me much protection and I said rather too many times I beg your pardon madam, I thought you were a statue. She glared as I walked away backwards over the toes of several assembled assistants. Sad when only minutes before I'd helped an old lady across the road. It could be the moment for me to swim the Channel both ways, French and British flags between the toes and the usual inflated French letters for buoyancy. I find all my acquaintances booked up. Even I suppose for their funerals. I say there, one says, are you booked in for a shit old man, better be, the best places are awfully crowded. God I miss the ways of Erseland where one was lucky just to wake for the next day's doggish proclivities. I am taking my colonic irrigations like a man and cry out only for town house, country estate and polo ponies as a little embellishment and garnish in my life. But to add to my dangerous difficulties I went recently to an all night do it your ruddy self laundry just opened here to cleanse my clothes at one A.M. when there wasn't a bugger in sight. I delicately stripped down and washed my shirt, socks and lacy underthings. A passing woman walking her unpleasant dog saw me and called the police. They arrived in force as I sat stark naked and lonely reading a copy of Country Life. Only that I bedazzled them with ecclesiastic and legal mummeries I would have been had up. As it was they helped me dry my garments and drove me home. You will gather from this that it is a far away time when one was pushed by nannie in one's pram looking down from one's lofty wheeled height at the ranks of other men below. All I now hear whispered at me from the unprivileged corners of this London world is, sir may we be of assistance in your failure. It's not too funny when one thinks of all the time spent growing one's eyebrows long in a good London club. But I still do have my little bevy of fluffy delights who polish my instrument like a doorknob before turning it open to frolic and frisson with my soul. Needless to add, a mare of much fortune eludes me more and more. And so, blessed are they who rat on their principles and trample their codes for profit, provided the friend is dear who suffers and dies betrayed.

By a pubic hair I still remain a member in good standing of the brave ruling classes.

Beefy

A smooth crossing of the Channel. Rearwards, in second class, people sang around a man who played a mandolin. And down in first class with the suspicious immigration officer as the ship plied its way. I sat before his desk as he thrust out his lower lip and sucked air between his dentures.

"How long are you staying."

"I don't know."

"Have you come for a visit."

"I don't know."

"How do you support yourself."

"Privately."

"You may be required to give proof. However you will be permitted to land as a visitor provided you don't enter employment or engage in any business or profession. And leave the United Kingdom not later than such date as may be specified by the Secretary of State."

And there ahead lay England. Suddenly a green and welcoming land. The great high darkness of Victoria Station. To taxi through the bustling streets. Where the people sauntered looking hopeful again. The fountain sprinkling under the leafy trees of Sloane Square. And dead ahead at the end of a straight road, the turreted red brick eminence of this peaceful hotel.

Balthazar B went to look at 78 Crescent Curve. To push open the heavy oak door. A scattering of brown envelopes inside. Footprints on the parquet. His boxes and trunks stacked in the hall. To walk in across the grimy dusty floors. All once new paint grown shades darker in the stale air. And this is where I would have sat and smoked perhaps a pipe. Might have been little laughing voices racing by. And no. I must not go on thinking. For the pain will never go away. You just go on and live. In the dust of desertion.

Still
Falling
Where last
I loved.

23

To walk out under the big crystal chandelier past the wide brown marble balustrade. Touch the brass handrail and go down the green carpeted steps. And out into this warm sunny day.

Take this morning stroll through the park, a light wind shaking the leaves. Couples lying on the grass. And striped sails fluttering on boats bumping across the Serpentine. An Afghan hound goes loping around the deck chairs. Nice to see an Alsatian locked in cohabitation with a little white poodle as the owners hysterically dance and belabour all around. And there two little babies, a boy and girl, come wading through the grass hand in hand. And I look up. A blue jay catches a moth. Now it lands to sit on a branch and devour and dine. As the tiny bits of moth wings come fluttering down.

And again to march out into life after lunch, a tune in my head. Step lively, stride long. Under a sky flooded blue. And over blackened slate rooftops and greening copper rain gutters clouds float puffy white and moisty. Turn this corner away from traffic humming on the mild afternoon air. The houses of this street all their red sooty fronts mellowed umber. And there, that's the house where I still might live. Behind the bits of ivy. Me and my volumes of comparative anatomy. Mr. Pleader, who comes after Horn and before Hoot, not to mention Bother and Writson, said yesterday these brooding blocks of flats nearby are graced with leading stage actors and psychologists. They graze here on these calm spring pastures. Of soft brick, gentle curtains, gleaming glass and goodish surnames. Terribly nice, all of it.

Balthazar B went through the double swing doors of this russet stone walled emporium. Suppliers of fancy goods to the Monarch. Past the ties, shoes and shirtings. The glove counter and the stairs down to the safety deposit vaults. Where many documents and various ready cashes have lain locked away between the mirrored walls, lonely in the fireproof silence.

Ahead the waiting hall. Vast marble room of creamy browns. Six fluted pillars hold up a ceiling lit with funereal glass trays shrouding neon lights. A gauntlet of dowagers in last year's wedding hat. Seated with unmarried sons in the green leather chairs. They confide little jokes. Nod and flicker timidly at their random passing friends. And sometimes they pause to talk of weddings and christenings. And my God. There. Is it, it must be. Beefy. And his clothes. As he sits dejected. Suede leather on his feet smudged with something like plaster and powdered cement. His grey flannels spattered with crusts of mud. But higher up near the throat he looks splendidly the same. Silk crimson hanky and a moss green cravat tucked in the neck of his yellow shirt.

"My God Beefy. I hardly recognised you."

"Yes. I know. Note the colours of my jacket match nicely with the encrusted clay. Clearly no tonsorial artist or tailor is doing his fortnightly nut to keep me beautiful. But my glands sustain in the lack of gaudery. Goodness I am glad to see you. I need a friend in my world these days. If I'm away from the building site much longer I'll be sacked. Say I'm shirking. When I have the most awful case of the runs. Together with my piles, which attacked recently, I can barely stand up. Chaps keep accusing me of not pulling my weight."

"What have you done Beefy."

"Done. Dear man I should like to know. Mostly it is what another has done. In particular dear old granny. I came to the last five pound note in my deed box after a catastrophic series of races devoid of tips from Zutu. And then I made another awfully ill advised attempt to harass granny, I tried to get a mortgage on the insurance of her life. And I am now situated in chambers in Bayswater. A polite word which upon map scrutiny admits of one having been pushed into Paddington. The tale is simple. I'm ruined. As you know the Public School Appointments got me my job on the stock exchange. After a prolonged safari in Brighton with a most saucy but impoverished debutante, I was fired. Upon many subsequent interviews I was finally offered another position. As a clerk. Can you imagine. I said not on your life. I will go and tear up earth as a navvy before I will stand behind a counter. I sounded so convincing, I believed it myself. Mesmerised by those suicidal words that's what I've done. After the first two days I was so blistered and tired I thought I'd soon die a natural death. Some days later climbing up the marble steps of the club, my hand touching along the reassuring brass gleam of the rail, I asked for mail. Hoping my trustees might have unearthed ownership of a deed to some country pub. But there wasn't even a bill. And just as I went across the lobby to the lift, an elderly rather red nosed member said to George the porter as I passed, that chap is soiled. Imagine. Soiled."

"O my God Beefy. You must let me help you."

"Wait there's more. Not all of it gloom. Just last week at my very bottom lowest when I'd returned to my tiny room. Put sixpence in the slot for a morsel of electric fire. Not for heat. Just for the encouraging glow in the gloom. I stared out back at the pipes and chimneys and the car parts yard below. Then I knelt down. God I was fervent. I really meant it. Knees sunk deeply in the threadbare broadloom. I promised and prayed, as a onetime member of the Church of Ireland, that if God would send some reasonable female creature of marriageable age across my path, in fact age immaterial, who was possessed of the wherewithal and whence I should get my hands upon it, I would forthwith, as decency allowed after the ceremony, covenant the church to two and a half percent of the income, after tax was paid. At that exact moment. Right over my head. The light bulb exploded. I was showered in glass and darkness. I also jumped ten feet. And as the room is six by nine I had to call my doctor. He bid me, tired as I was, to come round and he would look for breaks in the arm bones. Off I went to Harley Street. I was next to last at his ultra late Friday surgery. My unbroken legs crossed as I turned the pages of a magazine. And into the waiting room. There comes a young lady."

A rainbow of a smile bursting across Beefy's blustery freckled face, his wandering nose and wine tinted cheeks. As Balthazar B leaned forward in his light grey flannel suit sewn in the Rue St. Honoré with two horn buttons requested on the sleeves. A matron near by, long nostrilled, green suited, her lorgnette held up to an auction catalogue. An audibly tender moment really.

"Yes. There comes a young lady, Beefy."

"Ah. By the way Balthazar, that is a fine blue tie you're wearing with that elegant shirt. You're marvellously turned out."

"And you Beefy have not changed one bit. And what happened. There comes a young lady."

"Ah. Wait. My God I have an erection. Of the volcanic variety once again. Visions of richness always brings it on. Ah so. Yes. To be sure. The young lady. Who that moment came delicately in, in the best of leathers and fabrics. And I who had just crawled searching for forgiveness, off the wintry Hornchurch Marshes near some borax works to face a committee of ecclesiastics lined up inside a glassed, centrally heated pavilion. They were chanting quietly, I Know That My Redeemer Liveth. And then at the sight of me. They pointed. Go back, they said. Back to the marsh, dirty deed doing profaner, your redeemer does not liveth."

The nearby dowager shifting uncomfortably in her seat, turning for a moment to survey Beefy. As he leaned back legs spread wide to regard airily the randy bulge upon his person. The lady made a high pitched noise down her nose and jerked swiftly back to her auction catalogue of ceramic antiques.

"My God Beefy, the young lady."

"Ah the young lady. But you are so splendidly turned out Balthazar, so frisky and one might say fresh from France that it does my heart fair good just to see you."

"Yes Beefy, I've come all this way. And a girl came into the waiting room and then what."

"You must let me tantalise myself Balthazar. To me these days it means much. Let me digress one more delicious moment. The chaps at my building site when they saw me giving the cement a little extra wetting down. They cheered. Said it was the biggest weapon ever seen. It rather improved my day. Of course I know it's achieved a further grandeur it did not know at prep school. And perhaps not even as one prepared to take holy orders. But to have these chaps cheer. It's given me courage to again present this instrument to a mare who would exchange all her riches lain at my feet for a guarantee of frequent thrustings. Ah but back at the doctor's."

"Yes."

"Ah. Her name, listen carefully while I thrill it out between my sober lips. Listen. Angelica Violet Infanta. Doesn't that tell you much already. Angelica, from the Greek, Violet from the Latin. Those delicate tiny flowers found on grassy banks through woods. Infanta. From that latter one catches a tremolo of Debrett. I swim back to the shores of privilege out of the sea of the dispossessed. Saved from a lifetime of discomfort. But back at my doctor's. Medical treatment is the only thing left that granny pays for these days. And the dear man while he was examining my bones said, now Beefy there waits downstairs in my waiting room a girl of not too great looks perhaps but a marvellous fortune. When I returned to the waiting room I gave my most charming smile. But she was of course aloof. In fact positively ignored me. Being as I was and still am, in a state of deshabille. But on the good doctor's front door step. I lurked waiting. And did pounce. With a long prepared stream of lies. When the door opened and she appeared. I said I'm awfully sorry. Then I left an enormous pause. To let my villainous vowels sink in. Her eyebrows were rising. I attacked. Said I'd just rushed from rehearsals. Left my bowler and brolly in my dressing room. I'm a navvy darling in an uproariously funny stage play. I didn't say darling I must admit. But I made a further thrust. As always I'm the first to believe myself. I said you, my dear, are just the one one has been looking for. My leading lady in the flesh.

304

She began to open her mouth. I knew it would be fatal if ever she got anything out. Something odious like be gone cad. So I said. Say nothing please. Just come with me. I got her into a nearby wine lodge. Admiring her eighty quids' worth of tailoring she carried so presentably on her back. I extracted her address. Belgravia of course. I flung the necessary heirlooms into pawn. Bombarded her with red roses for a week. And now if only I can hold out. Keep the wool over suspicious eyes. Tonight I meet ma and pa."

"I'm terribly pleased for you Beefy."

"Balthazar so good to hear your word. When all is not well. When you know that out under the cloudy skies of London no one thinks in love of one. But now. The Violet Infanta. Niece of a Welsh peer. You know how utterly rich they are. She may mention Le Touquet a trifle too often for my comfort. Does rather hysterically laugh. But what matter. We'll get on. In wedlock I know I can grow to love her. For what she is. Stinking. Gushingly stinking rich. My doctor smiles every time he tells me of her ground rents and her father's connection with motor cars. Given me the runs, made me half demented. The slothful grandeur of it all. Our spiritual feelings are so in harmony. She's a rabid believer in the monarchy. And of course so am I. Ah Balthazar you look so untouched by life. The calmness of your existence. Back there in Paris. You must meet her. You must. Told her all about you. She thinks she has a friend you would adore."

Beefy's sun reddened hand reaching to lightly touch his cravat. And a finger flicks away a morsel of hardened mud from his knee. As mothers, aunts and nannies march by, irregularities of figure neatly corsetted under their tweed. Children in tow. On their way to measure for the school uniform.

"Balthazar, you do tolerate me so much. Why."

"Your charm."

"For that I shall send you by foot messenger six gull's eggs. Imagine though how God answered my prayer. Nearly within the hour. I even thought I might have caught a glimpse of him as the light bulb overhead exploded. I knelt with the backside out of my underwear and untold guilts from nursery days blushing on my face. I'm on my way. My rich mare lassoed. And till I get to the altar, I smash back my emulsion of poppy juice to keep my spirits up. I really know now that one's redeemer damn sure liveth."

"Beefy. I don't want to trouble you or be presumptuous. But I do think that you need a little help. And I'd like very much if you would accept from me an early wedding present."

"Balthazar, my goodness, you are a brick. You really are. What an awfully nice thing of you to say. Were I a heretic denying the transubstantiation and you minded, I must say I'd mend my ways forthwith. And my Lord I haven't really asked you how you are. How are you."

"I'm fine. Very fine. I had one or two low moments in Paris perhaps. But at the same time I rather caught up on some aspects of zoology I had missed."

"God suddenly the world at this moment seems so good. I mean one couldn't help wondering what was going to happen to us. To our caste. Me wheeling a wheelbarrow on a building site. Marvellous thing is, amazing how many places one can go, a wheelbarrow in front of you, shouting out gangway. I'm planning to use it to enter the Enclosure at Ascot with champagne buried in my little load of ice cold sand."

"Would you excuse me Beefy. Just for a few moments."

Balthazar passed to the end of the waiting hall. Between the elevators. And down the steps into the vaults. Pressing the black little button. A buzzer ringing along a corridor and footsteps approaching. Dark uniformed man lifting up his rings of keys to unlock and swing open this iron barred entrance.

"Good day, sir."

"Good day."

Heels clicking over the tiles along this passage and turning right into a mirrored room, a fan whirring quietly. The tinkle of keys and clank of a safe door. Great steel box lugged forth. Placed on a high table shelf behind the frosted glass door of a panelled booth. Turn the key, lift up the lid. Reach into the loneliness. To choose a stack of white storage crisp five pound notes. From the other stacks of French, Swiss, Dutch and Danish. Uncle Edouard always said keep a balance of currencies dear boy to cushion your horror if they all devalue at once.

And climbing back the carpeted marble stairs. Left between the phalanx of lift doors. Step aside politely for a high heeled toy poodle carrying perfumed customer. Beefy, my goodness, engaged in eager conversation with the dowager. He must practice on all old ladies. In the hope of handling granny. He lights up one's whole lonely life. With his fighting flaming flesh and bone. Now my God she's handing him her card. Enmeshed in his magic. And once he said at a distance people look different but when you talk to them they all become the same.

"Beefy. Here."

"Balthazar. I don't really feel I ought to take this."

"You must. Because it's my wedding present."

"You are a brick you know. But if the wedding should never take place."

A silence. And their both eyes look down. Upon the packed sheets of money. The dowager clears her throat. A waddling American goes by through the cocktail murmur of voices on this splendidly tremulous afternoon.

"Thank you unforgettably Balthazar. With the world gone dotty with greed you alone stand uncorrupted."

Beefy with a gentle gesture touched Balthazar. And put the wad of notes with all their curlicued embellishments in under his tweed. Giving them a reassuring little pat. He turned to his dowager friend and smiled. She smiled. One can weep with joy. To be at home again in London. Beefy's eyes as they always look for something in the middle distance. Never too close nor too far. He will hit yet the world a stunning blow. Crumple it in the mid section. And bring it back to life again with a dram of his poppy juice.

"Balthazar may I introduce you. Lady Bicuspid. I've just been telling her about great grand uncle. Who contracted fever tracing the source of the Nile. He was the first to find

307

the source of the Shannon for the Irish. It foxed the Erse for years. Poor devils. They were delighted when great grand uncle with a sample given him by my great grand father identified the water as being from a particular lake in China, called Shah Nun. For millennia it had leaked right through the earth. To trickle out in Ireland. That's how Shannon came to be its name. They gave uncle an immortal potato. The very original one they kept buried in a box at Tara. From which came all the others. Poor uncle. After his success in Ireland he thought he'd solve the Nile. Got knighted for his religious work among the savages. Who later, God rest his soul, knighted him with a spear where one does not want such a thing. They offered him up as a sacrifice in honour of the God uncle had revealed to them. They ate him. Without salt. It was awful. And dear lady. It appalls me still. The utter lack of gratitude and charity. Must rush now, but so pleasant meeting you like this."

"So interesting. I've enjoyed every moment so much, thank you. Young people don't talk to their seniors these days."

"Yes. I know. Not nice. But please God may we have this happenstance again. Been much rewarding to see the wealth of colour sparkling in eyes such as yours. An autumn splendour which only comes with the riper years."

"You are a dear boy."

"Goodbye, madam."

"Goodbye."

Beefy led Balthazar to the cigar department. There to purchase several packets to bulge out his pockets. On this lucid afternoon. He said he was going to distribute them to his mates on the building site. Where he would finish out the week. But alas he would still have to stay employed. Gainfully and continually or else forfeit the last remaining hope of granny's distant riches.

They parted with a wave at the entrance to the sweet department. Balthazar B went past the cheese and candles, by petunias and into the health juice bar. There amid a sudden throng of busty twice married heiresses he quaffed a mixture of blackberry juice and milk. And up through the various departments. To order furniture, enough for one. To sit and sleep upon.

The day of delivery in the door of 78 Crescent Curve. The men in pleasant green coats came. Set up the bed, table, sofa, chair, lamp and rug in the dining room. They thought me rather a little strange but I said it saves running around the house. I climbed up the stairs and stood there on the landing. Looking out back and into a small garden opposite. And saw lying back carelessly in a chair. A nearly naked girl. A towel just over her lap. Moving her head back and forth in the sunshine. A gleam on her small sharp pointed breasts. I was enchanted and somewhat saucily steamed. How gay and carefree and goodness, how London has changed. An older lady, looks her mother, comes out. Polishes her all over with an embrocation. As she now leans forward. Her pair seem to gain much in size. One wonders what other windows are alive with binoculars or unassisted eyes. Good Lord they look up. I step back. And wait. To peek again. From the landing next floor up. Ah the scene remains unchanged. I could run around and present my card. Placed neatly sticking up. I beg your pardon.

Out of
Beefy's
Wheelbarrow
Of ice cold
Sand.

24

The morning came when the parish magazine was pushed through the letter box. With a welcoming open letter to come and worship from the local vicar. And a week when I met the Angelica Violet Infanta, as well as her tall curvacious friend. We dined a foursome under the tinted cherubs painted on the ceiling of the Ritz. And danced around a champagne laden table hidden beyond the midnight curtains of Mayfair. The Infanta's laugh was deep throated and frequent. Her friend's was lighthearted and rare. And her name was Millicent.

Life easeful, moist and summery. In this most polite and courteous of cities. Grit and paper scraps tumbling in the gutter and people said sorry upon contact of an elbow. Smiles here now when needed. And words from the lips of Beefy. I kept appointments down in dark vaults near a candle to taste wine. Taxi engines trembled me a tranquil passenger, out to Mayfair and down to St. James. And sometimes I rode top the double decked red buses swaying roaring from stop to stop. Neighbours departed countrywards as weekends went by in Knightsbridge with unfussed burglaries on thick town house carpets.

I joined Beefy to play bezique at his club and dined off pheasant, claret and cheese. An afternoon on his day off he took me with a hamper of eel fillets, Scotch haggis from Perth, and boned and stuffed chicken in aspic and we sat with our wine surveying saucy antics in a private emporium of striptease. Beefy was climbing the road back up again. He said ah the Infanta, such is she as a girl and I as a chap that together we make a miracle.

I had a cook and Uncle Edouard's old butler, Boats, come one evening to give my first dinner at Crescent Curve. Magnums of champagne with slabs of tender steak and platters of garlic bread. Boats, retired a few years, was slightly enfeebled and very hard of hearing. And the crystal bowl of fruit salad he carried was dropped with one resounding pineapple splash. But there on that Thursday evening we drank a toast to the Violet Infanta and Beefy who announced their wedding. And I was asked to be best man.

I played tennis with Millicent. Who arrived smiling with tan legs in white socks and her racket and little box of balls. To volley, lob and smash me to smithereens all over the quiet and peaceful garden court. I stood so sweatily, spindly and white. And chasing her shots back and forth. Secretly I practised in an empty upstairs room against the wall. Breaking three rackets against the ceiling and knocking out four panes of glass. I met her parents. Both of them smiled. And leaned against their mantel piece. A marble little altar of propped up white invitation cards.

Millicent had long strong tan arms and splendidly muscled thighs. She stood straight and brown haired in flat shoes an inch taller than I. She moved wilfully forward her teeth flashing everywhere. Her serve was like a rifle shot and her back hand sizzled by. And each afternoon collecting up the tennis balls, I would watch her drying away her beads of sweat the other side of the court. Where she stood quite handsome. Elegantly serene. And pleasantly untouchable.

An evening we went to Soho for dinner. Each time I invited her I never thought she would say yes. She wore a close fitting orangy dress low cut over her breasts. And she listened and listened out of her lackadaisical brown eyes. With dark waiters crowding around. I stole looks down at her legs. Watched her buttocks wagging as she walked to powder her nose. And when she leaned forward I stared there too. A waiter doing so impertinently as well. I was so angered I lavishly overtipped him. Then we left for a nightclub. I finally moved to her close as she took my arm. She said out of the smoke and noise of the evening. Why Balthazar, it would not be impossible for us to go to an hotel. One weekend along the river.

From Crescent Curve I made lathered enquiries of river

hotels from Greenwich to Maidenhead. And she said yes when I told her. We were booked. My gladstone bag packed with my most favoured linen. A change of ties, four shirts and socks. An old volume on vertebrate morphology stuffed between. I would set forth in grey pin stripe. Change later to more casual wear. And there. She waited packed on that sunless north west corner of Harrods. As I came cruising in a hired chauffeured car along Brompton Road.

It had been an early afternoon of much sprinkling of the toilet water in all possible places. The combing and brushing of that awkward bit of hair. That jumps up from my crown. Sitting serene in this motor now. Distinctly headed west through Barnes across Putney bridge. Turn left to smile. And she puts out her hand and a finger striped gold with a wedding band. I had three times on lonely nights crossed through the park. Strolled the Bayswater Road. To hope to purely by accident meet Breda. But I never did. As the odd ladies went past whispering good evening dearie.

Reports coming in daily from Beefy were good. Back happily in his club. Employed as lift operator in one of the taller buildings. An improvement he said on the days crossing the stock exchange with slow gait so as not to expose his bare ankles devoid of socks. Awful dear boy when one can't sit down or walk too fast without fear of hiking up the cuff. But these days now living at his club crossing the lobby or marching down to breakfast in his elevator operator's uniform. Under the suspicious scrutiny of the members. But Balthazar, I tell you, George my old whipper, dear chap, spread the word among them that indeed I was of the foreign military, rank of major general in the Zanzibar marines.

Proceeding west through the middle afternoon. An hour or two before the rest of London will charge out to the countryside. We turn down a winding narrow road and go through this postern onto a gravel apron before a mullioned windowed door. With its little sign above saying so and so licenced to serve alcoholic beverages and tobacco on the premises. One feels a need of both right now. The hotel large and empty.

Across the lobby and through a smoking room where windows overlook the river cool and grey. The chauffeur carrying in our bags. One follows behind wondering what to do. I gave him a little something extra for himself. And tried to raise my eyebrows when I thought he seemed to wink at me.

At the polished oak reception desk I tinkled the little bell. A woman came. Busty in a rather over colourful flowered dress. Millicent standing with her everlasting smile playing across her lips as she looked down and bowed to sniff a vase of shrubs and flowers. I moistened my lips. Cleared my throat. And leaned forward imperceptibly.

"I have booked."

"Name please."

"Balthazar B."

"What's that."

"Balthazar. B is for B."

"O. Is it just one."

"O no it was for two."

"A double eh."

"Yes, I think so, please, with bath."

This big white book open. Where this lady points to say sign the register. And one does not know what to sign. Is it binding. To put down one great big B. Preceded by the tiniest written Mr. and Mrs. so that one can say I didn't mean it really. Evidence down through the years. Of deliberate saucy aforethought to indulge in shameless physical familiarities. Vile, low, shabby and inglorious. As I put the pen to this paper and tremble uncontrollably. Writing out across the page Mr. and Mrs. Balthazar B. So much larger than I ever meant it to be. And change my number from 78 to 94 Crescent Curve, and make it Mayfair instead of Knightsbridge.

A little man in a large grey suit took our bags to the room. Up a back staircase and down a long hall. Beefy said one should have as many rehearsals as possible for the honeymoon and he'd already played a solo on the Infanta's violin and she quivered and groaned on the high notes. As he shoved his stake as many times as he could into his claim. Flinging her down into seven leafed pink and purple clematis and rogering her right sharpish in the camelias where they both rolled ardently. My dear boy, of course one unzips the white dazzler and gets it into her before she can hear a sparrow fart. One merely whispers first, may I slip madam a gradual glissando. And here and now one walks hands atremble, heart beating far too fast. Into this room, bow fronted on the river. Big red flowered curtains, black narrow beams in white ceiling, pink and blue towels, and a crimson shade with tassels on the bedside lamp.

Millicent stands in front of the mirror combing back her neck length brown hair. Beneath the window a cherry tree. And beyond across the river a corner of a little field, great fat pink pigs lying in the grass. The door closed behind the porter. Our two bags side by side on the luggage rack the foot of the bed. And Beefy said whenever he looked with appealing honesty and purity of passion at some lady she would turn eastwards if any soft southerly attempt was made at her intimate acquaintance. Therefore it was frequently better to approach first with a gentle pastoral goose, oblique but deep enough to ruffle the female feathers. This led often to immediate and delightful bare arsed infamies without any prolonged further ado.

Balthazar B crossing the floor to stand close behind Millicent. And reach down, and my God I don't know quite how to give a goose. But must do something while I'm so near. Just put my hand I guess on her buttock and hope for the best as she slowly smiles in the mirror. And opens her brown eyes wide to look at me. My God how does one behave. Retreat now to give her time to pack. I mean unpack. Or wash her hands. Or rinse a pair of stockings as ladies often do. What a most awkward time of day. To stand here so close, my pole prepared as much as I am unprepared for anything. Still there is always that splendid solution to soothe and calm.

"Millicent, would you like to have tea."

"That would be nice."

We went down into the smoking room. Another couple of older years in the corner. Who raised their voices. To make conversation about the invention of the electric light bulb. The wife eagerly listening to what could only be her husband as tea is brought. Behaving as if they had never met before. In their twenty years of marriage and I don't suppose they have. Just like the moments when I touch Millicent and she answers by opening up that great big smile. What on earth will we ever talk about. Out now in the open over tea. She'll know at least that one is not beset with uncontrolled desperate passion. Or that the words I tried to get up out of my throat in the bedroom would have come out stammering. Not to have brought our tennis rackets. By which our relationship has volleyed back and forth and I've lost every game. Sealed with back hand top spin cross court passing shots. She sits so nonchalant, carelessly and beautiful and takes three lumps of sugar in her tea.

Again one starts back up the stairs. After a brief stroll along the river low on the banks with the lack of rain. Watching the muscles on her calves as she climbed. In her flat laced up walking shoes. Swallowing my breath, I followed along the hall. And I put in the key to open the door. Pushing it wide aside for her to go in. And remove the brown tweed jacket of her suit. She stands there in cream silk blouse and her string of pearls. Those little beads of refinement. I have come across so many times before. One feels now so absolutely full of Friday. Because if I didn't, no day of the week would mean anything to me at all. She waits again at the mirror. While I'm over now at the window. Making believe I'm watching the skiffs on the river. And a rather tattered little yacht going presumptuously by. Could be the very moment to change into casual wear. And she into hers and then I could suggest we lounge about devil may care before dinner. Or God damn it, go over and grab her now. Which I've never done to a girl before. Since they were always grabbing me. Time for a change. And here goes.

Balthazar B came across the red lilac carpeted floor. Wishing he were drunk in command of his person. To reach out and take Millicent's arms from behind in both hands. In the mirror again comes that smile. I've got to slowly turn her around. Force the issue from the front. And hear through one's memories one of Beefy's solemn cries. When you strike a blow in defence, dear boy, of carnal knowledge make it resounding. To see now Millicent's incredibly developed eye teeth, their sparkling points as she widens her smile. For me who, without a God to pray to, can never beg to be sent a sweet surprise. And I feel if ever her lips spoke I would hear them say, do not tax your energies unduly on my account. Her eyes look down over her shoulder where grasps my hand. But it was she who said. What about a weekend along the river. That night after she sat wiping her mouth in the restaurant where the waiter flexed his arm in emphasis when suggesting spinach. And the bill came and had me counting off pound notes for hours. Must break through her cool reserve. As Beefy did bust and break when he was a little boy. Living in his granny's big house. He had a carpet cannon with a gleaming brass barrel on its black iron carriage wheels. He brought it into position on the hall balcony and blasted down the huge crystal chandelier. He said choose a day dear boy when one has all one's nerve. Do it now. Regret later. For next after that is never. And dear boy remember it is simply not done to ever let your prick hang in a girlish manner. Don't wait for the moon to go green before grabbing her. With my voice quavering and breaking during these moments. Hearing a whispering Beefy. Outside an evening thrush is chirping. Bestir my bravery. But remember Beefy could beat her at tennis for a start. Spitting on his racket handle before serving like a spring snapping a trap shut. And then quietly and persistently reducing her to a sprawling lunging wreck. I thought it a wee bit ungentlemanly to serve that way to a lady. But changing court, adjusting his white cap and drying off with a pink towel, one heard him whispering quietly, my God the brute fleshy pliability of that girl. I put my lips on her neck under her hair at last. In the perfume smell. On a soft silky skin. A

316

little roughness of a spiked eardrop against my cheek. Turn her around and push backwards towards the bed. God forbid she should ever resist. Without even the nerve to ask her now to turn down the bed and undress. Just as I am when someone squeezes on a bench. I always get up and walk away. And goodness our arms are awkwardly engripped. Her lipstick close up rather bright. Reach my hand to go back of her head beneath her hair. Push a little more past these baubles caught between my fingers. My God what was that. Her pearls. Snapped. As she sits up. And they go bouncing. And make a sound as they reach the edge of carpet and roll on the floor.

"My pearls."

"I'm awfully sorry."

"They've gone all over the floor."

"I'll get them. I'll find them. I'm terribly sorry. Please don't upset yourself. I'm sure we'll find them all."

Balthazar B on his knees. Under the bed and dresser. Carefully picking up the whitish round little gems. Gathered into the palm of his hand. And a last two, way in under there. Take off my jacket and squeeze in, gathering plentysome dust on the cuffs and sleeves. Just one shirt gone and three to go.

Millicent sitting on the edge of the bed. Her hand brushing back her hair. Lifting her chin as she peered across into the mirror. I suppose I could tell her the funny little story of how Beefy goes racing round the streets, pushing open doors of painting galleries and screaming in, fakes. But instead I must to the bathroom go and button back together again one's double breasted coat. And take a timorous pee. Or tell her that Beefy said there are too many baronets mixed up with buggery these days.

"I do hope they're all accounted for Millicent. I'll put them in this envelope and take them to Asprey's first thing Monday to have them restrung. I am awfully sorry."

"They were my mother's."

"I am terribly sorry."

"Given to me on my twenty first."

"You are twenty three now, isn't that correct."

"Yes."

"Well what say we just. I'm sorry I've forgotten what I was going to suggest. I think I'll just go down for a moment to get some cigarettes."

"I didn't know you smoked."

"I haven't much done so before. As a matter of fact. I'll only be a moment."

Balthazar descending to the lobby. Crossing into the cozy oak panelled bar. The news of weather coming from the radio. A complex depression centered over England and moving west. Clouds and some showers are expected. Further outlook, rain moving east will cover all parts of southern England. And will not save me from melancholy and raving madness. As one steps to ask for a double brandy please. My God when will I ever become a man of the world. And put a noisy dirty lady sitting perched high on me spinning like a top, with her red hair waving and her light coloured shoes flying off against the walls. Perhaps it may happen after I have purchased my first cigar.

"May I have one please, that long one there."

"They're three and eight a piece, sir."

"That's very pricy but still I think I'll have one."

Balthazar B taking a sip of brandy and lighting his cigar. A little wooden bird behind the bar dipping and dipping into a jar. So hard to sit alone with one's thoughts now. After busting the beads. And chasing them all over the floor. Dear God when I think of the body of her. When all it needed was just to remain calm and look where one's hands were going. Up behind the hair. Get a newspaper now. And then one shall return. With some current topic of conversation. And have another try.

Balthazar B walked out across the lobby from the bar. To turn to look into the smoking room. The raised voices and opening front door and someone coming in. They say with cigars one doesn't inhale. You just go around puffing and stinking. No newspapers in the smoking room. Make an enquiry. Just wait till these two folk are served. Standing there

318

at the reception desk. Yes, right there, they stand in something familiar like a dream one had once somewhere and you think you're having it all over again. Because those two people, right there, in front of the open registration book. They look like the father and the mother of Millicent. And I'll just pass on now over here and wait. To stop. And turn again and look. My God. That is the mother and father of Millicent.

Balthazar B stood frozen thinly on the red tiled floor in his grey double breasted pin stripe suit. A silk shirt tiny knotted at the collar by a black silk tie with a three legged emblem sprinkled on it like stars. Millicent's mother and father turning as one, as the landlady pointed her finger right at me. And I took a deep intake of cigar. The smoke filling out my jowls and stacked and packed down my throat. To all explode at once. And send me staggering forward in a fit of coughing as these three folk watched. And two of them caught their breath. And two of them began to approach.

Balthazar B looking out from uncontrollably rolling eyes, gasping and speechless. The tints and hues of Millicent's mother somewhere near. And for no accountable reason one thinks of that distasteful English habit of wetting the finger and putting it in one's companion's ear. As Millicent's mother now points with her own finger towards the smoking room. Which one can hardly see. But follow this way. Beefy always ran to elderly blind old age pensioners to lead them safely across the street and have a joke with them on the way. As I step quite sordidly across into a blaze of socially ostracised eternity. Beefy always warned. Of what the English so expertly do. Is to take one's composure utterly away. Mine is gone. Left with only my green colour changing to alabaster white.

"As Millicent's mother I am shocked more than I can say. In fact Stephen please, would you order me a whisky, double. No need to go into why we're here, the fact is we are. And have seen the register with our own eyes. I am absolutely aghast and surprised at you. Certainly one never expected someone to whom the hospitality of one's own house has been offered to stoop as low as this. One can only ask now have we come upon this too late."

"No no you haven't."

"Where may I ask is Millicent."

"She's upstairs."

"I see. Poor girl. Taken to a place like this. Of all things. A hotel on a river. Is there an explanation. Or are you taking this matter casually."

"No madam. I'm not."

"Why aren't you speaking up. Or do you suppose more subterfuge will help. As since when is Crescent Curve suddenly in Mayfair. Or is the truth that you have deliberately taken my daughter here with the intention of ravishing her."

"No no I didn't."

"You didn't. You didn't ravish her. Is that what you're saying. With my daughter up there in the same bedroom, registered as Mrs. Balthazar B. You haven't ravished her."

"I know that my redeemer liveth."

"You what."

"I'm sorry. I don't know what I'm saying."

"That's very apparent. As is also that you don't deny abducting my daughter."

"I haven't done anything. Her pearls fell on the floor."

"Her pearls. O my God. Stephen. Did you hear. She had to fight for her honour. O my God thank you, I need that whisky. Millicent had to fight. It came to that. Her pearls strewn everywhere in the struggle. I must go to her."

"No no, they just fell apart."

"Fell apart. As you used force. On my daughter."

"Your daughter is much stronger than I am."

"O my heavenly God. In just one moment I think I shall get completely hysterical. Stephen go please and close that door. This could lead to scandal. Front page of every paper in Europe. My daughter forced to submit."

"Please I only weigh ten stone two. And your daughter Millicent weighs ten stone four."

320

"As if her weight mattered. At a time like this. And what may I ask are your intentions."

"Well I suppose to leave. As soon as possible."

"Leave. You mean walk out. Just like that. Millicent was presented at Court. She was outstanding as one of the leading debutantes of the season. And you, you're going to leave. Have you no scruples."

"Well I'm not awfully well at this moment. But perhaps later."

"Later. My husband Stephen here is in the motor trade. Some of our best friends pass on this very road outside. Not more than a few yards from the bedroom to which you dragged our daughter. How is she now going to confront some honourable gentleman who will hear of these heinous hours spent here in this place. Are you aware that she is in receipt of a written proposal from a peer of the realm."

"I'm sorry, I didn't know."

"Well she is. And that may be now ruined forever. One hopes one does not have to resort to sordid measures. But in the circumstances I have no alternative but to ask you. What are your intentions towards our daughter. Availing yourself as you so obviously have of the prerogatives of the marriage chamber. Can you answer me that."

Balthazar B his hands placed neatly palms down flat on each thigh. Stephen pretended to look out on the river. And I face these eyes accusingly glued to me as I sneak away cowering into the Austrian Alps and there am seen peeing on a defenceless mountain flower. Sitting here nearly waiting for one's second childhood to play games missed in the first. Without an erotic hope in one's future. Only antique collecting left to give one a sense of longevity. As the desperations come. When Beefy planned his ad in The Times. Gentleman of razor thin means, bachelor with own dog and gun, suffering slight nervous disability, glad to undertake light administrative work or, in clement weather, prepared to give time tending rose garden in return for congenial permanent accommodation where servants kept. While the present advertiser suffers some slight psychological impairment he is fluent in Urdu. Beefy what do I do. As I struggle heavy footed. Dying amid flashes of sunny memories. When Bella once sat, a picture of a funny little car she said was hers, and I laughed when I heard her say her car was not well, it had been long ailing, so she took it to the car doctor for a little bit of hammering and a little bit of fixing and a little bit of oil and the car doctor gave it medicine and it coughed.

"Coughing is all very well, my dear boy. That is all very well. One only hopes one finds a way out of this before it is too late. And Millicent pregnant. The matter lies with you rather than with us. For the moment anyway. I don't want to go on repeating myself, but what are your intentions towards our daughter."

"I have had good intentions."

"Continue."

"Yes I have had them. But I don't think I know really what to do with them. I know I'm not very good at making myself clear."

"We have until eight fifteen, so by all means continue."

"Well I don't know really, I happen to have had a fear of death."

"What on earth are you talking about. I want to know what your intentions are. And I won't leave this smoking room until I do. Then it will be quite clear to us what steps are to be taken to protect our daughter's interests."

"I only meant I was choking to death before. It's passed now. I have intentions."

"Yes, you have intentions."

"Yes I do."

"I see. Intentions to do what."

"Well I guess a lot of things."

"What lot of things."

"But I haven't done anything to Millicent."

"You haven't. Surely you must be joking. Stephen I think we had better reserve our rights and seek legal advice."

"O my God. Don't."

"Don't. Of course we shall."

"I'll marry maybe, if that is, I mean o my God, my trustees would have to approve."

"You'll marry maybe. O that's very nice to know. And also we can acquaint your trustees then fully."

"O God no. Please leave it to me."

"Well then. This perhaps is a little different. But you seem so sure Millicent will marry you."

"No I'm not."

"But you intend then to marry Millicent."

"I think maybe I do."

"You think. You'd better know."

"I know."

"I'm sorry to have to put matters like that. But one can't go on bantering and bandying."

"Yes. I'll marry Millicent."

"I hope you won't think for one second that either Millicent's father or I want you to marry Millicent if you would really prefer to worm away like a cad."

"O no. Not nice. A cad. Would you mind. I think I may require the use of a water closet. Thank you."

Balthazar rushing from the room. Across the lobby into the bar where he reached to grab his still waiting brandy as he passed. To feel the bowel beginning to move. As one rushed to get into these cool shadows and quickly lower drawers. No one has ever seen a kangaroo screw. Yet somehow I've been seen. And wasn't screwing. I could do worse. She's big and awfully stong with a lot of curves. Live with the constant fear of being beaten up by a woman in a fair fight. Beefy says without cash use courage and I'm without courage and can't use cash. And soon by the feel of it I'll have piles too. Chains winding round one with an eternal clank. Can't leap from the crapper here and go chasing so hopelessly after freedom. Only thing left now is to rest and ruminate without rusting. Be parsley sprinkled on everyone else's soup. The shadow's of her two nipples pressed against her beige silk. Her legs back and forth across the tennis court. The long tan muscles winking on her thighs. To catch a glimpse of her arse cheek as she wound up to serve. That's what I watched because she slammed so hard I couldn't see the ball. And her father seems to have two glass eyes. The Sunday I went to tea. Had a postage stamp of cucumber sandwich and declined a piece of cake. I agreed with everything they said to me. Given them such a headstart. They said with all Millicent's suitors the phone never stopped ringing. And her mother sighed when she said it would be such a rest when Millicent was finally engaged. And I wondered then how they ever knew my father had been connected with cement and wine, cars and pulp. How long I can hold out in here. Before Millicent's mother comes in and gets me. O my God. I am heartily sorry for myself. My ears are burning, they feel very red. They'll be searching my bag upstairs. Full of French letters. Must keep a grip. Millicent's breasts are multiplying right in front of my eyes. This is what one gets. Not staying home and reading the parish magazine. And Millicent's mother's eyes during the time she spoke to me, kept dipping and staring at my flies. And the words I was hearing. Have you any dirty habits you've come here with from abroad. For instance, the crabs. O my God. How can one ever be. Ideally suited for the world. And.

A
Popular
Personality.

25

The organ played, Balthazar B stood solemn and still. Millicent covered in white veils. A choir hired to sing. And all through the ceremony I needed desperately to pee. Listening through Millicent's four christian and one double barrelled names. Reeled off again and again. Millicent, Angelina, Consuelo, Trixie Butterworth Jones. Wilt thou have this man to thy wedded husband, to live together after God's ordinance in the holy estate of matrimony. Beefy handed me the ring. With this ring I thee wed with my body I thee worship and with all my worldly goods I thee endow. And a little boy followed by his mother running up the center aisle between all the morning suits and ladies' hats and crinolines, shouting in his high pitched voice, mommie mommie I must do wee wee.

This tiny chap had big green innocent eyes. And while other folk drew in their breath I turned to smile at him. He was a sweet looking little fellow. And Beefy too reached to pat him soothingly on the head and whisper and point at where he could go, in his short trousers, brown tiny shoes and red little jumper.

A house had been rented for the reception. From people who it seemed paid their rent that way. Millicent's father had whispered and asked before the wedding if I were able to effect a discount on the wine and spirits. I was alarmed and later surprised when it turned out I could. Millicent's uncles crowded me in the corner. One trying to sell me a used car, another who would give me the opportunity as a new relative to heavily invest in his newly opened ironmongery shop. And Mr. Pleader said at our last conference that the sum demanded on behalf of one's fiancée as a marriage settlement was excessive.

Beefy swept his way back and forth chatting gaily among the guests and made a splendid speech. He spoke of the bride's brilliance on the tennis court and said he knew her soup would be every bit as good as her serve. He gave me as a wedding present two cement cast replicas of the stray dog of long ago, little Soandso, for the front porch of Crescent Curve. Said they would scare away other dogs who would shit and make one skid on one's steps. And two gross of French letters got wholesale near Tottenham Court Road, beating the man down over the price until both were in an hysterical nervous sweat. Millicent smiled through everything. Even when Beefy after nudging numerous bridesmaids under the tit, waltzed up to her mother and slipped her one of his beatific gooses. She laughed delightedly as she disported tipsily explaining at length why I had no relatives.

The motor came, and changed and packed we piled in. The waving heads from the window. A last picture taken against a drain and bars of a fence. Beefy said Balthazar she is really beautiful but don't give her too much all at once. Wait till she likes it and then by God you can feed it to her like honey. She'll eat it and love it. He said the Violet Infanta was playing hard to get. But he was rogering items in between. He blew a kiss and said give my saucy regards to Dublin. And lastly yelling in the window as we pulled away. I won't be wiped out by the phenomenon of natural selection but shall triumph as the fittest with the fattest inheritance.

The train was delayed pulling out of Euston. A derailment, and widespread fog covering the Midlands. With smash and grab burglars emptying shop windows over the same area. Beefy said there is no criminal class as ready as the English to swing into action when the weather is ripe. Millicent wanted to know what was in the parcel Beefy gave me with such a smile. I said the first thing that came into my head, chewing gum. And when I looked and reflected on the two hundred and eighty eight condoms I was rather flattered. But a little mystified by the two dozen black ones found enclosed.

The night full of flashing light, twisted grey pipes of factories. By biscuit makers and piggeries and the shimmer of the canal. We pulled into Liverpool utterly late. Between the black sweating sooty walls. And missed the boat to Dublin. I felt everyone must know I carry all the French letters I do. Millicent looking up from her magazine in our first class compartment. As I looked at my watch. And she turned without a smile and said, you clot.

The grim bleak black station. The train emptying. Carts stacked high with mail. The smoking sighing locomotives and sulphurous smells. Liverpool covered in mist. A soft droplet rain staining footpaths with black sooty prints. Millicent in her all pale blue and pink. The great wide shady hat on her head. Sitting with teeth clenched on our stack of luggage. I phoned the Adelphi Hotel, sorry sir, all booked up. I phoned and phoned and the answer always the same. The strong midget professorial porter finally said he knew of a place. And a propos of nothing at all Millicent said that the announcement of the wedding in the paper had brought an avalanche of filthy literature and contraceptive advice. With my religious and gentlemanly feelings I was desperate to please. I said I'd get a taxi.

Up the dark grim cobble stone street. A wasteland of blackened rooftops and crazy chimney pots. In the shadows a dying plant in its flowerpot on a square foot of front garden before this house with a green door. Bed and breakfast, clean and select. In view of my wedding night I was glad it was both of these things. At the end of this long narrow hall a balding man eyes me rather suspiciously. Forge on, chilled hungry and begrimed, it hardly matters. Yes I have a double room for two. I said would he mind I would just go back and ask my wife. Just outside the door.

"I'm not going in there."

"Millicent everywhere is booked."

"You're such a clot, my God."

"Please it's just for tonight."

"Do you think I'm going to go into that place."

After much tugging. Embroidery and sheer fatigue. She

moved. Up the steps, one by one. Standing tall, her elegant legs silhouetted against the wet glimmering street. The man standing ahead of me in this barren green walled hall. His grey cardigan buttoned. A blueish cloth knotted at his throat. Raising his hand and putting his head to the side as he peered at Millicent. Her heels clicking on the floor, her head rearing with disdain. Outside the taxi pulled away. The landlord leaning forward, putting his hands on his hips.

"Ere ere now, there'll be none of that now. None of that in this ere house. I keeps a respectable premises and there'll be none of that ere."

"I beg your pardon."

"Don't you beg my pardon. There'll be none of that kind of goings on in my hotel. Plenty of them kind of places down on the docks the bottom of the hill for that kind of caper."

"I beg your pardon."

"O yeah, sure you do. You'll beg my pardon too when I lose my licence for keeping a disorderly house."

"This lady here is my wife."

"I've heard that one before."

"And I have a marriage licence to prove it. Furthermore I would have thought you'd take more care than to risk slandering callers at your guesthouse."

This grey skinned man retreating silently for a key. I couldn't believe my own ears at my forceful say. Just as one wanted to run. Millicent's eyes wide with fascination, when one would have thought it might have been umbrage. We climb up two flights of stairs. Into a square green walled room, two electric converted gas mantles on the wall. Yellow and blue triangles across the linoleum floor. To shut the door and put a chair up against the knob. Millicent standing in the middle of the room absolutely still. I say things to her and she refuses to speak. My bag with the two gross of French letters left behind checked in the station. I thought all the way up on the train that I might try one of those coloured black. Just for size.

The lights left burning. All the night. Millicent after two

hours leaning against the wall condescended to sit on a chair, hat on, wrapped in her coat. I sat fully clothed, elbows resting on my knees and my head in my hands in the center of the bed. To finally lie backwards and fall asleep. To dream of the brown envelopes on the floor of Crescent Curve when first I came back there from Paris. And pink envelopes started to fall and cascade down the stairs. Building up around me as I stood. I had Fitzdare's photograph in my hands. Which shook as I said Elizabeth. To see her small smile across her lips and the soft waves flowing back from her hair. The beads of light in her eyes shining like the beads of her pearls. When the clouds were grey and blue. Across the morning breezy sky of Fermanagh. Stood there. Seeing. Racing along the green edge of the sparkling lough. In that morning crystal air, the earthly God forbidden splendour of Elizabeth Fitzdare. And the words I hear.

"Take me out of here."

Millicent in the same position on her chair. One long leg folded over the other squeezing out a curving mound of flesh. A long hacking coughing and upheaving coming through the wall of the next room. Sound of water draining and a toilet flushing. The lids droop on Millicent's eyes and she snaps awake again. I must go and take an urgent and desperate pee.

"Did you hear what I said. I said take me out of here."

"Yes. I will. Just excuse me. I must go to the water closet. I'm sorry."

Down this hall past a door. Inside the springs of a bed rustily squealing. Pushing the latch on this broken water closet I cut my finger. And held it coagulating between the open crack of window. The morning light and foggy air. Back ends of houses and garbage strewn yards. A window lit. A girl stands spreading something on a piece of bread with a knife. She is pretty and sharp bosomed in a moss green sweater. Takes up a kettle in her hand. My pee comes out. Lean further towards the crack to see. And she's seen me. Makes a rude gesture with her fingers. Pulls a tattered curtain across the window. Send her an apology on my calling card. Tell her about the whole horrid mess because of derailment and fog. You girl, buttering your bread. I was only standing peeing. The morning after my wedding night. My soul strewn with a simple little hope to please my wife. My prick in my hand. From which I shake the last drops. And they go, with my tears down my cheeks. Into the toilet bowl.

Among these breakfasting figures I pushed a tray along a self service rail. Had coffee, two sausages, bacon and egg. Gritty around my collar. Greasy round the egg. Face feeling stiff with sleeplessness and grime. Millicent sat across the table and refused to eat. And after silence through the morning she spoke as we sat amid hotel palms for tea.

"Who is Fitzdare."

"Fitzdare."

"Yes. You were shouting it out in your sleep. And you writhed. It was quite horrid to watch."

As the ship cut through the water. And at dawn Dublin loomed in the west. I never said who Fitzdare was. Ten o'clock last night rung high up on the Royal Liver Building shaking the great birds atop held against the wind. The dark heaving pier. I had two bottles of stout in the bar before I went to bed. Millicent in the top bunk. The ship hitting a bit of rough sea. I undressed falling about the cabin. I was trying to find the ladder up to her bunk. My pole so hard I thought it would break. Feeling exposed and awkward when it waves about. Apologise and explain that it did it when least I knew why and often when I was only counting money. To now take it with me wagging up step by step to kiss her on the cheek.

"Get your drunken hands off me."

She reached out and shoved me on the shoulder. I fell from the ladder with a crash. And lay in silent naked agony. A terrifying pain across my shoulder and down my arm. Waking in a cold sweat in the dawn of this lower berth. The path of death so well worn by the many gone before. The brown plastic ventilator in the ceiling. Lifebelts in racks over the top bunk. A brass vomit bowl and a white chamber pot. Catching my breath with pain. Struggling to look out the porthole. The sea calm. A dredger, grey and still. Dublin lies flat and ahead, hills rising out around her. The Sugarloaf beyond Dalkey. The sky all faint blues. A squat row of the little houses as the ship turns round. Down those alleys went Beefy in all his degrees of devilment. See a pair of great iron hooks and the cables winching in the bows. Ships. The Manta. Netta from Rotterdam. The Glenbridge from Dublin.

An ambulance was called to the ship. I was lifted out on a stretcher staring at the sky. Millicent said she was red faced with embarrassment and all the French letters were confiscated. At the red brick hospital over the Grand Canal bridge. They said I had a broken collar bone.

But one
Day
Soon
I would
Be well
Again.

26

Crescent Curve was awake festooned from attic to basement
aflow with flowers. Carpets laid, cupboards and shelves fitted.
Sideboards and suites of bedroom furniture. All lavender
waxed and ordered by Millicent's mother and the bill sent to
me. To await the arrival after the honeymoon. As one listened
being taken on a tour of one's own house.

"In our way of life Balthazar a wife always has her own bed
and dressing room. Then there's a time and place for everything."

My shoulder was just but out of its cast. After a few weeks
of married life. Three weeks in Dublin. Where there had been
the French and Irish Rugby match during our stay. I tried to
smile winningly over my injury. As the French players
swarmed about one's wife. Saying in their language to her as
she smiled back. My God what a glorious cunt she is, how can
we get rid of the husband who looks like a crippled English
peer. And as I whitened and tightened my lips they licked
theirs at the sight of Millicent. And shook their heads at the
sight of me.

A Friday lunch I saw Beefy. Up in the top of Fortnum's. I
walked in. Having strolled from Knightsbridge. To find him
seated there. Resplendent in his lift operator's uniform, with
a general's lapels. The world so balmy. The sun slashing
through trees and streets. And he could tell that I carried a
tale.

"My God Balthazar, you're thinnish. You must eat more.
Dog food, that's where all the nourishment is these days
in England. The selected meats, liver, vitamins and minerals.
Honest nourishment at an honest price. Choice lean beef
finely chopped with proteins. I take a tin a day. But my God
Balthazar, what's the matter."

"Beefy. I don't quite know how to put this. Millicent and I have not yet cohabited."

"Good grief. Let's order lunch."

"My collar bone broke at the first try. Been in a cast ever since. But now I'm out. She doesn't seem to want me."

"Mandamus her. To commit the act."

"I couldn't do that."

"Then annul for God's sake. Annul."

"Do you think so."

"Get your trustees on to it. If you don't annul now you condone, you could be trapped celibate for the rest of your life."

"But I don't want to annul. That's a legal step and I somehow feel her mother would shout awfully loudly in court."

"Has she seen it."

"Seen what."

"Your tool, your private member. I mean does she hold it in horror or disbelief. Is she distressed at the sight of it."

"I don't know."

"Did she scream when she saw it."

"No. I think I may have when I fell. Is this usual in a marriage."

"But of course, I mean there are some who haven't laid hand to each other in all their years. Often makes for permanent unions. You mustn't worry. First thing is to get you some dirty literature and have it around the house. Few of these filthy books. You know the sort of thing, Lola stood there as the bishop or butler advanced his sheath upon the shaft well drawn back from the rosy knob of his stiff passion. Older members of the club who don't want to be bothered stimulating the wife often just throw her one of these tomes in the dressing room. Twenty minutes before dinner is served is thought to be a ripeish time. Millicent might just pick it up and get carnal minded."

"Isn't that a little distasteful."

"It's abominable but you must. I know a shop. Good chaps. Specialists. Answer your needs in a hurry. A portfolio

333

of the male nude may be your man. In the usual erected poses. Hate to bring up nationalities but you know how you French chaps wear white gloves so not to leave fingerprints on your pricks. Well, such photos throw English women into uncontrolled fits of passion. Buck up Balthazar. I'm now tying the last little strings on the Violet Infanta. We've decided to live at the Ritz. When I shall like any other civilised human being be able to spend my afternoons at the usual auctions. Chippendale's cheap at the moment. My trustees are delighted by my prospects. But you know I miss work on the building site. Good chaps to a man. There was a Padrick from Tipperary. Wore a chef's cap while on the job. He employed his culinary deftness he said in mixing the cement into which I always took a pee. He could fart in unison with the pneumatic drill. And goose one with the mechanical digger. I mean he could make it dance, there he was in the glass operator's cubicle playing the sticks and levers like a prodigy. He'd dig a hole into anything. Down into gas mains, electric cables, nearly every day there'd be an explosion, like open warfare. Ah but you Balthazar, you will overcome."

And parting at Piccadilly on that sunny afternoon, Balthazar B sped to Knightsbridge by tube. To attend a fortnightly visit to the chiropodist with nail trimming and foot massage. Later leaving the male nudes and one volume of dirty literature carelessly in Millicent's pink walled dressing room. On the afternoon of the Palace Garden Party five days later, she asked me before leaving with her mother, a propos of nothing at all, did I ever do anything sexual with other boys at school. In a black chiffon dress and an enormous black straw hat against her silken tan, she said do come and pick me up.

One was mystified by the faintly scheming way she looked. I walked the afternoon slowly down through Green Park. The rows of cars all lined up. A loudspeaker calling them one by one. I stood by the Palace gates. The crowds of commoners standing aside to let through the chauffeured cars. The splendour and elegance passing by. Top hats, monocles, ebony canes and fluttering tails. Silks and hues and flowing veils. And many many pearls. And finally Millicent grim with fury. Where was the car to come in and pick her up. What did I mean by leaving her to this disgrace. And I suddenly said shut up.

There was silence on this warm evening as we walked towards home. Up Constitution Hill, the Palace tinted crowds thinning through Belgravia. Their high heels, wide hats and powdered noses. Puffs of low white clouds. A westerly wind blowing a smell of new mown grass across the fresh green of the park. Along Grosvenor Crescent, the pillared porches, the high walls painted cream. Across Belgrave Square and through an empty echoing West Halkin Street. And one took comfort from the calm mellow brick of Knightsbridge where the moss lies quietly between the paving stones.

In my little study off the drawing room I went to check through my cellar book and enter newly arrived wine. And as usual to stack up and count the bills. Pouring in from Fortnum's and Harrods. From dress and shoe shops up and down Bond Street. And Millicent came in. Walked over as I sat with my pencil and paper weights. She gave me a little push and I drew back.

"How's the shoulder."

"I think it's fine."

"Come upstairs."

"What for."

"Don't ask me questions. Just come upstairs."

I climbed up the stairs following Millicent into her pink and blue bedroom. Reviewing in my mind the legal interpretation of the presentation of one's member. Private and erect. To the spouse present and duly open eyed. In this so silent house. There were couples sunning on the grass in the park. Others wrapped in arms. Millicent's wide black garden party hat on her dressing table. Two foot stack of magazines by the bed. And she in her stockinged feet. The big blue diary next her telephone. Booked every day for lunch and tea and all the fashion shows. She pulls the curtains across on the window.

Complained of the man across the street spying with binoculars. She could see the lens gleaming behind leaves of a plant he grew for camouflage. And I had walked in upon her once having a bath, to get a piece of her Paris soap. And she clutched her arms across her breasts and said get out of here. I made believe as I paused in the mirror that I was examining my eyebrows for dandruff. I had spent that day watching the men from Harrods come and go. With the latest samples in materials. Her mother brought friends to see our curtains and view the bathrooms, all four, and our big fat towels. Millicent's glass shelves covered in bottles of scent, her wardrobe full of shoes, handbags and scarves. And I sat staring at my laundry frayed cuffs, my missing buttons and holes in my socks. A man came to do her hair. And meals arrived from a restaurant. When one evening more than anything else in the world I wanted chicken kedgeree and rhubarb crumble. I asked her to make it. She just looked at me and said how dare you be so thoughtless and cruel. Now she looks at me, and is taking off her clothes.

"Balthazar we'll go into your bedroom so we don't upset my bed."

Millicent taking a towel and passing through the dressing room. A breeze blowing against the curtain in my open window. And one of the most marvellous things in the world is to be in bed on a train speeding through the night time countryside after a hot summer day and have moist cool air blow through the sheets. I thought on a day such as this there must have been sun bathing nude in the garden. But now the sun was sinking and may have sunk. She takes off her slip and lays it across my pile of zoology books. Waits like women sit and wait in Paris antique shops, spiders in a web. I feel a little breeze under my armpits. Millicent standing there stark naked. A sight I have never seen. Her triangle of dark brown curly hair and her soft swell of belly and navel like a small inlaid ear. My eyes closed as I saw her breasts. To think all this time both those things have been there. Lips dry. No voice in me. She beckons me with her finger. There are big leeches in the River Eure flowing through Chartres. Mind runs riot. I'm tempted to call for a taxi to take me across this carpet. Feel like an Algerian trying to sell a piece of Africa in an empty side street. With the vision now of all my trustees seated round. Intoning in ecclesiastic voices, the Lord blesses the dead who have done the brave thing instead of the smart. They take out pencil and paper. To make a proper record of proceedings. Mr. B has presented his member expanded to eighteen centimeters and the opposite partner in the marriage has not yet screamed. Mr. Pleader with opera glasses, Mr. Horn with callipers and Hoot with racing form. My mirror there. Where there is so much to see. As she leans right down and grabs it with her mouth. I stand with nervous hands at my side at attention. Looking down on her gleaming brown head of hair. Uncle Edouard said for something which is priceless a woman should charge nothing. Paid such a price already until this change in her. Tanned all over by the infra red of her bathroom ceiling. And sometimes away racing in the afternoon, I had visions of all her former admirers beating a path to the door. Drinking one's wines and gobbling down the caviar. Hands all over one's undressed wife. The lover's bare toes twiddling the knobs of my gramophone. The mysterious little absences one noticed among the wine bins. Which make me wonder now. How much blowing could go on without my knowing. Millicent carries her arse as if it were the last one on earth. Shops all through the morning till she needs a rest and goes to a shoe emporium to sit and buy shoes. The cold clarity of her nudity makes me thank God I have eye lids to close. Times she sat when I looked at her. All she wants to do is go out and dance in front of the world. Far from the cooking carrots and undusted window sills. To rush to a fitting for a brassiere. Why worry. There are still some immortal mistakes I cherish. Let the brain steam. And trustees record that it's now in her mouth. Beefy knows exactly when not to wear white shoes. And the postal boundaries all over London. Those where one can safely walk with holes in the socks and find cads who use brown envelopes. The boundary stone set in the curving sidewalk of Pembridge Square and Moscow Road. Where and when Beefy winces as he steps into Paddington. The world never knows you're so lonely. When you're leaning by some dark iron railings outside a slightly opened window. Listening to piano playing. Uncle Edouard said people look for arse when they look for art. And a little band of ruffians with a baby carriage walked by with a tame goose waddling after them. They looked for money and I gave them half a crown. I would stand solemn and prolonged at that red and brown brick world, transfixed by Sloane Street, Pont Street and Beauchamp Place. The white cheese cloth behind the polished windows, the turrets and transoms on the rooftops, the blackened tiles on the gables. And up high the odd weather vane veering above the whining traffic. I can't believe it's going into her down through the soft moist parting between her legs. As she gives out a frightening long howling groan. With the trace of a smile. Heard all over Knightsbridge. Never knew it meant so much to her. Been glad to slip it in before. Stayed by the hand of protocol and ceremony and broken collar bone. Gained in my first attempt. One is taught to be so nice. Wait till asked. Don't do that. And get nothing for the hesitation. When people seem to like it better if you elbow them around. I told her to shut up. I was just as aghast as she. Groans getting even louder now. What on earth am I doing to her. Playing a dirge down her nervous cord. The whole neighbourhood listening to the notes. And it's getting that kind of dark when the world can hear you pull your penis. The same one that Beefy said his building mate stained green on St. Patrick's Day. Now that I've got it in must make no mistakes, yet no one gets to the grave without tripping a few times. Her legs locked around my waist. Ankles waving her feet I see in the mirror. She must be a woman. But will never flick a spud into the boiling water. Or take needle to one's flies. With a wrist flicking beat up a mayonnaise. But she is as Beefy said, by merely shifting her hind quarter fractionally abaft, taking one's noble carboniferous tool eight miles up her jeroboam. This Wednesday. A

338

chime from my study clock below. The groans roll out longer
and louder from her parted lips. Echoing back across the
gardens. Voices below. Each thrust a sound peals out. Her
legs wrapped around me like two snakes. When you think
she's mad. Someone you've never met before. She strolled out
today between the parsons in gaiters and much purple cloth. I
saw a big blue prison van go by with the eyes staring out from
the little windows. And uniforms passing out the Palace gates
where one might ask not the rank but what's your nation. A
smile on Millicent's face. Where whenever I close my eyes. Is
it you Fitzdare. As I come near where I will go diving diving
down. Parting air with my hands. Brushing away Dublin raindrops. Hear bells ringing. Just like a front door. I told Millicent's mother I would on no account have chimes to be
modern. A bell would do. She said do forgive me. I did and it
was another invitation to come charging in with all her friends
just to say hello we've only time for a drink. But after two
they always stayed for three or four. And later I was handed
the whopping bill at a restaurant. Followed by the warnings
of one's trustees. Dear Mr. B, for the sake of future reserves
we would advise some restraint in current expenditure. Who
knows one day one might have heirs. As o my God I go with
everything crashing into her. And she gives out with a long
echoing howl and one hears the ringing and ringing of bells.
World falls down. A dust rises up. Voices saying, I say there,
I say there, you in there, we are citizens out here. And you will
be punctured at the end of her last long piercing groan.
Tightening and swallowing the length of my organ. Tell
Beefy what the nude male pictures with white gloves have
done. And the voices who cry out I say there, in there and
murder most foul. What. What murder. Whose are those
noises. And the knocks on the dressing room door. A voice
says do we have to break it down. Good Lord. What's this.
Don't get nervous. The nightmare continues. Sound of fiddling of keys. In Millicent's automatic lock to keep me out.
And a knock and hands hammering now. Balthazar B un-
ravelling from his wife's arms and legs, rolling from the bed

339

and standing up. Crossing the purple carpet to the dressing room door. To say to the other side press the button on the lock. And it opens slightly ajar. For there are. Distinctly people there. A nearby strange face with grey hair.

"Sir, there are gurglings going on somewhere."

"What."

"Gurglings, we've heard gurglings and groans."

"I beg your pardon."

"We've traced it up here. Had to come in your door. To investigate of course."

"What are you doing in this house."

"Sir, gurgling and groaning and some cries have been heard out in the garden. By my wife."

"Gurgling."

"Yes, quite. We have come to see by what authority it is being emitted. Sir. Then there were groans, long, long, piercing groans."

"I think you must be mistaken."

"O no, there are four of us. This other gentleman came with us. He heard it too. We met him on the street. We wish to know sir, by what authority these groans are being uttered. As it would appear from the sound that some embranglement is afoot. Sir, my God, have regard, you are without any garments, please."

"Pardon. But it is my house and I want to see the rest of you. The light's not awfully good."

"Yes, quite, we wish of course it were better too. On this investigatory mission. I don't think any of us, let me make that point quite clear, will be deterred by hollow answers. We are all here agreed we have heard the groans and moans."

"You are I think trespassing. This is my house."

"Look sir, that may be, but again I must make perfectly clear that we have entered upon the premises on a serious investigatory mission, in the manner, if I may say so, of vigilantes, and we would appreciate not being trifled with. If someone is in distress it is the duty of citizens to demand to know sir."

Millicent sitting upright in shadows, the sheets gathered around. A cow goes on grazing latterly the bull has been in her. Balthazar B bare arsed at the dressing room door, a Welsh traveller in Wales attired in national costume. Urgent whispers from Millicent get those damn people out of my room. Beefy said it was an inclination of Knightsbridge population to have a go. With fans, lorgnettes and furled umbrellas. To put down theft, slow up crime. And stop diabolical secret murder. Betwixt the damp warrens of masonry. The English hide their houses and the French always cut a little window in their trees. But one of those misty London evenings can come with the pavements moist and greasy black as the people thread darkly home through the streets. And the paper sellers' shouts go out. Echoing across the fog. Woman's torso found in Thames. Killer with a surgeon's skill. Floating remains found on foreshore of Wapping Old Stairs. Police search for missing head. A clue to the killer might be given by the expression on the dead person's face. A smile if the victim had long liked the assailant. Surprise and horror if she did not. The torso was well built. Now tarry sir, listen to the gore. The hairy hand, reaching. Cutting. Leaving blood and remains. On the foreshore. What does one answer in all this distress. To keep one's arse unbroken. Or police being called and possible arrest. Only left one thing to say.

"I know that my redeemer liveth."

"That's all very well and proper sir, all of us here I'm sure know that our redeemer liveth. But dash it all, that's exactly why we will not be sidetracked."

"Could we not all sing Abide With Me."

"Certainly not sir, this is not a joke. We demand to see in."

"No."

"Sir, you are asking to get force from us. Isn't that so, I didn't catch your name on the street sir, ah, Whitewang. Is that in one or two words, White Wang, ah two, good. Now isn't that so Mr. White Wang, we are being asked to use force here."

"I must ask you all to go away please. Out of my wife's dressing room."

"We shall not."

"My wife only is here. And she is quite well."

"How do we know that sir. My own wife is certain she recognised the cries of a downed female, if I may be so blunt as to use that term."

Balthazar swung wide open the dressing room door. Till now one has been so patient with the entire world. Tip toeing through a woman's dissatisfactions hoping too many of them will go unheard. Seems anyone steps in these days to infernally invade one's privacy. Treat them now to plenty so they won't be asking for more. One gentleman and lady in the forefront. One lady and one gentleman in the rear.

"My God sir, how dare you present yourself thus, to my wife."

"You're demanding to gain entrance to my bedroom. You are already standing in my house. Without my leave. And I again request you to go."

"Sir, attend to yourself. You are in a state of undress. I happen to be connected with the Admiralty and I am also a member of the Automobile Club."

"Well I should be glad then if you would promptly motor out of here."

"I think I speak as spokesman for the group, and God help me man I would appreciate if you were to cover yourself."

"I am quite as God made me."

"That sir is a matter between you and God. We all of us consulted at length in the street over the noises. Matters had to be taken into our own hands to insure that injury was not being done. Now that we are here we intend to succeed in the measures we have thus far taken."

"Did you hear a cry for help."

"No, I don't believe we did."

"Then I must ask you to leave this instant."

"Look sir, all of us are willing volunteers. Responding to what we feel is an emergency. I've had my time in Burma, sir.

I've been acquainted with this kind of thing before. When although there isn't an outright cry for help, one surmises quite properly that the presence of help is required. I wish sir, you wouldn't continue to stand there naked like that."

"What was your rank."

"Major and damn it sir, attend to yourself, I'm quite fed up talking to you in that condition, presenting yourself unadorned to my wife like that. Get back behind the door or a towel at least."

"I want you to clear out please."

"Not until we have had satisfaction sir."

"I said please go."

"Sir if you take another naked step forward in front of my wife I shall strike you."

"I'm sure your wife has seen privates before. I've spent half an hour in front of the Sorbonne like this."

"What you did sir, nude in front of the Sorbonne, is no concern of ours. And my wife has not seen privates before. Not even in tableau. And how dare you suggest she has."

"Have you no privates Major."

"As a matter of fact if you must know I received an injury to them in Burma. In the service of my country. Wretched wog had at me with a lucky shot. And sir I think you are being most ungentlemanly to stand there like that, cold bloodedly exposing yourself. And sir your organ is deliberately twitching."

"For the last time, please leave this house."

"I am umpiring this matter here, sir, with the full agreement of the others. I resent strongly my integrity being questioned. I have commanded men in foreign parts. But if I may say so, foreign parts are one thing, and facing your privates provocatively presented is entirely another. We want evidence that all in the room beyond is quite correct and no knavery has been committed."

"I shall take this coat hanger to you. If you don't get out of this house."

"I must remind you sir that every Englishman is duty

bound according to his code of behaviour to have a go wherever there is evidence of foul play."

"What evidence."

"We shall see."

"And if you don't."

"Well we shall of course retreat and enlist the aid of further authority."

"Followed closely by my legal advisers who will lash you with writs till your shoelaces dance in terror."

"Good God sir, we're only doing our best here. What about all the poor old dears in this street. What about them, they may even now cower thinking they will be next. They are not motor owners like we, and here I speak for myself as I do not know if Mr. White Wang is a motor owner."

"I'm not."

"O I see. But these old dears can't motor away to safety, peace and quiet. We of us who own motors must take care that the rights of those less fortunate are protected."

Balthazar B covering privates with the shoulder bulge of the coat hanger as there was a slight engorgement there. In the heat of this utterly unbelievable encounter. When one would prefer to be popping fresh strawberries down one's throat, right out of season. But one thing to do. Before these people try to fill me up with sawdust to make me look nice. Is to set the record right and send these folk scattering.

"Millicent would you please phone for the police. To come and have these intruders shown the door."

"Yes I will."

Alarm over the Major's face. He reached for his breast pocket spotted red hanky. And wiped away the moisture on his thin upper lip. Which he licks now. The nameless second lady quite at home feeling, as she passes, the satin of Millicent's counterpane. Mr. White Wang staring down at his shoes and up at the ceiling as the little group slowly moves backwards towards Millicent's open bedroom door. Balthazar B advancing. Nakedly.

"I wish sir that you would not keep advancing in that con

344

dition. Quite clearly there's been a misunderstanding but my wife's heart is not good."

"It appears to have had sufficient pumping adequacy to get her up here. And one would certainly hope to get her out. Go away please."

"We are going. Please let us. Without coming too close, there's quite a lot of light out here on the staircase. Marjorie please turn your head away. Look front. Please, for my sake."

Balthazar standing at the stair head watching the little group pass out and close the door. From the small reading room window one looks down. There gathered on the pavement. The vigilantes. Watched by the Colonel across the street in the window with his binoculars totally emerged from the plant leaves. One might now be advised to hang out a sign high over the front door. To those of you who do not recognise the groans of lust which one hopes will continue to come out of this house. To say to you, do not breach the privacy dear chaps, if you please. And when next you hear a scream. Look up at the night.

> The new
> Moon yawns
> To take
> A bite
> Of
> The sky.

27

The little fellow was born three days after nurse came to Crescent Curve with her hat of white daisies with big white petals on the back top of her head. She wore blue frequently and when out of uniform a grey sweater with two rows of amber beads. She smoked inhaling the air deeply and threw her head back shooting the smoke upwards at an angle from the horizontal.

A fortnight later nannie came. And nurse was slow to leave. In the long still tight lipped silences at table. No one having a second helping except of wine. Millicent wrapped up high with frills all over her bed. Delivered trays of delicacies by the fragile and hard of hearing Boats with his white hair flowing behind his ears. He had made his way from his tiny sea front cottage in Dorset. Travelling for three days, getting lost on stations, taking trains back to where he came from instead of where he was going. As I shouted directions to him down the long distance phone. Lodged safely now up top in the back room. With all his neat equipments laid ready about.

There were tremors of lighted warmth over the house. Between the black looks nurse gave nannie and nannie gave nurse. Neither ever passing the salt to the other and pushing butter and bread further away. Millicent muchly reclined in the middle of her bed having hair and fingernails done. The little fellow nuzzling in at the breasts. One nipple just a little larger than the other. The left one as a matter of fact. Millicent's right eye is a little larger than the left. Nature quite fussy in balancing things. Beefy came to visit. We had a private little talk in the library.

"Dear boy, I don't know what the Violet Infanta's advisors and principals want. I've told them granny will go to her maker any day and I will be immortally rich. They say they

346

are advised from confidential sources my granny will go on living for years and years, the reports say she has the heart of a twelve year old girl. It is all simply too too sad. The Infanta when I roger her says she's got to wank. Asked me if I minded her tickling herself off in that manner. I said don't be a miserable so and so, of course I don't mind. Of course you may wank if it gives an extra pleasure. Full steam to orgasm. Sometimes the Infanta wears an expression of staggeringly splendid stupidity on her face, utterly endearing. I'm frightened I may be becoming more fond of her than her money. She has an awfully beautiful back. Ah my God Balthazar, you're a father. I'm not even a husband yet. And from last week no longer an elevator operator. Too awful. I am about to reveal my address to the world as the Savoy Steps, a nice crooked little street behind the Monarch's church where there's no doorway to deliver an envelope to."

Beefy with his strangely delicate fingers playing with the stem of his glass. Boats entering, lifting up another bottle laid down in the ice. His hands shaking as he undid the wire over the cork. Which hit him on the forehead and nearly knocked him out. We sat there stilled by Boats' lofty elegance as he silently withdrew. And I asked Beefy, who has so often sailed through my life, yawing and heaving, cutting through the waves under a brisk following breeze, how had he lost command of his lift.

"It happened most unexpectedly. I'd been taking chaps up to the top floor throughout the afternoon. Had this Chinese coin with a hole in it in the palm of my hand. If I had a chap with me travelling alone, I'd mumble an aside that this was the tip the last passenger gave me. Worked marvellously time and again in producing a couple of bob. Anyway, I'm as usual conducting a most well run lift. Giving smart salutes to those passengers deserving it. And slipping out a morsel of a fart at others meeting with my displeasure, mostly of the untutored talkative variety addressing me without invitation. This is marvellously good champagne Balthazar. So good to see you sitting there. Happy in your own little buzzing home. Nice.

347

But me alas. I sped my elevator to the top floor. To take down some of the day's last passengers. There they were, an even dozen gents. Although all short, all extremely wide. They were pushing, all wanting down at once. Well I mean to say, one has had authority over a company of men in the field. I said gentlemen, the capacity of this machine is seven, the first seven please only. The entire twelve instantly crushed forward. I announced over the heads that we would plummet to the bottom of the lift shaft and if one gentleman would step back he could laugh himself sick at the sight. Well it was quite clear that they were not about to let one of their number get to the bottom first. A most horrid group. Fuck-pigs of multiplicities, distinguished as they were by jug handled ears and halitosis. They mocked my safety precautions. I announced once more that the capacity was seven. The pushing became even more prevalent. I was poohpoohed in an aggressive manner. Their cigars were starting to stick into the back of each other's necks. I thought you saucy chaps, you're all fiddling with each other's genitals at the closest of quarters. The lift was already swaying and groaning with the weight. Again I announced the risk. No one could bear to be the chap to step out and be left behind. The last bugger who finally squeezed himself aboard had his arse stuck in the doors. Wouldn't close. There was a general exhaling and he was fitted in. The mixture of smells was sickening. By the time they all got on they could have walked down. I thought well, stand by my post. A guardsman always. Of course I reckoned we were quite safe. I manoeuvered the power handle over to descend. Slowly. But we were picking up speed. The sixth floor passed by. The fourth flashed by. And the rest simply didn't exist at all. Not nice. I pressed and pulled and switched the emergency yokes. The whole gang of them shouting, what's wrong, stop it. I braced myself for the moment of impact at basement level. Or perhaps lower. And my lift which I had run without the loss of single life was suddenly a load of moaning trembling sweating jelly. Screams of legal steps and negligence and we want out. My God, I thought wistfully of my pedigree. And my most modest position. The alarm bell now ringing. Stifling smoke from cigars. Like a crematorium. One accusing another that he was breathing his area of air. A third that his lawyers would already be looking into his disappearance. Two chaps just behind me however were engrossed in discussing percentages of a deal. Thirteen of us trapped for twenty five minutes. Finally in the lobby there were police, fire brigade, lawyers, all taking dispositions from the lift travellers who had suffered moral disfigurement and spiritual bitterness in the disastrous descent. And would sue for damages. Each one pointing a finger at me. Balthazar. My dear man. Here you are, in life, where I should so much like to be."

Gallantly through dinner Beefy lightheartedly tickling the fancies of nurse and nannie. Through the somewhat long pauses as Boats got stuck outside the dining room door. His shoes far too big for him. The tray too heavy. Until the yells from cook brought us all running. Boats in the scullery covered in gravy and mint sauce. Beefy and I lifting the dear old gentleman bodily. Up to his bed. Putting compresses softly on his brow. As I had to rush to meet Alphonsine, an au pair arrived from France. In her soft grey suit, short cropped hair and pretty eyes. And quite extraordinary arse, much callipyge.

But again we were all nice and settled. Cook laying a place for Alphonsine. As she sat shy with her wine, slabs of lamb, rhubarb custard, port and cheese. Which Beefy and I brought up to Boats and he lay propped with pillows in bed, a purple tasselled night cap on his white head. His faint blue eyes and delicate long fingered hands. We poured his port and held it for him to his lips and slowly he revived and indeed was rather animated and cheerful. Spoke of his great old days with Uncle Edouard and before that in the grandnesses of Wales. When he went shooting and fishing. And met his first love. Until he finally fell asleep and gently snored.

349

Beefy and I sat there with the sleeping Boats. Quaffing a decanter of port. Quite silent. Tonight in England. Across all the stiff upper unmustached lips. Men not clever, not overly endowed with carnal prowess, but of normal pleasant appetites, only asking to enjoy their pudding in peace. Some with a quiet evening erection browsing through their erotica. Secure in their postal districts, or preferred counties. At slipper footed ease in their castles. And here in Crescent Curve where Boats busted the cut glass bowls one by one. To my cheered relief to see the last of these seventeen wedding presents purchased at the same sale finally disappear.

"Of course Balthazar. I was so depressed. Nothing seemed dandy randy and delightful anymore. Wondering if the sun would ever come up again. To be witnessed solitary in London. Known that one's diary entries are nil. That one's life doesn't merit having the hours booked up. I chose some fluff from the Bayswater Road. And announced my desires. She said that will be two guineas extra. I said guineas. She said yes, I'm not like the other girls, my fees have always been in guineas. Very cheeky she was. I said peruse my organ and pull it gently for me please. I sang my repertoire of Irish ballads. She said aren't you the straightforward darling though. I said usually I was rather more craven but wasn't at my best tonight. She had a quite nice little place. She asked me if I wanted to watch her ride for two more guineas her rocking horse in her transparent macintosh. Of course, I screamed, I want to see you ride. Then she asked me to give her a little fluttering of the whip across her what for. I said madam that will be exactly three guineas. She was furious. But you know, suddenly again I was awfully cheered. At that moment. And my God. What happens. The floor was quivering. And shaking. As I laid on the lash. I knocked her over. Both of us fell. And one's one leg and a knee of the other went right through a blasted cardboard patch in the floor. Came out through the ceiling below, in a room where they were showing the second house of a dirty film. Well I scratched my head. I really did. And calmly looked down upon the scene. Not nice. Boats dear man is snoring there, I may be giving him dreams. But upon my word, the debacle of the lift was most minor. There they were below. Dirty film goers. About fifteen of them. Trying to get out the door. Some through a blocked up window. I could catch a glimpse of the untoward film still flickering on its moth eaten screen. Of course they thought it was the police. Attacking from the top. I must confess I did myself whisper such a word. Thought it would frighten away complaints from below. Said this is the chief detective superintendent Beefy, everyone stay as you are. The thing was the chaps below were locked in. Pure murder. I recognised a titled cousin struggling in the dust and broken chairs to get out between someone's legs. Packed with peerage it was. One shouting out that he wished to call attention to the lack of sanitary provisions in a place of entertainment and was present there officially investigating the matter. Marvellous ruddy cheek of the chap. But enough Balthazar. I must go. Look how Boats sleeps. After his long gentle life. My God it makes one wish one had been born a butler."

Quietly leaving Boats' room. Past Alphonsine's door. Where Beefy bent to peek in the keyhole and put his hand up to his amazed lips. As I dragged him away and down the stairs. To bid him a fond goodnight out my front door. Standing between the two little statues of doggies. Beefy patting them on the head. I watched him walk away down the street. Until the shadow of his jaunty shoulders turned the corner. After this April third day. Back in there the little family I'd founded. To look up at the sky. Mountains of cloud tumbling across the tree tops down the street. Rain beginning to fall. I sigh. When suddenly one is left without a complaint.

The silent house. To pass back into my study. The wall now lined with volumes treating of the whole of the animal kingdom. Of the birds and snakes, of the monkey and the horse. Port left in the decanter on my desk. Sit at last for a little read of the paper. Sip the sweet splendour of this ancient fortified wine. And lay out the page. Of The Times. Announcing marriages, births and ruby weddings. And rows of deaths. Of all these pleasant ringing names. Adams, Blyth, Clutterbuck, Donoghue, Eliot. And.

FITZDARE. On March 31st, peacefully at The Manor, Co. Fermanagh, Elizabeth Astrid Benedicta Fitzdare, beloved only daughter of Raphael Fitzdare, in her twenty fourth year. Funeral private at The Manor. No flowers please.

28

I do and say nothing all these days. As I sit taking my meals silent and alone in my study, watching out on chill winds and sudden April snows. Beefy went to Scotland for another desperate and unsuccessful bid to prise loose funds from his granny. On his return I met him at his club. Sitting away in a corner. Suddenly I couldn't hold my sorrow. Pouring from me like a great ghost. And just as Beefy was that crushing day my Tillie was torn away. He put his arm across my shoulders. And walked me home across the park.

Poor old Boats went back into retirement. When he regained his feet again. And left me his knife sharpener and shoe horns as a gift. Nurse said goodbye in her big hat. Said she would miss all the wine. Nannie sat rigid and correct day in and out. Her narrow compressed lips and bustling starchiness through the house driving me out of my mind. Saved by the laughing and pleasing Alphonsine. Who went happily cleaning and telling me about her Paris boyfriend Jacques. Sometimes she wheeled the little fellow out in his pram. I could go and talk with her when I followed them to the park. And Millicent hearing me come one early evening into my room, stood at the dressing room door.

"You never take me out anywhere."

"I'm sorry."

"I'll bet. Where were you all afternoon. I'll tell you where. Talking to Alphonsine in the Dell in the park."

"I'm sorry but I don't care to get into an argument."

"I could kill you."

"Another time perhaps. I want to change."

"You're going to the ballet again."

"Yes."

"What right have you got to tell my mother to stay away from this house."

"Possibly a legal right. I'm not sure."

"I could kill you."

"Yes."

"Why don't you be a man."

"I want to change my clothes please."

On that occasion Millicent knocked over the furniture in my room. Broke the mirror with an ashtray. And heaved other glass through the air. Until Alphonsine came rushing in to see what the matter was. When a hair brush bounced off the side of my head and I saw stars. A cut across my brow. As Millicent charged, her fingers drawn up to scratch my face, and Alphonsine intervened.

"Madam you must stop, there is blood on Monsieur."

I sat on a righted chair. Millicent ran from the room. Went down the stairs and slammed out the front door. Alphonsine bathed my eye. And put a bandage neatly there. One further trial of strength was over. With a letter reaching me two days later. From her solicitors. An injunction would be sought restraining me. Not to molest my wife. With another letter a day after from my trustees, enclosing an envelope marked personal and postmarked Belfast.

The Temple
London E.C.4

Dear Mr. B,

Herewith a letter of which we are in receipt with the request that it be forwarded to you.

We should be glad if you will attend a meeting, convened by the undersigned trustees, in order that compensation paid to the trustees may be varied with regard to increased expenses now found incurred by the many recent contingencies. Please advise us of a time suitable to you.

Yours faithfully,
Bother, Writson, Horn,
Pleader & Hoot

Part this other envelope, black ink penned neatly on the cream paper. My hand atremble and my heart thumps hard. To see again this address.

The Manor
Co. Fermanagh

My dear Balthazar,

I know this letter will find you far away in your own life. And it is with the greatest sorrow that I write. But I feel you would have wanted to know. Elizabeth died the thirty first of March. And was buried here beside her brother and mother.

It is extremely hard to know how to say something when one learns that out of a desperate love there can come cruel things. It broke my heart to withdraw from my daughter's wedding plans. Elizabeth had an accident taking a hedge with her horse being caught by wire and she was thrown violently hitting her head. I could not face the doctor's verdict. Elizabeth after the accident never fully regained her complete self. But in her limited way she begged me not to say anything in the hope that she would get well. Neither of us could bear the thought that the possibility of marrying did not remain. Her love meant so much to her. And therefore to me. It was the only thing still perfect she had. Now that it is over I somehow feel that it would have been fairer to you had you known. And that I was wrong in a hopeless way. It was a father's love for his only daughter that made me not say for her sake. And I do most hope you will understand. She also asked as a final wish I should send you this enclosed.

Yours sincerely,
Raphael Fitzdare

Inside the pink envelope Balthazar withdrew a sheet of paper with a large lettered scrawl of two words headed, The Manor, Co. Fermanagh.

Dear Balthazar

And that night when finally I could sleep I dreamt a dream. I had had so many times before. In the darkness and night wind of that green land. Under the tall trees and waving grasses. Fitzdare sat by moonlight on her little brother's tomb stone in a wedding dress. And I would climb the hill up from the lough and cross to her and try to take up the white splendid vision in my arms. And wake with tears.

355

I had breakfast at my desk each morning brought by Alphonsine. Weather warming across London. The skies clean and blue. And sat with my feet up over the steaming delicious coffee and croissants. Which I covered with black-currant jam. Staring out my window over the lilac trees and across the walls at windows where perhaps there move other sad lives. When my private phone rings. The one man who knows its number. Pick up the black handle. And hear Beefy.

"Dear boy, joy. It is announced. Just as I finally threw in the towel. Put on your hat and coat and rush to the Edge-ware Road. Meet me the north east corner of Praed Street. Sorry to give you such sudden news. You know how one might pick up the best newspaper of a morning only to read that the Swedes are legalising incest. But for me I regain my rank. Valued by one's equals and honoured by one's inferiors. Of course I may add I am really a one orgasm man but I do guarantee some tempestuous thrustings in between."

"What's happened Beefy."

"It has happened. New shirtings, smoking jackets and ki-monos are on the way. The Ritz first stop. The Infanta and I have a little passionate caprice I'd like you to cultivate. Called the regal rapture. Balthazar you will think me entirely without humility. But you know I stand in front of the mirror now and I must say when I look at it, it's fully ready for rosy rogering in deep solitude. Corsica perhaps for the honey-moon."

"Beefy I can't understand what you're saying."

"We are marrying, the Violet Infanta and I, today. Awfully rush and much hush hush. You are best man."

And Balthazar B rushed to change his clothes. Gathering money from the bank. Only thing one has for a present. Put it in a brown bag with two apples they can eat wherever they go. Jump into a taxi heading to the meeting place up this straight grim road. The Violet Infanta in a blue suit and blue hat. Beefy in grey double breasted pin stripe and Trinity Dublin tie. In a panelled room four of us stand before this pleasant smiling man. Who frowned a little and looked up as Beefy convulsively exploded a helpless laughter out his lips. And said as we went to a nearby hotel, I hope no one minded, my laughter was all relief.

Outside there was a din of pneumatic drills and I bid them goodbye with a wave and kiss from my lips. The dark shadow of Beefy through the opaque taxi window. I shook hands with the Infanta's friend who boarded a bus. People part. One does not want to grow old in misery. Trickle down to death. Carry always with me now. My Fitzdare I married. Long ago in my heart. Her smile and all the rest of her. Walks with me. Told to one's face. By a wife who has trapped you. Because of your money. Stroll along this road through a thronged street. Lady shoppers testing tomatoes on the stalls. Past this female hospital. And over the canal. No taxis anywhere. Just wait and look. Before one goes into the tube. Watch that weary old dog bent up crapping in the gutter between two cars. Poor doggy having such a struggle. Like Beefy he may have piles. But codes as well because he doesn't foul the footpath. Pity there are not more doggies like him. My God he's taken umbrage at my watching.

The dog with its fat body wobbling on thin ancient legs sped up from the street at Balthazar, barking and biting round his ankles. As one moves most quickly down the steps into the tube. A lesson learned that some doggies want their privacy. Like his master standing at the door of his pub. A regular who goes back inside to ask for his usual. And drink beer in the quiet civility where no shins are chipped. Or privates displayed.

Go now and take a ticket anywhere. On the low round little trains. Roaring down their tunnel tracks. One will go to St. James and walk across back through the park. See the ducks and swans swooping in the air. Wish so much for Beefy to be glad. With his pretty bride. The two of them holding hands. Wed when the daffodils are gone. And Beefy said the Infanta said she married him because she liked men with big pricks so she wouldn't have to strain her eyes.

Stepping off the train. Walking down this grey station.

Bright shouting pictures on the walls. And suddenly stayed by a hand. To turn and look into the black face of a man.

"Escuse me sir."

"Yes."

"Do you live about here."

"No. But not too far away."

"Can you tell me how to get to the Foreign Office."

"Yes indeed. Just go out of the station into Petty France Street. Down Queen Anne's Gate, go right along the park. I think it is Birdcage Walk. Continue left along the park and then go right, up some steps, into what I think is King Charles Street. And that's the Foreign Office."

"Sir may I ask you kindly another favour. I have been watching you on the train. I have been riding the train for hours. Seeing all the faces. Just waiting until I could see a face of intelligence and humanity. Such as yours, the only face like that I have seen all day. I am a medical student. At Edinburgh university. And sir, believe me when I say I have waited to see a face like yours. One of sensitivity. An honourable face. Distinguished. I know nothing more about you except what I see. And sir, I know you have been to a university. Is that correct."

"Yes."

"You see I know. I can tell human beings and what they are. It is with the utmost reluctance I trouble you. The fact of the matter is sir. I have not eaten all day. I have no money. I am at my wits end. Everywhere I have gone I have been refused help. My shoes are worn out. Dear sir, could you give me the fare to Edinburgh."

Balthazar B looked into these dark pleading eyes. The black shining skin. And gracious manner. His shoes were only very slightly pointed. The missing buttons on his shirt and frayed cuffs nearly like my own.

"Please sir, before you speak, before you make up your mind. I want you to know that I am not lying. That I am genuine. Believe me. You are a professor."

"No."

"A member of the government perhaps. You know the streets so well."

"I walk here often."

"I can tell that you are important. I knew it as I watched you on the train all the way from Paddington on the Bakerloo Line to Charing Cross. You changed to the District Line to alight here. You see I do not lie. You are perhaps a member of Parliament."

"No."

"What are you sir. If I may just ask you."

"I'd hardly be able to answer that really."

"It is all right, you don't have to tell me, I understand you are someone important, and you do not want to divulge. I can see. Then you are a minister."

"No."

"You are of the peerage. Modesty prevents you from telling me. You have the carriage and demeanour of a lord. It is so clear to me that such is the case. Your clothing and the air about you tells me. But sir, upon my word of honour. Everywhere I have gone they want credentials from me. And I have left them with my landlady in Edinburgh and she will not send them to me because I have not paid the rent. That is the gospel truth. If I can get to Edinburgh my credentials will allow me to get further funds. And immediately I will send the sum back to you. Believe me sir. If I fail with you. There is no hope. Because it is only you out of all the hundreds of faces where I find love expressed with an elegance that simply no one else I have seen possesses. I do not ask you further. Believe me sir, I am aware that you may even be a member of the royal family. And that you would not want me to know. I offer you my watch as security."

Balthazar smiling to put this gentleman at his ease. The watch of poor quality held out in the pink faced palm of his hand telling the wrong time. His eyes full of sad resignation. Back those years, when one saw passing across college squares

359

black princely gentlemen with their white flashing teeth and splendid ways. Flowing colours of their robes and the grand aplomb with which they wore their tweeds. And there was Zutu. Great soothsayer of the horse and race course.

"Please. Do put your watch away. And don't worry. You do flatter me over much I think, but alas you have stopped the right man. I will help you."

"Sir. Upon my God I knew I could not be wrong. That no face like yours have I ever seen before. I do not try to flatter you. I know you would scorn such an attempt. I merely speak the truth that is forced up out of my heart by hunger, the dread of destitution and no one to turn to. I have tried everywhere. I would show you my wallet or some identification but I have none."

"You must not upset yourself further. I am walking out, perhaps you would accompany me."

"Yes. It is sir, as if Christ himself had given me a goblet of wine. Men such as you have courage in your heart and wear love upon your face."

"It's nice of you to say but I'm not so sure. You mustn't trouble to give me praise. I am happy to give you the money."

"I'll send it back, please I beg you to tell me your name and give me an address."

"I'd prefer just to make this a present. I give it in memory of someone else. I'd like you just to accept it. And we'll say nothing more. It's enough to get you to Edinburgh, first class on the train, and this, extra, for you to have a good dinner tonight. I had an uncle who always said a bottle of Gevrey Chambertin today gives the spirit its sleep for tomorrow. Goodbye. I wish you a pleasant journey."

Balthazar B turned, tears left in the dark eyes as he made his way away into the park. The weeping willow bending to the water, ducks steering their way to bread dropped from the railings of the bridge. Emerald gleam of their heads. Warm sun on one's back. Murmur of voices. Click of passing shoes. The late light of long London evenings in the sky. Beefy now in his riches. Told him Millicent threw much Silesian glass of the baroque period which crashed expensively around my ears. Out of which one day soon I'm sure lawyers will walk. Beefy said he and the Infanta would travel quietly to the edge of the Caspian Sea to indulge themselves calmly in fresh caviar, following which he would say Violet, bend over to allow admission of this valid concept. One hears a band playing. A man walking across the park with his shirt off, umbrella, bowler and attaché case in his hand. No end to sacrilege. Beefy said far too many folk these days were outfitting themselves without entitlement, parading about in the privacy of their homes as archbishops. Not nice.

Balthazar entered this public house. Down in a mews in Belgravia. Cozy, neat and quiet. Stand at the bar. I am going to lonely celebrate. Drinking bitter beer. Chew over my own dark musty thoughts. Some precious. Where they lurk like saved up little children's treasures. Touch them before they die. And if I die. Leave them to those who live. Like the furniture they auction behind those double calm green gold fringed doors of Sotheby's. Where I go under the gleaming creamy painted arch. And put my fingers across the satin and touch the delft. One is always taught to keep. The old wears better than the new.

Balthazar B goes out now, tipsy. Look up. After a big fat sun sank tonight. London glows against the cloudy sky. An onion man goes by. Pushing his bicycle, two last bunches bubbling over his handle bars. He stops. He blocks one nostril and blasts air through the other, sending his phlegm in the gutter. He smiles. Bonsoir. And salutes handing over his last wares of the day to this pleased gentleman.

Moving along Pont Street, Balthazar B singing O For The Wings Of A Dove, his onions strung fore and aft over both his shoulders. Up the steps of 78 Crescent Curve. To search through pockets for one's keys into this house. Turn and see the binoculars up at the window there. It's so friendly really that someone else cares so much about what happens in one's

361

house. And sir do focus down on me here and watch me bring in my onions. So French and fat and nice.

In the silent hall. Lights out. Go secretly in my study. Put lights on. Unload onions. Dumped on my desk. Beefy is right. It's the rich what gets the peaches, it's the poor what gets the punches. But does he know it's the squiffy as what brings the onions home. When the world's all grey. Settle my beer with a glass of brandy. Everyone gone to bed. And old Boats to Lyme Regis, just when I need him most. He could take one's watch from one's wrist and wind it. Sit my old self safely down. And sigh. Sniff this cask cured distillate of wine. And my God what's this. Papers strewn on the floor. And letters. Fitzdare's picture torn to shreds. O my God give me oblivion. From small small voices of small small men ashout in the world.

"O Monsieur. Monsieur. You are all right."

"Yes. I am all right."

"You have not seen the rest of the house. I have tried to clean it up as best as I am able."

Alphonsine standing in the faint light, her serious brown sad eyes. Her cheeks spotted with red. As she looks across at me. And I do not stand. Which stand I must. To brave against the wave of fear. I see in her eyes and comes crashing over me. With the chime of the clock. It tinkles and rhymes. Makes the little fellow crinkle up his nose and wave his tiny hands.

"What's happened."

"Monsieur. After you left this morning. I don't know what to say. It was bang, boom, bang. There was shouting in here. I came running. To see what the matter was. I find all the paper and picture torn. The drawers out of your desk. Madam said I was not to touch. Mrs. Davis was told to go. And nannie left with Madam and the little boy. I was told to go as well. But I do not have anywhere I can go. I have not enough money to go back to Paris."

Balthazar B sitting back down in his chair. Feel the silence of the house. I can wake in early morning and think again when my brain is pure. Rest now while Knightsbridge is asleep. My little fellow gone. I walked home across the wide open grass. Clouds of starlings in the sky. An urgent chattering thrush shot under the trees. Beefy gone into riches from which he may never return. If you have a waterfall of money crowds rush with buckets, bathtubs and thimbles. Only thing to do is ask them please wait in line, don't climb up each other's backs. Left now with Alphonsine. Who's been down on her hands and knees to clean. When Millicent has walked by. Now she stands there all distressed. Tears in her eyes.

"Monsieur I have made some supper. Please don't disturb. I will bring it."

To lose and lose. What you love. Put all this scattered paper in the fireplace. Let it go up in flames. Hurry up to die. So little reason left to live. Take a ship across the Atlantic, jump down into the cold waves. Should have made a fist. To shake in her face. But instead put some logs on the fire. Ready for another long night.

Alphonsine came in the door with a great black tray. A golden fold of omelet. Salad of tomato and watercress. On the onion pattern Meissen all neatly arranged. The space she clears at my desk. For wine and salt. Pepper and butter. Before even I can get up to help. A nice girl. Who loved the little fellow so. Saw her give him crushing kisses on the cheek. Fuss back his little wisps of hair. To make me wish I were he.

"Alphonsine. Don't go. Stay."

"If you like Monsieur."

"Please don't call me Monsieur."

"But, I must be frank, it is not proper that I should be now in this house."

"I know. Just sit. And have some wine with me. I've drunk too much tonight."

"You have many onions too."

"Yes I have many onions too. I like you Alphonsine."

"Yes I know. And I like you too. But just as we are here now is very much taboo. I must leave. It is very sad for me to go. To see your home like this. Here is your napkin. Is there anything else you would like I can get."

"No. Thank you. Just stay here with me."

Those afternoons when nannie was relieved from two to six. I went out. Past the French Embassy across the bridle path of Rotten Row, to see Alphonsine on the incline of grass. Facing the little pond and rabbits running in the shrubbery. Where we so often sat and had our laughing talks. Of her family and four little brothers. To whom she wrote every day and showed me pictures of. Under the acacia tree with the squawking geese swooping overhead as they flew each evening before sunset from St. James to the Serpentine. The little crowds of pigeons collecting. The black lamp standards, fat globes under an iron crown. The weeping willows and the ash. All surrounded by other nannies. All paid fourpence for our chairs. They whispered when they saw us. In blue and grey, white aprons and green cumberbunds. Frills above the biceps, white collars flowing from the neck. Sitting in their clustered circles. Where nothing was ever a secret. Till they said goodbye and come along Jonathan, Felicity and Nicolas. Alphonsine you look so nice now in your dark green sweater. And no pearls. How much longer does one remain a gentleman. Through those first days when you said you had no taste for tea. And later when I did just once help myself and pinched you on the behind. Just to hear you say, it is taboo Monsieur. I had tipple taken. And you tell me so much about Jacques that I always want to hear more. With the pain of jealousy. Ah Monsieur he has, how do you say, biceps. Stripped to the waist sweating he is debonair. He works hard in his family business. It is a small furniture factory in Paris. He drives fast his big car. He is not afraid to be very gay. He is below my social class but it means nothing to me. Then Alphonsine to my crestfallen face would smile and say, but ah Monsieur, he does not have the distinguished cultivation and handsomeness like you. And to her solemn face now that she always wears when a week is gone without a letter.

"How is Jacques Alphonsine."

"O he is all right I suppose."

"Will you see him if you go back to Paris right away."

"Yes of course."

"What will you do."

"O we will go if it is Sunday perhaps for a picnic. He puts down the cover of his car. We ride with our hair flying to the Parc des Buttes Chaumont. It is there that sometimes people commit suicide off the high bridge. Sadness is always in the happiness. We lie on the grass. We play the radio. We have our apples, sandwiches, cheese and wine. Jacques takes out his pocket knife, to cut what I might want from the apple or cheese. We go then to the Champs Elysées, it is dark, we speed back and forth. We go to the cinema. We have a lot of fun."

Beefy now. Owning perhaps much freehold land soon in Sunningdale. Up to his neck in his wedding night. As I'm up to mine in sorrow. With this girl who loved the little fellow and was so good and gentle to him. With her on the grassy incline of the Dell I was never despondent and miserable. Would lurk round the shop windows. Working up my courage to walk up and say hello. Always to feel a little tortured. When she would say, ah Jacques and I will holiday on the Riviera. I have bought my new swimming costume. Jacques looks so good in his. It is brief just over here. The stomach he has is flat like steel. And soon now she'll be gone. Like cherry blossoms when they were pink. Leaving leaves all green.

"Will he meet you in his motor."

"But of course, if he can."

"It has many cylinders, I suppose."

"But of course."

"How is Jacques' dog. Does he lift his leg on the better poplar trees."

"You make fun."

"Does Jacques kiss you when you meet."

"Monsieur you have drunk far too much beer and wine tonight to ask such questions."

"Does he kiss you."

365

"Of course. He takes what he wants."

"Does he ask."

"Of course not. I am there for his wishes."

"O dear, Jacques with his beaucoup force. Me with only wishes. I am homesick for Paris. The tiny little lives tucked away in the cement hives. The alleys. Hallways cool in summer and cold in winter. The restaurants full of wine and talk."

"That is nice, how you say that. I think Jacques if he would get to know you. Would like you."

"Has Jacques swum the Channel yet."

"Now now you make a joke of Jacques. He is young but he thinks old. He would not do something so foolish. A man is best with a young body who thinks old."

"He can swim."

"Of course. Like a shark. Just like he drives his speed boat through the water."

"Does he steer with his toes."

"O I will not talk about Jacques with you tonight."

"Please. Do. This is the most delicious omelet."

"I should not sit here."

"Why."

"We could be noticed. That man across the street. Is always watching. You know of course he sent a note."

"No."

"Yes. He said that he could see the shadow of my underthings drying on the little line I put in my room. He asked if I mind awfully removing it. He said it is not elegant for the street. I look out last week and he is dressed as a woman going out his front door. I knew it was him."

An aircraft flying overhead. Means the wind is from the west. Moist air stream over Knightsbridge. Where big and little dogs trot down Sloane Street. Debutantes in their polka dot silk dresses. To rowing and tennis. As I was off to the Dell. Stopping, looking into the window of Cobb the butcher. With his Scotch beef of the finest quality. Cooked one Sunday so splendidly by this girl with her understanding eyes. In love with Jacques. Who said I am not pretty and beautiful like your wife. But Alphonsine you can cook carrots to taste like caviar. Or even carrots. You say you must be discreet in another woman's home. And be faithful to your Jacques. And I wish you weren't.

"Monsieur perhaps it is not the time to say but you do make me laugh. In bed at night I think about what you have said to me in the park. And I laugh to sleep."

"I like you Alphonsine."

"You know I do like you too. You are very kind. You are too, very beautiful. I should not say that to you."

"Once you put your fingertip on my nose."

"Yes when you pinched me where you shouldn't."

"Tonight I have brought home the onions. Have more wine."

"I have had too much already."

Chimes go on the clock. My little note here, to go to the shoe maker to have my shoe tongues adjusted. These carpets fitted. All over this entire house. A shell. To keep alive with my dreams. Beefy where ere do you be. Just when you said service at your club was getting offhand and slack. Your voice so sad, spare and clear. Across clipped grasses. When England was all so new to me. Hear it still in my heart. On this London evening. Go so often to lone sad sheets. Beefy says worry makes you put on the undergarments backwards. End up standing in the gentlemen's convenience scrabbling and tearing in an unseemly fashion to grasp one's particular. And you take out under the sky one more guilt to wear among all the gay faces prancing by in vanity. Clinging by fingernails to districts, not to drop to social oblivion below. Near sighted nearly tripping so that they don't notice one. Never be without a leek or onion, the smell keeps you out of the whirlpool of dispair. Go into middle age along Pall Mall and up St. James. Downhill gliding through still air. Laugh and keep the gall bladder without grief. Explain how sorry you are that you are not good at mixing with people on all levels. Just the topmost. Where bargains bring bliss to an Englishman's eyes.

367

But if you're not booked up the whole world is against you. Loneliness makes you look at other people. And they look away. Even faster. In their own loneliness. And Beefy in his long struggle to marry said the beads of sweat freeze on the brow and drop with a metallic clank to roll into a lonely corner of one's coffin room. Will it ever be autumn again. When the yellow leaves fall curled on the deep green grass. Press my lips to the ground of Fermanagh. She lies there.

"What do you think of, looking so sad."

"Things."

"What."

"O how the geese gather together in the gloomy of St. James Park. The ones who come flying over our heads when we sit in the Dell. But there are others who fly for the night into Buckingham Palace Gardens. They have a pedigree."

"O you are funny."

"You have a tâche de naissance on the neck Alphonsine."

"I think your eyes are very busy Monsieur."

"Come over here."

"No."

"Why."

"I must not. I must go away. Back to Paris. I am not happy to do so when your home is like this now. But it would not be proper to stay."

"Don't go."

"I must. It will be goodbye. It is sad too. I have liked it here. Sometimes I feel to go to Paris is like a grave. All the way from Calais looks like graves. The eyes of everyone are like lizards. But then when I am at last in Paris I go speeding in Jacques' car and we are gay."

"Is Jacques hairy."

"O la la. Jacques has not a hair. A little of course on the leg. And where he should have hair. On his chest he has a gold cross. With Christ. A tattoo. It looks how do you say, high style."

"Is he a good driver."

"Ha. Magnificent. We go so fast like a shot across Paris.

368

Honking his horn. The tires squeal. His car is big, others get quickly out of the way. He is always the master. We will make such a good husband and wife together. We would not be perhaps too rich. We would not have all the things but what does it matter, we would have enough."

"Is Jacques very strong."

"O la la. What a question. Strong. How do you say, like the reptile with the constriction. He wrap around and squeeze like so. He makes the shoelace of me."

"He might squeeze out your life."

"Ah he leaves just a little so that I will recover."

"Jacques sounds so musculaire."

"You are being naughty I think. But of course I tell you many times already he is musculaire. In the bathing costume he is superb. Bump bump bump it go over the stomach."

"Does he put dressing on his hair."

"A little perhaps. Otherwise he is so very casual. He likes the tight trouser. Like a glove over the hip. Sometimes he hangs the open shirt outside. When he goes in the evening to the cafe. He say hello hello to all his friends. He laughs. He pushes away the others from the pinball machine who make a low score. He waves away the praise over his shoulder as he makes a high score. He never tilt the machine. He move the hip just so and his shoulder just so and makes the ball go in the skill hole."

"Does Jacques ever look awful when he gets up in the morning."

"Never. He is refreshed. Touches the toes, one two, one two. It is so beautiful when he shaves. He pats the toilet water over his face. Women they all turn the head when he goes by. I save all my money to buy my swimming costume and it is very extravagant but that is why. To feel confident and when Jacques looks at me and I feel he is proud. He does not notice then the other women."

"I had a big car once. Perhaps I could have won a race with Jacques."

"O never. You would not stand a chance."

"O dear, have some more brandy. I feel a need of champagne."

"A little. Tiny bit."

"Why wouldn't I have a chance with Jacques."

"He drives fast. Wears the sunglasses of course. It is so funny. We come to the stop light. The cars they are there waiting to start. Bumper and bumper like so. They are even, at the line. The drivers they look at each other, like down the nose from the engine to the wheels and they think ah monsieur will be left in the dust. At Jacques, they think, ha not much that car. Ah but Jacques he does not bother to look. He look straight ahead, he know what will happen. His hand is ready to steer, so relaxed like it would hold a cigarette, so bored he is. And his foot is ready on the accelerator. Tap tap it goes with impatience. For he know what is to happen. Inside himself he laughs as they look at him. The lights change, he is so bored, he gives them a second to get away. Then only for a moment he allow himself ah just a tiny smile. He is bored. Completely he is bored. He press the accelerator to the floor. One arm is across the back of the seat holding the cigarette. He give the ash a flick. And zoom we are going. A little smoke rise from the wheels on the street. The others they are thinking with a smile that he has been left standing. Then it is so funny as Jacques comes like a bird, he go by to leave them in the fume. And he puts the cigarette to the lips, he raises the one eyebrow. He sends out the little puff of smoke from the nose. And he is yawning. And that is that. He is of course so absolutely bored with his speed."

"Jacques is a winner. But Alphonsine it is I who bring home the onions. Jacques would be bored being so fast he would not bother."

"Ah yes, you are sweet."

"But how has Jacques become so formidable."

"He was born a winner. He works hard. When you are asleep, he has already worked half a day. His father, his brothers, the sister, they too are at work. He has but time for a quick cup of coffee in the morning. When you are only having your bath at eleven, with the pine scent. And you are on the bed till twelve in the towels."

"You have spied on me."

"Only a little. You have spied on me through the keyhole."

"Only a little. What would Jacques do if he knew."

"O he would kill you. First like so, to the jaw. Then he would come with the uppercut. He is fast like a cat."

"Ah Alphonsine let us toast my death at the hands of Jacques."

"I have had so much already."

"We both need just a little more I think. Even Christ on the cross on Jacques' chest would join us tonight. But if Jacques were here he might kill me, slowly perhaps."

"It would not be bad, it would be over at once. But to try to make a fight, ah another thing it would be. It would be an abattoir for you. It makes me laugh to think. You and Jacques. So funny. Snap would go your head. Jacques then would come in with the chop. Chop chop. With the downward motion. Whoops, like a chicken who lose the head. O it would be funny. Like the tiger he would fight. He has machines for the hand to squeeze, in and out like that, one two, one two. To make the hand strong. In his underwear I see him. It is tight. The belly like little mountains."

"O dear, I am not musculaire."

"You are distinguished. Jacques is not distinguished. But I have enough distinguishness for the two of us. We do not worry who is your family. Where is your chateau. Who is your uncle. Your tailor. How is your accent. The English they are like parrots. The women squawk. So nervous. They do not get enough love. It is very sad. They go to Italy and they have it up the backside. I do not think that is satisfactory. It make the accent go high. It hurt the arse too. I am high. O la la, what am I saying. I have far too much to drink."

"Alphonsine may I just say it's good to listen to you."

"You are so flattering to me. Jacques does not flatter. He

commands. Like a matador. But brave like the bull. When he comes and it is time to take me. I lie there on the bed. He is there, only in his brief. I but wait."

Crackling fire. Snapping of embers and the licking light across the room. Two photographs of Trinity, taken from my window in the square, hanging there against the oak panelling. A rainy day it was then. And wheels go by on a wet street now. Got my onions in before the rain. Pull the drapes closed on the window. Alphonsine sits back on the leather cushioned chair, feet tucked up, shoes off, in her tight grey slacks. Millicent said she probably looks like a cow when first she wrote. And I knew she didn't. From her handwriting. Her strokes so light and tentative. A strange little love grew up the moment I saw the way she crossed her t's and made the capital letter I. This blue delicate trembling vein on her ankle. Brought her here with her two large brown leather bags. We hardly talked all the way in the taxi. She spoke English and I answered in French. She wore a man's watch on her wrist. Her eyes were smiling so gleaming and shy. They somehow reach into one's life and touch it gently. I carried her bags up and she said her room was very pretty. At night Millicent put instructions written out and posted on the wall in the kitchen. Under au pair. And others under cook. After Boats left. And I would take them down. But once Alphonsine saw it when she came to make cocoa and blushed all over her cheeks. She could hardly speak and swallowed a lump down her throat. I said to Millicent you are never to do that again. She said why not she's French.

"You sit so how do you say, dejected. I should not tell you such things. I see what they do on your face. Even though I make a little joke, it is not nice. I suppose I do not tell you what is really the truth. When sometimes on my day off. I walk. I go to the shops. Up the Park Lane down the Oxford Street. And. Yes. I have thought of you often. I would wish I was back with you and the little fellow at the Dell when you come to the park. I would be bored by myself. I would be hungry too. I would be too stingy to have lunch. All the time when I was saving for the swimming costume. I come to a bun shop. Look in the window. I stand next to an old lady. She is hungry too. I count the number of raisins in the bun. To find out which is most. I go in the shop. I ask for that bun. I say no. Not that bun. That bun. I laugh. He mixes up the buns. I say wait, you have lost my bun and I must count all the raisins again."

"I will make your salary higher, Alphonsine."

"O no. I could not accept. I did not tell the story for you to say that."

"Let us have some champagne."

"O I am so light already in the head."

"It clears the palate. Refreshes the spirit."

"You are funny."

"I am not Jacques."

"Now now. You hold what I say against me. You know I have already said now what I shouldn't say. That it is often I think of you. But what good is it to think. You are another woman's husband. I have no right to think like that. It is not good to tell you these things. I have already made such a mistake to be here in your private room like this. But I want to be. So I am. And it is very wrong."

Balthazar bowed to put his lips briefly touching her hair. And went down the dark cellar stair. Along the cool corridor to the wine vault door. In here among the bins. Find something quite unforgettable in the straw. The two of us left in this house. No reason why for one night it should not be a happy home. I suppose if I were strong enough to lift it, the only defence against Jacques would be a chair. But if I got it up above my head he might punch me in the belly. So hopeless. I'm not even awfully good with sabre or foil. By the sound of him he could also beat me at squash. Only my palate would win. Challenge him to deciphering champagnes.

Alphonsine taken the tray away. All the other little scraps of paper gone. The cushions fluffed up. Scent of wood smoke. And one day when I went a walk along Brompton Road and entered the Oratory. Where often I go for peace and solitude. It was middle afternoon on a coldish day. A couple came and knelt at the altar. All alone. Then a priest came out. He performed a wedding ceremony. These two people wrapped up with each other's love holding hands. No cheering, singing and hats and rice and champagne. Just a priest's soft voice gently joining them. I thought how sad but then how beautiful. Two people together against all others. And me their only witness who watches. In the empty church. Send them out of my heart some good little wish. When one never believes in miracles. I saw one small one happen. At the moment they were wed. A ray of sunshine came striking down from the church dome and shone upon their heads. To light up their world.

"I could not drink more."

"To celebrate."

"No no. I could not when your wife has gone. And the little fellow too. I would never celebrate such a thing."

"It's to celebrate my friend's wedding. Beefy."

"Ah. Le Comte. O la la. Who would marry him, he is such a one. What things he say. How is that funny one, that it is the rich what gets the prunes and it is the poor what gets the shits. I laugh."

"Your eyes sparkle."

"Ah you are. Are you not. Making it a bit risky here. But it is nice to feel so good. I like when the light goes on your hair. It is like the electric that one touches. But taboo. I am above Jacques' class. You are above mine. And you are very rich."

"I am poor."

"Ha ha, I see how you live, you could not be very poor. Do not think I do not know the champagne we are drinking. It is not for poor people. You do not fool me."

"I want to kiss you."

"No."

"Why."

"Because it is taboo. Who is he on the wall, clinging to the cliff."

"That is my Uncle Edouard."

374

"He looks nice."

"Yes he was."

"O something happen to him."

"Yes. He is in his grave."

"O I am sorry."

Balthazar rising from his chair. To step near Alphonsine. Her hair gleaming. She is alive. No grave. She is France. Like all the piers from Calais to Boulogne where men stand and fish. And starfish lie crushed and sun dried along the quays. The towns now lit bright with neon lights. But the fishing boats still come and go. Just as when I was a little boy. The car ferry was moving away. Trawlers coming in from distant seas. And white little sailboats like butterflies, their wind slanted wings out on the grey green water. Fresh blue sweeping across the skies. Each day lay out upon my dreams somewhere near the edges of land and water where the eye could see. Married I was as voices sang. Walked stiffly slowly up the aisle. Needing to take a pee. My afternoon already darkening. My hands are on you. Alphonsine. Takes so little flesh to make a curve. And there's a flat wall of red brick on the corner of Pall Mall and St. James against which one can lean. And with you Alphonsine tune our ears to vespers. Tea with crumpets and gentleman's relish. Jacques takes what he wants. And I must ask. To pardon my ancient expression. And the tremors of trouble bubbling behind the kneecaps. Hard pressed by evil. Snatch delight in these selfish times. Soft to kiss. Take up our memories in the Dell. Hear a Beefy beatitude. Blessed are they who out of a sea of human frailty climb aboard a piece of arse when it floats by.

"No, I think we must not. Please."

"Why."

"It is not that I do not wish to. But I must stay here no longer. Please. It is very sad but it is so."

"Alphonsine. Let us sleep in the same bed."

"What difficult things you ask."

"Please."

"You want me. I want you. But why should we be allowed.

375

Everybody passing on the street. They look. They want. But why should they have."

"No one wants you as much as I do. And I may never drink enough again to have the courage to ask you. I know it."

"I am thinking you are as wicked as you are sweet. You have such a way with you."

"Do I leave Jacques standing in his tracks."

"O la la. You are bold."

"Watched you through the keyhole."

"Of course I know you watch me. It was so funny. I move this way and I move that way. I was so naughty. And you are so English to look through the keyhole. I am so embarrassed but I laugh at the same time. As I hang the towel slowly over the hole. It is le Comte Beefy who put you up to it. Both of you outside the door looking. I give you the towel like a curtain at the end of the performance. But Jacques would be jealous. He sometimes say at the end of a letter we are finish, that I have the affair in London. He has his dog. His boat. He says when he wants to make me unhappy that he likes his dog better. And I am only second."

"You are first with me."

"I cry a little. I miss the little fellow. I love him so. He has eyes like you. Now it seems so sad. I do not say to you all your wife said to me. I cry too because I do not want to go back to Paris. I would like always to be friends with you. But maybe it is not possible to be friends between a man and a woman. You never see me cry before. But please. Tell me. I want you to tell the truth. When you look through the keyhole. Do you think when you see it, that my bottom is too big."

Alphonsine looks down into her glass, head bowed. My study bells chime. One waits. And in the silence comes the distant boom of Big Ben. Lit up looking down on the Thames. Where it ebbs flowing up against bridge ramparts. Carrying all the French letters away. Alphonsine come with me. Don't say no. Bolt the doors. The windows. Only thieves can get in. Monsieur I am so ashamed. Take your arm. Both of us stand. Offer up your face. Lids closed over your sad dark eyes. Taste your tears. Apple smell of your mouth. The last bell of twelve comes over the rooftops. Climb slowly each stair. Kiss and hold tight on the landings. Up to your room. Undress your big bottom in the darkness. Ripe and round. Put my arms around you. Stand flesh to flesh. Till the day grows light up the valley of the Thames. My little fellow will not see the sun come up the street and gurgle in his crib and smile. Down on your hands and knees to clean this house. When I was aloof and mortified. Safe in my comfortable habits, sailing through little miseries. Lay me on you. You say I am so hesitant and shy instead of sportif and musculaire. That I have everything I want. But one never wants what one has. Except more of you. All through this night. As I see a streak of light. At a door opening in dreams. To let in things it's sad to know. And it's morning in Knightsbridge. Back in my room. When I was in yours. The world swirls. Fades light and dark. I rise up from bed. You sit all dressed again.

"O Balthazar. You are awfully sad, you had so much to drink."

"What happened."

"You were so sweet. So kind. So very drunk."

"O God."

"You will be better very soon."

"What happened."

"O it was nothing. You say you love me. You say you love someone else who's dead. O la la, such a pickle. You say you will buy me a little cottage with roses round it by the sea. Then you fall asleep and snore."

"I am sorry."

"You are a saint. You say such wonderful things to me. I will never forget. Go back to sleep. Later you will wake and feel better. Go to sleep."

Back to darkness on the crisp pillow with an uncrisp head. My eyes will open sometime again. Where I dream sitting at a white table cloth. On a crimson carpet. Pink spots on pottery. Lights glow and waitresses move to and fro. In this mauve illumined room. Vichy water on the bedside table and

377

my red glass decanter. And at the window. A fluttering like butterflies. Moth wings beating against a shade. White winged figures. Roses in their hair. Am I dying. Smiles upon their lips. Quiet gleams from their faces. Tip toeing across the carpet. Towards me. To touch the hem of my coverlet and raise it gently up to my neck. Take light lemon flavoured water, wipe my lips and brow. Hear them all humming now. Is it the first chill day of London winter. When clouds lie striped on a western sky. And a wind blows cold and clear down Jermyn Street. Warm inside like Christmas. And there they stand. In summer. In all their beauty. Waitresses. Pouring tea. A flavour of blessing.

> At a time
> Told by
> A sea's sad
> Big clock.

29

A man in a belted mackintosh and brown trilby hat stood by
the lamp post with a newspaper and sometimes a shooting
stick across the street from 78 Crescent Curve. And when he
was gone a letter arrived from a firm of solicitors with reference to protecting the interests of their client Mrs. Balthazar
B. I read it in bed over a breakfast brought me by Alphonsine.
After which I sped immediately somewhere to an auction.

And one Wednesday when the air was quite pleasant,
taking a crowded bus from the middle of Sloane Street.
Which jerked and swayed with a rather playful driver. I fell
back upon a small white wisp of woman standing just behind
me. I could hardly see her under her red felt hat and red
tweed coat. And out came her saddened little voice.

"Please don't, you're pushing on me."

"I'm terribly sorry madam."

"Well would you please be more careful and hold on to
something. I know the bus is pulsating but if you crush me it
would be awful. Because I am so tiny and weak."

The bus lurched on as I clung dearly with my hogskin
glove. Holding life and death over the minute creature behind
me. And suddenly the vehicle stopped abruptly and one was
swung helplessly. I fell again upon the little person. As she
cried out in her most forlorn voice.

"There you have done it once more. You are a big person
and you continue to fall on me a little person."

To the end of Sloane Street I was thrown back on her again
and again. Her small voice rising in its pleading high pitched
manner begging for mercy. The entire bus viewed me with
such disfavour and then suddenly with umbrage that I
alighted before we turned into Knightsbridge and took a taxi
the rest of the way. At the estate agent's I gave my require-

ments. And they said they had just the thing nearby. I walked with the man and viewed the commodious premises a couple of floors up overlooking a little piece of green grass and trees in Mayfair. I walked the long corridors and peeked into the ancient musty rooms. In and out of the servants' quarters and the large kitchen that reminded me of Uncle Edouard with its tiling and great ranges.

At 78 Crescent Curve Alphonsine was packed to go. Each day I pleaded for her to stay just one day more. To hope she would change her mind. And when she would not leave her room and then later come to me, her eyes red with tears, I knew a letter from Jacques had arrived. But slowly through the evening she would cheer once more. On fillet steak, mushrooms, camembert and Grand Echezeaux. As organ concertos trumpeted on my gramophone she would sit reasonably pleased, sewing buttons on my shirts and darning my socks.

A card arrived from Beefy. Rather risqué but antique. A lady with her finer points exposed and garlands in her hair. His tightly minutely scrawled message I deciphered under my magnifying glass.

The Sunny South

My dear Balthazar,

We cast our clothes from us again last night as we have done many the nights previous. The Violet Infanta has a sweetness of character of which I was totally unaware. Our room overlooks the harbour. Our toothbrushes stand together on our little shelf over the washstand and her childish flimsy garments are strewn on an odd chair. I have on, my dear boy, my rust brick coloured slacks, sunglasses and sandals. The dear girl weighs a cool fifty eight and one half kilos. Very flat on the belly, she is. A marvellous space between the thighs through which I get morning and evening breezes when necessary. She's my mare, dear boy, we trot off on the trail together, soon followed, I hope, by little Beefys. Now that one waits in nonchalant comfort I dream each night of what colour socks I will wear to my granny's memorial service. God willing it should come. But one dark note was sounded in the night when a couple moved in next door. This room it would appear is of cardboard walls. Chap and his wife from Orpington, Locks Bottom to be exact, very south London if I may say. Me and mine were up to some rather very naughty and nervy tricks together when in the middle of one came these raised voices doing their accounts of the day together. Adding up tips, price of postcards and where they were robbed, cheated and miserably duped beyond, it seems to me, belief. It didn't half put me off my canter, but being cheated was the least of it. My dear boy, both were poisoned by some fish dish or other. And the toxin was only at that moment getting a grip on them. They yawked, howled and bitterly complained through the entire night. Having ruined two of my most flagrant caprices I went into a rage on the third just near dawn and put my fist clean through the wall. This appeared to cure both of them but brought the owner. He promptly did his nut and his own amazing caprice but was silenced by a note of large denomination. However the world is colourless without war. My banker loves me now. And by the time you get this I should be back visiting estate agents to get fitted properly out for the future. I hope you manage to read my minute scrawl. And one little beatitude, blessed are they who do not eat poisoned fish and yawk for they will refresh themselves with filthy multiple perverse practices in the night.

Love,
Beefy

Alphonsine laughed as I read her the card. And we rejoined to bed. She took each stocking carefully down from her legs and asked if I could feel a breeze come through the space between her thighs. She blew me as I watched the ceiling turn white. Which it was already. And I asked would she come with me when my new flat was ready, no one would know we were there. But her cheeks flushed and she sat up still and silent, the pink buds on her breasts, to shrug her shoulders. Till one knew there was nothing else one could say. And dressed I turned in the hall. She stood on the bottom stair. Beefy had rung on his return. I said I was off to see him. She stepped up to me in the hall and stood on tip toe to kiss me on the brow. She gave a sad and silent little smile. A mist in her eyes and watched me go out the door.

High in the grey great hotel. At the end of a long hall. A door swung open in greeting. The tanned brimming face of Beefy in a purple kimono, straw hat and Trinity scarf. Cowhide bags in an open bedroom closet. The Violet Infanta sitting demurely, her dark hair waved back and two blue eyes in her triangular face. She said a shy hello, grabbed her bag, swung her tweed skirt and left for a hair appointment. To leave me sitting in a fat chair as a bucket of champagne came in.

"Isn't she an absolute darling. My honeymoon was more than I ever anticipated. Little sad the Infanta was no virgin for the occasion. But excellent sport. After years of struggle at last washed up safe on a secure financial shore. Drew out cash at her bank this morning. Chap called me back and said there was some mistake. I riposted right sharpish, I said yes, that you leger scribblers are not at prep school learning a bit of civility. People of course hate to be invited to love you. But it is an awful responsibility guiding her riches through the shoals. So many fortune hunters around these days. Haven't had a look see at her share certificates but when one does one will know what sand banks to avoid. But Balthazar you look thin. Strained. How is all your little farm."

"Millicent vacated."

"Good God. That is sad. For good."

"Yes."

"And the little fellow."

"Took him too."

"O Lord no. That's awful. O dear I don't like that one bit. I mean she did once or twice try to brain you but that's all part of it. But buck up. Come, there now, have a sip. Better and more gracious days are coming."

Good to see Beefy looking so well. But not to put a pall upon his triumphant return I withdrew. The trains trumpeting in and out of Victoria Station. To points south and east across the Continent, Paris, Vienna and Istanbul. Gentle fall of soot and smut. Newspaper hawkers shouting over the roar of traffic. London in its shallow bowl of tidy green squares and parks. The distant hills rising north, south and west around the Thames. To walk away from that hotel with a strange sense of sad. Cross Belgrave Square and pass a stream of ladies in flowery dresses and big straw hats. Back up the steps of Crescent Curve. To an empty house. With none left but me. And an envelope under the paper weight on my desk.

Dear Balthazar,
    I have left because I think it is best. I go back to Paris. I leave your dinner, nice mayonnaise lobster, in the fridge.
                                    Love from
                                    Alphonsine

To wake this day in a lonely house. As Beefy phoned. Moving from hotel to hotel. In search of one befitting his future. While I sat staring at Uncle Edouard clinging to the side of his cliff on my wall. Unable to see further than tomorrow. Wandered at a late hour across the park to the Bayswater Road. To hope by accident to run into Breda. But never a sign of her. Until Beefy stood suddenly in the hall of 78 Crescent Curve with his arms outstretched in doom.

"Balthazar, they've done it to me, I've been had. It will mean prison. It may have all been planned and plotted. She hasn't a sausage to her name, my violent Infanta. God help me if she hasn't Irish blood and relatives, all without social credentials. And what is worse, quids."

"Beefy, this is unexpected news."

"My dear boy I'm bankrupt. Fortunately I had lunched off oysters and a dozen gull's eggs out of season. Before my bank manager says to me, when I was just calling to pass the time of day, he said what on earth do you think you're doing. And the dismal facts were revealed. A huge Infanta cheque I'd paid into my account bounced right over St. Paul's. Everyone who has eyes in London saw it. I taxed the creature with it. I

383

said your cheque bounced. She looked utterly innocent and asked why. I said because you don't have sufficient funds. Then the awful words came. She has had all these months a credit of eighty seven pounds fifteen shillings in her account and could prove it. I said if you do my dear girl, I am up the spout for thousands as I stand here. My bank manager thinking all this time that granny had been shoveled under. All rather hysterically horrid. I was found last night dear boy in a Mayfair doorway, protruding onto the pavement. Some gentle kindly taxi driver lifted me up and I groaned to him an address. Took me to the club. Had a little note pinned to me, Dear Guv, you are no lightweight, but good luck to you. You are a merry gentleman. And I did the worst possible thing. The most heinous thing of my life. I confronted the Infanta. Just over an hour ago. I struck her and she went down. I haven't got it in me to commit murder. I fell upon her sobbing. Worst thing of all is, I love the dear girl. I mean we've had our awkward moments when I wanted to put it where I have done previously in others. And where too she finally welcomed it with delight. Although radiantly new to such proclivity."

"Beefy I am to the cellar. I will be back."

Beefy's words so loud in the silent house. As he sat there in his plus twos. At any minute he would make for the highlands and lie himself amidst the heather. To creep down at darkness into his granny's manor. And scare her to death. With a goat's skull. The time come to take slowly now upon one's palate two rare bottles of golden wine. Full of musky death sipped by the living to give life. With fresh lobster to go with Alphonsine's leftover mayonnaise.

"Balthazar you are a brick, to purvey this gonadal wine when it is most needed. And you know what else happened. On this fatal day. Only moments ago. A marvellous thing to befall any British subject. But me. I was on my way in one awful hurry to the merchant bankers in the City. Can you imagine, Masterdon. A power in the banking world. Actually ready to help me. Well my God, what happens but I get instantly into the most atrocious traffic jam. Thought best to get out and run the remaining three or four miles. And there I am standing on the pavement. Motors bumper to bumper, choked in all directions. When a car, a large vehicle of polished glass, coat of arms, flags on front fenders, stops right in front of me, my nose nearly at the window. I thought for one instant it was granny, so help me God. That's the way she goes about terrorising all her tenants. I had simply so much on my mind I froze. Dressed of course like this I should have been miles away in heathery landscapes. But there I was a British subject standing a little to the left of the middle of my prime. And sitting barely two feet from my incredulous face was the Monarch. Locked right in the traffic. Facing me, Beefy, just before bankruptcy. My first instinct is as always to check one's personal dress. Then I instantly came to attention. My hand half way up to salute. I was the only one on the pavement for miles. And I dropped my arm again. The Monarch turned and looked at me. I knew it was written all over my face that I had been corrupted by my nannie at the age of six and thereafter led steeply down the path of infamy and wretchedness. And that this morning I had to take an umbrella to crap under the drips from the club cistern above. I was not worthy of the Monarch's gaze. But I knew it was essential to look back with all the fair play and loyalty at my command, right in the Monarch's eye. One realises in a moment such as that, that the Monarch is always there, head of the ship of state to whom one can appeal in spirit when life is most rough. That the Monarch speaks for truth when you know damn well everyone is lying through their litigation. The Sovereign, always the resistor to the irresistible impulse, steadfast in jostling. Never unnerved in national turmoil and sorrow when from the Monarch's eyes the tears must fall. And it was clear from the very polite indifference in the present gaze back at me that no tears were shedding for my disaster. I knew I had to salute at that instant, hoping desperately the car would move on. But it didn't. The Monarch stared at me. I thought I saw an imperceptible raising of one eyebrow. And

385

you know it's a feeling no foreigner would ever understand. That I wanted it somehow known that I was loyal, unbought and non fishy. Locked as one was in this eye gripping awkward manner. I couldn't hide my face in my hands. Or run. I wanted to almost say finally. Please don't look at me shattering the atoms down my spine. God how unworthy I was at that moment. Then the traffic began to move again. And the Monarch smiled at me. God help me if I didn't grow faint. And rushed straight here."

"Beefy do help yourself."

"My God what yummies. By whose hand was such mayonnaise wrought."

"Alphonsine."

"A true darling. O dear what will a chap like Masterdon say, awaken as I must memories of pulling each other's pecker. What a time to be without the bullion when so many beastly delicious freedoms abound. I nearly slid off your steps dear boy, only my good eyesight kept me from upending and writhing besmirched in awful doggie befoulment."

"I regret to say the dog across the street has learned that your little bow wows are only stone. He wee wees over them and they're rather stained on their little noses."

"By God Balthazar let us get some women and to hell with everything. Launch a major orgasm. There is that one you know, to which one mounts climbing up through those precious seconds and at the pinnacle explodes an imperceptible part of one's soul. The cream upon one's milk spilled without a pagan's apology. Which makes for serenity in one's life. God you know, you sit there so beatific and never beastly Balthazar. More than anything I'm sad for what has befallen the Infanta. She just lay on the floor holding her dear little hand to her face, not knowing what hit her. A defenceless creature struck down. And suddenly it seemed as if she reposed beneath a great marble arch on a bed of flaming roses, dead. I threw myself on her like a tearful child. Sorrow makes me awfully randy. Gave her a molto adagio rogering which was more in my later manner I felt than my usual earlier one. It defies me how I've got so fond of her. I suppose that in her own little way she is such a vulnerable creature and it would break my heart to see the world do her harm. As it is, the world is about to dump it on me in bulk."

"Beefy I'd like very much if you would allow me to help you."

"Balthazar, you are princely like no other and I'm touched. But so help me God, granny at her age can't go on befoggling me. Now that life is so terrifying and my fear of death nil I'm ready once more to have at her. She may be tough but by God I have taken the last of her diabolical, regrettable, shirty, shabby and tawdry antics. However, enough. Let us go in search of women."

A taxi with a jocular driver trundled them to Soho. Along with bottles of the golden wine, two dozen quails' eggs and bowls of the mayonnaise and lobster. They settled in the third row of the strip club. Packed out with a queue along the wall. And somewhat sulphurous with match lighting. The splendid friendly greeting to Beefy from the gentlemen at the doors. And a chap in the last row emitting a great gasping sigh after each act. Said to be a member of the peerage. Whose hand clapping could be heard as a lady skipped on stage wearing nothing but a well known old school tie.

As the lights blinked on in Soho and streets filled with night time traffic Beefy walked out with Balthazar into the evening, the wicker hamper balanced on his head. Past the doorway lurkers and book vendors busy with the toil of keeping their public satisfied. They lean over their wares with smiles and greetings. Beefy raising an ecclesiastic hand in blessing. To finally flag a taxi which roared off to a Mayfair address.

"You know Balthazar I have that feeling which comes when one is leaving the building site on a Saturday afternoon, a good week's work behind one. Even though I was mostly curled up asleep in an empty sewerage pipe. Yet will I see myself lodged in Sunningdale, carpeting laid thick under the occasional tables strewn with cigarette lighters. The Infanta has the most interesting mole on the back of her thigh. In my leisure moments perusing her skin, I found parts of her unaccountably beautiful. About the armpit she is quite elegant. All I wanted to be was a great ecclesiastic. Offering up prayer in the sanctuary of a cloister with a fountain and ornamental waters. Amid moisty green swards and orangeries. Stamping out the lonely evil habits rife among civil servants. Calling upon solicitors to do penance and barristers to beat their breasts in contrition. Of course I'd also twist the ears of shopkeepers who put on airs. The Infanta has an incredible knack of cradling the balls. Gently squeezing them at the appropriate time. And I have been diabolical to her. Here we are. Wait Balthazar. I shall bring on the girls."

The taxi sped under a purple London sky. One's street lamp glowing and illuminating the expression of utter indifference on the face of the gentleman across the street as he raised his binoculars to view Beefy, two girls and two little dogs rushing up the steps of 78 Crescent Curve. Beefy in my doorway pointing a finger. And with a voice of window rattling resonance.

"I say, you sir with the binocs. You are clearly an impostor. Get out of that nun's habit immediately."

Sounds echo through this house where all has been so silent. My canes, my little prints of Dublin on the walls. As these two ladies of pleasurings fix their hair and tie up their dogs to the leg of the kitchen table. And Beefy holds out some fare. The rare faint blue of a shelled quail's egg in the palm of his hand.

"Welcome girls. Here is the invalid tray of goodies with the turtle and calves foot jelly. Your host, Balthazar. Isn't he a beautiful gentleman. While others are cunning and deceitful, he remains always witty and kind. Let the necklines plunge now. I'll paint your portraits for a start."

The girls giggled chased by Beefy through the house. They oohed and aahed to his gallant gooses given through bed and dressing rooms. Balthazar butlering with the buckets of ice brought forth. And champagne corks popped. Beefy mounting the dining room table upon which so many crystal cut bowls had crashed from Boats' trembling hands. He skidded back and forth in his socks. And shouted out gospel according to Beefy.

"Girls amid this forest of definitive degeneracy let us fan the appetites and incite the mind with black underthings. While I tremble over the extraordinary liberties pending. My old granny won't die. Lives on and on eating her own home-made jam, weaves her own cloth, sips heather honey and dandelion wine, and quaffs pot still whisky. No laughing matter. Her grandchild has been doomed to taking much roughage to clear the bowel. Ah both you girls have shallow navels. Which of you again is from Ongar."

"Me Winetca, your grace."

"Don't flatter me with title my dear girl. I am not quite that titular. But come into my little anglican communion. Up here you dears. Caper for Beefy. See how you gavotte. Neither of you I am sure send your vicar anemones on his birthday. No niceties remain. Such inclement changes have been wrought in England. Hardly a beastly beatitude is left. Stop that kissing and embracing girls. Too early. That caper is reserved for further and better particulars later. During my scripture lesson. Yes, pour the champagne on each other."

Balthazar sitting in the corner of the candle lit dining room. As Beefy dances away all his disappointments suffered. He lives on as if the world will bounce up again when you drop it. Yet one knows a terrible little sad secret stays in his heart. Which I read one day long ago. And found he was just a little boy like me chilled on an evening desert of sorrow. Even as he now gleefully puts a glass of wine to his lips. And slapping a narrow hardened buttock of Edwina. How did he get to us down through the centuries. To stand stark naked as he does. A belt around his belly, embracing the ladies of light fingered love.

"Girls I must caution you on that recent posture. Edwina

remember you are the daughter of a long distance lorry driver and he would be ashamed. Can't you see my friend Balthazar is quite stricken with the outrage of your engripment."

The cries and screams of laughter. These three on the table pouring champagne on each other when suddenly the girls' poodle doggies came charging into the room. Trailing broken leads. Rushing to the sound of their mistresses' high pitched squeals. Beefy up into the air as one little doggie mounted a chair and nipped him about the legs. And he came down again with the other doggie's teeth clamped over his ankle. A swift kick upwards dislodging this clinging animal towards the ceiling and across the room to come crashing down on the candelabra formerly glowing gently on the sideboard. A mite of light left to see Edwina casting her bottle which crashed against the door. Just a little to the side of Beefy's head.

"By God girls you will get what for. The battle is on. There'll be false eye lashes everywhere I can tell you. My trustees will have at you with their canes long after I am done. Swipes across the tit and arse with my cutlass is not good enough for you."

Balthazar B tip toeing out into the hall. The battle raged inside. An awful dog smell coming from the kitchen. In the disturbed peace of what was once my home. And will no longer be. After tonight. Because I am going to march up these stairs. An outsider in Beefy's games. I've only ever been able to play with one. Take away this vase full of dying yellow flowers. Pour all the unicellular animals down the sink. Pack up a bag of clothes. And do so without a sound.

The two girls chased by Beefy followed by the little doggies came charging up the stairs. Their heavy breathing as they passed and went up another flight. And the floor rumbles in Boats' former room. Then all is quiet. And echoing down the stairs the voice of Beefy, that's very fine girls, very nice. Thank you. More please. I now anoint you. Winetca of Ongar of the shallower navel. And you Edwina of the long nipple from Nuneaton. But dear girls I should much hate to serve supper to any of your distant relatives.

In darkness one turns away. To go and sit and wait in my study. So sobered by sadness. And too awfully shy to ever feel delight. Go down the stair. All Beefy's beatitudes. Blessed are they who wear God's garters and sip champagne from the cupped hands of naked women for they will keep their pricks and palates young. Beefy never casts a stone. Stands alone with his dark devilments held aloft victoriously. The scream of a little dog. Sounds just like the small person I fell upon in the bus. You are a big person and I am tiny and weak.

Balthazar B sat in his study chair. A tired head leaning. The sounds distant upstairs. One is all alone. When you stop somewhere in your life and look at the love spilled from your hands. Hear the little fellow chuckle. He would reach up and take my finger and tug. And try to see me with his wide open believing eyes. To grow I hope when he does to rear up anew from each misfortune. And never know the sad little secret untold in Beefy's stout heart. Read all those years ago, fallen on a tiny piece of paper from his diary he kept at school. I picked it up from the floor between our beds and saw his tight little scrawl.

I want
A mommie
And a daddy
Please
Help me
Somebody.

30

From a high sunny room in the red brick turreted hotel Balthazar B looked out over the trees of Hyde Park. At night the Serpentine waters glitter in moonlight and flash up sun in the morning. 78 Crescent Curve was up for sale. A family residence in a favoured part of town. Broken furnishings of its last gallant night were being repaired for removal with Uncle Edouard's desk and chair to Mayfair and the rest to Sotheby's for auction.

Beefy entrained for Scotland on one last heroic beseechment to his granny. I walked the longest and loneliest streets of London. Taking a bus this late afternoon to Putney to stroll along the river in a park. Tankers and barges swept past on the ebb tide. I put a foot on the railing and listened to the shouts of oarsmen lifting their racing shells from the river to put them away for the night. And the park keeper came ringing his bell. To close the gates and leave it quiet under the big old plane trees. The birds breaking evening silence in a little churchyard where I passed reading gravestones to wait for a bus on the bridge.

The lamplights on as we move along. The conductor pulling his buzzer cord on the ceiling. Handing customers tickets and rummaging in the pennies of his big leather bag. The houses pass to make one think of all the lands of London, from Paddington to Wandsworth, Shoreditch to Dulwich. Grey streets packed with lives under rooftops and rooftops. Chimney pots puffing slow smoke from the precious fires tucked away in the bricks.

The bus stops at a crossing. A shoemaker and an antique shop. Pavement stacked with bathtubs. A woman waiting on the curb. For the bus to pass. Her face. A brown cloth coat tucked up tight at her throat. Eyes staring ahead on this chilly night. The cheekbones and chin and eyes. The bus begins to move. Those bones and contours. In a face that seems so old. And gradually becomes familiar. As my mind peels all the time away. To hope that it isn't when I see that it is. That woman, careworn and sad. Must grab the handrail to get up. But no, sit back again. What could I ever say. Everything seems so late. That I can hardly believe but know that waiting there was Bella.

Back at the hotel a letter from my mother. From Paris to say she was poorly and hoped I would come. Please bring pictures of Millicent and the little fellow. I place her missive over another. A quite threatening one from solicitors. Not nice. And hardly knowing what I was doing. I took a taxi to Euston. Caught a night train. Stepping out in the morning after tea and biscuits in Liverpool. Stared at the big blackened building of steps and huge pillars across from the station Spent the day wandering to take a ferry across the muddy river to Birkenhead and go up and down along the rows and rows of red brick houses, reading the curious names of the streets. And at night to stand at the ship's railing to see again the iron birds high up on the Liver Building. The clock tolling a quarter to ten as the mail boat headed out on the water. Past the lightships. And great cargo vessels waiting to steam into the Mersey.

In the misty Belfast morning I took a taxi. Out through the smoky streets. The driver said he would ask his wife if he could drive me to Fermanagh. And he read a newspaper while drawn up by the side of the road. And I in this early afternoon went past the gate once held open on a broken hinge and now closed and padlocked. I stepped on stones and climbed over a broken part of the wall. And walked lost for a while. Brambles scratching through my trousers. To think I am here in trespass. Something I would never do. And look for where the land rises crowned by a wood. Cross this pasture. I know where I am. She lies just up there in the trees. Look down as I walk over her grass. And through the little iron gate in the wall. I come here to say hello and not goodbye. A piece of

393

granite stands tall and plain. Next to another half its size. Two words make your name. And underneath the years that lived your life. Primroses and violets grow here where you lie. You will never go away. See all of you through the tears that cover my eyes. Wind blows in the yew. Soft red berries dropped with a green shadowy seed. The musty smell of boxwood. When you looked at me and I looked back we each said all our words. It matters only what private things we know and have never spoken. Or will ever speak. Take up the years that come. To carry you with me wherever I go. Face any loneliness. Know I'm not alone. You the only one I ever told about my lost little boy who was my first son. Wish I could blow hoots from the hollow of my hand and make the owls answer back. Tonight I will be in Dublin. From the train through Dundalk. I'll walk across Trinity in the morning. Around its flat green velvet squares. See you again as you passed beneath my windows. I'll look from the roadway where your bedroom window was and at the house in which I first heard you speak to me. Never to know all those suffering creatures your hand and voice gave comfort in hospital. Putting bravery in old men in fear of death. And these tears that fall from me, they'll help your grass to grow. Goodbye Fitzdare. Goodbye.

The day windy as I went out to Collinstown. And the plane rose in the sky over Dublin south towards London. I could see along the coast and count the towns, Dalkey, Bray and Greystones. And the train we took through tunnels and up on cliffs looking down on a wintry shore in summer. Leave Ireland now. With part of it mine. Where it has your grave.

Balthazar B climbed up the steps and through the doors of the hotel. Up more steps to the man at the desk handing across two cables. To wait to be in my room knowing certainly from whom one was. Open the other first. Stand by the window. As rain pours down. And makes the roofs of the cars below gleam as they pass.

URGENT YOU COME TO PARIS WHERE YOUR MOTHER SERIOUSLY ILL   DOCTOR PIERRE

I will never catch my breath. From one place to another. And never believe that people who travel get ill. Beefy is travelling. This cable from Perth.

AM ENROUTE PLEASE CHILL CHAMPAGNE FOR RATHER UN-
BLESSED MAN WITHOUT BEATITUDE   BEEFY

In the dining room I sat near the window. Eating curled little pieces of toast with my escargots and steak tartar. Food to give one fortitude. And plan a life. Of how I no longer want to live. Performing comfortable habits. In London in spacious antique splendour at addresses more gracious than glad. Walking grey wall to wall carpeting in amphibious leathers. Keeping one servant, a secretary and female pug dog. My income big and private. To go each autumn whisking by train and boat to Paris to have a pair of riding boots made. Uncle Edouard said be wary with new friends and wise with old wines because it is sad that riches overshadow both good looks and an endearing demeanour of which you are possessed, my Balthazar. Journey to America, twice a year, once by sea, once by sky and you can marvel at the criminalities and cruelties of opportunity. You will reach an age when the past amazes you as much as the present. Then you will wonder if poverty held any sensual features you might have missed staying at the best hotels. But dear boy, you will find nothing better than good breakfast coffee or cake. And in the countries providing it, rise early. And remember do not be too overwhelmed with shyness for it is nice to sometimes weep in the face of beauty. And last. Be careful not to catch the crab.

Two bottles of champagne chilling in my rooms above. Eat one's strawberry ice cream. A group of youngsters laughing gaily waltz by through the room. My life lies as much behind as it does ahead. Won't matter now how I live it. That couple smile with a waiter over their bowls of caviar. Two dowagers sit sipping sherry and reading their menus. Winter comes and will bring smoke and fog to London. When the air sniffs sharp. And the streets are wet. Curtains drawn and everyone waits. For spring to blow the big cold grey clouds away. Order

395

a cab for morning. Make my reservations on the train. Go out from Victoria, in a big comfortable chair amid the panelled walls and polished brass. And the little lamps with pink shades. By Battersea look down to see the dogs wagging tails in the dog pound.

Beefy stood with his hunting cap dripping rain and a worn brown leather briefcase hanging from his hand. As bells strike ten P.M. About his lips the trace of a smile. His face the bow of a ship ready to ply all seas and crash cutting through any storm.

"Balthazar. The sight of you is so welcome. The train of course was derailed. I ended up having to take a car through half the night through a lashing gale and pouring rain. But o let me just sit down. What a splendid drawing room. How quiet. Tucked away up here. That suit. You used to wear it at Trinity."

"Yes."

"It's charming. I like your colours. The soul needs a little pink here and a little magenta there."

In this green carpeted room. A writing desk. Two flowered sofa chairs. And round mahogany tables. Driving mists of rain tumbling over the tops of trees out the window. Where the lights are dotted across the great dark stretches of park. Beefy's shoes scuffed and sodden. A white hanky tucked up his shirt cuff. A golden one peeking from his breast pocket. So much said on his face. And were he alone I know it would be ablaze with worry. His hand falls from his wrist and his veins stand out blue. We will pour out the faint ash scented wine.

"Beefy how did it go."

"Not nice."

"O dear."

"Yes. I shouted at granny. I shook my fist and said I know that my redeemer liveth. After plunging through deep rutted gullies, shortcuts I knew from boyhood days, my man motoring me was in paroxysms. Kept complaining about his suspension. Then when we got in granny's gate we were surrounded by her four Irish wolf hounds. Took half an hour before I could charm them into doggish naughties with each other. And then I rushed up the steps and the door was locked. Finally had to climb through a window in the pig curing room which by day looks like the most gruesome sort of mortuary. And by night should be avoided altogether. My gout was aching in both my big toes and I could hardly walk. Cold, hungry and terrified I'd meet someone in the halls. As it was I fell promptly over an ancient fire apparatus, started wrestling for my life with the damn hose. I was completely hysterical. Near tears in fact. Thought I'd wake the whole house. And that Swithins would come beetling down out of some unnoticed direction in his wheel chair. That's how he gets around these days, keeps his walking stick across his lap and larrups the rest of the household across the arse, all except cook to whom he does other daredevil delights. Thank God everyone in that mansion is hard of hearing. Stood outside the billiard room. Thought it would only take a cue, one little tap on granny's birdlike head. But I just haven't such greed within me. I mean frighten her to death certainly, that's quite natural. But at four A.M. to clock her one on her nut. Not nice. So there I was, in her bedroom doorway. Trying to look a vision of terror in my hound's tooth knickerbockers. Good old Irish custom to frighten the life out of the old ones. I thought I was doing very well when she sat bolt upright in bed. Her night cap on. Me shivering drenched to the skin wearing my diabolical demeanour. She knocked over her bedside water. Turned on the light. And said how dreadful of you to come in with your muddy feet on the carpet. My God Balthazar she has vinegar for blood. I said granny, I am up the spout, I must have twenty thousand immediately. Her tiny old hand was opening and closing on her stick lying by her on the bed. I said granny, twenty thousand. Balthazar she let out with a blood curdling peal of laughter. The hundreds of little old ladies I've helped across the street, flattered and indeed danced with. And all granny does is pour herself a dram of her own special brew from her distillery. And suggests to me that I go make cocoa in the kitchen. If I'd had the cue stick it would have been the end of her. How can she at her age remain so hard and soulless. I said the family name was about to be disgraced. She said pity. Her elegance crushed me. I mean she sits to an evening drink covered in black silk and eight rows of pearls. I know for a fact she smashes back two brown eggs laid by two pet hens at breakfast, steam pudding in the evenings. On Sundays she devours a kipper with a dram of the pot still. She gardens six hours a day. I finally dropped to my knees. Bowed my head. Said I beg you for the sake of my own newly wed, the pure Violet Infanta, who is having a little one to carry on the name, nineteen thousand will do. Balthazar, she replied don't dare to insult my intelligence with such impertinent humbug. Then I thought I would at least let her have a jolt of the truth. I said how does it feel with so many people waiting for you to die. You know Balthazar, the wind stopped, the trees were still. You could hear a flea fart. And she said my dear boy, what a refreshing question, it is no end of comfort and solace to me each day I live, to have so many concerned for the day I die. Nice of you to ask but I will die at my own convenience, not yours. Balthazar, I withdrew. Stood a few last moments in the hall, looking up at a portrait of me and my cherubic face as I posed in white breeches and black hose against a backdrop of foliage, a little hat in my hand and a big brown dog sitting at my side. And high up over the damp walls other portraits of the family's horse thieves, imposters and cads who married rich widows. And then the little old fashioned drawings of granny's distilleries. And suddenly as I was leaving she came to the balcony railing at the top of the stairs. Said go make yourself hot cocoa. And in the chapel you will find my private prayer book. On page three hundred and ninety three you will see an item marked. Try to take it to heart. O God Balthazar. Must quaff a glass of this fine liquid."

"Beefy you mustn't give up."

"Actually I didn't. In fact she was rather kind. She had underlined, the ungodly, and him that delighteth in wickedness doth his soul abhor. And there pressed between the pages was one hundred quid. Dawn was breaking over the highlands. Although it seemed to light up the horror of my affairs I left at least hopeful. Got on the train. But along the Cromarty Firth I fell asleep and had a nightmare. Stretched out sooty and grimy. A second class passenger on a first class crimson seat. Dreamt a meeting had been convened of Europe's hotel owners where they passed a nasty resolution reinforced with a vote of confidence to blood hound me up and particularly down every glen from Caithness to Argyllshire. Fleeing holding my chilled balls. Blood hounds favour them as a canapé you know. I scampered into the higher hills where the heather would give the hounds hayfever and I could sleep peacefully bedded down under the herbs. Then I was seized, the hounds were upon me, one had me by the finger. I woke up God help me with my hands right round the throat of the conductor as he gasped for air in front of my incredulous eyes. His dentures, full upper and lower, sunk into and hanging from my index finger. I blinked my eyes. Saw these pale teeth and membrane pink plastic. The conductor had difficulty mouthing his words. During which moments I apologised profusely. He took off his coat, shook it, and his tickets fell out. I helped pick them up. Said I had had a dastardly trip under great strain and was chilled to the marrow. Five minutes later he came back with his teeth in and presented me with a miniature bottle of one of granny's pot still highland malts. Craziest thing of all he'd been a groundsman for granny before he worked on the railroad. He remembered me as a little boy. Recognised my grown up features as I lay asleep on the seat. Said I used to sit in the heather and hold a bunch of flowers sniffing them in my hand. Will sit now sniffing writs instead. My trustees are so old. Haven't the strength left to rise up in my defence. Poor old Mr. Smart. When last we lunched he was handling a breach of contract action in which the relevant papers and torts became affixed by gum to his trouser bottom. Poor old chap looking round his room for them. And then walking across Lincoln's Inn as they fluttered from his backside. When everyone else is gone

from one's life, only trustees are left. Balthazar you of all
people give me hope. Why."

"Perhaps because I am a beatitude."

"Yes, that's it, you are. Well I am now about to set off to
Maida Vale. Take up the battle from there."

"Beefy I'm off to Paris in the morning. And I'd like you
to take this. Just a cheque."

"You are a prince. But no. I have my plans. I will stand at
Marble Arch. Look up that straightaway, an old Roman road,
from which only the very hardiest ever return. But Beefy
shall. You'll hear the beating of the drums. The Almighty
may have me by the balls now, but soon I will be tickling
his."

Balthazar B crossed with Beefy the darkness of Hyde Park.
Shadows of trees looming. Up the long wide path under the
gas lamps towards Speaker's Corner. Their feet grinding on
the gravelly path. A westerly sky with a fresh new air. Blowing
east down the side streets of Mayfair. To follow where the
cool dark rain clouds had gone. And Beefy stopped. A wet
yellowing leaf fluttered down. At the end of this path. He put
out his hand.

"Balthazar, when anger leaves one, so does life. And the
world has an instinct. Waits to deliver blows at the moment
when it knows it will hurt most. Not nice. And you. You put
out a kind and helping hand. I'll never know why. But thank
you. And I say goodbye. Because I know you will understand I
could not bear to be a burden. Nor do I want to be presumptuous but we've been good friends. I head out past the electri-
cal supply stores. And others selling garments to the outsize.
Like an actor to whom death has come so often on the stage
that when it arrives in life I'll only want a little limelight."

Balthazar B stood watching the chunky figure go. Until he
was out of sight. Carrying all his secrets he will never tell. Out
there to the wasteland wilderness. And I go back. Across the
wet grass. Hear the ducks nesting for the night. Along there
the little fellow rolled and was gathered up in the arms of
Alphonsine. See the room where I've left my light. Looks like

400

a castle against the sky. Wait for green on the traffic light to cross the street. Beefy had little sewing hands. They'll be joined when he's promoted to glory. And I stop right here. Because something has happened. To make me wonder what it is. And hope it's warm and dry. But I know it's damp and cold.

Like
A mother is
When
She dies.

31

Today smashes down, sunlight flickering through the trees. And the ducks and geese fly by. Reach out and run my hand over the green little hills of Hyde Park. Sit with breakfast and stare. A pot of fragrant steaming coffee on the linen table cloth. Warm brown toast and honey. Instead of kippers and whisky which got Beefy's granny so far.

Balthazar B went down in the lift. This morning dressed with a little something for everybody. A pink silk shirt, a Trinity tie and black Manx tweed. People going to the dining room for breakfast. With their newspapers tucked under arms and wives ushered ahead. I stand packed to go. Feel no sadness. To know my mother's dead. Or that I'll climb the winding hill over the cobble stones to the ovens atop Père Lachaise.

In this hotel lobby, pull on my black capeskin gloves. Slide a hand into the crimson silk. Tighten my fist on the grip of my bag. Go slowly down these steps. Out through the doors. To the autumn air. Free and clear. Last night as I fell asleep, all the lamps along Rotten Row went off one by one in my head. Woke with a coo of pigeon and backfire of a car. And wondered will one ever walk abroad again on the brimming countryside laughing in the green. Where the seeds fly from thistles standing sharp leafed strangers in the fields.

There will be the little line of people waiting to board the steamer. The harbour may be heaped with waves. Mail loading from derricks swinging a great net. I'll be watching as I always do. The clank of chain and cables dripping water. A capstan grinding as it tugs the bow out towards sea. With the last shouts and bustle.

Stand here on Knightsbridge pavement in the public domain. Where so much of one's life began. To wait for a taxi to

take me just a little further away. Aboard the train. Out of
London and England. Across the grey Channel. To bury a
mother. And chase others gone goodbye in my years. Calling
after their names. Come back again. Where that countryside
sings over your grasses matted by wind and rains fall in sunshine. Don't fear when some nights rise up wild. Go walk in
heather along a narrow path. Seagulls glide and curlews cry.
Reach up and gather all this world. Before dark or any other
people should ever come. And find you sheltering. As all
hearts are. Worried lonely. Your eyes quiet. By the waters
cold. Where the sadness lurks so deep.

It doth
Make you
Still.